PLEASE DON'T BE TRUE

BOOKS BY PHYLLIS REYNOLDS NAYLOR

Shiloh Books
Shiloh
Shiloh Season
Saving Shiloh

The Alice Books
Starting with Alice
Alice in Blunderland
Lovingly Alice
The Agony of Alice
Alice in Rapture, Sort of
Reluctantly Alice
All But Alice
Alice in April
Alice In-Between
Alice the Brave
Alice in Lace
Outrageously Alice
Achingly Alice
Alice on the Outside
The Grooming of Alice
Alice Alone
Simply Alice
Patiently Alice
Including Alice
Alice on Her Way
Alice in the Know
Dangerously Alice
Almost Alice
Intensely Alice
Alice in Charge

Alice Collections
I Like Him, He Likes Her
*It's Not Like I Planned It
    This Way*

The Bernie Magruder Books
*Bernie Magruder and the Case
    of the Big Stink*
*Bernie Magruder and the
    Disappearing Bodies*
*Bernie Magruder and the
    Haunted Hotel*
*Bernie Magruder and the
    Drive-thru Funeral Parlor*
*Bernie Magruder and the Bus
    Station Blowup*
*Bernie Magruder and the
    Pirate's Treasure*
*Bernie Magruder and the
    Parachute Peril*
*Bernie Magruder and the Bats
    in the Belfry*

The Cat Pack Books
The Grand Escape
The Healing of Texas Jake
Carlotta's Kittens
Polo's Mother

The York Trilogy
Shadows on the Wall
Faces in the Water
Footprints at the Window

The Witch Books
Witch's Sister
Witch Water
The Witch Herself
The Witch's Eye
Witch Weed
The Witch Returns

PLEASE DON'T
BE TRUE

Dangerously Alice

Almost Alice

Intensely Alice

PHYLLIS REYNOLDS NAYLOR

Atheneum Books for Young Readers
New York · London · Toronto · Sydney

ATHENEUM BOOKS FOR YOUNG READERS
An imprint of Simon & Schuster Children's Publishing Division
1230 Avenue of the Americas, New York, New York 10020
ATHENEUM BOOKS FOR YOUNG READERS is a registered trademark of Simon & Schuster, Inc.
For information about special discounts for bulk purchases, please contact Simon & Schuster Special Sales at 1-866-506-1949 or business@simonandschuster.com.
The Simon & Schuster Speakers Bureau can bring authors to your live event. For more information or to book an event, contact the Simon & Schuster Speakers Bureau at 1-866-248-3049 or visit our website at www.simonspeakers.com.
Book design by Mike Rosamilia
The text for this book is set in Berkeley.
Manufactured in the United States of America
This Atheneum Books for Young Readers paperback edition March 2011
4 6 8 10 9 7 5
The Library of Congress has cataloged the hardcover editions as follows:
Dangerously Alice / Phyllis Reynolds Naylor.—1st ed.
p. cm.
Summary: During fall semester of her junior year of high school, Alice decides to change her good girl image, while major remodeling begins at home and some important relationships begin to change.
ISBN 978-0-689-87094-1 (hc)
[1. Self-perception—Fiction. 2. Conduct of life—Fiction. 3. High Schools—Fiction. 4. Schools—Fiction. 5. Family Life—Maryland—Fiction. 6. Maryland—Fiction.] I. Title.
PZ7.N24Dam 2007   [Fic]—dc22   2006024181

Almost Alice / Phyllis Reynolds Naylor.—1st ed.
p. cm.
Summary: In the second semester of her junior year of high school, Alice gets back together with her old boyfriend Patrick, gets a promotion on the student newspaper, and remains a reliable, trusted friend.
ISBN 978-0-689-87096-5 (hc)
[1.Friendship—Fiction. 2. High schools—Fiction. 3. Schools—Fictions. 4. Identity—Fiction.] I. Title.
PZ7.N24Aln 2008   [Fic]—dc22   2007037457

Intensely Alice / Phyllis Reynolds Naylor.—1st ed.
p. cm.
Summary: During the summer between her junior and senior years of high school, Maryland teenager Alice McKinley volunteers at a local soup kitchen, tries to do "something wild" without getting arrested, and wonders if her trip to Chicago to visit boyfriend Patrick will result in a sleepover.
ISBN 978-1-4169-7551-9 (hc)
[1. Coming of age—Fiction. 2. Summer—Fiction. 3. Maryland—Fiction.] I. Title.
PZ7.N24Iq 2009   [Fic]—dc22   2008049047

ISBN 978-1-4424-1721-2 (bind-up pbk)
These titles were previously published individually.

Dangerously Alice

For Becca

Contents

1
LABELS

I had to hear it from Pamela. But then, the fact that she told me, and that she wasn't going back, sort of put a seal on our friendship. Ours was the real McCoy. So I couldn't figure out what was bothering me most: that Liz and I hadn't been invited or that our old gang was breaking up.

She told us about it on our ride to school that Monday. And to make things worse, we were riding the bus—one of the last places you want to be when you're a junior. Seniors would walk to school in snow up to their knees before they'd be seen on a bus. But Pam and Liz and I don't have cars of our own, and there was no one that morning to drive us. We sat close together on the backseat.

"This is the second time they've done it," Pamela went on as we listened uncomfortably. "Very hush-hush. The rule is that no one can speak. You can't move a deck chair or make any kind of noise, but you can do . . . well . . . almost anything else in or out of the water." She laughed.

"And everyone's naked?" Liz asked.

"In the pool, yes."

I couldn't help smiling a little—partly remembering the skinny-dipping we'd done at Camp Overlook two summers ago and partly thinking how Mark Stedmeister's parents were pretty strict about alcohol and drugs at their swimming pool, but completely oblivious to the fact that Mark and some of his friends were having midnight swims in the nude.

It was too painful to ask Pamela outright why Liz and I hadn't been invited, too scary to think that Pamela was being pulled away while we were being left behind. So I took the mature route and said, "Well, it sounds fun to me, Pam. Why do you say you're not going back?"

"For one thing, when you know you weren't invited the first time around, you can't help but feel that your invitation is borderline," she said. "But afterward—when we put on our clothes and drove to the soccer field so they could smoke and drink and talk—it was nothing but a big, malicious gossip fest. Boy, Jill and Karen . . . Brian, too . . . can rip into somebody faster than a tank of piranhas. Just mention a name—any name of anyone in the whole school—and in a matter of seconds, he's totaled. And you get the feeling everyone's expected to take a bite."

"I didn't think guys did that," said Liz. "I always knew that Jill and Karen were into it big-time—who's in, who's out—but I'm surprised that the guys are interested."

"Hey, they're interested in *Jill*—her body, anyway. And Karen, now that she's practically Jill's twin—hair, clothes, makeup, nails—parrots whatever Jill says. Whatever turns girls on turns guys on, you know that," Pamela said.

"So how did you get invited?" Liz asked. "And what did they say about *us*?"

Pamela just shrugged it off as though it weren't important, but we weren't letting her off that easily.

"I'd overheard Jill and Karen talking about the 'Silent Party,' or 'SP,' as they call it," Pamela explained. "I was nervy enough to ask what it was, so Karen described it for me—probably wanting to see if I was shocked. And when I wasn't, she asked if I wanted to come. I said 'Sure,' and asked if you guys were going to be there. She made this sort of face and looked at Jill, and Jill shook her head and said 'No.' And then she added, 'DD.' And they both laughed and walked off."

I tried to think what DD could possibly stand for. Dried dandruff? Dead as a doornail? Liz and I looked at each other, clueless.

"They speak in acronyms these days," Pamela went on. "When Jill and Justin and Mark and Brian and Keeno and Karen and some of Brian's other friends get together, they've got the whole student body divided up into groups, and each group has a label."

"Oh, every school does that," I said. "Walk in any high school, and they'll point out the Geeks, the Goths, the Nerds, the Brains, the Jocks, the—"

"That's not the kind I'm talking about," said Pamela. "Jill and Company divide the kids into the Studs, the Players, the Sluts, the Clueless Virgins, the Christian Virgins, the Freaks, and even *these* are broken down into UJ (Ugly Jock), TM (Typhoid Mary—don't touch), AG (Anything Goes) . . . you get the picture."

"And DD?" I asked.

Pamela dismissed it with a wave of her hand.

"*Tell* us!" Liz insisted.

"Dry as Dust," said Pamela. "But don't you believe it. I can only imagine what they'd been saying about me before I went and what they'll say now when I don't go back."

Dry as Dust. I felt my throat drying up just to hear it. This meant that somebody—some *bodies*—found me boring. Uninteresting. Unexciting.

Pamela grabbed my hand. "Who are *they* to decide who everyone else is?" she said. "And you know what Jill said they'd called *me*? Before I'd had the guts to come to their party?"

"What?" we asked.

"SS," said Pamela. "Serious Slut. I was mortified, but laughed it off. Yeah, right. Ha ha."

"They actually *told* you that?" Liz asked.

"Yeah. To see if I could take it, I guess. Boy, make *one* mistake, and you're labeled for life. After New York last spring, Hugh must have done a lot of talking."

We digested that for a moment or two, remembering what Pam had done in a hotel bathroom with a senior. Then Liz said, "It's hard to imagine Justin going along with all this. When I was going out with him, he seemed too nice to be so petty and malicious."

Pamela shrugged. "He's in love with Jill, and love is blind. Jill just laughs off all this gossip as a hobby of hers—labeling people, that is. And at some point in the evening, I asked the others what label they'd give Jill. This was at the soccer field later. They'd been drinking, and the guys were cutting up. Brian said BB for Beautiful Bitch. Justin suggested LM for Love Machine. It was sort of like Jill had never considered what others might think of her. I couldn't tell if she was flattered or annoyed, but I knew by the look on her face that she didn't appreciate the question. Didn't appreciate *me*. I won't be invited back, you can bet, and if I am, I won't go."

I suddenly put my arm around Pamela. "*We* appreciate you!" I said.

"More than you know," said Liz.

This second week of my junior year, I sure didn't need any more hassles. Every minute of my day was filled with something, but I didn't know what I could give up. All juniors had to take the PSAT in October, ready or not, and I worked for Dad at the Melody Inn music store on Saturdays. I was the roving reporter for the junior class on our school newspaper, *The Edge*; I still belonged on stage crew in the Drama Club; I got up ridiculously early three mornings a week and ran a couple of miles to keep in shape; I visited Molly, my friend with leukemia, once a week; plus, homework was heavier and harder than it had been last year, and geometry was a killer.

"I feel like I'm going under for the third time," I told Sylvia, my stepmom, when I realized I hadn't called Molly all week. If anyone should be complaining about life, it's Molly.

"I know the feeling," said Sylvia. "I felt it every Friday for the first year I was teaching. But by Monday I'd usually recovered."

"So there's hope?" I asked. "The teachers are merciless! It's like theirs is the only subject we've got. 'Make an outline.' 'Write a paper.' 'Research a topic.' When you multiply that by five . . . !"

"Well, teachers are hassled too," said Sylvia. "If their students don't do well, it's the teachers who get hassled by their principals. And if test scores are down for the school, the principals get hassled by the supervisors."

Sometimes—more than I like to admit—Sylvia gets on my nerves. It's like I tell her about a problem, and she's always got a bigger one. I wasn't interested right then in teachers' problems. I wanted to talk about *me*. *A little empathy here, please.*

"I'm not talking about test scores, I'm talking about assignments—about the timing of assignments," I told her. "When teachers get together in the faculty lounge, why don't they space their assignments so they're not all due at the same time?" I asked.

"Probably because we've got a zillion other things to think about," she said. "My guess is that after you get in the routine of a new semester, it will seem more bearable. If nothing else, you'll probably find at least *one* thing you can look forward to."

She was right about that. His name was Scott Lynch—a tall, lanky senior, our new editor in chief on the school newspaper. He was smart, like my *old* ex-boyfriend, Patrick, and knew his way around; he was thoughtful and caring, like my *new* ex-boyfriend, Sam, one of the photographers for our paper. When I walked in the journalism room after school for our meetings, Scott would give me this big, warm, welcoming smile that enveloped me like a hug. As though he'd been waiting just for me. But then, he did the same to the rest of the staff, including Jacki Severn, features editor.

Jacki's not a real blonde, like Pamela Jones, but her hair's gorgeous, and on this day she looked even better than usual. Great top, great jeans, great makeup.

"Idea!" she said when we'd pushed two tables together and sat down for our planning session. "If students have to read the stuff we write every two weeks, they should at least know what we look like. I think we should have a group picture taken for the front page."

Now I knew why Jacki was all spiffed up. I'd washed my hair that morning because I'd been running, but I hadn't taken time to blow-dry it.

"Not the front page," said Scott.

"Well, *any* page," said Jacki.

There were four guys on the newspaper staff: Scott; two photographers, Sam and Don; and Tony Osler, sports editor.

Scott, Don, and Tony are seniors, and I seemed to have a thing about seniors this year. Of my two latest boyfriends, Patrick and Sam, Patrick has traveled all around the world with his parents—his dad is a diplomat—and sometimes he acts incredibly sophisticated. But he's a couple of months younger than I am, and he can also act incredibly juvenile. Sam's a junior too, like me, and sweet as honey, but sometimes I felt I was out with a little boy. I'd never dated a senior, and right now I was crushing on Scott.

None of the guys on the staff were remotely interested in having their pictures taken, and I voted with them. But all the roving reporters this year were girls, one for each class, and they voted with Jacki, along with the layout coordinator. So the vote was five to five. Miss Ames, our sponsor, broke the tie with a yes vote and went next door to get the chemistry teacher, who came over and took our picture. Jacki seated herself in the first row beside Scott, and the rest of us gathered around them.

"A little closer," the chemistry teacher said. "The guy on the end there—move in real tight next to the girl in green."

"With pleasure," said Tony, and put one arm around me, his hand on my ribs. I could feel his breath in my hair. Almost imperceptibly, one of his fingers moved a little under my arm, not quite stroking my breast. An electric shock traveled down my spine, but I didn't move away. And then—*flash*—the picture was taken and the group dissolved.

"Okay. Back to work," Scott said as we sat down at the tables again. "Here's what the classes have decided for Spirit Week."

A lot of high schools had been doing it for years, and though we'd always had a homecoming dance usually attended by the juniors and seniors, we'd never had Spirit Week—a time for students to bond and show loyalty to the school and its football team. Each day during Spirit Week, the students—and sometimes the teachers—came to school in crazy outfits, decided on in advance. So our school had assigned the freshman class to choose the costume for Monday; sophomores got Tuesday, juniors got Wednesday, seniors Thursday, and the faculty would choose the dress for Friday.

"Here are the votes," Scott read. "Monday, Pajama Day; Tuesday, Beach Day; Wednesday, Mismatched Day; Thursday, Wild Hair Day; and the teachers chose Victorian Day for Friday."

"Are you sure that's not Victoria's Secret Day?" asked Tony, and we laughed.

"Don't I wish," Scott said. "Nope. Victorian England."

The freshman and sophomore roving reporters were already chattering about what they would wear.

"Somehow I thought we'd be a little more original than that," said Jacki.

"Well, what we need are ideas for next year, and here's where you come in, Alice," Scott said, his blue eyes smiling at me. "Would you go around asking for suggestions so we can get people thinking about Spirit Week next year? Making it a tradition?"

"Sure," I said, lost in the blueness of those eyes. They were topaz blue, like the Caribbean Sea I'd seen on postcards. "I can do that." Scott could have asked me to climb up on the school roof and recite the Gettysburg Address and I would have said, *Sure! I can do that!*

Dad had let me use his car that day. He lets me have it sometimes when I've got something going on after school if Sylvia can drive him to work. I stopped by the CVS drugstore on the way home to buy a new steno pad and some eyeliner.

Jill and Karen were smoking at one of the little tables outside Starbucks next door. I hesitated for a second, and then—taking a chance to see if I was really as DD as they thought—I walked over to them and asked if they had any suggestions for Spirit Week next year. When Jill saw me, she gave a sort of half smile and took another drag on her cigarette.

We've never been buddy-buddy, but ever since I stopped letting Jill and Karen use my employee discount when I worked at Hecht's last summer, I've felt they've cooled even more toward me. And after what Pamela told me, I was sure of it. Just the way they excluded me from their conversations some of the time. Once or twice I'd even had the feeling they'd turned away and whispered something to each other when they saw me. Their smiles seemed to have double meanings. The way they'd light up a cigarette, then glance my way. Just little things like that.

I know that a couple of times I've fanned their smoke when they lit up, and I've tried not to be so obvious about it, but I hate inhaling the stuff. This time, though, I tried to ignore it.

"Hi, Jill. Hi, Karen," I said. "I'm doing a short piece for *The Edge* with suggestions for next year's Spirit Week. Any ideas?"

"What kind of ideas?" asked Karen. She tilted her head back and blew the smoke straight up.

"How to dress. Hawaiian Day. Stuff like that," I told her, and added laughingly, "Tony Osler's already suggested Victoria's Secret Day."

They laughed too. "Hey, I'd go for that one," said Jill. "Bikini Day, maybe?"

"All right . . . ," I said.

"We could do Twins Day," said Karen, and she looked at Jill. "You and I could team up."

"That's a good one," I said, and wrote it on the back of my hand with my ballpoint. I really needed that steno pad.

"Or Preppie Day, and half the school would already come dressed for it," said Jill, who dresses more like she's going to work at Saks than going to school.

"That makes three," I said. "Thanks. I'm off to buy a steno pad."

"There she goes! Alice McKinley, Girl Reporter!" Karen sang out as I walked away.

I know that Karen and Jill look on my little job for the newspaper with amusement, but what else is new? This semester was already a grind. I'd missed a couple days of school that first full week when we went to Tennessee for my grandfather's funeral, and I still had a paper to write for one of those assignments. The only solution I could see was to stay up late at night till I got caught up. Bummer.

Still . . . the truth was, our old group wasn't the same. Until recently, we'd simply thought of ourselves as "the gang at Mark Stedmeister's pool." Now our differences seemed more important. I know that some of the kids think I take life too seriously, but . . . well, sometimes I do. That's me. Also, word had gotten around that I'd chickened out over the summer when Brian was going eighty in a forty-mile zone in the new car his dad had bought him and that I'd made Brian stop and let me out. I felt that some of the kids were still talking about it.

"So let them talk," I told myself aloud, and headed for the cosmetic counter. This was my junior year, and I had some decisions to make about my future. Jill had already confided that her number one objective was to marry the wealthy Justin, and as for Karen, she said she either wanted to marry rich or get into fashion design.

I'll admit that, other than going in to talk to the school counselor about a career, my immediate goal wasn't any more noble: I wanted to get Dad to relax his rule that I had to go six months without an accident before I could have any friends in the car with me. Finally, knowing how much I needed the car for after-school stuff, he'd said that he might—*might*—shorten it to five months instead of six, but I couldn't so much as get a traffic ticket during that time. This would mean I could have friends in the car with me by Thanksgiving, not Christmas. Just the thought of Gwen and Liz and Pamela in the car, with me at the wheel driving them somewhere, was number one on my "can't wait" list.

* * *

Lester came over on Sunday to rake leaves. The trees seemed to be shedding earlier this year, and he said it would make things easier if we did a first raking now.

I was glad to see Les back in our old routine. After he and Tracy broke up last month, I was afraid he might become a recluse or something. My twenty-four-year-old brother is getting his master's degree in philosophy next spring. I guess I always thought of philosophers as the hermit type, but that doesn't exactly fit Lester.

"It looks like you're going to make it, Les," I said as we raked, the bamboo tines of the rakes making *scritch scratch* sounds in the grass. "I mean, your degree and everything. I've still got all that ahead of me, and I haven't even taken the PSAT yet. I'm scared silly."

"Of what?" he asked.

"If I do poorly on the PSAT, I'll probably bomb on the SAT," I told him. "If I bomb on the SAT, I won't get into college, and if I don't go to college, I'll probably end up cleaning public restrooms on the night shift."

Les looked over at me. "Congratulations, Al. You just beat your all-time record. You went from a potential high to a major low in four seconds."

"But it's true, Lester. Life is just a series of hurdles, and no one ever tells you that. Right now everything's riding on that PSAT. You get over one roadblock, you've got another staring you in the face."

He laughed. "Well, *some* people *like* to have 'next steps' to look forward to. Some people *like* to have challenges. Ever think of that? Think how bored you'd be if everything came easy."

We raked in silence for a little while. Then I asked the question I'd been wanting to ask him for the past month. "When Tracy said no—when she broke it off—was that a roadblock or a challenge?"

"No getting around it, I was disappointed."

"You'd been dating since January, Les. Do you look at it as eight months wasted or what? I really want to know how you deal with it."

"Not wasted. I don't look at the time I've spent with *any* girl as wasted. I feel I learned something from each one, and . . ." He grinned. "I certainly had a good time."

I ignored the good time part and concentrated on the learning. "What did you learn?"

"About the kind of woman I'm looking for," said Lester.

"What kind is that? What did you learn from Loretta Jenkins?" I asked.

"She was never my girlfriend," Lester said. "But I was around her enough to know that I wanted a girl with her feet on the ground. Which was definitely not Loretta."

"Marilyn?"

"That I wanted a girl a little more . . . uh . . . physical. Like Crystal."

"Then what was wrong with Crystal?"

"I wanted a girl more sensitive . . . like Marilyn."

I wondered if I was naming these girlfriends in the proper order. "Lauren?" I asked, remembering one of Lester's instructors at the university.

"Too fickle."

"Eva?"

"Too sophisticated."

Should I go on? I asked myself, but I did. "Tracy?"

Les sighed. "With Tracy, I thought I'd found it all. But she broke up with me, remember. For Tracy, her family came first." And then he said, "Nobody's perfect, Al. I could fall in love with somebody tomorrow who's as different from me as night from day."

"That's scary, Lester," I said.

"That's life," he told me.

By staying up three nights in a row till twelve—two o'clock, one night—I finally finished the last assignment I'd missed when we went to Tennessee. I'd researched the Marshall Plan for World History and finished a list of suggestions for next year's Spirit Week for the newspaper:

- Victoria's Secret Day
- Towel Day
- Egyptian Day
- Twins Day
- Preppie Day
- Bikini Day

- Pimp 'n' Ho Day
- Garage Band Day
- Body Part Day
- Celebrity Day
- Crazy Hat Day

Scott was really pleased, and he gave my shoulder a squeeze when I turned in my list before homeroom the following morning. "Nice going!" he said. "We'll run it next time. Garage Band Day! I like that!"

That one shoulder squeeze was enough to make *my* day. I would have liked a Scott Lynch Day just to be able to tag along behind him for six periods.

I was beginning to feel, as Sylvia thought I would, that I was getting into the routine of things. That I was getting a grip. As I refreshed my lip gloss in the restroom after lunch, I came to the conclusion that I looked pretty good. Only a zit or two I couldn't cover with foundation, and if I was lucky, as the orthodontist said, I might get my braces off by spring.

I was putting a little blush on my cheeks when Jill and Karen came in the restroom.

"Alice!" Karen said, and looked genuinely glad to see me. "Did you do the essay question on *The Great Gatsby*? You know . . . that comparative thing?"

"Yes, and I was up until two in the morning finishing it," I said.

"I'm *drowning* in homework!" Karen said dramatically.

"Absolutely *drowning*! I just couldn't get to it. Could I see yours? Just to get some ideas? I'll paraphrase it; I won't copy."

I had spent at least three hours struggling with that essay. I had come up with what I thought were original ideas for looking at F. Scott Fitzgerald's other works—finding trends, contradictions, repetitions. . . . There was nothing Karen could paraphrase that wouldn't take my original ideas and run with them.

"Oh, Karen, I can't," I said. "I worked really hard on that piece, and I want to keep the originality."

"Just this once?" she pleaded. "I'll be careful." I could see a crease deepening in her forehead.

I shrugged helplessly. "I can't. Sorry."

She turned to Jill as they left the restroom, and I heard her say, "Told you! MGT."

2
MGT

Liz, Pamela, Gwen, and I decided to make it Girls' Night Out—
to go to the Homecoming Dance together. Jeans and sweaters.
We'd argued about the kind of shoes to wear, though. Pamela
said she was coming in the tightest pair of jeans she could find
and her silver stilettos with ankle straps. She also wanted an
escape clause: If any of us got asked to go with a guy, that girl
was free to back out. So much for loyalty. But it didn't happen,
so we entered Spirit Week as a team. Monday through Friday
were costume days; Friday night was the football game; and
Saturday night was Homecoming Dance in the gym.

The Friday before, at our lockers, Liz said, "Mom's going to drive us to school on Monday, seeing as how we'll be in pajamas." Her locker's next to mine. They say you're lucky if your locker's next to a gorgeous girl's because all the guys will stop to talk to her and you can have the leftovers.

That was only partly true. Elizabeth was one of the most beautiful girls in school—long dark hair, thick black eyelashes—but she was also shy around people she didn't know, and that makes some kids think she's stuck-up, which couldn't be further from the truth. She's as brunette as Pamela is blond. I wear my hair shoulder length, Liz wears hers long and straight, Pamela still prefers the short layered look, and Gwen—who's African American—changes her hairstyle every couple of weeks. We never know what she'll try next.

"So what are we going to wear on Pajama Day?" I asked. "I'm just going in my T-shirt and flannels."

"Oh, but you've got to wear bunny slippers or *something*!" Liz said. "If we're not going to be outlandish, what's the point?"

The point, actually, as Scott told us, was to get the whole school doing something together to build school spirit and help the football team win one of its biggest games of the season. I couldn't see how bunny slippers contributed to that, but I told her I'd think of something.

"Listen," I said. "Do you know what MGT means?"

"Monosodium glutamate?" she guessed, stuffing some books in her bag. "Oh, that's MSG. I don't know. Where'd you see it?"

"I heard Karen say it to Jill when she was walking away from me the other afternoon."

"Just . . . MGT?"

"Yeah. And I don't think it was complimentary."

Liz shrugged. "Who knows? Who cares? It's just another stupid label. Did you ever hear either of them say anything *nice* about anyone?"

"Probably not," I said, and let it go.

It was a zoo at school on Monday. Mostly it was the cheerleaders, the class officers, the newspaper staff, the faculty, and maybe one fourth of the junior and senior classes who came to school in their pajamas. But at least a dozen showed up in animal slippers of one kind or another—big, fluffy bunny slippers like Liz's; cow slippers that mooed; pig slippers that oinked. Pamela had on a pair of duck slippers that quacked each time she took a step.

Jill came in tailored black satin pajamas with lace trim; Karen's were trimmed in fake fur. Penny, however, wore the same red flannels with the trapdoor seat that she'd worn the night of my coed slumber party two years ago—the night she and Patrick faked a kiss for the camera. That was probably the beginning of my breakup with Patrick. I felt that old familiar pang in the chest and was surprised that, after all this time, I wasn't over it yet.

The teachers were the funniest, though. Our principal came in his pj's with a pillow tied to his back like a backpack. The chemistry prof brought a teddy bear. One teacher even came in her pajamas with a pacifier on a string around her neck, and our English teacher had bedtime storybooks scattered around the room. It was a blast.

The one person who didn't quite get it was Amy Sheldon, or "Amy Clueless," as some of the girls call her. We've never decided what makes her tick, but Amy marches to a different drummer. On Pajama Day it appeared that she had simply got out of bed that morning, put on her shoes and socks, then her coat, and came to school—hair unbrushed, one thin, wrinkled pajama leg hiked up above her knee. She thought it was a "come-as-you-are" party or something.

"This is fun, isn't it, Alice?" she said, laughing, when I saw her in the hall. "My mom didn't believe we were supposed to come to school in our pajamas, but I showed her, didn't I? Didn't I, Alice?"

I thought of the teasing Amy had endured since she'd moved from special ed into the regular classrooms. She was undersized for her age, her features not quite symmetrical, and when she talked, her voice seemed too loud for such a small body.

"You sure did," I told her.

Probably because the cheerleaders got involved and all the class officers, too, more kids took part in Beach Day on Tuesday. No one could wear bathing suits, but we could wear shorts. When we changed classes, the halls were filled with the squeakings and squishes of dozens of flip-flops. During P.E. the gym teacher gave us an exercise to do with beach balls, and almost every T-shirt had a slogan on it—the kind you'd see at the beach: EAT ME FOR DESSERT and LIFE IS A BITCH and GOD IS COMING, AND IS SHE PISSED!

I cut my lunch period short to put my name on the sign-up

sheet outside the guidance counselor's door. I wanted to talk to her about majoring in counseling in college—what courses would be helpful now, what colleges have the best programs, stuff like that.

She wasn't in her office. There was a sign on her door that said GONE SWIMMING, but I took the clipboard off the hook and penciled in my name for the following noontime slot. As I was putting it back, Karen and Jill and another girl sauntered by the doorway in their cutoffs and halter tops.

Karen's sandals had sequins on them. Jill wore a huge pair of dangly earrings made of seashells.

"Oh, Alice!" Jill said, taking in the situation with the kind of condescending smile she's been giving me lately. "Having problems already?"

That's the first thing anyone thinks about when you go to a counselor. What I should have said was, *Isn't everyone?* What I said was, "I just want some career information. I'm thinking about majoring in counseling in college."

"*Counseling!*" Jill said. "Spare me."

"Why?" I asked.

"With all the glamour jobs in the world, you'd pick *counseling*?" Karen exclaimed. "Gee, why not grow soybeans or something. Now, *there's* an idea!"

Jill laughed. "No, I've got it! She could design closets."

They were really getting under my skin. "I like the thought of working with people. I think it would be interesting," I said.

"Oh, absolutely!" said Jill.

"MGT!" Karen murmured as they turned in at the next doorway.

"What's that?" asked the girl who was with them.

And Jill answered, "Miss Goody Two-shoes."

I didn't react, just kept walking, but my cheeks felt hot. It was as though there were one gauge inside my body registering my discomfort level and another registering my self-esteem. The first one was rising; the second was bottoming out. Did I really care what Jill and Karen thought of my career plans? Evidently. I hated that they got to me so.

Forget it, I told myself.

You can say that, but how do you actually *do* it?

By Wednesday, Mismatched Day, at least half the students were in the swing of things. We came to school not only in different-colored socks for each foot, but in hideous combinations of colors and patterns. Pamela, all 105 pounds of her, came in a fur jacket on top, shorts on the bottom, a different earring in each ear. I made sure Sam took a picture of her for our paper.

It's interesting how well Sam and I get along now that we're not going out anymore. He seemed so hurt the day we broke up, and I felt so awful, so guilty, I wondered if he'd ever be the same again. But as soon as he got a new girlfriend, he was happy as a clam. Happier, maybe. Sam's probably one of those guys who's in love with love. As long as he has a girlfriend, life's good.

"I wish Spirit Week went on all year," Pamela said. "School would be more fun if we could dress in costumes all the time."

"Let's all go over to Molly's after school dressed like this," I said, showing off the lace-up boot and red knee stocking on one leg, the black net stocking and high-heeled pump on the other. Gwen had her brother's car for the day and said she'd drive.

When I went to see Mrs. Bailey at noon for my appointment, I found her wearing a baseball cap and a football sweatshirt. We laughed at each other's getup.

"Well, I'm not getting a whole lot of work done this week, but I'm having fun," she told me, and gave me a welcoming smile, then waited.

"I've pretty much decided that I want a career working with people," I began. "I used to think I wanted to be a psychologist, but I'm not sure I could get through a doctoral program. Statistics and everything. And the more I think about it, I want to go into counseling."

I expected her to get all enthusiastic, but she just nodded and smiled.

"Well, a degree is only one thing you need to consider," she said. "The other half is personality—your ability to empathize. How's your patience factor? Are you a good listener?"

"I probably do a better job of listening than I do of being patient," I told her. "But I can learn, can't I?"

"Definitely," she said. "You'll want to bone up on psychology and sociology, anthropology, literature . . . anything having to do with people. . . ."

We talked for ten minutes or more, and then I asked, "What's the best thing about being a counselor?"

"Good question," said Mrs. Bailey. She thought a moment before answering. "I think it's helping students connect with their real selves; helping them find out what they really, truly, down in their heart of hearts, want to do or be, not necessarily what their parents want them to be. And now you're going to ask what's the worst part, right?"

I nodded, and we laughed.

"Time," she said. "Not enough of it. I wish I could spend twice as much time with every student who walks in here. *Three* times as much. There are too many forms to fill out, reports to write. We're given too many tasks that aren't in our job description. But there's no perfect career, Alice. There are always going to be pluses and minuses."

So there, *Karen and Jill!* I thought as I left her office. Your *careers won't be so perfect either.*

At lunch Penny was showing us a fashion magazine article about how burlesque had influenced the fashion industry over the years. There was a photo of a 1930s fan dancer, supposedly nude except for a large Japanese-style fan covering part of her body; a 1940s-type bubble dancer who performed nude, half hidden by large bubbles blown from a fan behind the footlights; burlesque dancers who used large ostrich feathers to hide their bodies and tease the men. And then the magazine showed pictures of fashion designers' dresses with fantail pleats for the bodice; large round globes, like bubbles, decorating a neckline; dresses made of beads and feathers. . . .

We were laughing at the hairstyles in those old photos.

The heavily mascara-lined eyes, the heavily rouged cheeks, the pouty lips. That same afternoon as I headed for my locker, I was approached by the roving freshman reporter for our newspaper, a shy girl who looked relieved to find an upperclassman—*any* upperclassman—she knew.

"Scott wants me to do a poll on what people plan to do after college," she said.

"To do?" I asked. "Like . . . travel?"

"*Be,*" she said. "What do you want to *be* after college?"

"Bubble dancer," I joked.

And she actually wrote it down and put my name after it. I laughed out loud as I opened my locker and put on my jacket. *Chew on that for a while, Jill and Karen!* I thought. Miss Goody Two-shoes indeed!

Molly was definitely thinner and feeling pretty sick when we saw her. She smiled at our mismatched clothes, but it was a smile that looked as though it were holding back nausea.

"You guys are great to come by, but I'm the 'Puke-Up Kid' right now," she said.

We didn't stay long. We did the talking mostly—Pamela told her about the first three days of Spirit Week and how we were all going to come to school the next day with the weirdest hairdo we could think of. Then Pamela's voice fell flat when we realized that Molly didn't have any hair at all under her bandana. In fact, she'd lost her eyebrows and eyelashes. You think of a head being bald, but not a face.

"We'll come back another time when you're feeling better," I said, signaling the others that I didn't think she was enjoying our company much.

"Yeah? When will that be? I wonder," Molly said plaintively.

"You're going to beat this, Molly," Gwen said. "Be strong, girl."

"You don't still work at the lab, do you?" Molly asked her.

"No, that was a summer internship," Gwen said.

"Then you don't really know if I'm getting better or not, do you?" asked Molly.

"No," Gwen said truthfully. "I don't. But I'm going to picture you well and strong and gorgeous."

"Good," Molly said. "I want to be a redhead next time, with hair down to my waist."

"You got it," said Gwen, and Molly closed her eyes.

Downstairs her mom said, "It's been a trying week. She can't seem to keep anything down, and she's behind in her school-work. She's discouraged and scared, and so are we, frankly, though the doctor says this is all to be expected."

"I'm praying for her," said Elizabeth.

"Thank you. I really appreciate it," said Mrs. Brennan. "One of her sisters is in town visiting now, and that should help too."

Outside, Pamela said, "Maybe we ought to start a fund drive and collect money for her."

"For what?" asked Gwen.

"I don't know. For whatever you need if you have cancer," said Pamela.

"We're not doctors, Pam. We don't know what she needs," Gwen said, and didn't say much more as she drove us home.

I think that most of the school came on Thursday with their hair a mess, literally. All colors of the rainbow. Spiked, frosted, peaked, molded, zigzagged, cornrowed, teased, and even shaved.

On Friday the wild hair was replaced with top hats and high stiff collars, only to be discarded that night at the football game, where we wore wool jackets and fleece-lined boots and cheered our lungs out, even though we lost by three points to the rival team. To be frank, I never really understood football. I cheer when everyone else is cheering and sit down when everyone else sits.

We were getting some good stories and photos for the next issue of *The Edge*, and during the second half of the game— for the third quarter, anyway—Scott Lynch and a couple more seniors sat with us, Scott next to me, thigh to thigh. I figured my junior year couldn't get much better than this and that I would remember this night, this moment, this warmth against me for the rest of my natural life.

On Saturday night Gwen got her brother's car again for the Homecoming Dance, and I went to Liz's house in my best tight-fitting jeans and a low-cut sweater. Liz did my makeup, and I did her hair, and we both looked eighteen when we left her house and climbed in Gwen's car, Pam in the front seat. Liz's little brother waved to us from the house.

"Tonight we are going to *howl*!" Pamela announced over her shoulder.

"Ow-ooooo!" I yipped, and we laughed.

The gym was decorated with streamers in fall colors, and a DJ played the music, taking requests and playing our favorite songs. He'd also recorded our school song and had a local band tape different variations of it.

There were a few slow numbers, the lights dimming. The four of us danced together on the fast numbers, drifted away during the slow ones, but as I was leaving the floor near the end of the evening, someone swung me round and pulled me toward him. Tony Osler.

"Dance?" he said as he began moving with the beat.

"Do I have a choice?" I teased, smiling back, glad to have at least one serious dance of the evening—and with a *senior*, at that!

"All right, *may* I have this dance?" he said, grinning at me.

"You may," I said.

Tony's about my height—brown hair and eyes, nice-looking but nothing spectacular. Husky. We were cheek to cheek for a while, and sometimes I felt he was pressed just a little too close. But I'll admit I didn't object.

"So," he said into my ear, "I've been meaning to ask you a question."

"Yeah?" I said.

"How many of those answers were true?" he said.

"What answers?" I asked, pulling away a little to look at him.

"You know—on that 'Predict Your Future Love Life' questionnaire that Brian Brewster sent out."

I should have known he was still thinking about that terrible trick Brian had played on me, when I'd answered some extremely personal questions online without knowing that all the answers had gone to Brian.

"That silly thing?" I said. "It's old as Methuselah. It must be the way Brian gets his kicks. I just wanted to stir him up a little."

Tony held me close again and whispered in my ear, "Stirred *me* up a little."

"You're easily stirred," I said.

"Well, all I can say is that you look good tonight," said Tony. "Good enough to eat."

And this was exciting to a girl without a boyfriend. A girl with braces. A girl of average intelligence, average everything, who hadn't been kissed since last spring.

3
ANNABELLE

Everyone says to get a good night's sleep before you take the PSAT. They say to eat a high-carb breakfast, don't have a quarrel with your parents, and if you can't answer a question on the test, go on to the next one and come back to it later. But you can do all these things and still be terrified.

Sylvia had invited Lester over for dinner and made an extra pumpkin pie for him to take back home and share with his roommates.

"Give me some sample questions, Les," I said.

"Al, it's been so long since I was in high school, I don't even remember taking a PSAT," he said.

"I don't care," I told him. "Make up something, and see if I can think clearly. Anything at all."

He took another helping of peas and onions. "If 'X' equals the number of women seeking eligible men, and 'Y' equals the number of men seeking eligible women, and 'Z' equals the number of men and women with cell phones, how many couples will hook up?" he said.

"Be serious," I told him.

"Alice, I think the best thing you can do at this point is put the test completely out of your mind and watch a movie or something," Sylvia said. "That test isn't going to define you for the rest of your life."

Dad grinned at me. "No matter how you do, you can always work at the Melody Inn."

"Yeah, right," I said.

After dinner I called to see what everyone else was doing. Gwen was reading a novel, Pamela was doing her nails, and Liz was planning to take a half-hour soak in the tub. I decided to go for a long walk in the fall air, then come back and watch a video.

I was thinking how much I liked our neighborhood—how much I liked Elizabeth living across the street and Pamela only a few blocks away. We'd been friends forever, and at least that much hadn't changed. But Lester had moved out, Sylvia had moved in, and what I had thought would be the perfect life with the teacher of my dreams for a stepmom turned out to be not quite so perfect after all. She just had her own way of doing things, and sometimes she seemed too much the teacher here at home. But Dad loved her, and I was glad they married. Besides, I only had two more years to live here full-time before I left for college, and that gave me a funny feeling in my stomach.

I was about four blocks from home when I heard someone call, "Hey, Alice!"

It was Keeno, Brian's friend, the guy from St. John's. His last name was Keene, but everyone called him Keeno.

I grinned and walked over to where he'd pulled up at the curb, then rested my arms on the open window. "Hey!" I said. "When did you get the wheels?"

"Dad finally caved and bought me a car. It's a secondhand, fourth-owner, with a hundred thousand miles on it, but it moves. What are you doing out by yourself? Running away?" he asked.

I laughed. "PSAT tomorrow. I'm trying to calm my nerves."

"I took mine last year," he said. "Not so bad."

"I hate tests," I told him. "I think I'd actually enjoy school if we never had to take tests. I get stomachaches and headaches, and my hands perspire. . . ."

"Want to go for a ride and relax a little?" he asked. "I'll drive slow and play soft music and let the wind blow through your hair."

I smiled. "No, thanks. I need the walk, but it doesn't stop the worrying."

"Then I could drive seventy miles an hour, and at least you could worry about something else," he said.

"Not that." I laughed.

"Starbucks? A caramel latte? Ice cream?"

"Naw. I'm just out clearing my head. Thanks. So where are *you* going?"

"Oh, just cruising around looking for pickups. Drugs. A little robbery, maybe. Nothing big."

I laughed again and backed away from the car. "Don't get caught," I said. He waved and pulled away.

When I got home, I watched an hour of *Gone with the Wind*, then fell asleep.

The next morning I wasn't nearly as worried as I had been the day before. Now that the day was here and there was nothing more I could do about it, I read the comics at breakfast like I always do. And as it turned out, I think I did okay on the test. I was sure of maybe 60 percent. A lot of kids finished before me, including Gwen, but I calmed down and tried to see it as an adventure. An experiment. We wouldn't get the results till December.

I decided that one thing I could do to make myself more interesting was to actually learn football. I don't know how I grew up to be so sports-challenged, but I did. When the gang gets together, the other girls seem to know about fifty yard lines and halfbacks and fullbacks, while I sit hunkered down in a corner chair wishing I were watching almost anything other than football. But no one is going to invite a girl over to watch football if she cheers for the wrong team and doesn't know it. No girl like that would be the life of the party. There was only one person to call.

"Lester," I said on Sunday, "will you be home this afternoon? I really, really need a lesson in football, and I was wondering if you were going to watch the game."

"Yeah, we're watching it here," Les said, meaning he and his roommates. "Come on over if you want."

I arrived with a bag of chili-flavored corn chips and some brownies. I was a little embarrassed that Paul Sorenson and George Palamas were there too, but I tried to ask only about things that really confused me. Les and I were on the couch, Paul was in an easy chair on one side, George in the contour chair on the other.

"Okay, you know who the Redskins are, right?" asked Lester.

"Yes, I'm not a total idiot. The guys in red and orange," I answered. "And the Cowboys are silver and blue."

"So far so good," said Les. "Now, at each end of the field, you see two goalposts. Those are in the end zones. One end of the field is Washington's end zone. The other is Dallas's. A team scores if they can get the ball in the other team's end zone. If they do, it's a touchdown, worth six points. They get an additional point if their kicker can kick the ball between the other team's goalposts. Questions?"

"No, I think I understand that much," I said. "It's all the stuff between the two end zones that I don't understand."

"We'll get to those one by one," said Les. "But you can't think straight unless you have a beer in your hand. In your case, a can of Gatorade."

I watched for a while in silence. Les glanced over now and then to see if I had any questions.

Finally I said, "See, Lester? *See?* This is why I like basketball better than football. In basketball you can't take your eyes off the ball even for a second or somebody might score. It's easy to understand. If the ball goes through the basket, you score. What's to understand? But all these guys do in football is huddle and *talk* about it first. 'Just *do* it,' I want to say. Just get out there and *do* it! And even when they do move, it's only for a few seconds and you can't even see the ball."

Suddenly, however, as Dallas was moving down the field, there must have been a fumble because a Redskins player had the ball. He whirled around and ran . . . and ran . . . and ran for Dallas's end zone. One Cowboy after another tried to bring him down, but he made it, and I was on my feet yelling my lungs out.

"Touchdown! Touchdown!" I screamed. "We got a touchdown!"

I looked around. No one else was cheering.

"What?" I said. "*What?*"

"Sit down," said Les. "There was a flag on the play."

I stared. The Redskin who had been doing a victory dance between the goalposts suddenly stopped. A referee switched on his microphone and waved his arms, but I didn't understand a thing he said. All I knew was that the touchdown didn't count. Turned out it wasn't even the Redskins' ball. So what did the players do then? Went into a huddle and talked about it.

At school the talk was of the PSAT, Halloween, and the Snow Ball. Because Halloween fell on a Wednesday this year, no one seemed to be planning anything. We were simply too busy, for one thing. Too much homework. And we certainly weren't going trick-or-treating anymore. As for the Snow Ball, I hadn't been asked to go as a freshman or sophomore, and suddenly, as much as I'd liked going to the Homecoming Dance with my girlfriends, I wanted to go to the Snow Ball with a guy. To be asked by a guy. And not just any guy: a senior. And not just any senior: Scott Lynch.

I tried to figure out the odds of his asking me.

Pro: He'd sat next to me for a while at the game.

Con: He was a popular senior; I was a junior.

Pro: The way he smiled at me.

Con: He smiled that way at everyone.

Pro: He'd squeezed my shoulder once.

Con: So what?

When we had our staff meeting on Wednesday after school to lay out the photos and write-ups of Spirit Week, I tried to catch Scott's eye and see if there was any spark. See if his smile lingered a bit.

"Hey, Alice!" he called. "Look at this one."

I went over to the layout table and stood as close to him as I dared. The photos Sam had taken of Mismatched Day and Pajama Day and Wild Hair Day were lined up across the table. Scott was pointing to a close-up of my legs, the one in red stocking and boot, the other in net stocking and heel.

"Yeah!" said Tony, grinning. "Let's use that one!"

"Sold!" Scott said, smiling at me, that luscious, wide,

lip-stretching, teeth-gleaming smile. Then, to Don, he said, "Show me your five best shots of the football game and the Homecoming Dance, and let's see what we've got. We'll do a double-page spread." As he passed by me in the narrow space between table and desk, Scott's fingers rested on my arm for just a moment. I wanted to put my hand over his and keep it there forever.

Later, as I wrote down my assignment for the next issue, I found I had made elaborate *S*'s and *L*'s in the margins all up and down the page.

I didn't have Dad's car that day, so after the staff meeting Jacki Severn dropped me off at the corner nearest our house. She was reciting some of the Halloween parody she'd written, which was funnier on paper, I hoped, than it seemed when she recited it aloud. The gist of it was that it was the one holiday of the year when everything was the opposite of ordinary—when ugliest was best, the grosser the better. . . .

"I've got this great idea for the Snow Ball issue," she said just before I got out. "There's this computer graphic of icicles, and I want them hanging from the top of each page, with pictures of couples dancing on the double-page spread."

"Sounds good," I said. "You going?"

"Hope so," she answered. "If the right guy asks me."

I felt sure that her "right guy" was the same as mine, and my heart sank. I trudged the half block to my house feeling about as gray as everything around me. The sky looked more like November than October, and the wet leaves clumped on the sidewalk were depressing. I wished I had *some*thing to look forward to that weekend. That *some*body was giving a party. *Any*thing. It seemed like most of my life now was dictated by something else—namely, school. When to get up, where to go, what to read, what to wear, when to eat . . .

I opened the front door and put my books on the hall table. As I hung up my jacket, Sylvia called, "Alice! In here! Come see what I've got."

"What?" I asked, and walked into the living room.

Sylvia was standing by the fireplace holding a cat in her arms. It was a white cat with irregular patches of black on it, not especially attractive. The eyes were yellow, and the cat was probably about a year old. Not a kitten.

I stared at it. Then at Sylvia. After Oatmeal died when I was in fifth grade, I'd made up my mind that when I got another cat—*if* I got another—it would be *what* I wanted, *when* I wanted one. Dad had surprised me with the cat in the first place, and Sylvia was surprising me now. I didn't want something to love and lose again without having any say in the matter.

"Whose is it?" I asked, unsmiling.

I saw a flicker of disappointment in Sylvia's face at my reaction.

"Well, right now it belongs to one of the teachers at school, but she's having a back operation and asked if I could keep it for three weeks." She bent her head and rubbed noses with the cat. "Her name's Annabelle."

"Oh," I said, and sat down on the couch, making no move to go over and pet it.

"The thing is," Sylvia continued, "Beth—my friend—is going to need a second surgery after this one, and a cat's a little more than she can handle. If we *want* to, she'll let us keep Annabelle. Otherwise, I guess we'll have to find her another home."

"Yeah, a cat's a lot of work," I said.

Sylvia studied me, then sat down on a chair across the room, Annabelle on her lap. "I wouldn't mind the work," she said. "I think I like having one more thing to love."

"Well," I said, picking up a magazine and flipping through the pages. "Whatever you want."

"It's not just what I want, Alice," Sylvia said. "I only agreed to take her because I thought we all might enjoy a pet."

"I already had a cat," I told her. "And I'd sort of like to be in on a decision before it becomes a fact."

"Of course," Sylvia said. "We won't keep her if you don't want to."

"But see? Now I'm the bad guy!" I protested. "I'm put in the position of saying no, and I hate that!"

My voice was too loud, I knew. Annabelle's ears lay back for a moment, then perked up again.

For a short while Sylvia just sat stroking the cat. Then she said, "You're right. I'll see if somebody else at school can take her, and if you're ever ready for a pet, you can choose it."

"Thanks," I said. I got up and started toward the kitchen to get a snack. Suddenly the cat leaped off Sylvia's lap and dived for my ankle. I could feel her claws like pinpricks through my sock.

"Ouch!" I yelled, giving her a little fling with my foot.

Sylvia laughed. "Oh, she was just trying to catch that long string on the bottom of your jeans," she said. "It was dragging on the floor."

"Well, she grabbed my ankle, not the string," I said, rubbing my foot.

"Come here, you!" Sylvia got up and picked up the cat, and I went on out to the kitchen, furious that I had to play the role of spoiler.

When Dad walked in the door that evening and saw Annabelle, he said, "Well! What have we here?"

Sylvia came out of the kitchen and said, "I'm afraid I should have asked first, Ben, but Beth, at school, is having back surgery tomorrow and I agreed to keep her cat for three weeks. If you think you can stand one for that long . . ."

"I certainly don't mind," Dad said. "A cat on my lap might feel good on a cold fall evening." He looked over at me, and I stuck my nose in my geometry book again, hating myself as I did it, angry at Sylvia for creating the situation in the first place.

I really didn't want to be difficult. I hadn't planned this. But I would like *some* say in my life. I hate when things just *happen* to me. Like, *deal* with it, Alice! So much of my life is planned by others that I can't even choose my own pet?

Things were too quiet at dinner. I tried really hard to pretend that nothing had happened. But as I talked about school, my voice sounded unnatural. Sylvia's was too polite. Dad could sense that something had gone on between us. I looked up once and saw the glance that passed between them and knew right away that when dinner was over and they were alone, she'd tell him everything—like what a snot I'd been.

I guessed right about Dad and Sylvia. Around nine o'clock, when I was sitting at my computer Googling twentieth-century poets, Dad came to the door of my room.

"Al?" he said. "Sylvia says she's not going to keep Annabelle. Is that what you want?"

I lifted my fingers from the keyboard. "Yes. And . . . ?"

"Well, I think she's really fallen in love with that cat. I'm afraid it would break her heart to give it up."

"So? Keep it. Why are you asking me?" I said coldly.

"Because she feels really bad that you're against it."

I whirled around in my chair. "Okay, what do you want me to do, Dad? Just tell me and I'll do it. Go downstairs and say that I always wanted a cat named Annabelle? Why do you even ask me stuff when there's only one right answer? Either I cave and say, 'Great! Let's keep her!' or I'm the bad guy and Sylvia's upset. Do whatever you want and leave me out of it, will you? When there's a decision to be made where I have some real input, let me know."

Dad's voice was strained and matter-of-fact. "Okay," he said, turning, and went downstairs.

That wasn't what I wanted either. I wanted him to stay and discuss it with me. *All* my feelings, not just this. Now, no matter what happened, somebody would be mad. Things were just too tense with Sylvia around! Sometimes it seemed as though she didn't even *try* to fit into the family. Just went off and did things her way.

I went in the bathroom, filled the tub with hot water, and soaked awhile, sinking in up to my chin. For two cents, I thought, I'd go to the Humane Society tomorrow and come home with a dog. *I had no idea I'd fall in love with a dog like this!* I'd say. *It would break my heart to give him up.*

I tried to be really nice to Sylvia at breakfast, and I think she was trying to be nice to me. Dad was all business, like he wasn't going to take sides, and Sylvia and I would have to work it out ourselves.

Annabelle was batting a spool of thread around the kitchen floor. It pinged against her water dish, then sailed into the dining room. It smacked against the opposite wall and came spinning out into the middle of the floor again, making Annabelle jump. I almost laughed, but caught myself in time.

Dad kissed us both good-bye when he left. It was a perfunctory kiss on the top of my head, but at least it was a kiss.

"Life sucks," I told Pamela that day at school.

"Don't I know it," she said. "What happened?"

I told her about Annabelle. "It's not enough that I say, 'Okay, keep it.' I have to be *happy* about it! I have to say I want it! I have to lie!"

"So lie!" said Pamela. "Here's the way I look at it, Alice. You give in on this one, and then Sylvia owes you big-time. Someday you're going to want something from her, and then you can pull out all the stops. All you'll have to say is, 'Remember Annabelle?' and you'll get what you want."

It made sense, but I also realized that if I expected Dad to let me have friends in the car when I drove—to move the date up from December to November—I'd better start making concessions now and quit making waves. But it took some time before I could get the words out.

Sylvia came home late from an after-school meeting a few days later, and we worked together in the kitchen, cutting up beef cubes and celery for stir-fry.

"Listen, Sylvia," I said. "I want to clear the air about Annabelle. She's not my cat, and this is your house as well as mine. If you want to keep her, I really don't care, as long as I don't have to look after her. I mean, as long as we understand that she's your cat, not mine."

"Of course, Alice. But our relationship means a lot more to me than Annabelle. Are you sure of this?"

"Yeah, I am. Someday maybe I'll want to choose my own pet and maybe it will be something *you* don't want, who knows?" I said. "But it's okay. You like this cat, and it's silly of me to object."

"All right. And I'll take the responsibility for her—feeding, brushing, trips to the vet, litter box . . . ," said Sylvia. "Thanks, Alice. I'm really surprised that I'm so fond of her already."

I felt better then. I'd had my say, and even felt I understood Sylvia a little better. Maybe women who'd had hysterectomies and couldn't have children of their own needed pets more than others, I thought.

Dad and Sylvia celebrated their first anniversary on October 18. Dad left work early, Sylvia came straight home from school, and they got all dolled up and went to the Four Seasons restaurant in Georgetown for dinner, with tickets to a show at the Kennedy Center later. I played the part of the magnanimous daughter who babysat an ugly cat without complaint while they were gone.

Annabelle really was fun when I let myself admit it. I left my bedroom door open, and she sauntered into the room, tail straight up like she owned the place. She meowed a couple of times, then jumped up on my bed and started purring, kneading her paws into my bedspread.

"Go away, you conceited fur ball," I told her, scratching her under the chin. "Who made you Queen of the Universe, anyway?"

It was most fun to watch Annabelle at my window. She was an indoor cat, Sylvia said, never having set foot in the great outdoors. But she quivered and crouched in the pounce position when a bird landed on a branch nearby.

"You don't know what you're missing, kid," I told her. "There's a big wide world out there, and you're stuck inside forever."

On Halloween night, I stayed in to study. I told Sylvia I'd man the front door, though, and I wore a tall black witch's hat. When the doorbell rang, I'd answer with a large bowl of candy in my hands.

First the Milky Way bars disappeared. Then the Mars bars and the little packs of M&M's. Tootsie Rolls were the last pieces chosen.

I was just about to turn off the porch light at nine o'clock, signaling that we were through with the treats, when a group of six rowdy kids came to the door. As I answered, my witch's hat tipped to one side and fell off. I stooped to pick it up, and in that one moment I saw Annabelle slip through the doorway and out into the night.

4
CRUSHED

"Sylvia!" I yelled. "Annabelle's outside!"

"You let her *out*?" she cried from the other room, where she was grading papers on the dining room table.

"I didn't *let* her out. She slipped through the door," I said. The kids, seeing that I was distracted, reached in with both hands, grabbing candy by the fistfuls.

In the light from the porch, I could see the cat on the sidewalk below, sniffing the air, her quivering tail straight up. But as the children went galloping back down the steps, she disappeared into the bushes.

"Alice, I told you she's *never* to go outside!" Sylvia said, pushing past me in the doorway and hurrying to look over the porch railing. "I didn't want her to even get a taste of outdoors! Now she'll always be meowing to go out."

"Well, then you should have locked her in the basement or something while the kids were trick-or-treating," I said defensively, going out on the porch and down the steps.

"Annabelle!" Sylvia called. "Here, kitty, kitty, kitty!"

Unless she knew something about cats that I didn't, I doubted Annabelle would come just because Sylvia called her name. Do cats even *know* their names, and if they do, do they care?

Sylvia came down, and we crouched by the azalea bushes, parting the branches with our hands, trying to see into the darkness.

"Annabelle?" Sylvia kept calling. "Here, kitty! Here, kitty, kitty, kitty!"

The branches scratched my hands, my cheeks. I knew *this would happen,* I told myself. This wasn't my cat, yet here I was outside in the dark when I had a ton of homework waiting for me.

We moved along the row but couldn't see anything. A car was coming down the street a little too fast, and Sylvia jerked upright, staring at it, expecting, I'm sure, to hear the squeal of brakes and the cry of an injured cat.

"I'll get a flashlight," I said, and went back inside, then came out with two of them, handing one to Sylvia. "Let's check around the side of the house."

"She may have run across the street or even followed a child home," said Sylvia, and her voice had a slight accusatory tone. I didn't answer.

We shone our flashlights on the holly bushes and the rho-dodendron. I got down on my hands and knees and crawled through to the back, shining my light along the base of the house. The ground was wet, and I came back with muddy knees and with twigs in my hair, but not with Annabelle.

"Oh, Alice!" Sylvia said in dismay. There was that tone again.

"Well . . . ," I said, and paused. "I've got to turn in a paper tomorrow, and I'm not even halfway done. I'm going back inside."

Sylvia ignored me. "She'd walk right in front of a car and not even know what it was. A dog could tear her apart in seconds," she continued.

I took a deep breath and held it. "Maybe if we opened a can of tuna, she'd smell it," I suggested.

"That's an idea," said Sylvia.

I clumped back in the house and found the tuna. I opened it, then brought it out and handed it to Sylvia. She held it out away from her as though it were a magic wand and slowly turned around and around in a circle, like she was casting a spell or something. But no cat materialized.

Still another group of Halloween stragglers was coming up the walk, but we waved them off.

"Well, I'm going back to my homework," I said.

"I'll keep looking," said Sylvia.

Inside, I settled down again with my clipboard and refer-ence books. Fifteen minutes went by. Then twenty. Twenty-five. I began to feel awful, and angry that I did. I remembered how terrible it had been back in fifth grade when I found my cat dead on the kitchen floor. But it was almost more horrible imagining what might be happening to Annabelle this very minute. I wondered if I *should* have stayed out there to help. Then I heard Sylvia's footsteps on the porch, and she came in. No cat.

She headed for the hot air register and stood there hugging herself.

"What am I going to tell Beth?" she asked plaintively. "What if she wants Annabelle back?"

"I don't know," I murmured.

"I'm going to take a hot bath and go to bed," she said suddenly, and leaving her papers scattered on the dining room table, she went upstairs. I heard water running in the tub.

Dad was at a concert listening to one of his music instructors play the oboe, so I was going to get stuck with the job of telling him what had happened to Annabelle. I studied until ten fifteen, when the doorbell rang again. I debated not answering. No kid should be out this late. But I opened the door a crack and peeped out. There stood Lester.

"Trick or treat?" he asked. "Dark chocolate, if you've got it."

I laughed, and he came inside, reaching around me for the candy bowl.

"You came all the way over here for some candy?" I asked.

"No. I had to pick up something at the mall, so I swung by here and saw you were still up. Figured you might have some candy left."

"Take it all," I said. "It'll keep me from eating it."

"Any idea what that can of tuna is doing on your front porch?" he asked. "Trying to ward off vampires or something?"

"No, it's bait," I said, and told him about Annabelle and how Sylvia was so upset, she'd gone to bed.

"*That's* a bummer!" he said.

"I *knew* this would happen, Lester," I said irritably. "Sylvia swore she'd take complete care of that cat, but that's never the way it is."

"I know," said Lester. "Dad said the same thing when I begged for a dog."

"I'm sounding like *Dad* now?" I asked.

"As long as you don't start looking like him, you're okay," he said. "Give me a bag for the rest of the candy, and I'll take it off your hands."

"You're a first-class moocher," I said fondly, but we encourage him because it's one way to guarantee we'll see him now and then. I got a bag from the kitchen and filled it up.

As Les opened the door to leave, he suddenly paused, his hand on the knob. "She's baaaaaack!" he said.

"Annabelle?" I said, moving up behind him.

"And she's got *com*pany!" Lester said.

I stared. There were two cats competing for the tuna can, nudging it this way and that as they fed. One was Annabelle, and the other was a large orange tomcat.

"Omigod, get him *away* from her, Lester!" I cried.

But all Les had to do was open the screen, and the tomcat leaped to the top of the railing and sailed down into the bushes.

I ran out on the porch and scooped up Annabelle as Les brought the tuna can back inside.

"Well, well!" Lester said. "Looks like she got herself a boy-friend!"

"Les, what are we going to *do*?" I bleated.

"About what? This isn't Annabelle?"

"Of course it is, but she's never been out of a house before! She's never touched grass or smelled a flower or seen a male cat until tonight!" I told him. "What if she's pregnant?"

"Yep, let a female loose for one night, and she goes wild," Lester said.

"Les, this is serious!" I cried.

Les put on his serious face and shook his finger at Annabelle. "*Bad* kitty! Bad, bad, bad!" he scolded.

I took Annabelle out to the kitchen and let her lick out the tuna can. "Do you think I should call a vet?" I asked. "Should we take her to an animal emergency room or something?"

Les stared at me. "For *what*? A morning-after pill? Are you out of your mind? You don't even know what she did."

"I can guess."

"Maybe the tomcat just smelled the tuna."

"And maybe he smelled *her*. What if she has a litter?"

"So take her to a crisis center! Capture the tomcat and test his DNA!" Les said in exasperation.

There were footsteps overhead, and then the stairs creaked and Sylvia appeared in the kitchen doorway in her robe.

"I *thought* I heard voices down here," she said. Then she saw

Annabelle. "Where did you *find* her?" she asked delightedly, kneeling down beside the cat. "Is she okay?"

Les frowned at me and gave an almost imperceptible shake of his head.

"She's fine," I said. "I guess the tuna lured her back."

"You naughty little girl!" Sylvia said, picking Annabelle up in her arms. "You're never getting out again, so I hope you enjoyed yourself!"

"Oh, I'm sure she did," said Lester. "Probably more than we'll ever know."

I was telling Pam and Liz about the Annabelle episode at lunch the next day.

"Can you believe it? Her first time out, and she comes home with a boyfriend," I said.

"Man, I wish *I* had that kind of luck!" said Pamela. "I'll bet he was all over her too!"

Karen and Jill were standing near our table with their trays, looking to see if there was a better option somewhere else. It was raining, though, and most of the kids had stayed inside, so all the tables were taken. The girls took the last two seats across from me.

"Who you talking about?" asked Jill. "Who was all over whom?"

I caught Pamela's eye. "Tom and Annabelle," I said.

"Who are they?" asked Karen, taking a bite of her ham salad.

"Oh, you wouldn't know them," I said. "Sylvia brought Annabelle home one night. Friend of a friend."

Liz was hiding a smile behind her napkin.

"And the minute their backs were turned, Annabelle's out the door. Five hours later she's back with a boyfriend," Pamela said, poker-faced.

Jill set down her Sprite. "She's staying at your place, Alice?"

"Unfortunately," I said.

"What's the boyfriend like? Some bar bum? Did you meet him?" asked Karen.

"Orange hair. Big. You could tell he had only one thing on his mind," I answered, and quickly wiped my mouth.

"And Sylvia just let him come in? He spent the night?" Karen exclaimed. Pamela and Liz and I were trying desperately to keep from laughing.

"No. Lester found them together on the porch and sent the boyfriend packing, but Sylvia will forgive anything," I said.

Liz stifled a giggle, and Jill glanced quizzically at her.

"But what did Annabelle have to say for herself?" Karen asked.

I couldn't keep it up any longer. "Nothing," I said. "She only purred." And Pam and Liz and I broke out laughing.

Jill gave me a disgusted look. "I might have known," she said. "The only girl at *your* table who will ever get some is of the feline variety."

Pamela bristled. "There are other tables in the cafeteria, Jill. Help yourself," she said.

Jill laughed if off as though she'd been joking. But she and Karen continued their conversation in a low voice, and it seemed to be about a lingerie sale at Victoria's Secret—definitely, they appeared to be saying, not for the likes of us.

The day *The Edge* goes to press, we pile in Scott's car and anybody else's car who can drive, and we take the new copy to the printer. Then we go to the fast-food place next door and eat dinner. Meatball subs and fries.

"Come on. We can seat three up here," Scott was saying from behind the wheel. "Alice, you squeeze in between Jacki and me."

He was smiling at me with those incredible eyes. The middle seat was a kind of fold-down affair between the two bucket seats, and I had to sit at an angle, my legs to one side, so that Scott could move the gearshift. That made my upper body closer to him than it would ordinarily be. I was almost leaning against him.

I could smell the scent of his leather jacket, the shampoo traces on his hair, the male-armpit deodorant smell.

"Everyone buckled up?" he asked, turning the key in the ignition. "There's no belt for you, Alice, but if I crash, I'll grab you, I promise."

Crash! I wanted to say. *Please crash. Just a little fender bender, that's all. . . .*

My left hip was pinned against his right hip, my left shoulder touching his right. I could feel any move he made with the gearshift, every turn he made of the wheel.

Jacki Severn was prattling on and on about the pictures she *wished* we'd gotten to accompany her feature articles this issue, and Sam, in back, was explaining how shots like those were so difficult to get. Tony and the sophomore roving reporter, sitting with Sam, were arguing over one of the referee's calls in the last football game. About the only people in the car who weren't saying anything were Scott and me.

Didn't that mean something? I wondered. Was he conscious of the warmth of our bodies pressed together there in the front seat? Was he thinking about me like I was thinking about him? Ignoring all the chatter and just thinking how close our bodies were right then? I think this was the closest I'd ever been to Scott Lynch in my life, and I loved it—the smell of him, the feel of him, the way he laughed, smiled, breathed. . . .

The printer is way out in Gaithersburg, a thirty-minute drive, depending on traffic, and I wished it were thirty hours instead. I wished it were just Scott and me, and we'd leave everyone else at the restaurant and he'd drive me home and we'd park and . . .

We all trooped inside the print shop and waited while Scott and Jacki went over a few details with the printer. Then we went next door to the sub place and took a table.

I wanted to sit beside Scott, but Jacki got that chair, so I sat across from him instead. I took a chance and gave him a big smile. "Looks like I got the best seat at the table," I said, smiling knowingly.

He smiled back. "Ketchup?" he asked when our food arrived, and handed me the bottle.

It was like I was waiting all evening for the perfect time to talk to him. I was so aware of him—so full of him—that I hardly tasted my Coke or fries. He had a funny little wrinkle at the corner of each eyelid and three tiny moles at the side of his jaw. There was a faint blond mustache above his upper lip. If you could fall in love with a face, I guess I was in love with his. I wanted in the worst way to run a finger along that mustache. It was crazy. *I* was crazy for crushing on him like this.

Jacki got involved in a conversation with someone else, and I saw my chance.

"So," I said to Scott. "What do you do when you're not working on the paper?"

"Study," he answered. "Fill out applications for college. What else?"

"Which colleges?" I asked.

"Ithaca, University of Michigan, Ohio State. . . . I'd like to go into journalism. Either that or architecture, I'm not sure."

"You'd be great at either one, I'll bet," I said. "But what do you do for fun?"

He grinned. "Oh, go to the movies. Go bowling with my cousin. Rock concerts. Jazz. Sailing in the summer. What about you?"

"I love movies too," I said, hoping he wouldn't ask the name of the last one I'd seen. "I like theater . . . I like to write . . . I love dances."

He took another bite of his meatball sub, so I barreled on: "Thanksgiving's so early this year that they moved the Snow Ball up to November," I said. "November thirtieth. I heard that the decorating committee is going all out."

"Yeah," he said. "I heard that too. It's going to be like an ice cave you have to walk through to get in the gym."

"That should be fun," I said, and looked right into his eyes. I was smiling my special smile, just for him. At least, it felt special. I could feel the air on my teeth. I waited. Scott went on eating.

"My dad's manager of the Melody Inn over on Georgia Avenue," I said, hoping I didn't sound desperate. "We've got a great collection of CDs if you ever want to come by."

"That right?" he said. "Thanks. Maybe I will." Then he reached over and swiped the pickle off Jacki's plate, but she caught him and slapped his hand, and he laughed.

It hurts so much to like someone who doesn't see you as anyone special. I felt right then as though I could have been a doorknob. A chair. A comfortable old shirt, maybe. I wondered if this was what it had felt like to Sam when I broke up with him—that hollow feeling in the stomach. The dryness in the back of the throat. The thick feeling on the tongue, like it's too big for the inside of your mouth. All I wanted to do was go home, curl up, and sleep.

Maybe Jill and Karen were right, I thought. Maybe I *was* a boring Miss Goody Two-shoes and I'd be the last girl on the newspaper staff—no, the last girl in the whole high school—Scott would take to a dance.

When the next issue of *The Edge* came out, there were some leftover pictures from last month's Spirit Week, including the one of my legs with a different shoe on each foot. And on the last page of the paper was a little filler by the freshman roving reporter, titled "Thoughts on Careers from Upperclassmen":

Ann Haung—chemist
Dan Kowalski—criminal lawyer
Scott Lynch—journalist
Holly Morella—business
Erin Healey—physical therapist
Sean Reston—veterinarian
Alice McKinley—bubble dancer

5
SURPRISE OF THE NICER VARIETY

The following evening before dinner, Dad and I were doing the final raking of the yard. I had decided that for the month of November, I would focus so much on driving very carefully, obeying the rules, helping out at home, and getting along with Sylvia that Dad would *have* to let me drive with friends along in the car. My six-month probation period would end the last week of December, and Dad had all but promised he'd reduce the probation period to five months.

"Are we still on for the week after Thanksgiving?" I asked pleasantly, plucking a leaf off the sleeve of Dad's knobby wool sweater.

He looked at me blankly. "We had a date or something?"

"The car!" I told him. "You said if I didn't get in an accident for six whole months after I got my license, you'd shorten the waiting period for driving with friends in the car from six months to five months."

"Oh. That," said Dad. "We'll see. If you can go all that time without an accident or a ticket and do your homework, clean your room, help with housework, cook some meals, wash the windows, shine my shoes . . ." He grinned.

"Hey! No fair!" I said.

He laughed. "Concentrate on driving safely, doing your homework, and getting along with Sylvia, and we'll make it November," he said. "The last week, now. Not the whole month."

The fact that he mentioned Sylvia meant either that she had been telling him things that had gone on between us or that he'd been noticing on his own. I hated the thought that they might be talking about me behind my back. But as soon as the rakes were put away, I went inside and e-mailed my girlfriends.

We're on! I typed. *By the last week of November, I can have you guys in the car with me!*

Hooray! Liz e-mailed back. *Let's have another Girls' Nite Out.*

Yeah, seconded Pamela. *But make it special.*

U mean go sumplace special? wrote Gwen.

Pamela: *Yeah. Someplace sexy.*

I circled the last week of November on my calendar, first in red, then green, then blue. There it was for me to see first thing when I opened my eyes in the mornings: the week I would really begin to feel like an adult.

* * *

It was a good thing I'd agreed to be on my best behavior because Dad dropped a bombshell the following night. This time he made sure that I was in on the original conversation:

"I got a call today from Frank Kroger," he said, "the manager at the construction company. He's made a new offer, so I want both of you in on the decision."

I looked up from my shrimp stir-fry. "About remodeling the house?"

"Yes. As you know, we were planning to start right after New Year's, but one of their contracts fell through and they've got a crew with time on its hands. Frank said they'll give us ten percent off the initial price if we can start now."

Sylvia put down her fork. "*Now?* Before the holidays? Like . . . ?"

"Tomorrow or the next day," said Dad.

Sylvia gasped. "But . . . we're not ready!"

"They'll be tearing down the back of the house with us in it?" I cried.

"No, they'll leave the back walls intact as long as they can," Dad explained, and added, laughing, "You won't have to undress in front of the neighbors or anything."

"What would we have to do to get ready?" asked Sylvia.

"Keep out of the men's way, mostly, and put up with trucks coming in and out, bricks and lumber in the yard, a Porta-John out by the street, noise. . . . If you think it will be too disruptive over Thanksgiving and Christmas, we'll wait."

Sylvia sat thinking it over. "Ten percent's a pretty big savings,

Ben," she said. "It could help us buy new furniture for the family room. But I hate the thought of all that mess at Christmas."

"I know," Dad said.

"We could go live in a hotel for a few months!" I said brightly.

"Great suggestion, Al. That would take care of the ten percent savings," Dad said.

"Well," Sylvia said finally. "We don't plan to have company here for the holidays, so why don't we go ahead with it? What do you think, Alice?"

"If they start now, when will they be done?" I asked.

"Probably February or March," said Dad.

"And it *would* be nice to have it all done before spring," said Sylvia.

To be honest, what I was really thinking about was how I would feel if Scott Lynch *did* invite me to the Snow Ball, and when he came to pick me up, he'd see that ours was the house with the blue Porta-John in front. But I wanted to be mature and reasonable, and I *especially* wanted Dad to let me drive my friends in November, so I said, "I think it's a good idea to start early too. Let's do it now and get it over with."

The next day I came home from school to find stacks of lumber and a load of cement blocks in our side yard. The day after that a truck delivered the Porta-John. The third day a cement truck was making deep ruts in the yard as it backed up over the curb. Men were pushing a huge wheelbarrow back and forth, and there was constant hammering from the back of the house.

REMODELING BY ACE ARCHITECTS, read a sign.

"Welcome to the madhouse," I said to Les when he came by later to see what was going on.

"They're really going through with it, huh?" he said.

"Yep. The new addition will be a family room off the kitchen and a study off the dining room, with a powder room in between. And a screened-in porch off the family room. Upstairs it will be a master bedroom suite with a bath, two walk-in closets, and a laundry/linen closet."

"Wow!" said Les. "Now that I've moved out and you'll be going to college in a couple of years, they must be expecting a lot of grandchildren."

"Yeah," I said. "Get busy."

I walked to homeroom on Friday hugging my books to my chest. I hate dragging a backpack from class to class. I was thinking how utterly, completely, totally ordinary life was. Really. I was an ordinary girl with ordinary hair and ordinary clothes, making ordinary grades, and I wouldn't even have an ordinary home to remember after I left. It would be changed forever. I was trying to figure out how I felt about that.

On one level I didn't want it to change. I wanted the same old thing I loved to come back to. If anything was going to change for the better, let it be *me*, I thought. My life. My personality. My grades. My future. *Anything*. Let me be remembered as *anything* except Miss Goody Two-shoes—the nice, dull, sweet, obedient, ordinary, dry-as-dust Alice McKinley.

"Alice, Alice, Alice!" Amy Sheldon yelled at me from half a hallway down. "Do you know how many girls in our school have a name beginning with 'A'?"

I hate it when she yells to me like that. I shook my head.

"I don't either. I just thought maybe you knew," she said as she got closer. "But we're two of them. That's one way we're alike!"

I ducked through the doorway of my classroom, glad I didn't have any classes with Amy, and sat down in the middle row, third seat from the back, as always. Mr. Hertzel makes us sit in the same seats each morning to make taking attendance easier. He goes over the announcements, reminders—all the housekeeping details of our school life—and then we listen while the office plays the national anthem and we say the Pledge of Allegiance.

I was only half listening to Mr. Hertzel talk about what was and was not appropriate use of our lockers—decorating with balloons on birthdays was appropriate; painting our lockers was not—when Tony Osler suddenly walked into the room and stopped at the teacher's desk. He was wearing a dark blue pullover with his jeans, an orange-striped shirt collar sticking out the top. Surprisingly cute.

Mr. Hertzel stopped talking and turned to look at Tony.

"Could I speak to Alice McKinley for a moment?" Tony asked, bold as brass.

I stared. *Wha . . . ?*

Mr. Hertzel frowned. "This can't wait till after the bell?"

"Not really," said Tony.

I thought maybe I was supposed to get up and go out in the hall, but Hertzel gave a disgruntled nod and Tony came right down the row, stepping over backpacks, till he got to my desk.

"Alice," he said, leaning down and lowering his voice a little. "Would you go to the Snow Ball with me?"

My God! I couldn't believe it! A senior walking into a junior's homeroom and asking *me* to the Snow Ball, in front of everyone! A junior who still wore braces! I was dumbfounded! Amazed! Excited! Thrilled!

"Okay," I said, my face heating up.

He smiled at me, turned around, and stepping over the backpacks on the floor again while everyone grinned and looked at me, he left the room.

A couple of kids clapped, and even Mr. Hertzel smiled a little.

Karen is in my homeroom, and she looked the most astonished. When our eyes met briefly, however, she quickly looked bored, but I knew that I wouldn't have to tell a single person who I was going to the Snow Ball with. By noon everyone would have heard the news: Miss Goody Two-shoes was going to the Snow Ball with a senior who was definitely *not* an imitation of Patrick Long or Sam Mayer. He wasn't like Scott Lynch, either, I realized with a pang, and now that I'd committed myself to go with Tony, I couldn't go with Scott even if he asked.

You only live once, I told myself. And I knew Pamela or Gwen would say, *You go, girl!*

* * *

"Is it true?" Pamela asked when she saw me in the cafeteria. "Karen said Tony walked in the room, interrupting the teacher, and asked you to the dance in front of everybody!"

I smiled happily as we walked our trays to a table. "That's the way he did it."

"You're really going with *Tony*?" Liz exclaimed. "Gosh, Alice!"

"*What?*" I said.

She grimaced a little. "Isn't he sort of . . . you know . . . fast?"

"I don't know. I guess I'll find out," I said flippantly.

"Wow!" said Pamela.

Gwen just gave me a benign smile and went on eating her salad. "Every so often a girl has to go a little wild," she said.

"You *approve*?" asked Liz.

"She didn't ask *me*," said Gwen. "What do I know?"

Strange how that incident in homeroom made a difference, though. I felt more attractive. Older. More sophisticated. It was just so weird, the way Tony interrupted the class. Just took over. Whatever I thought of Tony Osler before, I was as excited as anything now. He always had been sort of flirty with me. Curious about me, maybe.

I saw him in the hall on the way to Spanish that afternoon. He playfully grabbed my arm and pulled me close to him.

"Didn't embarrass you, did I?" he asked.

I laughed. "Not really. I think you shook up Hertzel, though."

"Just wanted to get my bid in before you were asked by someone else," he said. "See you." And he was off.

I wondered what that meant. Had he heard that someone else was interested? Somebody else might ask? I felt a little sick to my stomach. What if that someone was Scott?

But by the end of the day I learned that Scott Lynch was taking a girl from Holton-Arms, the exclusive girls' school in Bethesda. It would undoubtedly be someone who wasn't stupid enough to tell the world she wanted to be a bubble dancer, blowing her one good chance to let guys know she had given her future some thought. I told myself I didn't care. If private school girls were Scott's taste, then I'd never make the grade. And besides, I insisted, Tony would be more fun.

Dad was watching the news that evening when I told him.

"I got asked to the Snow Ball today," I said, curling up on the end of the couch. Dad says that as soon as we build the family room, the TV goes in there.

"Oh?" he said, then listened to the commentator another fifteen seconds and switched the set to mute when a commercial came on. "Who you going with? Patrick?"

"Patrick!" I stared. Was Dad living in a time warp or what? "Dad, I haven't gone out with Patrick for the last two years!"

"I knew that," said Dad, grinning. "But since you're not going out with Sam any longer, I figured maybe Patrick was back in the picture."

"No," I said. "I'm going with a senior. Tony Osler."

"A senior, huh?" Now I had his full attention. "He the same fellow who drove you to that Halloween party last year?"

"Yes. He drove a bunch of us. It wasn't a date or anything."

"How well do you know this Osler boy?" he asked, and kept the mute on even though the commentator was back again.

"Well, this is my third year on *The Edge*, and he's been on the staff the whole time. I guess you could say I know him pretty well."

"Safe driver?" asked Dad.

"We've had this conversation before," I reminded him.

"Anyone else going with you?"

"I don't know yet. We'll probably double with somebody," I said.

"Well, make sure to get all the details. If I know where you'll be all evening, I won't volunteer for parent chaperone," he said, and laughed when he saw the horrified look on my face. "Don't worry. Just like to shake you up a little."

I decided to be the very best daughter I could—until the end of the month, anyway, when I'd have earned the privilege of having friends in the car with me. I took a load of laundry from the dryer and carried it upstairs to iron the collars of some of my shirts. I'm not fond of the "slept-in" look, where the front edges of a shirt are curled and wrinkled.

We leave the ironing board up in Lester's old room, so I called downstairs, "Sylvia, I'm going to touch up a few things. Anything you want ironed?"

"Oh, *would* you, Alice?" she called back. "There are two shirts of Ben's hanging on a closet doorknob and a blouse of mine on a chair. Those and a few of Ben's handkerchiefs. That would be great."

We couldn't see out the back windows of Dad and Sylvia's bedroom anymore because the workmen had stretched a heavy sheet of plastic on the other side of that wall to seal out noise and dust until it was time to take the wall itself down.

Dad and Sylvia really did need more space, I realized. There were two big closets in their bedroom, but one had shelves instead of clothes racks, and we used it to store extra blankets and pillows. Suitcases took up the lower half. The other closet was crammed with Dad's clothes on one side, Sylvia's on the other. I could smell the scent of Sylvia's perfume as I pressed her blouse and put it back in the closet. I wondered what kind of clothes my mom had worn. Whether she would have had so many nice things—the silky dresses, the sling-back pumps, the beautiful sweaters with the gorgeous colored yarns. Les said she usually wore slacks. Was Sylvia sexier? Would Dad remember my mother's scent?

Then I remembered our visit to Grandpa McKinley just before he died—how he mistook me for Mom. "Marie," he kept calling me, and I was glad, for him, to be her.

Well, I told myself as I ironed the clean handkerchiefs, *I'm not her, and I can't be her, and I can't be a replica of Sylvia, either. All I can be is me, whoever that is.*

When I took my own shirts back to my room, I found Annabelle asleep on my bed.

"Don't get too comfortable," I told her. "When their new bedroom is finished, off you go."

6
SPEAKING OF ANIMALS...

I was taking Speech as my elective, and was almost as nervous about that as I was about geometry. The problem was that Gwen helps me whenever I don't understand something in Geometry, but no one can take your place in speech. You're so alone up there. At least in geometry, when you have to go up to the board to prove a theorem, all you need to do is get it right. But if you have to memorize Edna St. Vincent Millay's "The Dragonfly" and recite it in front of the class, you not only have to get the words right, you have to think about expression and volume and voice quality and the fact that your armpits are wet and your knees are knocking.

I knew I needed it, though. If my career was going to involve people, it was important to know how to speak distinctly and be comfortable in front of groups. But Mrs. Cary took off two points for each "I mean" or "Y'know" or "like" and it's hard not to include those when you're talking extemporaneously.

In the ten weeks since the semester began, we'd recited poetry so that every word was articulated; we'd memorized lines from a play and presented them with great drama. We'd described the workings of a machine; given instructions for making pizza; and practiced introductions. But last Friday, Mrs. Cary had given us a new assignment:

"Choose a controversial subject, something you feel strongly about, and give a three-minute talk defending your position," she said. "Don't memorize it and don't use notes. You'll be graded primarily on your passion and your persuasiveness— how successful you are in getting us to agree with, or at least understand, your point of view."

I was thinking about that as I walked to second period on Monday morning. I felt strongly about injustice and prejudice and torture and rape and animal cruelty, but these weren't exactly controversial issues, Annabelle notwithstanding. I was pretty strongly against hunting and trapping. But someone could argue that if I wore a suede jacket or leather shoes or a fur-trimmed cap, my heart wasn't really in it.

Then I remembered an article I'd read about a woman who worked in a medical research lab, but she was really a spy for an organization that watches for cruel treatment of laboratory animals and then publicizes it. I still remembered the photo of the cat that was trying to walk again after they'd broken its spinal cord.

When I took my seat in World History, Patrick said, "Ah! The girl with the furrowed brow."

"Yeah," I said. "I'm trying to think of a controversial subject to present in speech class."

"Socialized medicine, the Palestinian cause, capital punishment, statehood for Puerto Rico . . . ," said Patrick.

I looked at him long and hard. "You know what?" I said. "Your brain is so full of stuff from your accelerated program that it's just spilling over."

He laughed. "Is that a problem?"

I wondered if he was still seeing Marcie, the girl he'd taken to the Jack of Hearts dance last February. "Don't you ever think of anything *fun*?" I asked.

"All the time," he said. "Whenever I can squeeze it in."

"Yeah? I didn't see you at the Homecoming Dance. Are you going to the Snow Ball?" I asked.

"No."

"See what I mean? Why not?"

"Because I'm visiting colleges that weekend. A friend invited me to Bennington," said Patrick.

I wanted to ask whether the friend was male or female, but this was undoubtedly to check out schools, knowing Patrick.

"You going to the dance?" he asked.

"Yes."

"Oh? Who with?" he wanted to know.

"A guy from *The Edge*."

"Sam?"

"No," I said. "A senior. Tony Osler."

Patrick blinked. "Tony? You're going with *him*?"

"What part of 'Tony Osler' don't you understand?" I joked.

"All of him," said Patrick.

"Why? What do you mean?"

"I don't know. He just doesn't seem your type, that's all," Patrick said.

The teacher was looking around now, checking his attendance book.

"So what *is* my type?" I asked. If he said *sweet* or *nice*, I was going to go out and get a tattoo.

"Hmmm," said Patrick. "I'll have to think about it."

All that said to me was that I was so unremarkable, so plain, so vague, so *vanilla*, that I couldn't even be typed. I reached for my history book and buried my face in the pages.

Neither Elizabeth nor Gwen got asked to the Snow Ball, strangely enough. Liz couldn't get up the nerve to ask a guy herself, so she wasn't going. Gwen said she didn't want to ask someone because she didn't want to buy another dress. I was sure I could get a date for Liz in a minute if she'd let me, but she hates that and made us promise we wouldn't. She can't stand the thought of somebody having to be prodded to ask her out.

Pamela, though, got asked by Tim Moss, a guy in her English

class, and Tony had said they could go with us. He'd be driving his dad's Buick LeSabre for the night, not his little Toyota.

"So what are you going to wear?" Liz asked me. She didn't seem to mind talking about the dance, even though she wasn't going. But that's Liz. I don't think there's a jealous bone in her body.

"I don't know," I said. "I hate spending money on a dress I'll probably only wear once or twice. But my other dresses don't fit so well."

"What about Sylvia? Won't she help out?" Liz asked.

I shrugged. "I don't know. I just don't feel like asking her. I don't want to be . . . indebted to her, you know?"

"What are you talking about? She's your stepmom!" Liz said.

"I know. But we've got . . . issues," I said.

"Doesn't every mom and daughter? Listen, just for kicks," Liz said, "let's go to that consignment shop that sells prom dresses."

"*Used* dresses, you mean?" I said.

"Yeah, but who cares? They're clean, and they look like new. If you don't like anything, we'll leave," she said.

We went after school on Tuesday without telling anyone. I'd made sure I had on my strapless bra and decent pants. A little bell tinkled as we entered the store.

A girl and her mom were the only customers present.

"May I help?" asked the clerk. "What size are you looking for?"

"About an eight," I guessed.

She led me to a rack against the wall. There were a dozen dresses in my size, their hems almost touching the floor. "Look through these, and tell me if you want to try anything on," she said, and went back to the counter.

Liz started sliding the hangers backward, pausing at every dress for my reaction.

"Too frilly," I said of a pink ruffled organza.

"Too severe," I said of a midnight blue dress with a collar.

It was easier to reject than to like a dress. We were down to the last three—a red dress with a back cut so low, I'd probably have to leave off my underwear; a gold sparkly dress that looked as though it had belonged to Barbie; and a slim black dress with a halter top and knee-high slits on both sides.

We lingered over the black one.

"It's simple," said Liz. "Non-fussy."

I looked at the price tag. "The price is right!" I said. "I like the top."

"Try it on," said Liz.

We dumped our backpacks in one corner of the open dressing room. There were no cubicles, no doors to close, just a couple of mirrors on the wall. I slipped out of my jeans and top and slid the black dress down over my head and arms.

"Oh! Wow!" said Liz, starting to smile. "Don't look yet." She zipped up the back, then tugged a little on each side around my hips. "Now stand on your tiptoes. Pretend you're in heels," she said.

I turned toward the mirror. There stood a sexy-looking girl with strawberry blond, shoulder-length hair in a black halter-top dress that hugged her hips. I moved one leg to the side, and the slit opened up.

"Sex-y!" Liz said, grinning.

"Slink-y!" I said, turning slowly around.

"You'll need to wear heels and hold your tummy in, but it looks great on you," Liz said.

There did seem to be a slight bulge in front, but a pair of Spandex panties should take care of that, I decided. I had the typical little bulges of fat on my outer thighs just below the panty line—not a lot. Just enough to show I'm female.

"Buy it," said Liz.

And I did.

Most of the research I did on using animals for experimentation came off the Internet, but it was enough to make me sick. Some of the material was accompanied by photographs, and some pieces were on video.

The day I was to give my three-minute talk, I felt queasy at breakfast and wondered if I was coming down with the flu. I realized finally that having to tell the class about the horrible things I'd been reading made the stories that much worse.

Four of us gave our talks that morning. Brian Brewster argued for lowering the drinking age to eighteen. If you're old enough to marry, to be a father, and to be sent to war, he said, then you ought to be able to have a beer now and then.

Another guy argued against capital punishment and talked about the number of people who had been put to death for crimes they hadn't committed.

A girl, believe it or not, actually got up in front of the class and gave her three-minute talk on why girls should remain virgins until they're married.

A lot of kids clapped for Brian. Maybe half the class clapped for abolishing the death penalty. Nobody clapped for the girl. Then it was my turn.

I hoped I would get through my talk without breaking into tears, because my voice was trembly. I began by saying that animals were not put on this earth for us to use in experiments, especially those in which they suffer a lot of pain. I described the dog used in a military experiment to test the effects of nerve gas, as though scientists didn't already know. As the vapor rose, the dog began licking his lips and salivating, then he lost the use of his hind legs and lay down, whining, moaning. Then he began to drool, and he died.

A couple of girls covered their faces.

Live rats, I told the class, were immersed in boiling water for ten seconds, then infected on the burned parts of their bodies. Others were shaved, covered with ethanol, and "flamed" for ten seconds.

I described the nine rhesus monkeys strapped in chairs, vomiting and salivating from total-body irradiation. The goats suspended from slings and shot with high-powered weapons for military surgical practice. The baboons who suffered artificially induced strokes by removing their left eyeballs to reach in and clamp a critical blood vessel to their brains.

"And for what?" I asked, and ended with, "Some primates eventually go insane from terror and isolation. A few university laboratories have been reduced to animal torture chambers. Since animals can't tell us of their excruciating pain, we have to speak for them and abolish once and for all the use of animals in medical and military experiments."

I sat down and found myself swallowing and swallowing to keep from crying as a lot of kids clapped for me. Why does hearing your own voice crack make you feel even more emotional? Why does the sight of even one girl with tears in her eyes make tears well up in your own?

It wasn't the way I'd wanted to present my argument. I'd wanted to come across as professional, concerned, knowledgeable, articulate, and very much in control. Instead, I felt my legs shaking and I had to pee.

"All right," said Mrs. Cary. "Comments, anyone? How would you rate her delivery?"

"It was very passionate," said a girl.

"Too emotional," said a boy. "I found it distracting."

"Sometimes I missed a word because it sounded like she was trying to speak and swallow at the same time," said another girl.

"Too over-the-top," said Brian. "Like violins should have been playing in the background. She gave only the worst examples."

"Yeah, but if those things really *are* happening, why *not* tell the worst?" said someone else.

The only thing that saved me from further dissection was the bell. We ran out of time, and Mrs. Cary gave me a B. All I could think of was how glad I was it was over.

* * *

Actually, we *were* going to have company for Thanksgiving. My cousin Carol from Chicago—Aunt Sally and Uncle Milt's grown daughter—was coming to Washington with the "nice young man" Aunt Sally had told us about, and they wanted to spend Thanksgiving with us.

Dad hung up the phone after talking with Uncle Milt and relayed the message to Sylvia and me as we worked at the dining room table. Sylvia was grading papers on one side, and I was doing my geometry on the other.

"It will sure be nice to see Carol again, won't it?" Dad said, smiling broadly.

Sylvia just stared at him. "They're coming for Thanksgiving *here*?" she cried. "Ben, the front yard's all torn up! It's so tracked and muddy, the workmen put down boards for us to walk on!"

Dad looked nonplussed. "But the inside of the house is still okay, isn't it?" And when Sylvia didn't answer, he said, "We'll just take them to a restaurant, then. We'll have Thanksgiving dinner out."

Sylvia sighed. "Oh, I don't want to do that. I can roast a turkey. It's just . . . things are such a mess. I was hoping we wouldn't have company here until after all the remodeling was done."

But I was excited. "Carol won't mind at all!" I said. "How long are they staying, Dad?"

"Well, I don't know exactly," Dad said. "Milt didn't tell me."

"But . . . are they staying *here*, with us, or in a hotel and just coming for dinner?" Sylvia asked.

Dad looked crestfallen. "I didn't get that straight, honey. Milt and I got talking about his heart medication, and all he said was that Carol and her boyfriend would be dropping by for Thanksgiving."

Sylvia put her face in her hands, but I was ecstatic. I couldn't wait to see Carol's "nice young man." I was betting he'd be *hot* hot!

"If they stay here, where am I supposed to put them, Ben?" Sylvia asked. "Do I put them in the same bedroom? Are they even engaged, did he say?"

Now we were getting down to the important stuff! I looked from Sylvia to Dad and from Dad to Sylvia.

"Beats me," said Dad. "I guess I should have asked more questions. All we can do is play it by ear."

"I'll help get ready for them!" I said quickly. "I'll put fresh sheets on Lester's bed and help with the pies and the vacuuming."

"We'll all help, Sylvia," Dad told her. "Carol is family. She'll just have to take us as she finds us."

"You're right," Sylvia said. "Just let me concentrate on the rest of these papers, and when tomorrow's over, I'll put my mind on Thanksgiving."

I guess since they weren't *her* relatives—not blood relatives, I mean—she couldn't be expected to go nuts over them. But she could have shown a *little* more enthusiasm.

We got a call from Aunt Sally the day before Thanksgiving. I had just put a pecan pie in the oven, and Sylvia was making the pumpkin.

"Now, I know you're busy," Aunt Sally said to me, "but I wanted to wish you and your family a happy Thanksgiving and say that I hope Carol and Lawrence won't be too much trouble for you."

Lawrence? Carol was dating a Lawrence? I think Lester and I had watched an old movie once, *Lawrence of Arabia*.

"What kind of trouble would they make?" I asked. "We're excited to see them."

"Well, I think we're all a little nervous when we meet someone for the first time," she said.

"Why? Is Lawrence an ex-con or something?" I joked.

"Mercy, no! He's a very nice man, Alice, and I want to get to know him better myself. I don't know how serious they are, but I think they've been seeing each other a lot."

"So what do you want me to find out for you?" I said, knowing exactly why she'd called.

"Why, nothing, dear!" she said.

"Not even how old he is?"

"Well, I'm guessing around thirty, but I could be wrong," said Aunt Sally.

"Should we ask what kind of work he does?" I questioned.

"He's in business, that's all I know."

"Should I ask how much money he makes?"

"Gracious, Alice! That would be rude! Of course, if they ever marry, we'd hope he could support a wife and children," Aunt Sally said.

"What about his family?" I asked.

"I don't know if he has any brothers or sisters, but it might be nice to find that out too," Aunt Sally said, getting enthusiastic.

"Do you want me to ask Carol if they're being 'intimate'?" I tried not to laugh.

Aunt Sally gave a little gasp, and I knew she was probably getting pink around the neck and ears. "Now, Alice, you just stop!" she said. "My goodness, I would never ask anything like that."

"Well, if I find out anything good, I'll let you know," I said.

"Have a nice Thanksgiving, dear," she told me.

"And hugs to Uncle Milt," I added.

Lester came over early on Thanksgiving to bring in wood for the fireplace.

"What do you know about this Lawrence guy?" he asked me as we crumpled newspaper to put under the logs.

"Not much," I said. "Uncle Milt said he's here for a convention or something and that Carol decided to come along."

"That's not much help," said Lester.

"Well, *I'll* bet he's tall and dark with a thin mustache above his lip and that he rides horseback through the desert in the moonlight," I said. "Lawrence of Arabia!"

"*I* think he's five foot two and wears a bow tie," said Les.

The bell rang, and we all turned toward the front door.

7

LAWRENCE OF ARABIA

He was big, he was blond, and he was built like a boxcar—not at all what I'd imagined. His head, his jaw, his hands, his entire body were square, and he had shoulders like the frame of a rowboat. I think I saw Les wince a little when Lawrence shook his hand.

"We're so glad to have you!" Dad said, hugging Carol, and then Carol hugged me.

"I've wanted Larry to meet you for the longest time!" she said.

So not even his name would be "of Arabia," it seemed. Larry it was.

Unless they'd left their bags in the car, I guessed they weren't planning to stay overnight. And after all that scrubbing I'd done in the bathroom too!

"So this is Lester!" Larry said. "And this must be the inimitable Alice?"

"Inevitably," said Lester, and everyone laughed.

I wanted in the worst way to sneak off and look up *inimitable* in the dictionary, but I decided to treat it as a compliment and returned the smile.

Dad took their coats, and Sylvia ushered them into the living room. "I thought we'd start with a glass of something in front of the fire," Sylvia said. "I've got some sherry and some sparkling cider. Which shall it be?"

I immediately set to work filling glasses as Carol and Larry sat down on the couch across from Les. I figured that if Larry didn't ride horseback across a desert in the moonlight, then he must play fullback for the Minnesota Vikings, but he didn't.

"I'm in the hospitality business," he told Dad in answer to a question. "Working my way up the ladder in hotel management."

"Now, that's an interesting business," Lester said.

"And practical," Dad added. "There will always be a need for hotels."

I noticed the tender way Larry brushed back a lock of hair from Carol's cheek. The way her hand sought his on the couch between them. I think Dad noticed it too, because he just beamed like a proud uncle. We all liked Carol and wanted life to go well for her.

"What on earth are you guys building out there, anyway, a swimming pool?" Carol asked. "When we walked up your board sidewalk, Larry said, 'Are you sure this is the place?'"

We laughed.

"Isn't it a mess?" said Sylvia. "But it'll be worth it once we're done." And she went on to describe what it would be like—the study, the family room, the master bedroom suite. . . .

"But they forgot one thing," said Les.

Sylvia turned. "Really? What?"

"Hot tub and sauna," he said, and grinned.

We gathered at the table in anticipation of the beautiful turkey Dad carried in from the kitchen. He began to carve while the sweet potatoes and cranberry sauce made the rounds. There's nothing that makes you feel more like family than to sit at a big table passing the food from one person to the next.

After dessert Dad got out some old photo albums with childhood pictures of Carol in them, including one of eight-year-old Carol, her girlish arms impulsively hugging a startled Lester, five, who was standing straight as a mop handle, arms at his sides, his face turned toward the camera with a "what-do-I-do-now?" look. We howled.

"The opportunity of a lifetime." Lester grinned and shook his head. "Gone forever."

Larry told us about growing up in Red Wing, Minnesota, and going ice fishing with his father when the Mississippi froze over. And he and Dad discovered they'd both attended Northwestern University.

I wanted Carol and Larry to stay all weekend. I wanted to hear that maybe Larry was going to be transferred to Washington to run a hotel here and that they were marrying in the spring. Finally Dad said, "You're staying with us, aren't you, while you're in town?"

"Oh, no. We're staying at the Capital Hilton," Carol said, to my disappointment.

But then she looked at me, pursed her lips, and said, "You know, Larry has an early-morning session tomorrow, and he'll be in meetings all day. Why don't I stay here tonight so Alice and I can chat some more? Then I'll take the Metro in tomorrow and be there in time for the business dinner."

"*Would* you?" I cried. "Bunk with me, like old times!"

I saw Larry squeeze her shoulder. "Well . . . I'll miss you . . . but I think I can manage to live without you for one night."

"Great!" Carol said. "I'll just need to borrow some pajamas."

"I might even have an old pair around here somewhere," said Lester.

"She'll sleep in a pair of mine, Les," Sylvia scolded. "We'll get you whatever you need, Carol."

After we said good-bye to Larry, Carol went out on the porch for a private good night, and then we all gathered in the kitchen to do the dishes and clean up the place.

"Ah!" Carol said when we were finally done and had trooped into the living room to enjoy the fire. "Bring on the marshmallows and the fluffy slippers!"

We had no room in our stomachs for toasted marshmallows,

but shoes came off, and Les and Carol and I sat down on the rug. In fact, Carol lay down, a sofa pillow under her head and her toes pointed toward the fire.

"Still working for that nursing association?" Dad asked Carol.

"Yes. I'm the assistant director now."

"Hey, nice! Congrats!" said Lester.

"It only pays half of what Larry's earning, and I'd have to give it up if we ever leave Chicago," she said, "but I enjoy the work."

"Are you still in the same apartment?" Les asked her.

Carol winced slightly. "Not anymore. I moved in with Larry the day before yesterday, and Mom doesn't know. I'm still trying to think of a way to tell her."

"Well, the first time she calls your apartment and the phone's been disconnected, that should do it," Les said.

"I've just told her my phone's not working," Carol confessed.

"Your mom's a big girl now, Carol," Dad told her. "She can handle it."

"Well, maybe. I'm just worried about how she'll react between the time I tell her and the time she decides to accept it."

Around ten o'clock Dad and Sylvia said good night and went upstairs. Carol sat up and hugged her knees, watching the fire. "What about you, Les?" she asked. "How's *your* love life?"

He told her about Tracy and how that had turned out.

"Gosh, I'm sorry," Carol said. "It's only a matter of time, though, till the right girl comes along."

"How do people know that?" I asked. "How can anyone say for sure that you'll find someone to marry?"

"Statistical probability," said Carol. "And the fact that there are a lot of 'rights' out there. It's not as though there's only one person in the whole world for you to marry."

That was comforting somehow. I think girls sort of grow up with that "Some Day My Prince Will Come" attitude, as though there's one guy out there searching for you, and you worry whether or not he'll ever find you.

At eleven I told Carol I'd go up and use the bathroom first, then get in bed.

"I'll be up pretty soon," she said.

I washed, brushed my teeth, and put on my pajamas. I figured it would be midnight before she and Les said good night, but twenty minutes later I heard Lester's car drive away, and here Carol came, wearing the pair of pajamas that Sylvia had left in the bathroom for her.

"I think I've got a new toothbrush around somewhere that you could use," I told her.

"I don't need it. I keep a fold-up kind in my purse," she said, and crawled in beside me. The only light in the room came from the streetlight.

"So . . . ," I said, turning over on my side and getting ready for a long chat. "How did you and Larry meet? Was it romantic?"

Carol laughed. "Not very. I was at this nursing convention in Boston. I'd been out for a drink with two of my girlfriends after a long day of training sessions, and I went back to my room in the hotel about midnight. I'd only been in the room once, when I'd signed in and taken my bags up, and I couldn't remember the number. So I got out the 'welcome slip' to see what the number was. The clerk had written it down, but I mistook a nine for a seven. And there I was, at half past midnight, trying to open the door of Room 607 instead of 609."

"How embarrassing!" I said.

"I'm turning the handle and pushing and trying to put the card in upside down and everything else I could think of. And finally, down the hall, the elevator door opens and this man starts toward me. I was terrified. I mean, here I am out in the hall all by myself in the early morning, and I can see he's heading straight for me."

"What did you do?"

"I stepped over to the fire alarm box on the wall and put my hand on the lever. When he gets about twenty feet away, I say, 'If you come any closer, I'll pull it, and I'm not kidding.' And he says, 'Miss, believe me, I'm here to help you,' and just then the door to 607 opens, and a man in his shorts and T-shirt says, 'What the hell do you think you're doing?'"

"Which one was Lawrence?" I asked eagerly.

"The man in the hall, the one in the suit. The guy in the room had called the desk and said someone was trying to break in. Larry was manager-in-training that weekend, so they sent him up to see what was going on."

We both laughed. "Oh, Carol, I can just *see* you!" I said.

"The guy in the shorts says to Larry, 'Stop her before she

wakes the whole floor,' and Larry says, 'Miss, I think you have the wrong room. Could I see your card, please? I'm the manager.'"

"And then what?" I asked.

"He opens the door to Room 609 and tells me if I just calm down, he'll treat me to dinner the following night. I was embarrassed right down to the bone!"

"And did you go to dinner?" I wanted to know.

"No. I had other plans and told him I'd be going back to Chicago the day after. He said, 'Well, I'll be working in Chicago after I finish here in Boston, so why don't you give me your phone number and we'll do it another time?' And we did. About four months later I get a call from a Lawrence Swenson, and after that we started going out. And fell in love."

I sighed dramatically. "I hope I'm that lucky someday."

"Well, I can think of easier ways to meet someone, but it's a story we laugh about now," said Carol.

We were quiet for a moment or two. Then I asked, "So why'd you move in together? Why don't you just get married?"

"Because I want to be sure," said Carol. "I had one bad marriage, and I don't want another. I keep reminding myself that I thought I was in love then, too, so I want to make sure I'm not deluding myself a second time."

I thought about that. "Some people live together for seven or eight years and *still* don't know if they're ready to marry," I said.

"I think if you have to question yourself that long, you're *not* ready," she said. "Larry would get married tomorrow if I gave the word. But I want to wait a few more months to be certain. I wouldn't hurt that man for the world."

She had been lying on her back all this time, and now *she* turned over and faced me. "So . . . what's new with you? Are you going out with anyone special?"

"Not really," I told her. "But I've got a date for the Snow Ball—a guy named Tony."

"Yeah? Nice?"

"Well . . . yeah. I guess," I said.

"You guess? Is he hot? Is that the attraction?" asked Carol.

I grinned. "Yeah, pretty hot. And he's a senior."

"Aha! Has your dad met him?"

"Yeah."

"And?"

"Dad's not too crazy about him, but I had a long talk with Tony last year. He's a different person when he talks about himself and his feelings and everything," I said. "He just seemed to need someone to really open up with."

"Hmmm," said Carol. "Hot and needy, huh? That's a lethal combination."

"Why?"

"Oh, he makes you think you're the only one who understands him. And then he's in your arms, and you're stroking his forehead, and one thing leads to another. . . ."

I laughed nervously. "We're just sort of friends. Nothing like that. We're on the newspaper staff together."

"Uh-huh . . ."

"I had no idea he was going to ask me. He just walked into homeroom one morning and asked to speak to me. And in front of everyone, he asks if I'd go to the dance with him."

"Wow!"

"Yeah. I was like, 'Omigod, and he's a senior!'" I said.

"Uh-huh . . ."

"That was pretty exciting."

"Sounds a little like me and my sailor," Carol said. "I was sitting in this deli near campus, and I could see this sailor at another table, looking at me. My girlfriends had left before I did—I was studying for a test—and he came over and asked if he could sit down."

"Were you thrilled?"

"Sure. You know—a man in uniform, all that stuff. We talked awhile—he was stationed in Chicago—and he asked if I wanted to go for a walk. There was a little park nearby. I was through with classes for the day, so I said sure. I mean, what can happen to you out on the sidewalk on a warm March day? We got along real well and started going out. He was wild and crazy and made me laugh. It was so much more fun than sitting in class, studying for tests, that four weeks later, when he was on leave, we eloped. I left the university, and we got married and went to Mexico for a honeymoon. I sent Mom and Dad a postcard, letting them know. And I never realized how deeply that hurt them till I was older."

"They didn't like him?"

"They didn't even know him. Had never met him. I'm their

only child, and I didn't even include them in the wedding."

"Oh, man. And then?"

"After a year or so, he was still wild and crazy, but I didn't laugh about it anymore. I found out he was seeing other women, and after the divorce it took me a long time to get my confidence back. I started going to night school, taking business courses, and eventually got my degree and a job as secretary for this nursing association. And . . . I've been there ever since."

"And now you're the assistant director! Yay for you, Carol!" I said.

She rolled over on her back again and pulled the covers up under her chin. "Yeah, I have to tell myself that now and then when things are rough. 'If you survived that marriage and that divorce, you can survive anything,' I say. Looking back, I think, 'Was that really me?' A girl who would leave college and marry a guy she'd only known for four weeks?"

"It must have been, because you did it," I said.

"One part of me, anyway," said Carol. "It's like I didn't even know the rest of me—the other part. Had to find that out the hard way."

"Well, I hope you and Larry will be very happy and you'll love living together and you'll get married and you'll never be sorry," I said.

"And I hope you have a great time at the dance and that all your hotshot fella does is talk," she said.

"Well, I hope he does a *little* more than that," I told her.

8
THE QUARREL

It was as though the last week of November, circled on my calendar, was a blinking neon light. My eye fell on it as soon as I entered my bedroom. It was like "the first week of the rest of my life." I could drive the car with friends in it and go wherever I wanted. Well, almost. Around the area, I mean. And, of course, the Snow Ball was Friday night.

Just as he'd promised, Dad let me have the car that Monday, and I drove Liz to school, but I could hardly wait for a "Girls' Night Out."

"Where shall we go?" I asked the others in the cafeteria.

"Did we decide on a night?" asked Liz.

"Yolanda wants to be in on it too," said Gwen, referring to her friend from another school who hangs out with us now and then.

"Great," I said. "I can fit three in the backseat."

"I heard about this student hangout in Georgetown where they card you but put a bracelet on you if you're under twenty-one. You can sit at the tables like everyone else, but they won't serve you alcohol. Great band," Pamela told us.

"Yeah, that's Edgar's!" said Gwen. "My brothers love that place."

"Let's do it!" said Liz.

"There's a cover charge, though," Pamela told us. "Let me get the details, and then we'll decide."

"And dress like college girls!" said Liz. "I know just what I want to wear."

"*Hot* college girls!" Gwen corrected. "College girls out on the town!"

I felt as though everything about me was different—my walk, my talk, my voice, my face, my hair. . . . Little by little I was getting inducted into adult life, and it felt very, very good.

On Tuesday, Liz's mom drove us to school, and as soon as we got inside, Pamela came racing down the hall toward us.

"Did you check your e-mail last night?" she asked me.

"No, I went to bed early. Why?"

"We're on for tonight!" she said. "Can you do it? There's no cover charge on Tuesdays, and some guys from St. John's are going to be there!"

"I think I can do it!" I said. "Liz?"

"Probably, if we're not out too late," she said.

"We can go early and eat there," Pamela told us. "They've got sandwiches and stuff."

We asked Gwen at lunchtime, and she said she could make it. Everything seemed to be falling into place, like the gods had prepared the way.

"Tonight it is," I said, and we set a time when I would pick each girl up. We'd split the parking fee in Georgetown.

All day I mentally tried on jeans and tops and belts and shoes. I felt like I could scarcely wait to get to college. To be a college student. It was so completely satisfying to be the driver for Girls' Night Out—driving around, picking everyone up, tooting the horn in the driveway, my high-heeled shoe on the brake pedal. Dangly jangly earrings, I decided. Earrings and heels—and the tightest jeans I owned, most definitely.

Sylvia wasn't home yet when I got in the house. I took my books up to my room and worked on geometry so I wouldn't have to do it later. Did a work sheet for history, started reading *I Know Why the Caged Bird Sings* for English, but I was too excited to concentrate. I decided I'd rather drive Dad's car. Sylvia's was nicer, but Dad's was smaller and a little easier to handle, and I'd be driving into D.C.

Every so often my computer would ding, and I'd check the e-mail.

Heels? asked Gwen. *Yo says stilettos.*

Whatever uv got, I replied.

See if you can stay out til midnight, Alice, Pamela wrote, *in case we want 2 do sumthing with the guys after.*

Fat chance, I thought.

At five I showered and put on fresh makeup, my best jeans, and a silk shirt. Everything but my heels. When I heard Sylvia in the kitchen, I padded downstairs barefoot.

She had rolled up the sleeves of her blouse and was rinsing off spinach leaves at the sink.

"Well!" she said. "You sure look spiffy!"

I smiled. "Where's Dad?"

"He's in Baltimore at a conference," she said.

"Baltimore?" I asked. "When will he be home?"

"Around ten, I suppose. Why?"

"Oh no!" I cried. "I wanted to use his car. Sylvia, can I drive yours tonight?"

She glanced over at me, hands on the colander. "Why, no, Alice! I'm going to a teacher's retirement dinner."

"Tonight?" I wailed. "Oh, Sylvia, I promised my friends! We're having Girls' Night Out, and we heard about this fabulous place in Georgetown, and there's no cover charge on Tuesdays!"

"Well, this is the first I've heard about it," she said, giving the colander another shake and setting it down on the counter.

"It's the last week of November, remember? I've been waiting all this time to have friends in the car with me, and there's no cover charge on Tuesdays, and some guys from St. John's are going to meet us there. . . ."

"One of the other girls will have to drive, I'm afraid, because I've got to have my car," Sylvia said. "I'm sorry."

I was desperate. "But can't you go with someone else or take a taxi? Just this one night?"

Sylvia turned and faced me, glancing quickly at the clock, and I could see she was in no mood to argue. "No, I can't. I'm taking Beth, and she's recovering from back surgery. I've got my car seat adjusted especially for her, pillows and everything. You'll just have to go with someone else."

"But there are medical taxis!" I said. "You know, for handicapped people. You could call one of those and—"

"Alice, I am not putting Beth in a taxi. I told her I'd pick her up, and I'm taking my car," Sylvia said firmly.

Tears welled up in my eyes. "How can this be happening?" I cried. "You and Dad both knew I've been looking forward to this week for a long time! For months! I even have it circled on my calendar!"

"If you reserved our cars for the entire week, nobody told us," said Sylvia, moving past me to get something from the refrigerator. She sounded impatient and irritated, but not half as angry as I was.

I wouldn't give up. "It just seems like it would be easier for you and Beth to go with someone else than for me and four of my friends to completely rearrange our plans," I said, selfish as it sounded.

And it certainly sounded that way to Sylvia, because she snapped, "Well, it's not! And if I were you, Alice, I'd quit the arguing and start calling my friends to see what else we could work out."

I already knew the answer to that. I stormed out of the kitchen and on upstairs and grabbed my cell phone. There was no point in calling Liz because she only has her learner's permit. I called Pamela's number.

"You're *kidding!*" she cried. "*No*, I can't get the car! Even if Dad was home, he wouldn't let me drive to D.C., and anyway, he's out with Meredith. Alice, you've *got* to make her let you. She *owes* you one, remember?"

I called Gwen.

"No deal," she said. "Dad's out shopping at Best Buy, and Jerome's the only brother here. He's got a sports car, seats two. We'd still need a second car."

"What are we going to do?" I asked, holding back tears. "Yolanda? Can she drive?"

"Don't even think it. She's having a huge fight with her folks. I think we'd just better pack it in, Alice. We'll do it another time."

"But I'm all dressed! I did my nails and everything! Even my toenails!" I wailed.

"So did I. Bummer."

"There's *got* to be a way!" I said. "I'll call Lester."

"Good luck," said Gwen.

I called, but he wasn't home. George, one of his roommates, answered and said that both Les and Paul, the other roommate, were out for the evening. I was almost too angry to cry.

Sylvia appeared in the doorway of my room. "Alice, I've left a shrimp and spinach salad in the fridge for your dinner," she said.

"I don't want it!" I said. And then, "It just seems to me, Sylvia, that since I caved on the subject of your cat, you could do this one favor for me! This is *huge* for me! Everyone's counting on it."

"If you let me know something in advance, sure," said Sylvia. "But not tonight, and I'm sick of arguing about it." She turned and started down the hall.

I felt the blood rushing to my face, anger almost choking me. "And *I'm* sick of *you!*" I said, leaping up to slam my door, and I found myself stepping in something warm and mushy. I looked down to see that Annabelle had been in my room and had thrown up on my rug, right next to my high-heeled shoes. *On* one of the shoes! And Beth, the woman who was ruining our plans for this evening, was the one who had given her to us.

I went ballistic. I yanked open the door and screamed, "And take your cat with you! She puked all over my shoes! I never wanted her here, and you know it!"

Sylvia turned around and stood looking at me. It wasn't the calm, beautiful face of the teacher I'd loved back in seventh grade. In fact, there was a flash of anger I hadn't seen before.

"You don't have to scream to make a point," she said, carefully enunciating each word.

"Well, nothing else works!" I cried. "Everything is *your* way ever since you moved in here. The cat, the cooking, the remodeling—*every*thing! If you think *I'm* unreasonable, you've forgotten what it's like to be sixteen and have four other girls depending on you."

"Then perhaps sixteen is too young to have any empathy for a woman in pain from back surgery who's going to be driven as carefully and gently as I can manage, to a teacher's retirement dinner that she has been looking forward to for a long time," said Sylvia icily.

"I *do* have empathy, but you could go in a taxi for the handicapped, and you know it. All you have to do is call one!" I said.

"And if you and your friends want to hire a taxi to take you to Georgetown, all *you* have to do is call one," Sylvia said.

I lunged for the door, my toes still squishy with cat puke, and slammed it. Then I opened it and slammed it again as hard as I could. I heard plaster fall between the walls.

I sat down on the bed breathing hard and crying from both rage and shock at what I'd said. Sylvia knew that we could never afford a taxi to take us all the way to Georgetown. Half of me knew that I had behaved abominably, and the other half knew that this was long overdue, that always, *always*, whatever I wanted came last. I grabbed an old T-shirt beside my bed and wiped the cat puke off my toes. I wanted to take it out in the hall and shove it in Sylvia's face.

Liz called and said that Pamela had called her. "It's off, then?" she asked.

"I don't know, I guess so," I said as I heard Sylvia's car drive away. "I'm so angry, I can't even think."

"Well, maybe it's for the best," Liz said. "I've still got some homework to do." But I knew she was disappointed.

Gwen called and said that she and Yolanda were going to rent a video. Then Pamela called to see if Sylvia had changed her mind. I told her what had happened.

"Shit," she said, and hung up.

I was too angry to concentrate. Every time I put my mind on my history book, I could see only words in front of me . . . letters . . . and I found myself reading the same paragraph again and again.

Of course Sylvia was right. I knew it even as I was yelling at her. I hadn't told either her or Dad that I wanted the car for that night because I hadn't known until that morning that we were going. And I was a selfish pig for suggesting that she and her friend change their plans just for me.

At the same time hadn't she and Dad known how much this week meant to me? Hadn't I been talking about it forever— about being able to drive my friends somewhere? How many times had they heard me mention "the last week of November"? How could they not have realized I'd want a car—*any* car— every chance I could get?

As my breathing slowed, I tried to calm down. But every time I looked at my carefully polished nails, tears rolled down my cheeks again. The guys from St. John's knew we were coming. Pamela had passed it on. They'd be waiting for us, and here we were, stuck at home. I looked down at the cat puke on my rug and felt the surge of anger once again. I just wanted to do something to get even . . . I don't know what. Running away was the first thing that came to mind, ridiculous as that was. Just go somewhere and sit for five hours and make them worry. I remembered when Pamela had had a fight with her dad once, and I'd smuggled her into my bedroom. Her dad went nuts looking for her. Maybe Sylvia wouldn't even care.

I got up finally and cleaned up the vomit. Fortunately, I was able to get it off my shoes without it leaving a stain. I took off my clothes, my silk shirt and tight jeans, and hung them up, putting on my pajamas instead. I felt drained. Exhausted. Also a little scared. If Sylvia told Dad what all I'd said to her, I bet he'd move the date for the end of my driving probation period back to December or even later.

Around nine o'clock I went downstairs and ate a bowl of cereal, ignoring the salad Sylvia had left for me. I watched TV for a while but turned it off when I heard Sylvia's car in the driveway.

She came in and, without a word, put her car keys on the mantel. Her light brown hair was windblown, and she looked trim and tailored in a periwinkle blue blouse with matching slacks and a black sweater.

I took a deep breath and said, "Sylvia, I'm sorry for spouting off earlier. I was just really mad."

"I guess I was pretty mad too," she said, turning.

We studied each other, knowing there was a lot more to say. I had expected her to immediately offer me a hug or something, but she didn't.

"I just . . . I guess I thought that everyone . . . like you and Dad . . . knew how much I'd been looking forward to this week. That I'd want a car as much as possible."

"You're not made of glass," Sylvia said, and she sounded tired. "We can't know what you've planned unless you tell us."

Was she going to forgive me or not? I wondered. There was still a slight edge to her voice.

"Well . . . whatever," I said flatly. "But I would like to ask a favor—that you not tell Dad about our . . . our argument."

She didn't answer right away. Seemed to be considering it. "It's something he should know, perhaps," she said finally.

"No, I don't think it is. I think it's something we have to work out ourselves," I told her. "And I'd really appreciate it if you didn't mention this to him."

She looked at me for a moment as if debating it still, and in that moment we heard his steps on the front porch.

"All right," said Sylvia. "I won't."

Dad came in and took off his coat. "Feels a little like snow out there," he said, "and if it does, I'm sure glad I'm not back on the beltway." He smiled at me, then at Sylvia. "Oh, it's good to be home," he said, and, to Sylvia, "Nice of you to wait up."

"I just got home a few minutes ago," she said, and I saw a hidden message in the glance she gave him. I knew then without a doubt that the minute they were alone, she would spill the whole story. I didn't know whether to stick around as long as I could to keep her from telling him or to go to bed. If I stalled, she'd only tell him later, so I decided on bed.

"I think I'll go on up, Dad," I said, going over and kissing his cheek. "Hope you had a good conference."

He gave me a quick hug. "It was okay. Too long, though. Speakers could have said what they had to say in half the time."

"G'night, Sylvia," I said, and went upstairs.

I know she'll tell him! I thought. She was lying through her teeth! I went into my room, closed the door just hard enough to be sure they had heard it, and then, with my light out, I carefully opened it again and crept to the top of the stairs, listening for the sound of their voices.

Instead, I heard them going around turning out lights. The click of a lamp. The clank of the dead bolt on the front door. They were coming upstairs!

Sylvia would tell him after they went to bed!

Suddenly a wild impulse swept over me. I reached back and silently closed the door to my room, then went down the hall into their darkened bedroom and opened the door of the blanket closet. Pushing the suitcases to one side in the lower half, I crawled in and pulled the door almost closed, all but the last inch. It took only five or six seconds for me to realize that this was a mistake. A terrible mistake. But it was too late, because they were coming down the hall, and the next thing I knew, they were in the room.

9
ON IMPULSE

I couldn't believe what I was doing. Couldn't believe I was sitting on the floor of their bedroom closet, hugging my knees, watching Dad take off his shirt and tie, Sylvia remove her sweater and start to unbutton her blouse.

". . . not worth your time?" Sylvia was saying.

"Not worth a whole day and evening, that's for sure," Dad said. "Heard a few things that will be helpful in the store, but I don't think I'll go to a management conference again. How did the dinner go?"

I held my breath.

"Well, we got off to a rocky start . . . ," Sylvia began.

My anger began to swell.

". . . Beth is really in a lot of pain. I don't think she should be trying to get out and do things so soon, but she wanted so much to attend Millie's dinner. I'm glad Joyce went with us, because I needed help getting Beth out of the car."

I began breathing again. Maybe she'd tell him after they got in bed. But then her voice might be so soft, I wouldn't be able to understand what she was saying. I'd probably hear Dad, though, and he'd explode!

"You're a sweetheart," Dad was saying, and he went over to put his arms around her, caressing her back. She was in her slacks and bra now. "You look tired, honey."

"It's been quite a day," said Sylvia.

They moved out of my field of vision then, and when Sylvia passed in front of the closet again, she was in her knee-length nightgown. She went across the hall to the bathroom, and I could hear water running, the lid of a jar dropping onto the counter. The sliding of the medicine cabinet door. Five minutes later Sylvia came back into the room, and Dad crossed the hall in his shorts.

My heart pounded. What if they needed an extra blanket? What would I say if he opened the door? What *could* I say that he would ever understand? I was sixteen, not six.

When Dad came back, he turned the lock. My eyes widened. The lamp went off by their bed, and I heard Dad's grateful sigh as he climbed in and lay down. Only a small nightlight near the baseboard gave any light to the room.

". . . come here," I heard Dad say.

Murmurings.

". . . not that tired . . . ," said Sylvia.

Dad said, "I'm so hungry for you . . ." And I knew they were going to make love! The look that had passed between them down in the living room didn't mean that there was something waiting to be said, but that yes, it was a good night for making love. That's why they had both come right up.

Omigod! I should leave! I shouldn't be here! I told myself, my head throbbing from guilt and shame.

Another murmur from Dad. An answering murmur from Sylvia.

"Let me help," Dad was saying.

A little giggle from Sylvia. "I think my arm's caught in the sleeve."

He was taking off her gown!

There was no way I could leave the room without unlocking their door, and even in my bedroom at the end of the hall, I often heard that loud *click.* I sat with my hand over my mouth, my eyes as big as coat buttons, horrified. Rustlings and murmurings . . . murmurings and rustlings . . .

My face felt so hot, I thought it would melt. My mouth, my tongue, my throat were dry. I sat with my forehead resting on my knees, my eyes shut tight with embarrassment. And then . . . the bed began to squeak, a rhythmical squeaking, and I put my hands over my ears. *I should not be listening!* This was a horrible invasion of their privacy. If Sylvia thought I'd been bad before, this was bad beyond belief.

I pressed my hands against my ears harder, harder, tighter and tighter, and kept whispering in my head, *Don't listen, don't listen, don't listen,* to drown out anything that might slip through.

I'm not sure how long I sat there like that, shutting out all the sounds that I could. Five minutes? Ten? I was supposed to be getting more mature as I got older, and this was one of the worst things I'd done—worse than anything I'd done in grade school.

Finally, my hands aching from the pressure of pushing against my ears, I relaxed my fingers and found that the squeaks and rustlings had stopped. Only an occasional murmur came from the bed.

". . . every inch of you," Dad was saying, his voice relaxed and sleepy.

And finally there were footsteps on the floor. I saw the shadowy silhouette of Sylvia's nude figure slipping into a robe, and then she left to go into the bathroom, leaving the door to their room ajar behind her.

I waited fifteen, twenty seconds and was grateful for the sound of Dad's deep, steady breathing. I pushed the closet door open a foot more, then crawled out on my hands and knees, pushing it almost closed again behind me. With my heart in my mouth, I crawled across the rug, through the doorway, and on down the hall toward my room.

The bathroom door opened before I could open my own door, and I crawled behind the stair railing, cowering in one corner. But the bathroom light went out before Sylvia stepped out into the hall, and I heard her footsteps once again and the closing of their bedroom door.

I went inside my own room and buried my face in my pillow. I felt as though I were running a fever, my head was so hot. The shame of what I had done! The shame of it!

Then another sound. The *click* of the front door. Soft footsteps. Silence. After a minute or two the sound of someone rummaging through the refrigerator. Lester!

I leaped off the bed and hurried downstairs, practically falling on the last step, and threw myself into the kitchen.

"Lester!" I whispered, holding on to the edge of the table. "I've done an awful, terrible thing!"

He was holding a glass in one hand, orange juice container in the other. "Are the police on the way?" he asked.

"*Listen* to me!" I gulped. "I just . . . I just . . ."

Something about my face—the flush of it, perhaps—caught his attention, and he put the orange juice on the counter. "What's wrong?" he asked. "You sick?"

It came out in breathy spurts. "I was mad at Sylvia . . . and wanted to see if she'd tell Dad . . . what I'd said to her, and I . . . I hid in their closet, and they just had sex."

Lester put down the glass. "You *what*?" he said, disbelieving.

"It's awful, I know! I didn't realize they were going to do it. I wanted to hear what she told him after promising me she wouldn't, and she *didn't* tell him. They made love instead, and I *heard*!"

Lester kept staring at me, shaking his head. "I can't believe you did that," he said.

"I can't either," I wept. "How am I going to tell Dad?"

"What?"

"I've got to apologize, and he'll be furious," I continued.

"No," said Les.

I looked up. "What?"

"You don't have to tell him. And you shouldn't."

"*Why*, Lester? It's a terrible thing I did. I'll never feel right again if—"

"Al, listen to me." Lester came over, took me by the shoulders, and sat me down in a chair. "For once you've got to be an adult. You're never going to mention this to either Dad or Sylvia. This is something you've got to keep to yourself."

I just stared at him. "I'll never be able to face them again! Every time I look at them, I'll remember, and—"

"And you won't say a word," Lester said sternly.

"I've . . . I've never kept big things from Dad before," I cried. "I have to know he forgives me."

"This is going to be one of the most grown-up things you'll ever have to do, Al," said Lester, "but you've got to deal with this yourself. You've got to save Dad and Sylvia the embarrassment of knowing you were listening to something very, very private. It's not like they were in the next room and you couldn't help but overhear. They had every reason to believe they weren't within hearing distance of your room."

I shook my head. "I'll never feel good about myself again if I have to keep this all bottled up," I cried.

"Yes, you will, because you'll be a better person, knowing how absolutely wrong you were tonight."

If I thought it would be hard to tell Dad what I'd done, somehow it seemed a lot harder *not* to confess. I suddenly wished I were Catholic. If I were Catholic, I could go to a priest and tell him what I'd done, and he would tell me how many Hail Marys it would take to be forgiven. At least, I think that's how it works.

"Lester," I said plaintively, "pretend you're a priest."

"What?"

"I want someone to tell me I'm forgiven."

"You're forgiven."

"You're not God."

"Then pray to God."

I sank back in the chair, arms dangling at my sides. "What makes me do stuff like this, Les?"

He was rummaging through the refrigerator again and pulled out a slice of pound cake. "I don't know," he said. "Mixed-up chromosomes or something. Anyone saving this pound cake?"

"You can have it," I said.

"What's with the shrimp and spinach salad?"

"You can have that, too," I said. And as Lester began to eat, I said, "None of this would have happened if you had been home this evening when I called and had agreed to drive five girls to Edgar's in Georgetown."

"If I had been crazy enough to drive five girls to Georgetown, I'd be the one with the mixed-up chromosomes," said Les.

I got down some graham crackers and drank a little milk. "Where were you this evening, anyway?" I asked.

"Took a woman to the movies, if you must know. Just a

friend, not a date," Les said. "I wanted to get something to eat afterward, but she had to get home. And since we were in Silver Spring, I naturally thought of stopping here after I left her off. If I'd known you were upstairs hiding in a closet, I would have come earlier and dragged you out."

"I guess you're right about never telling them," I said. "I'm glad you came by, Les. It's always good to talk about things with *some*one."

I put my glass in the sink, and as I started for the stairs, I heard Les say, "Go, my child, and sin no more." And I smiled for the first time that evening.

It was a strange couple of days, those days before the Snow Ball. When I woke in the mornings, it seemed as though hiding in the closet were just a bad dream—that it couldn't possibly have happened. Then I knew that, no, it really was. It really did. It really had.

I was quieter than usual, but I was good around the house. I helped without having to be asked. Did everyone's laundry, not just mine. Had salads waiting in the fridge when Sylvia came in. Set the table. But I kept finding it hard to look right at Dad and Sylvia when we were talking, as though they suspected. Maybe I had left the suitcases all pushed to one side, and they guessed. Maybe I'd left the closet door open a little too wide.

But once, as I was putting fresh towels in the bathroom and peeked into their room, I saw that the closet door still remained open the same few inches, and when I had a chance, I pushed all the suitcases together again. I don't think they ever noticed. It was, though, as Lester said, a secret I'd have to carry with me all of my life. The only redeeming thing was that I had, supposedly, become a better person because of it. Of that, I wasn't so sure.

By Thursday evening, however, I was a little sick of feeling guilty. My friends had simply put our plans to go to Georgetown on hold, and now I was thinking about the Snow Ball the next night. Liz and Gwen were going to spend Friday evening at Molly's, they told me, having a "foodless" party, as Molly gets nauseated so easily. They were going to bring over balloons and *Saturday Night Live* videos, and Gwen and Liz were going to demonstrate the steps to some new dances. I hoped that I would be that generous when a dance came along to which I wasn't invited: spend the evening with someone who was too sick to go.

When Sylvia came home from school Friday, I'd already showered and was in my underwear and strapless bra, doing my hair. She tapped on the bathroom door, and I cut off the dryer.

"Anything I can do to help?" she called.

"Well . . . you could zip me up once I'm in the dress," I said.

When my hair was dry, I curled it, then let it cool down while I put on my dress. Just as Liz had done, Sylvia pulled the material down around my hips where it tended to bunch.

"This is really a knockout, Alice!" she said. "I don't know if we ought to let Ben see you in this or not. He might forbid you to leave the house!"

We laughed together then, but somehow her laugh seemed forced, and I wondered if she felt the same way about mine.

I was ready before Tony got there. He was late, in fact, and that made me feel a little strange. Then I realized he probably didn't want to have to spend any more time than necessary in the same room with my parents. I noticed the relief on his face when I answered the door.

"Come in and let Sylvia take a picture," I said.

Tony was wearing a black tux with a red ruffled shirt. I'd never seen anything like it. He looked like a bullfighter or a flamenco dancer or something, but with his tux and my dress, the red made a nice contrast.

And then we were out the door, and Dad was calling from the porch, "Take good care of her, Tony." And I could not believe that he added, "Drive with both hands on the wheel." Talk about embarrassing! I'll bet even Dad was embarrassed after he said it.

Tony started the car, then slid one hand over to my knee and laughed. "Now, where *else* did he think I'd put my hand?" I laughed too and let him keep it there.

Pamela was in a salmon-colored satin gown and black stiletto heels. It had thin spaghetti straps and was cut low in front. If she leaned over too far, I swear she would have popped right out of the dress. Tim, her date, was in a midnight blue tux and smelled of aftershave.

I felt very adult and sexy as the Buick glided along the streets, and a singer's sultry voice came over the speakers. There was no snow yet. There rarely is this early in Maryland. None that sticks, anyway.

"I wonder why they hold the Snow Ball so early if it never snows?" said Tim. "Why don't they wait till January?"

"Maybe it's like some primitive ritual," I suggested. "Like a rain dance. If we put on costumes and perform a dance, it'll snow."

"Hey, you ought to write a story about that for *The Edge*," Tony said.

We had reservations at an upscale Thai restaurant in Bethesda, and I think we were about the two most attractive couples there. Everyone was looking at us and smiling, and I thought how great it was to be sitting in a room full of adults, being served like adults, Tony and Tim paying with credit cards like anyone else. Then it was on to the dance.

The entrance to the gym was just as I'd heard it was going to be: Couples entered one at a time through a Styrofoam cave—something like an igloo—with fake icicles hanging down around them, and stepped out onto the gym floor with swirling, snowflake-shaped strobe lights flashing across the floor and the roof of the gym.

Tony checked my jacket—Sylvia's, actually—then whirled me out onto the dance floor. He held me so close, I felt like we were a grilled cheese sandwich. But I liked the scent of his cologne. Liked his firm grip. Liked that at last I was wearing the shoes I couldn't wear to Georgetown last Tuesday. Liked that being in Tony's arms helped make up for not meeting new guys from St. John's.

Then we were cheek to cheek during a slow number, and Tony whispered, "Oh, baby . . ." in my ear. I closed my eyes and enjoyed the throb of the music, the beat of the drum.

When the band took its first break, Pamela and I went to the girls' locker room, where girls had gathered to repair their hair and discuss their dates.

"Oh, man!" Pamela said. "You two looked *hot* in more ways than one. And this was only the first set!"

"What do you mean?" I asked.

"The way you guys were dancing. If you don't have the hots, he sure does."

I brushed it off. "It's a dance! What do you expect?" I said.

Jill and Karen were there looking fabulous, as usual, and I think Jill was surprised to see me in a black halter-top dress.

"Something of Sylvia's?" she asked innocently.

"No," I said. "I bought it."

Karen looked me over quizzically. "I could swear my aunt had a dress just like that. I know she did! Same size and everything, but I think she gave it away."

"Imagine that," I said, and moved off. I wouldn't let anything ruin my evening.

Couples were still arriving when we went back upstairs, and just as the band started up again, someone else came through the ice cave and stood staring at the couples merging onto the dance floor.

It was Amy Sheldon, and she was alone.

10
IN THE BUICK

"Well, look what the wind blew in," Tony said.

We could have danced together or apart on the next number, and Tony chose together. I could see Amy over his shoulder, standing at the entrance in a pale green dress with a voluminous ruffled skirt.

"Looks like a head of lettuce," said Tony. "She is one weird girl."

"Just a little slow," I commented.

We were swallowed up by the other dancers, and I couldn't see her anymore. We danced past Jill, her arms around Justin's neck; past Lori and Leslie, both wearing white tuxedos; past

Karen and her date; everybody looking more glamorous than we'd ever seen them in school. Then I caught another glimpse of Amy, looking a little dismayed, talking with one of the teacher chaperones.

The next number had a South American beat, and the teachers who had been standing on the sidelines before now moved slowly, unobtrusively, around the edge of the dance floor. Tony chuckled. We knew what they were looking for—"grinding," which the principal had already announced would not be permitted: couples thrusting their pelvises together front to front or back to front. One girl tested the limits by turning her back to her partner and bending over slightly, but it was a fun dance and the band was great.

"Hey, Tony! Nice shirt, man!" said Mark Stedmeister, who was there with Penny.

Pamela caught my arm at one point and told me that one of the thin straps on her gown had snapped loose, so the next time the band took a break, we went to the locker room again, where teachers had put out a supply of safety pins and tampons and Band-Aids.

As we entered the restroom, we saw a small crowd of girls at one end, all gathered around a girl in the middle. I felt my throat tighten when I saw it was Amy.

"Where did you get that *beautiful* dress?" one girl gushed as the others stifled their laughter.

"It's so . . . so *springlike!*" said someone else. Amy was smiling back, glowing with their attention.

"With all those ruffles, doesn't she look like a . . . a Christmas tree?" said the first girl.

"More like a cupcake," said another, and now some of the girls were giggling openly, but Amy didn't get it and smiled even more broadly.

"Let me pin that strap for you, and then I'm going over to rescue her," I murmured to Pamela as the girls chattered on.

We found the pins, and I slipped my fingers down the back of Pamela's dress to fasten the end of the strap in place.

"You're going to have to be careful not to make any quick movements, or it might come undone," I said. "I doubt the pin will hold all night."

"The dress is so tight, I think it could stay up by itself," said Pamela.

I glanced at her breasts bulging out over the top. "I wouldn't count on it," I said.

When the strap was secure, I turned to find Amy and saw that she was going back up the stairs to the gym, the gaggle of girls following at her heels. Then my eye caught a long trail of white fluttering down the back of her dress, and suddenly I picked up the hem of my skirt and ran after them.

On ahead, I saw that, on the long trail of toilet paper pinned to the back of Amy's dress, someone had printed in black eyebrow liner, DON'T I LOOK STUPID?

Just as Amy reached the floor above, I pushed through the crowd and grabbed her shoulder. "I think your tag is showing," I said, stopping her. "Here. Let me fix that for you."

Amy smiled and dutifully stopped as the other girls cast sullen smiles at me and went on by.

"Spoilsport," one of them murmured.

I crumpled the paper up and threw it in one corner, but Amy was blissfully unaware.

"Gosh, Alice, you look so pretty!" she said. "Who'd you come with?"

"Tony," I said. "Tony Osler."

"Oh," said Amy. "Well, I didn't know you were supposed to come with a date. I thought there would be lots of singles here, like at proms and stuff."

"Well, there's no rule against it," I said. "Who drove you?"

"My dad. He's coming back at eleven to get me." She sighed and looked at the big gym clock. "That's a whole hour from now."

We moved around the line of couples waiting to have their pictures taken.

"Alice," she said suddenly, "would you be my partner for the photo? Dad gave me the money." She opened the ruffled matching purse in her hand and pulled out a twenty-dollar bill.

"But . . . I . . . ," I began awkwardly.

"*Please?*" said Amy. "If I'm all by myself, it won't look so good. We don't have to hold hands or anything."

I saw Tony coming toward me, motioning for me to get in line for the photo.

"All right," I said to Amy. "Stand behind us, and after Tony and I have our picture taken, I'll go up there with you."

"Thanks!" she said. And then, to Tony, "Hello, handsome!"

Tony rolled his eyes and moved over beside me, then groaned when he realized Amy got in line behind us.

"It's a beautiful gym, isn't it?" she babbled on. "The decorations almost make you feel cold! I mean, when I came through that igloo, I had to touch the icicles to see if they were real."

Tony put his arm around me and turned me toward the front of the line, but Amy went right on talking: "I like your dress, Alice. It's really sexy. Isn't she sexy, Tony? I don't think I look sexy, but I think I'm pretty in this dress. It was my aunt's. I think it was a bridal dress. No, maybe a bridesmaid's. Always a bridesmaid, never a bride. That's what they say."

We watched Jill and Justin stand before the sparkly background of snow and ice, Jill looking like a movie star, her slim waist accented by the silver lamé dress she was wearing. Justin had started wearing a small goatee, and they looked so grown up.

When it was our turn, Amy called out, "Next! Step right up and get your picture taken, Mr. and Mrs. Tony Osler!"

I felt my face turn crimson. Tony turned to Amy and said, "Put a clamp on it, will you?" We stepped up on the low stage and posed in front of the snow scene, but I could tell that my face would show up orange-red in the picture. I wanted to wait till my face had cooled, but it was too late. The photographer was already positioning our shoulders just so.

When we were finished, Tony started to lead me away, but Amy stepped up on the platform.

"Just a minute," I said to Tony. "I promised Amy . . ." I could barely face the camera, I was so embarrassed. The other couples stared.

"What the . . . ?" Tony said.

The photographer looked confused.

"Just take it," I told him, my face redder still.

"Okay!" he said, putting us shoulder to shoulder. I heard giggles from some of the girls. "Looks good to me!" said the photographer. "Hold it right there."

"Thank you, Alice," Amy said as she followed me off the platform, but all I wanted to do was get away, and Tony obliged by sweeping me out onto the dance floor and into the crowd.

"That's enough of that," he said.

I put my cheek against his and didn't look for Amy again.

Tony wanted to leave early and go to a party at a friend's house, but I'd promised Dad I'd tell him if we went anywhere else, and I knew he'd give me the third degree. Would probably want to talk to the friend's parents. It just wasn't worth it. I told Tony I couldn't. I could tell he was disappointed, but he was a gentleman about it, and we stayed almost to the end of the evening, leaving a little before midnight.

I had a one o'clock curfew for the night, but Pamela's was twelve thirty, so we headed straight for her house. Tony parked beyond it so that she and Tim wouldn't have an audience when they said good night. As though they hadn't been saying and kissing good night in the backseat for the last twenty minutes.

Once we dropped off Tim at his house, however, Tony said,

"We still have a half hour left," and parked beside a soccer field. The LeSabre had a bench seat in front with controls on the steering column. Tony pushed a button, and the front seat slid noiselessly back six inches. He kept the CD player on as well as the heater. I lay back in Tony's arms with my legs curled up on the seat.

"You smell good," he said.

"So do you. I think you're wearing my brother's favorite men's cologne," I told him.

He kissed me, one hand slipping under my wrap and around to my bare back, caressing my skin. "I've liked you ever since you joined the newspaper," he said. "Jealous as hell of Sam when you were going out with him. Didn't work out, huh?"

"Sam's a nice guy," I said simply.

"But . . . ?"

"He's a nice guy," I repeated, laughing a little. I wasn't about to trash-talk Sam or any other boy.

"Okay," said Tony. We kissed again. He was an excellent kisser—slow and gentle at first, then harder and more urgent as he hugged me tighter. . . . I nestled my face against his neck, letting scenes from the evening play back in my mind. The way Jill had looked at me in the halter-top dress, as though Miss Goody Two-shoes had finally managed to surprise her. The remark Karen had made about her aunt giving away a dress just like mine. The embarrassment I'd felt standing beside Amy to have our picture taken.

Well, right now MGT was sitting—lying—in a Buick LeSabre with a senior in a tux, who was gently caressing my right breast through the material. I felt the tingle of excitement each time his finger approached my nipple, withdrew, touched it, withdrew. . . .

I drew a sharp breath and felt the muscles of his face draw into a smile.

"Like that?" he asked, doing it again.

I didn't answer; just let him do it some more. He reached behind my neck and undid the fastener of the halter top. Then he slowly pulled it down, exposing my strapless bra. Just as slowly, he undid the bra and let it drop on the floor. I was lying in his arms with my bare breasts looking up at him, and he leaned down and kissed them.

It was exciting and a little scary to feel the wetness in my pants, my nipples tightening and standing up straight, as if they were begging for more. I drew in my breath again when his hand explored my thigh—investigating the long slit in my dress, tickling me gently behind one knee as the music played on.

"Oh, baby," he breathed in my ear. I wished he would think of something else to call me but "baby," but I liked the urgency in his voice. Then his hand was under my dress, moving up my thigh to my panty line. I knew it was almost one o'clock, and I gently took his hand and pulled it away.

"I've got to get home," I whispered, and we kissed—a hard, almost biting kiss from Tony. I reached down for my bra, my arm crossing his lap, and I could feel the hardness inside his trousers. He fastened my bra for me and hooked the closure on the halter top.

We slid the car seat forward again, and Tony turned the key in the ignition. But when we got to my house, he smiled and said, "I think I'd better not get out in case your dad waits up. You know . . ." He motioned to the front of his pants.

"Okay," I said, and smiled at him. "'Night, Tony. It was a great evening. Thanks."

"'Night, baby," he said. "*Next* time . . . !"

Dad had left the lamp on in the hallway, but otherwise, the living room was dark. I took off Sylvia's wrap and hung it in the closet.

A minute later I heard soft footsteps on the floor above. Dad appeared at the top of the stairs in his pajamas. "You back, honey?"

"Yeah," I said.

"Anybody with you?"

"No. Tony's gone on home," I answered.

"Have a good time?"

"Yeah, we did. I'll tell you about it in the morning," I said.

"Okay. Now that you're safely home, I can go to sleep," he said.

"G'night," I called.

My body still felt flushed and excited. I picked up the hem of my skirt and went quietly upstairs, then slipped the dress up over my head and hung it in the closet. My bra came off . . .

my shoes . . . my underwear. . . . I crawled into bed and relived the scenes in the car. Tony's arm around me . . . his finger on my nipple . . . up my thigh to my panty line.

My own fingers caressed my breasts under the blanket. Then my stomach, then between my legs, and finally I finished what Tony had begun in the car.

As my breathing returned to normal, I gradually opened my eyes to the darkness of my room—the shadows cast by the streetlight. I wasn't such a Miss Goody Two-shoes anymore. It had been exciting being in the car with Tony, letting unfamiliar hands explore me. I shivered again just thinking about it. *Next time . . .*

11
EDGAR'S

I rode in with Dad the next morning to my part-time job at the Melody Inn and decided to tell him as much as I cared to about the dance before he had a chance to ask. If he had to prod things out of me, he'd figure there was more beneath the surface, which, of course, there was.

"The gym was all shimmery with glitter, just like a mountain snow scene," I said, "and the band was great."

"You went to a restaurant first?" he asked.

"Yeah. Thai. One in Bethesda. It was really good," I said.

"And . . . after the dance?"

"Well, we stayed almost to the end, the music was that good.

Then we dropped off Pamela and her date, and Tony brought me home," I said.

Dad turned at the corner of Georgia Avenue and drove another block before he asked, "You didn't invite Tony to come in?"

"No. It was almost one, and I'd danced practically every dance. I was tired," I said.

"Well," Dad said, "I'm glad you had a good time. I guess I'm going to have to get used to your going out with boys I hardly know."

I smiled. "Guess so, Pops," I said.

The store had been decorated for Christmas during the week, and I found the Gift Shoppe—the little section under the stairs—wreathed in evergreen and tiny twinkly lights.

"If I stand behind this counter, I'm going to feel like I'm onstage," I said to Marilyn, Dad's assistant manager. She's married now and happy as a clam.

"Just wanted to add a little excitement to your boring Saturday job," she explained.

"Well, this is your first Christmas as a married woman," I said. "Now, *that's* exciting. What are you getting Jack?"

"I've been saving up for a new guitar for him— a really good one," she said. She and Jack are both folksingers. "Ben says they go on sale next week— the Christmas bonus sale—and with my employee discount, I think I can afford it."

Dad had ordered a lot of extra stuff for the Gift Shoppe because people who've never been in our store will come in looking for Christmas gifts for musician friends. In addition to bikini underwear with BEETHOVEN on the seat of the pants and long silk scarves like the keyboard of a piano, we had coffee mugs with Mozart's face on the side; music boxes with dancing bears on top; tie clips in the shape of a clef sign; earrings like tiny violins; T-shirts with part of the "Hallelujah Chorus" on the front; and little wind-up drummer boys. Customers came in as soon as we opened, and we were busy all day.

David, the young man who started working for Dad about a year ago—the one who's trying to decide if he should become a priest—shared a sandwich with me at the little table and chairs we keep for employees back in the stockroom.

"Now, why do I think that last night was special for you somehow?" he asked, studying my face.

It took me by surprise, and I instantly felt my cheeks redden, as though he'd seen through the window of the Buick.

"I—I don't know. Why?" I said.

"Hmmm. Must be your hair," he told me. And then I remembered there was still some glitter in it, and I relaxed.

"You're right, it was," I said. "The Snow Ball at school."

"Nice time?"

"Yeah," I said. "Great band. So how are things with you?"

"I'm going home for Christmas," he said. "New Hampshire. I want to talk over my decision with my folks. See how they feel about it."

"Your decision about the priesthood?" I asked.

He nodded. "To tell the truth, I also want to visit a woman

up there that I've been serious about for a time. See how I feel about giving her up, if I go that route."

"How can you do that, David?" I asked. "What about *her* feelings?"

"That's what I need to discuss," he said thoughtfully.

"I don't mean you shouldn't become a priest, but . . . I mean . . . if you're serious about someone, how can you just give her up?"

"Because I might be even more serious about the church. If I'm married to a woman but have a love affair with the church, it's not fair to the woman. If I join the priesthood and have an affair with a woman, it's not fair to the church. I've got to figure out which I love more."

"But a lot of married men are ministers!" I protested, rooting for the woman, whoever she was.

"I know," said David. "But until the Vatican decides otherwise, it's a choice I have to make."

I rested my chin in my hands. "Why is life so complicated, David?" I asked.

"To keep us from being bored," he said.

Liz wanted to hear all about the dance and invited Pam and me to sleep over on Saturday night.

Pamela was as happy as I'd seen her in a long time and kept saying, "Tim's so *nice*! I didn't realize a guy that cute could be so nice."

"Wow! Talk about stereotypes!" I said. "Cute guys have to be players, and plain guys have to be nice?"

"No, it's just that he's so quiet at school—you don't notice him much," Pamela went on. "He doesn't stand out in a crowd. But get him one-on-one, and he's funny, he's smart, he's thoughtful. . . . Isn't it strange how some people get along better with just a few people around, and some people enjoy a crowd?"

"Just goes to show how labels don't mean a thing," I said.

"But what we really want to know is how did he say good night?" asked Liz, and that broke Pamela and me up.

"What? . . . What?" she kept asking, poking at us.

"What you really want to know is how far he got, Liz, not how he said good night," I said with a laugh.

"Well, that, too," she confessed.

"From the sounds in the backseat, I'd guess they'd been saying good night for the last half hour before we got them home," I joked.

"Hey, he's a good kisser," said Pamela.

"French kisser?" asked Liz, all ears.

"Yeah," Pamela said dreamily. "French and Irish and Italian and Russian, all put together."

"What's *that* supposed to mean?" I asked.

"That he kisses everything in sight—my lips, my ears, my neck, my shoulders. . . ."

"And . . . ?" we urged her on.

"That's as far down as he went," said Pamela.

"*Listen* to us!" I said. "We're worse than guys. We give guys a bad rap if they kiss and tell, and we're doing the same thing."

"Yeah, but we're not spreading it around school," said Liz. "This is just among girlfriends. And so . . ." She grinned at me. "How about you and fast-track Tony?"

"Well, he got a little farther than my shoulders," I said, grinning.

Liz and Pamela crowded closer and glanced at the bedroom door to make sure it was closed. "*How* much farther?" Pamela wanted to know.

"We did a Liz-and-Ross in the front seat of his car," I said. That's what we've called it ever since Camp Overlook the summer before last, when Ross, this boy she met at the camp, kissed Elizabeth's bare breasts—the furthest either Pam or I had ever gone with a guy at the time.

"Ah! The halter-top dress!" said Liz.

"Ummm, nice!" said Pamela, imagining it. "If you had seen them on the dance floor, Liz, they were as close as the pages in a book. Hot, hot, hot."

"You really like him?" Liz asked me.

I cocked my head and paused a moment. "I sure liked what he was doing."

"And the slits on the sides of your dress?" asked Pam.

"He got up as far as the panty line, and then it was time for me to go home," I said.

We all sat soaking that in for a while. Finally Liz broke the silence: "Does this mean the three of us are 'experienced' now?"

Pam and I howled again. No one can say things quite like Elizabeth.

"We're not 'used merchandise,' if that's what you're think-ing," I said. "And we're still virgins."

"But for how long?" asked Pamela.

We put a pillow over her face and turned on the TV. But I was wondering the exact same thing. *You really like him?* Liz had asked. *I sure liked what he was doing,* I'd answered. And it didn't take what I'd learned at that sex education course at church to know that there was a difference.

It was awkward seeing Tony at school on Monday. There were only two boys in the whole school who had touched parts of my body I'd never allowed anyone to touch before—Sam and Tony. Sam Mayer was always so much a gentleman that I never wor-ried he'd talk about me to other people. But Tony?

I avoided the hall where his locker was located and ducked in an empty classroom once when I saw him rounding a corner. But at lunchtime he came looking for me in the cafeteria, and I'll have to admit it was exciting to have a senior interested in me. When his eyes met mine, I could tell immediately what he was thinking. I tried to pretend it was the last thing on my mind.

"Hi, Tony," I said, hoping to sound casual, while my friends watched intently.

He smiled down at me and put his hand on the back of my neck, his fingers caressing. "Hi, baby," he said. "How ya doin'?"

Liz had left the table to use the restroom, and Tony slid into her seat. He put his arm casually around my shoulder, one finger stroking the side of my face, and I felt the familiar tingle in my groin. I liked having his attention. Liked the way Jill and Karen at the next table kept glancing over, then pretended they hadn't.

"How'd you like the dance, Tony?" Penny asked from across the table.

"Grrrrreat!" he said, giving my shoulder a noticeable little tug to show everyone it was me who made it great.

People went on discussing the dance then, and Tony concentrated on me. He was rubbing my earlobe between his fingers. "So . . . ," he said, lowering his voice. "We going out next weekend?"

"Where to?" I asked.

"Does it matter?" he said.

I laughed nervously. "Of course it matters. Dad has this thing about 'purpose' and 'destination.'"

"Okay," said Tony. "Purpose: to be with Tony. Destination: uh . . . Tony's house? If my folks aren't home?"

"Yeah, right," I said.

The bell rang, and he gave my waist another squeeze. "Okay. See ya," he said, almost too abruptly, and left. I stared after him, wondering if I'd been *too* casual, *too* unresponsive, *too* inhibited. A senior had just asked me out, and I hadn't acted very enthusiastic. Then I reminded myself that he hadn't asked me *out* so much as he'd asked me *over*. There was a difference.

"Alice," Gwen said, nudging my arm. "That was the bell."

I picked up my tray and carried it to the counter, then followed the other girls into the hall.

* * *

We did our postponed Girls' Night Out that Tuesday. Dad let me use his car after getting out a map and showing me the best route to Georgetown. "If you get off on a side street, you'll find it's pretty narrow," he told me, then rapped me lightly on the head. "Please try not to dent my car."

"I'll drive slow," I told him, "and we're going to pay to park in a garage, so I'm not going to try to parallel park in Georgetown."

Once everyone was in the car, I was surprised myself that Dad let me go. With one or two friends, maybe, but not four— three in back and one in front. Liz sat with me and read the directions from the map.

Everyone was chattering and laughing and making a lot of noise, and the first thing I did was go through a stop sign. The girls shrieked and laughed.

Okay, I told myself. *This is serious.* "You do the talking, Liz. I have to concentrate," I told her.

I know you can cause an accident by going *too* slow and making cars go around you. But I followed the speed limit, and—forty-five minutes later, with Liz holding the map—I finally merged into one horrific traffic jam on Wisconsin Avenue in the Georgetown section of D.C.

It was easy to see why the area was so popular. People crammed the sidewalks, meandered through traffic in the streets, and cars moved at a crawl, people leaning out of windows, shouting to each other. Snowflakes fluttered through the air, which added a holiday touch. I think every shop was open, every display window lit up. Pamela and Gwen and Yolanda in the backseat were calling our attention to funky dresses in store windows, lace-up boots, fur-trimmed jackets, beaded T-shirts, but all I wanted was to get Dad's car to the parking garage without bumping into anybody.

When the car behind me gave us a little tap with its front bumper, I almost freaked out and wondered if I should get out to inspect it, but Gwen assured me it was a bumper tap, nothing to worry about. When I finally pulled into a parking garage, I could feel a trickle of sweat roll down my back and under the waistband of my pants.

We walked five abreast along the sidewalk, and I let out a loud "Who-eee!"—glad to be free of the car I'd waited so long to drive.

"We're here, girlfriends!" Pamela said. "And we're *babes* tonight!"

Yolanda, with her cinnamon skin, probably looked the best, in five-inch knee-high boots so tight, they fit like stockings. I don't know how she could even walk in them. Her fake fur jacket had a hood that fanned her face and certainly attracted a lot of attention.

"Look!" she cried, pointing to a guy with a pot-bellied pig on a leash. "Omigod, where else would you see *that*?"

"People are probably saying the same thing about you!" Gwen teased.

It was like we were in New York all over again, five suburban girls going ape over the sights of the city.

At Edgar's we lined up with the others and obediently

accepted the "under twenty-one" bracelets when we were carded at the entrance. We took one of the few available tables and ordered our drinks— all nonalcoholic, of course. Gwen ordered nachos and potato skins for all of us, and we wolfed them down but made our drinks last.

The band lived up to its reputation. Pamela went for the lead guitarist. "He is so *hot!*" she purred, one leg crossed seductively over the other, her high-heeled shoe balancing on the end of her toe.

Seated on a sort of platform at the back of the room like we were, we could see everyone who came in—what they were wearing, who they were with.

"You know what?" Gwen said between numbers. "We are the most dressed-up girls here."

Stunned, we looked around. She was so right. We spotted a few women in dresses and heels, but almost everyone else had come in loafers and jeans and denim jackets.

"We've got 'suburbs' written on our foreheads, practically," Pamela lamented.

"They *definitely* know we're in high school," said Liz. "I'll bet most of these people are George Washington or Georgetown U students. Maybe we ought to leave and go buy some loafers." As if we would.

The guys from St. John's never showed up, probably because Pamela had forgotten to tell them we were coming, but the room was almost too crowded for anyone else. The man at the door was shaking his head at the people outside. Six guys managed to squeeze in just before the door was closed and were trying to beg extra chairs from nearby tables so they could sit together in the back.

Pamela asked if they'd like to share our table.

"That's a table?" one guy said, seeing that it was scarcely big enough for our drinks. "Sure! Thanks!"

We scooted out to make our circle larger so the guys could crowd their chairs in. One guy was still left without a chair, so Liz gave him hers and sat on his lap. They turned out to be nice guys, students from GW, who were showing an out-of-town friend a good time.

It was pretty clear to me that they had come to hear the band, not to pick up girls, because they were talking music among themselves, and Gwen guessed they were music majors. None of them made a move, none of them did more than a little flirtatious teasing, and when they decided to move on, none of them asked for our phone numbers, and we concentrated on the music again.

Suddenly Liz gasped, "Look!"

The five of us turned to see ten guys wearing nothing but sneakers and Santa Claus caps come streaking through the club. They were coming, in fact, right toward our table, and they were singing "Santa Claus Is Coming to Town." In harmony!

Everyone started cheering and clapping, and—as we gaped in surprise—the first two men lifted the caps off their heads and plunked one on Gwen's head, the other on Pamela's. We shrieked with laughter.

As the men disappeared out the exit, people were saying, "Who *were* they? Who *were* those guys?"

The emcee said, "Well, folks, we've just had a visit from the University Men's Glee Club, showing their naughty parts and doing their bit for Children's Hospital." More laughter and cheering. He looked at us. "I know you'd like to keep them, girls. The caps, I mean. But if the two of you would please go around the club collecting money for the hospital, the men will return tomorrow—fully clothed—to pick them up. Thank you."

Pamela and Gwen had a great time going from table to table, holding out the Santa Claus caps. Almost everyone put a dollar or two in them, and the manager came over and explained that it was an annual thing. The guys discovered they could collect three times the normal amount if they streaked through the clubs naked, no matter how beautifully they sang.

"Did we pick the right night, or *didn't* we?" Gwen said when the girls came back, breathless, having turned in the caps with the money.

"And to think that we saw it on Mulberry Street!" Liz said, quoting an old Dr. Seuss book, and we laughed some more.

I looked at Liz and realized how far she'd come from the girl she had been back in junior high, complaining that she had never seen a naked man or boy in her entire life. She had seen statues and paintings, of course, but not a live nude male. And, trying to be helpful, I had gone through stacks of *National Geographic,* paper-clipping photos of naked men in other cultures, but they always seemed to have a spear or shield in front of the very thing Liz most wanted to see.

She caught me grinning at her. "What are *you* thinking?" she asked.

"Just happy thoughts. You and nude men and all that," I said, and she gave my ankle a kick.

We decided at last to leave and visit the shops, and we soon discovered that heels aren't good for walking, much less shopping. But we bought some great earrings at a ceramics shop and watched Yolanda buy an outrageous thong at a sexy lingerie store.

Finally we went back to the garage, pooled our money to pay for the parking, and I confidently drove us home, knowing that with each block we traveled away from Georgetown, traffic would be lighter, the distance from home would be shorter, the roads more familiar. And then it was back to our old neighborhood, and I was very, very glad to be home.

"Both your car and your daughter are back without a scratch," I announced as I came inside and gave Dad his car keys.

Dad gave me a small smile. "That's good to know," he said, but his face looked tired. Serious. *Now* what had I done? I wondered. For half a minute I thought that somehow he'd found out about Tony and me in the car. Then he said, "We got some disturbing news tonight, Al. Milt's had a heart attack and is in the hospital for a coronary bypass tomorrow."

I stood without moving. "Is . . . is he going to live?" I asked.

"Carol said not to worry, that his condition was stable. But she thought we would want to know," said Dad.

I sat down slowly and looked over at Sylvia, who was curled up at one end of the couch, hugging her knees, then looked back at Dad. "Four people I know have had heart problems!" I said shakily. "Mrs. Plotkin died; Uncle Charlie died; Grandpa died; and now Uncle Milt!"

"Milt's alive, Alice, and expected to live."

"But if it could happen to him . . . ," I began, and couldn't finish.

Dad understood. "Care to sit on my lap?" he said. I hadn't heard him say that since I was nine or ten. Like a child, I obeyed. I went over and sat on his lap, leaning back against him. My eyes were welling up already. "I know it's scary," he said, patting my leg, "and maybe you're afraid it will happen to me." I sniffled. "Well, Milt's been having heart problems for some time now," Dad went on, "and I'm doing what I can to lead a healthy life. I'm taking blood pressure medicine and watching my cholesterol, so I expect to go on living for some time yet."

"But so did Uncle Charlie," I mewed. "He thought he would go on living so long, he got married!"

"I know. His death surprised us all. But if I have any say about this, I'll be here to watch you get married someday and to play with my grandchildren."

I swallowed. "Are we going to go to Chicago to see him?"

"Carol says she doesn't think it's necessary. They got him to the hospital quickly after his attack, and the doctors feel they've minimized the danger. She'll let us know if we're needed. Right now she's with Aunt Sally, and she'll stay until Milt's home again."

I was quiet for a while, my head against the side of Dad's face. "The awful thing about life," I said finally, "is that we have to die."

"Yep," said Dad. "All the more reason to enjoy every single day we have. Did you have a good time tonight?"

I got up and went over to sit on the couch beside Sylvia. "Yes, except we were vastly overdressed. I bought some ceramic earrings. . . ." I took them out of my purse and showed them to Sylvia.

"Ooh, I may ask to borrow these sometime," she said. "They're beautiful!"

"And we shared a table with some college guys who weren't very interested in us," I said.

"Even better," Dad said, and smiled.

"But I don't think I want to drive to Georgetown again anytime soon," I told him. "Traffic was awful."

"Then that was a good introduction to city driving," said Dad. "I'll admit I had some second thoughts when I watched you drive away. But I'm glad you're home safe. My car, too."

When I went upstairs, I lay facedown on my bed for a while and thought about Uncle Milt and Aunt Sally. About Carol and what she must be feeling about her dad. What should I say to Aunt Sally when I called? What should I say to Uncle Milt?

I wished I could put a magic bubble around each person I loved and protect them always. And then I remembered that once Dad had said the same thing to me. *About* me. And I loved that he loved me that much.

12
TAKING CHANCES

Tony hadn't come near me at all on Tuesday, and he didn't come by my locker on Wednesday morning, either. I knew he was in school because I saw him with some other guys outside the physics lab. My fear that he'd ask me out—ask me *over*—gave way to fear that he wouldn't. When I'd seen him on Monday, Miss Goody Two-shoes had opted once again to be the cautious junior, the inhibited Sunday-school girl, the unexciting Alice McKinley. It was like being on a seesaw. You can feel like a child and an adult, one right after the other.

The weather was freakishly warm for December 5, almost springlike, though we knew it wouldn't last. After geometry I sat by the window in World History, the sun warming my arms, eyes half closed. Patrick slid into the seat next to me and glanced over.

"What's this? Hibernation?" he joked.

"Yeah," I said dreamily. "Wake me when it's spring. This sun feels so *good!*"

"Heard you went to Edgar's last night," he said. "Pamela was talking about it before school this morning. Have they got the same band—Blood and Tonic? I heard them once, and they were great."

"Yeah, same band," I said. "I didn't know you took time to do anything fun, Patrick."

"Hey, a guy's gotta live!" he said, and then the teacher started talking, and the class began.

Later, as Pamela, Liz, and I went down the corridor to the cafeteria, we saw that kids were taking their lunches outside and eating on the steps. Sitting on the walk.

"Yes!" said Pamela. "Let's sit on the sidewalk and bake in the sun."

Up ahead we saw that one of the office staff was taping up photos of all the couples who'd had their pictures taken at the Snow Ball. They were arranged in two long rows, one above the other, with a sign that said you could pick up your copies in the office.

"Omigosh, let's look!" Pamela squealed as we walked along the rows of smiling couples.

The office secretary taped up the last one and took her empty box back to the office.

"There's Jill and Justin," said Liz. "My God, look at that dress! And Karen!"

"Here's me and my date," said Pamela. "Not bad!"

"Lori and Leslie," I said, moving on. "Penny and Mark. . . ."

Some of the couples looked a little geekish, but most were more glamorous than we'd ever thought they could be. And then, right in the middle of the second row, was the photo of Amy and me, my face the color of sunset, Amy looking pleased and proud.

"Alice?" Pamela said, coming to a dead stop. "What happened? Where's Tony?"

I glanced frantically around. The photo of Tony and me was farther down, separated by eight or nine pictures. If anyone missed it, they'd think I came to the Snow Ball with Amy. I could feel my face burning all over again.

My first impulse was to take the photo down, but then it would be obvious one was missing. "Amy came alone and begged me to be in her picture with her," I explained tersely. "Come on. Let's get lunch."

Blindly, I made my way over to the cafeteria line, paid for a sandwich, and went outside with Liz and Pamela. I found a space on the concrete wall by the steps and hoisted myself up, wishing that the sun could evaporate me, that I could just disappear. It was chilly without a jacket, but the sun felt delicious, and I let my legs dangle, face turned toward the sky.

There was a low roar in the distance, gradually getting louder as a motorcycle came into view and careened slowly up the curved driveway in front of the school, a definite no-no.

Tony and a bunch of guys went over to look. A few girls, too. The cyclist seemed to be a friend of Tony's, because Tony gave him a slap on the back. It was a sporty-looking cycle, a Kawasaki Ninja, bright yellow with orange streaks and a black seat.

"Looks like it belongs in a circus!" Liz commented from the steps below.

Tony turned around to call to a friend, then saw me sitting on the wall.

"Hey, Alice!" he yelled. "Come and get a look at this."

My heart began to race. I put down the rest of my sandwich and slid off the wall.

"Alice . . . ?" Liz said, but I kept going.

At the curb Tony introduced me to his friend Steve. "Hey," Tony said, "how about taking her for a ride?"

Steve grinned at me. "Sure," he said. "Hop on."

Everyone was looking at me.

"I—I don't have a jacket," I said.

Tony slipped off his leather jacket and put it on me. It was too big, and I had to shake my fists to get my hands out. But I put one leg over the seat behind Steve, clutching his shoulders, and sat down.

"Hug me around the waist," he said, and I had barely put my arms around him when the motorcycle roared off, tipping so far to one side that I was sure we were going to fall over.

If Steve was saying anything, I couldn't hear him. Anytime I tried to look around him, the wind blasted my face, and I had to bury my forehead against his back to keep things out of my eyes. I felt as though my hair were flying off my head, and my fingers had a death grip on the sides of his jacket. I didn't know where we were headed—Georgia Avenue, maybe—but every time the cycle leaned to one side, I tried to lean the other way to keep us upright.

"Relax!" Steve yelled when we stopped at a light. "Just go with the flow. You like it?"

"Uh . . . yeah!" I gulped. "Great bike!"

"Got a twin-cylinder four-stroke engine with dual overhead cams," he said.

"How long have you had it?" I asked.

"'Bout a month," he said, and I lost the rest of the sentence because the light changed and we were off again, weaving in and out of traffic. I wondered if he could feel my arms trembling on either side of him.

"Aren't I supposed to be wearing a helmet?" I called.

"What?" he yelled.

"A helmet!" I called back. "Aren't I supposed to be wearing one?"

"Yeah, but I left my extra at home. You enjoying this or not?"

I guess I wasn't sounding positive enough. "Love it!" I lied. "Great day for a ride."

"Yeah. We've got an event coming up New Year's Day, if it don't snow. I know a fella you could ride with!" he shouted.

"Oh, sorry! I'll be out of town," I lied again.

At the next light he said, "Well, I better get you back," and when we got the green, he careened around a corner. I don't know if our feet scraped the ground or if I only imagined it, and by the time we got back to school, the bell had rung and people were going inside. Tony was still waiting at the curb.

"How was it?" he asked, helping me off the cycle. I took off his jacket and gave it back.

"Great!" I said. "Terrific motorcycle."

Tony and Steve gave each other a sort of salute, and then Steve took off again.

"So! Decided to live dangerously for a change, huh?" Tony asked me, giving my waist a quick, almost impatient tug.

"Hey, life's always dangerous," I said.

"You only live once. Gotta do what the spirit moves you to do," said Tony. And when we got inside, he said, "See you at the staff meeting after school."

I guess, just like me, Tony had two sides to his personality, maybe more. Once when he drove me home from a staff meeting, he'd just wanted to talk—about how he feels he's a disappointment to his dad, who'd hoped he'd be a big sports hero or something. But because of his heart defect, he has to settle for being a sportscaster or sportswriter, and maybe he won't even get that kind of job. This week he's Mr. Hot Stuff, the Wandering Hand Guy, friend of Motorcycle Guy. Which was he, really, or was he both? Would the real Tony Osler please stand up? And then, the bigger question: Who was I?

In speech that afternoon Mrs. Cary faced the class. "Most of you did a pretty creditable job of choosing a topic you strongly believe in and giving a persuasive talk," she said. "A number of you backed up your talks with excellent research. We heard sales pitches, you might say, against the death penalty, for lowering the drinking age, for spreading democracy in the Mid-East, against using animals in research, pro-abortion, against gay marriage—we covered a wide range of topics here in class."

We basked in her praise.

She continued: "Most of you are taking this class because you want to be able to stand up before a group and speak easily, naturally, without too much nervousness."

"I took it because I couldn't get mechanical drawing for my elective," some guy said, and we all laughed.

"Well, that's legitimate," Mrs. Cary said. "But to be a good communicator, you also have to be a good listener. You have to be able to sift through what you're hearing to sort out the logical from the irrational. So here's your next assignment: I want each of you to take the same subject you chose before and give another three-minute talk, this time taking the opposite point of view."

There were surprised groans and protests, but she went on: "So if, for example, you argued against capital punishment, now you have to defend it to the best of your ability. And once again, you'll be graded on how well you research your argument and how persuasive you are in presenting it to us."

"You should have told us about this assignment before we decided on our topics!" said the girl who had argued in favor of chastity before marriage. "This isn't fair!"

"Not fair to examine some of your beliefs?" asked Mrs. Cary.

"I'm not asking you to change your minds. But teaching you to *think* is more important than teaching you facts, in my book. The assignment is meant to help you examine a topic from another perspective."

I picked up my books at the end of the period and stalked out of the room. After all I had read about the suffering and torture of animals used in medical research, I now had to *defend* it? Brian and I practically collided going out the door. He had to give a three-minute talk on why we should *not* lower the drinking age.

Amy Sheldon caught up with me halfway down the hall.

"Alice!" she called, and came running alongside me. "I've been meaning to ask you a question." Her voice was particularly loud and irritating.

"Yeah?" I said, not even slowing down.

"Do you think there's something wrong with me because I'm fifteen and I still haven't started my periods?" she asked.

"How should I know?" I said impatiently, rudely. "Talk to your mother! Ask your sister! Ask your aunts! I'm not a doctor." And I shoved through the glass doors at the end of the hall and clattered on down the stairs to my locker.

By the time I got to the staff meeting, Tony had seen the photos in the hall, and he wasn't happy about the one of me and Amy.

"I took it down, what do you expect?" he said.

I was relieved, to tell the truth, but what I said was, "Amy will be disappointed. She'll be looking for her picture."

"Then she can go to the office and buy a copy," he said.

"That made *me* look like a jerk. What d'ya want people to think? We went as a threesome?"

The staff was debating which photos from the Snow Ball we should publish in the next issue of *The Edge*. Not the photos taken by the professional photographer, but the candid photos caught by Sam and Don. We obviously couldn't use them all. Scott suggested selecting a few of seniors with seniors, since this was their last year to attend the dance, but after that was settled, he still seemed unhappy with the paper.

"We're just doing the same old stuff, month after month," he said. "We need to come up with something different. A real story. An exposé or something."

"About the Snow Ball?" asked Jacki.

"Forget the Snow Ball. Something that'll get attention. Make waves."

"Like what?" asked Don, who looked like a linebacker. "Follow a teacher after hours and report on his nightlife?"

"Something offbeat but with a purpose," Scott said. "Everybody think about it. If you get any ideas, call me. There's still a big hole in the paper we need to fill by the deadline on Monday."

Tony drove me home after the meeting in his Toyota. When we got to my street, he pulled over to the curb and parked a block away. Then he reached for me across the gearshift, which was awkward enough, and kissed me. His right hand slid under my jacket, felt its way up my side, and cupped my breast, squeezing and stroking.

"See you, baby," he said, letting me go, and as soon as I was out of the car, he rode off.

I don't know when I'd felt so down on myself. Tony . . . the picture of Amy Sheldon and me together at the dance . . . the MGT and DD tags that Jill and Karen had labeled me. . . . People might even drag up stuff from last semester—how I'd taken a sex ed class at my *church*! I felt depressed and angry and confused and sad—a whole soup of emotions, all at the same time.

At dinner I heard myself saying, "Why hasn't Lester been over for dinner lately? It's like a morgue when he's not around." I was instantly sorry because it really wasn't true.

Dad looked at me sharply. "Ex*cuse* me?" he said.

"I'm sorry," I apologized. "I just miss his jokes." And then, when neither Dad nor Sylvia replied, I added, "I've had sort of a bad day."

"Well, so have I, so don't take it out on us, please," said Dad.

I swallowed the bite of potato I'd just taken and looked around the table. "Uncle Milt's not worse, is he?"

"No, Sal said his surgery today went off without a hitch. We should know more in a few days. But our plans to rent the store next to us fell through, and I really wanted that space for an annex," said Dad.

"Oh, I'm sorry," I told him, and we continued eating in silence. Finally I said, "Do you think the owner would reconsider?"

"We don't think so," Sylvia said. "He's going to rent the space to a restaurant."

That sounded interesting, and I wanted to ask what kind of restaurant, but that didn't seem appropriate. I knew Dad's heart was set on expanding the store. After dinner he said he had a headache and went upstairs to lie down.

"I'll do the dishes," I told Sylvia.

"Oh, I'll help. Sometimes it's good just to be doing something with my hands instead of my brains," she said.

I carried plates and silverware to the sink while Sylvia rinsed them off and placed them in the dishwasher. Finally I said, "Did you ever feel like saying, 'Will the real Sylvia Summers please stand up'?"

Sylvia looked at me and smiled a little. "About once a day in high school. In fact, a few times in college, as I remember."

"It's sort of what I've been feeling lately," I told her. "Like sometimes I don't even know myself."

"Want to talk about it?" she asked.

"Not particularly," I said.

"Okay." She went on stacking plates.

"Anyway, that's why I've been sort of irritable, I guess," I explained. "Sort of uncertain."

"I know the feeling," said Sylvia. "Sometimes when we try to please too many people, we get caught up in things that just aren't us."

"Well," I said quickly, "I don't plan to repeat what I did today, that's for certain."

Sylvia looked at me intently. "Well, whatever it was, I'm glad," she said.

13
THE CITY AT NIGHT

There's one cure for feeling so completely lousy and low that I can barely stand myself. That's finding someone who's a lot worse off than I am and concentrating on her for a while. The first person who came to mind, other than Amy Sheldon, was Molly, so I drove over there after dinner.

The thing about Molly Brennan is that she's always lived "in the moment," whatever it was. As a member of stage crew, Molly gave one hundred percent to each performance. She was one of those girls who, when she was talking with you, made you feel like you were the most interesting person in the world.

She'd never had a boyfriend, never had a date, never been

kissed, but was simply too busy to care. "It'll happen when it'll happen," she'd tell us. "I'm ready!" Meanwhile, she joined clubs, worked on committees, took flute lessons, learned to scuba dive, got good grades, had a zillion friends, and . . . got leukemia.

The hard part about visiting someone who's seriously sick is you feel you have to say something encouraging. Something cheerful. Something funny. And if you don't *feel* encouraged or cheerful or funny, you wonder what good your visit will do. And then you find out that just being there is what's important, even if you don't say anything. If you don't do anything but hold somebody's hand, it's something.

"She's had a rough week," Mrs. Brennan said when she met me at the door that night. "She's made it to only a few classes this semester, and she's really too sick to go at all. She's discouraged."

"Shall I go on up?" I asked.

"Go up and ask if she wants you to stay. She'll be honest. At least she'll be glad you cared enough to come by," Mrs. Brennan said.

Molly was asleep when I came in. I just sat by her bed and watched her sleep. Sat looking at her bulletin board—at her blue ribbons and trophies and pictures and photos and notes and silly little mementos—what a full life she'd had before.

She stirred and sighed, flopping one arm over the edge of the bed. Her eyes fluttered, opened slightly, closed, then opened wider, staring at me.

"Hi," I said. "Just wanted to come by and say hello to Sleeping Beauty."

She smiled. "My mouth tastes like gym socks," she said, her lips dry, sticking together.

"Day-old socks or week-old?" I asked. She closed her eyes again.

"I feel yucky," she said finally.

"I know," I told her.

"My bones ache and my gums are sore and I feel like I'm going to upchuck and I have no energy at all."

"We all knew it was going to be rough, but I guess you're the only one who can tell us just how rough," I said.

"Yeah," she said. "This morning I was thinking about all the lousy times in my life: the time I got stung by a nest of hornets and my face was swollen for a week, and the time I lost my best friend's key chain . . . the bone I broke in my foot . . . the usual miserable things that happen to a person in a normal life. . . . And I would gladly relive them all just to trade in what I've got now."

"I can understand that," I said.

She was quiet for a while. Then she asked, "What are they saying . . . about me at school?"

"That you're sick and you're getting treatments and that you're a fighter," I answered.

Molly's mouth turned down a little at the corners.

"I always thought I was too, but now I'm not so sure." A single tear rolled down her cheek.

I reached over and stroked her hand. "*I'm* sure, Molly," I said. "You're going to give this old thing everything you've got."

I didn't feel any better when I left Molly's, but I saw life with a little more perspective. I called Gwen, though, and told her how afraid I was for Molly.

"You don't think she'll die, do you?" I asked shakily. "I thought you said the doctors were optimistic." Gwen had had a high school internship with the National Institutes of Health last summer when Molly was sent there for evaluation, so she knew some of the inside stuff.

There was too much quiet at the other end of the line.

"Gwen?" I said.

"I don't know," she answered. "Maybe I was wrong."

I stared blankly at the wall. "What do you *mean*?"

I heard her sigh. "You know how they tell you that when you're sick and you go for the results of your tests, you should always take someone with you?"

That was news to me. "No . . . ," I said.

"Well, you should, because if it's serious, they've found, you'll only hear about thirty percent of what the doctor tells you."

"And . . . ?" I said.

"When I saw Molly in our lab and she told me she had leukemia, I asked the doctors afterward just how serious lymphoblastic leukemia is—the kind she has. What they said was that usually this is a disease in younger children, and the cure rate for them is especially high. What *I* heard was that the cure rate is high. What I blanked out was that the cure rate for people Molly's age maybe isn't that good." I heard Gwen swallow.

"Gwen!" I gasped. "How long have you known this?"

"Since September," she said in a small voice. "I've been doing some reading, asking questions. . . ."

"You never *told* us!" I said accusingly.

"I know. I got everybody optimistic, and there are still a lot of reasons to be optimistic for Molly. But I thought she'd only be in treatment for a year, and it's the first big block of treatment that can last for a year. She'll be in different stages of treatment for two or three years."

"Oh, Gwen!"

"I feel awful," she said. "Guilty and sad and everything that goes with it. I had no business saying anything at all. But there *are* things in her favor. Technical things . . ."

Just like Gwen said, my brain didn't focus on "things in her favor." It focused on "two or three years." I started to cry.

"It's just hard . . . to know what to say to her anymore," I wept.

"Tell her she's in the best possible hands, which is true," Gwen said. "Tell her that her doctors are experts at this stuff. Tell her that if one drug doesn't work, they'll try something else. And hope, Alice. Hope is powerful medicine."

"I want her to live, Gwen," I said.

"So does everybody. Have you ever met one person who doesn't like Molly Brennan?" Gwen said.

The more I thought about Molly, the more I thought about life and making every day count. And making every day count meant taking chances. Maybe I *didn't* take enough chances. Maybe that's what got me the MGT image with Karen and Jill, not that they were my role models. What if I *had* run away for a while that night I was so mad at Sylvia? In fact, what if I'd called Liz to go with me, and we'd both disappeared for a day or so? We sure wouldn't be DD after that!

Suddenly, without even running it past the automatic censor in my brain, I picked up the list of staff members for *The Edge* and called Scott.

"Whuzzup?" he answered. I could hear his TV in the background.

"It's Alice," I said.

"I know," he said.

"Busy? I could call back."

"No. It's okay." I heard the TV cut off.

"I was thinking about a story we could do for the paper," I told him. "Why don't I go out some night with another girl and pose as runaways in Silver Spring. No money. No ID. Then I'll write up the story."

"You want me to get expelled?" said Scott. "I couldn't assign something like that. You could get beaten up or worse!"

"Then send some guys along to keep an eye on us—take photos," I said, my mouth running on ahead of my brain, hoping that Scott would volunteer.

There was a pause. "I don't know . . . ," he said. "What exactly would we be trying to say?"

"Well, a lot of kids have miserable home situations, and even if they don't, I'll bet everyone's had a big quarrel or something where they just really wanted to take off for a day or two," I said. "We could show the reality of what it's like being out in the city at night with nowhere to go. Or we could show what resources *are* available without getting the police in on it."

"Wow," Scott said. Another pause. Then, "Who would you get to go with you?"

"Oh, I know someone. She'll do it!" I chirped hopefully.

"Let me think about it, and I'll call you back," he said.

Yes! I thought, my heart pounding, and immediately phoned Liz.

"Listen, DD," I teased.

"Don't call me that," she said.

"Well, that's the way some people think of us," I told her. "So . . . you want to do something wild and get your picture in the newspaper?"

"And get grounded for the rest of my life? Not particularly," she said.

"Okay. *Without* your folks knowing about it, but showing everyone at school just how gutsy we can be?" I said.

Now she was interested. "Doing what?"

"It'll be an article for *The Edge*, but they won't use our names. Two girls sneak out late at night and, watched over at a distance by two guys to keep them safe, pose as runaways. We won't have any identification or money on us, and we'll see just what help is available to two girls at night in Silver Spring."

There was a three-second pause. "I'll do it," said Liz.

"You *will*?"

"It's wild and exciting and fun, and we're doing it for a purpose," said Liz. "When?"

When Scott called back, I could hear the excitement in his voice. "Here's the deal," he said. "I didn't even check with Miss Ames because I can guarantee she'd say no. Too dangerous, and the school would be responsible if anything happened. So you're on your own. I've called around, and Don and Tony have agreed to be your backups—keep an eye on you—and Don's going to get some night photos if he can, silhouette-type. We've got to keep you anonymous. I can't actually assign this—can't condone it. All I can say is that if you turn in a good story, we'll run it, with a statement saying we didn't give our permission but felt it was worth publishing."

"Deal!" I said excitedly.

"The guys'll call you and set it up for Friday. If you can turn in the copy Monday morning, we can get it in this edition. And, Alice," he added, "be careful."

The dead bolt on our front door makes a loud *click* when you turn it, so we didn't lock it after us. Liz and I went down the steps in the darkness. She had come over to spend the night on Friday, and we'd carefully prepared our "look." Old baggy jeans that looked as though we'd slept in them, because we had, in preparation. Wrinkled T-shirts. Smudged jackets, dirty sneakers, dirty hair, no makeup.

Dad and Sylvia had gone to bed around ten thirty, so we called Tony on my cell phone one hour later and told him we'd meet him and Don at the corner.

"Ready?" I asked Liz as we checked ourselves one last time in the mirror.

She put a folded piece of paper on my bed.

"What's that?" I asked.

"Just in case," she answered.

"Can I read it?"

She didn't say no, so I picked it up.

> Dear Mom and Dad,
> If anything happens to me,
> I did this to be helpful to
> any girl who's alone in the
> city at night.
> Love,
> Liz

I decided that Liz's letter was explanation enough if we disappeared, and we crept noiselessly down the stairs.

Tony's Toyota was parked at the corner. "Where to, girls?" he asked when we climbed in. "Where's this undercover operation going to take us?"

"Let's say we hitchhiked here from some other place in Maryland, and they let us off in Silver Spring," I said. "I think the first thing we'd need is a restroom."

"Alice the Practical," said Liz.

"Okay. There's a twenty-four-hour Texaco just off Georgia, I think," Tony said, and off we went.

There's not a lot of activity at midnight in Silver Spring, I discovered. Tony parked a block away from the gas station, and we all got out. The guys stayed about twenty yards behind us, and Don had his camera set for night photos.

Liz and I went inside the Texaco. A young man was sitting behind a bulletproof glass enclosure and looked up when we entered.

"Could we have the key to the restroom?" I asked.

He studied us for a minute, a small bulge between his lip and his cheek where he'd tucked his tobacco. "Water's off," he said. "Sorry."

I could tell right away he didn't want us using his restroom.

"Aren't gas stations supposed to be available for travelers?" I asked.

"You got a car?" he asked.

"No, we're walking, but look, we're not going to sleep in there," I told him.

"Or use drugs," put in Elizabeth.

"We just want to clean up a little and use the toilet. And we really, *really* need to go," I told the man.

He reluctantly took a key down from the wall and slid it through the change slot in the glass wall. "Five minutes," he said. "You're not out in five minutes, I'll use the master key."

Liz and I went to the bathroom. Of course there was water.

When we brought the key back, I said, "Do you know anywhere we could stay for the night? Any shelter for women?"

"Don't you got no place to sleep?"

"No," Liz told him. "And we haven't eaten since this morning."

"Well, I don't know where you could sleep. But here . . ." He pushed a package of peanut-butter cheese crackers through the slot, and I think that Don, outside, got a picture. We thanked the man and started off again.

"You taking notes?" Tony asked.

"Mental notes," I told him. "Liz will help me remember the details."

"I'm hungry," she said. "What if we really *hadn't* eaten all day? Let's go to the all-night diner and ask if there are any leftovers we could have."

We walked the five blocks to the diner. There were a couple of workmen eating the blue plate special and an elderly man with a piece of lemon pie.

"Help you?" asked the middle-aged woman behind the counter.

"We don't have any money," I began, "and—"

The waitress cut me off. "Sorry. We don't give food away." She took another swipe at the counter with her rag, her face in a frown beneath the hairnet.

"Well, we were wondering if we could wash dishes, maybe, for a sandwich. We haven't eaten since this morning," Liz told her.

"We can't allow customers behind the counter. Insurance regulations," the woman said.

"Could we wipe tables, then? Stack trays?" Liz wouldn't give up.

"You see any tables need wiping? See any trays?" she asked. "You girls don't look very malnourished to me. I suggest you go back home and get your act together."

It was embarrassing. It was as though she saw through us. As we left the diner, Don got a photo of us, the woman glaring after us in the background.

It was almost one now, and a light rain was starting to fall. Liz and I huddled together in the doorway of a store, and the guys stood on the steps of a building across the street.

"What exactly are we doing now?" Liz asked.

"Keeping out of the rain," I said.

A police car came by. The cop in the passenger seat looked over at us, and the car slowed. It turned around in the intersection and cruised slowly back again. The driver rolled down his window.

"You girls need any help?" he called.

"Should we ask him if he knows of a shelter?" Liz whispered.

"No. We're minors. They'd take us in," I whispered back.

"We're okay," I called. "Just keeping out of the rain."

"It's late," the officer said. "Really shouldn't be out on the street like this." He nodded toward Tony and Don on the other side. "There are a number of people around who would probably like to know you better," he warned. "I'd go home if I were you."

"Oh, those guys are okay. We know them," Liz said.

"You know those fellas over there?" the policeman asked.

"Yeah, they're friends of ours," Liz said.

"They're just keeping an eye on us," I told him. This time the driver turned off the engine, and both police officers got out of the car.

"Omigod!" I said to Liz. "They must think we're hookers and that Don and Tony are our pimps!" I stood up and ran toward the cops, who were now walking across the street. "They're okay! They're okay!" I called. "It was all my idea!"

The policemen looked at us, then at the guys. The camera didn't help. I had to explain how we were researching an article for the school paper and the guys were along for protection. Don and Tony had identification as staff members on *The Edge*, but Liz and I had nothing and wouldn't give our names.

"Well, I'll tell you what. This sounds just crazy enough for me to believe you," the first policeman said. "But there's been some gang activity going on that we're watching out for, and I wouldn't want you getting involved in that in any way, shape, or form. You kids call it a night and go home, and we'll let it go."

"Okay," said Don. "Thanks." We walked down the block and all got in Tony's car.

"I guess that about does it," said Tony.

"No!" I protested. "We've still got to be turned down for someplace to sleep. I mean, what if it was five above zero and it was snowing and . . ."

"I know a home where some priests live," said Liz. "We could try there."

"Let's do it," I said.

"Then we can go home?" Don yawned.

"Then it's a wrap," I promised.

Liz directed them to the rectory, and once again, Tony parked a block away. Liz and I got out and started toward the house. We were halfway up the block when we heard a car cruising down the street, slowing when it got to us.

"Oh no, the police are back," I murmured, but when I turned around, it was a light-colored van with some guys in it. Men.

"Alice!" Liz said shakily.

"Keep walking," I said.

"Hey, girlies," a guy called, hanging out the passenger side. "What's the hurry?"

We didn't answer.

The driver leaned over and yelled, "Wanna go someplace for a beer?"

When we didn't respond, he said, "Hey! Don't act so friendly!"

I remembered the guys who had followed us on the board-walk last summer—how scared I'd been then and how we'd ducked into a stranger's house where all the lights were on. There were no lights now. Not even at the priests' house, and I had no idea how many men were in the van.

"Hey!" the first guy yelled again, and this time the van came to a stop. "It sort of hurts my feelings when a girl won't even give me the time of day." He started to get out, and we started to run. My heart was beating like crazy, and Liz was making frightened little bleating noises. There were pounding footsteps behind us, and someone grabbed my arm—not to stop me, but to speed me on. It was Tony, and Don stood like a wall between us and the van at the curb.

The men in the car hooted, and the first guy got back in again. "They got their big brothers looking out for them. Let's go," he said, and the driver gunned the motor and off they went.

My chest hurt with both the running and the fright. Even Tony was out of breath.

"Now, *that's* got to go in the story," he said.

"If I ever stop shaking!" I told him, and my voice trembled.

"They could be back, possibly with more," said Tony.

"This is our last stop," I promised. "Then we'll go home."

Liz pressed her finger to the doorbell, and we heard the *ding-dong* from inside. Don and Tony waited on a porch across the street.

"Oh, man!" I breathed out. "What if there had been a whole gang of men in that car, Liz? What if even Don and Tony couldn't fight them off?"

"Don't even think it, don't even think it, don't even think it," Liz murmured. "I'm nervous enough already."

We must have rung three times and stood there for five or six minutes before a light finally came on inside. An elderly man answered the door without speaking. I felt embarrassed for waking him.

"I'm sorry," Liz said hesitantly, "but we don't have anyplace to go, and we're afraid to be out on the street. Some men just tried to pick us up, and we were wondering if we could possibly stay here just for tonight."

The man opened the door wordlessly, and we stepped inside. He motioned us to his study, then came in and lowered himself into his chair, one arm leaning on the desk, nodding toward the sofa against one wall. He was in his pajamas and robe.

"I'm very tired," he said, "so I'm not quite coherent, but somehow I get the feeling that you girls haven't been out on your own for very long. Am I right?"

We sat down. "Yes," I said, wishing he would hurry and tell us to go home so we could call it quits.

"Problems at home? Fight with your parents?" he asked sleepily.

We nodded.

"Is there someone you'd like me to call?" he asked.

"No. We don't want anyone to know where we are," Liz said. "It's really very complicated, but you wouldn't turn us away if you knew the whole story. It's not that we're desperate, we just need to know if we could stay here overnight."

"If men are out there trying to pick you up, it sounds pretty desperate to me," the priest said. "There's the sofa for one of you, and the other will have to sleep in a chair. Bathroom down the hall. We'll be waking you at seven in the morning, because I have an eight o'clock mass and appointments starting at nine."

He stood up and pulled the belt of his robe a little tighter around him. "Good night," he said, and walked unsteadily back into the hallway, slowly climbing the stairs.

Liz and I stared at each other.

"That's it?" I said. "What are we going to *do*? The guys are out there! They want to go home!"

"Turn the light off and on and signal to them?" she suggested.

"Are you nuts?" I said. "We've got to leave, Liz!"

"I'll write a note," she said. I rolled my eyes and rested my forehead on my arms while Liz took the priest's memo pad and wrote:

> Dear Reverend,
> I'm afraid we came on false pretenses, because we're really doing a story for our school paper about what happens to homeless girls in Silver Spring and where they can go to get help. We promise not to use your address in the story, but thanks for your kindness.
> E and A

We turned off the light behind us and carefully opened the study door. Except for a dim hall light, the house was dark, and we tiptoed step by step over to the big front door with the little stained-glass window at the top.

"What if it sets off an alarm?" Liz asked.

"Liz, we've got to leave, regardless!" I insisted.

I put my hand on the doorknob and turned it.

"Good night," a voice behind us said, and we wheeled around to see the priest sitting up there on the landing, leaning wearily against the wall. "Next time you get an idea like this, bag it, okay?" he said. "Promise me you'll go straight home, and I won't have to tell the police I'm worried about you."

"We promise!" Liz said, and this time we meant it.

We all trooped back to Tony's car. We'd talked about going for coffee or something afterward, but we were simply too tired.

"Hope my photos turn out," Don said. "I'd like to get at least two or three we could use."

"Thanks, guys," I said. "I think we'll get a good story out of this."

"Remember to mention the two fabulous hunks who saved your lives," said Tony.

Fifteen minutes later, at quarter past two, he dropped Liz and me off at the corner, and we slipped back into my house.

No one was up. No light was on. No message from Dad or Sylvia. But the note Elizabeth had left on our bed—the "just in case" note—was gone.

14
SECRETS

When I rode to the Melody Inn with Dad the next day, he wasn't very talkative, but that was fine with me. I didn't know what he knew—*if* he knew—and I was too sleepy to try to sort it out. I hadn't had more than four hours of sleep. Liz had gone straight home that morning and back to bed. I leaned my head against the seat, my eyes closed, hands in the pockets of my jacket. Once the store opened, phones would ring, customers would mill about asking questions, clerks would call to each other, kids would troop to the practice rooms upstairs with their instruments for Saturday-morning lessons. It was good now just to soak up some quiet. But it was a jumpy kind of quiet with Dad lately, and any little thing could set him off.

He parked behind the store as usual, and we went inside. Marilyn was plugging in the coffeepot as we passed, and she studied us both.

Later, when she brought money over to my cash register, she asked, "Everything okay?"

"Okay how?" I asked.

She gave a little shrug. "Between you and your dad?"

"Sure," I said. "Why wouldn't it be?"

"No reason," she said quickly. "Your dad's been a little edgy lately."

"Yeah, we've noticed. The annex thing," I said.

"That too," said Marilyn. I looked after her, puzzled, as she took the box of twenties, tens, and ones over to David's cash register.

Halfway through the morning, a friend from school came in to buy new strings for his guitar. We stood there talking a few minutes, and even though I edged toward another customer who was looking peeved and impatient, I didn't stop our conversation. Suddenly Marilyn seemed to appear out of nowhere and waited on the woman.

When both the woman and my friend were gone, I said, "I know, I know, I shouldn't have spent so much time talking."

"Yeah, you really need to be a little more careful right now, Alice," she said. "Don't do anything more to upset them."

More? I thought. *Them?*

"Anything other than what?" I asked.

"Just stay on good terms with them till things blow over," Marilyn said, and then, "Your dad needs me over there. I've got to go."

"No, wait!" I said. "Stay on good terms with *who*? What are you talking about?"

And over her shoulder Marilyn said, "Sylvia knows." She crossed the floor.

I stared after her. What did she mean? Knows *what*? Knows where Liz and I went last night? Knows about Tony and me in his Buick? About me hiding in their *closet*? Was I living in a fishbowl or what?

I tried to get Marilyn's attention after she'd finished helping Dad with a sale, but she avoided me. I waited till I saw her go in the stockroom for something, then followed her back.

"Marilyn, what were you trying to tell me?" I asked.

"Oh, me and my big mouth," she said. "I just don't want you to get in any more trouble, Alice. Just a little tip from me to you, okay?"

I felt my scalp turning warm, but I had to ask. "What do you mean, any *more* trouble?" If I had to die of embarrassment, let it be here with Marilyn, not a stranger.

"Your dad's grumpy lately because he didn't get the annex, and he's been jumping on everyone," Marilyn said. "If he saw you chatting up that guy and ignoring another customer, he'd be on your case in seconds flat."

"So what does that have to do with Sylvia?" I asked. Nothing was making sense.

"Listen, Alice," Marilyn said. "Sylvia dropped by over lunch on Wednesday because Ben had left his glasses in her car. We both saw you on that motorcycle with a guy during school hours. . . ."

I felt as though my brain had broken into a dozen pieces and was trying to realign itself. "That was just . . . it was only . . . I didn't even know him!" I said, every phrase making it sound worse.

"I've got to get back out there," Marilyn said, reaching for the violin bow a customer had wanted, and quickly ducked through the curtain to the main room.

I stood there trying to remember the route the motorcycle had taken. Yes, I think it had turned onto Georgia Avenue, and I could well imagine we might have gone as far as the Melody Inn. And yes, it was over the lunch hour, and we'd stopped for a light. . . .

My throat felt dry as I went back out to the Gift Shoppe counter and pressed the START button for two girls who wanted to see the earrings in the revolving glass case. *Why didn't Sylvia say anything to me about the motorcycle incident? What's she waiting for?*

When I'd wrapped up the girls' earrings and made the sale, I went over to where Marilyn was looking up an order. "Just tell me this," I said. "Does Dad know?"

"I doubt it, because Sylvia and I were both looking out the window, trying to decide if it was you, and Sylvia said, 'Don't tell Ben.' And, of course, I haven't."

All afternoon it haunted me. All I could figure was that some-where, Sylvia was keeping score, tallying up my misdeeds, so that someday, when she really wanted to wallop me, she'd have all these grievances at once to tell Dad. And it probably included last night. She'd undoubtedly tucked that note Liz wrote in a drawer. It was ridiculous and childish and completely unfair to suspect this, yet I couldn't help it. It was as though Sylvia were a ticking time bomb.

Well, I thought angrily, *at least I'm shaking off that MGT reputation.* How many other girls had been invited to climb on the back of a stranger's motorcycle and ride off into the noonday sun? And yet, all the while I knew, *This isn't me.* Just like all the while Tony was playing with my breasts and I was enjoying it, I knew, *He's not the one. Not really.* You can do things, say things, feel things that—down in your heart of hearts—you know you aren't serious about, and yet, it's like a big deal to everyone else who reads a lot more into it than is really there.

At school, when Liz had finally asked me what all had hap-pened that noon on the motorcycle, I'd said, "We rented a motel room, made mad love, and he dropped me off at school again in time for the bell, what else?" She'd laughed, and so had I. But Sylvia, I felt sure, wasn't laughing.

As soon as I got home from work that afternoon, tired as I was, I wrote up my story and e-mailed it to Scott. He was prob-ably out for the evening, because an hour went by, two, three, and there was no response. Then, just before I went to bed, I got this:

Alice, you're a wonder! It will probably
get us both in hot water, but I love it.
Hope the photos turn out. S.

I knew I'd treasure that one e-mail forever (*Alice, you're a wonder!*), but why couldn't he have added, *But I'd love to be in a hot tub with you!* or something?

Lester finally came by for dinner that Sunday night.

"Where have you *been*?" I asked as he slid in across from me at the table.

"You mean I've been missed?" he asked.

"When you go close to two weeks without even *calling* . . . !" I scolded.

Lester grinned and reached for the scalloped potatoes. "Okay, so I met this girl."

"Thought so!" said Dad.

It had been four months since Les and Tracy broke up, and now he was back in circulation again.

"Can't keep a good man down, can we?" Sylvia joked.

"Did you meet her in grad school, Les?" I asked. "Not one of your instructors again, is she?"

"No, no. She's an aerobics instructor, actually, and a part-time student. I just know her from the gym. We've been going out some. Nothing serious."

"Well, we've missed you," said Sylvia. "Have some salad, Les."

He helped himself. "I heard about the annex deal, Dad," he said. "That's a bummer."

"Oh, I'll survive," said Dad. "I was just so sure we'd get it. The owner seemed to like the idea. But I guess the restaurant folks wined and dined him, and he liked their idea more."

"On the other hand," said Lester, "it's possible that people who come to the restaurant will discover your store."

"That's what I told him," said Sylvia. "He could put up a schedule of music classes in his window. Show people that here's a place a kid can get trombone lessons. Where you can hire a good piano tuner. Buy a guitar. It's not all bad."

"Anyway," said Dad, "that's water over the dam. But while you're here tonight, Les, I thought it would be a good time to call Sal and see how Milt's doing. He left the hospital today."

"Sure," said Les.

I hate group phone calls. You never know whom you're talking to next, and you have to keep the whole conversation generic. When Aunt Sally's on the line, though, all Dad has to do is hold the phone away from his ear and her voice comes through loud and clear. It's like she's addressing a school assembly.

"Milt's sleeping right now, Ben, but he's doing just fine!" Aunt Sally was saying. "The doctor says he's like a new man, and if we continue the medication and diet, he could live out his normal life span."

"That's just great news, Sal! It really is," said Dad, pleased. The rest of us cheered in the background so that Aunt Sally could hear us.

"And Carol's staying for a few days more," Aunt Sally continued. "Her phone hasn't been working in her apartment, so she brought a suitcase here, and it's so good to have her! She's out right now, and I think she's bringing home some take-out food."

Les and I exchanged looks, knowing that Carol still hadn't told her folks that she'd moved in with her boyfriend. Secrets, secrets . . .

"Sometimes," Aunt Sally went on, "good things come out of bad, and I think we've become closer as a family because of Milt's heart attack. Is Alice there, Ben? I want to say something to her."

I reluctantly took the phone. I love my aunt, but whatever she had to tell me, I didn't want the whole family to hear.

"Hi, Aunt Sally," I said. "We're so glad that Uncle Milt's home now."

"So are we," she said. "I just wanted to say, Alice, that things like this make you realize that every day is precious. Each day is a gift to be enjoyed to the fullest. But when I was waiting outside the emergency room for Milt, I wrote a poem, and I want to share it with you. You always did like my poems, didn't you?"

To tell the truth, the only poem of Aunt Sally's I remember is one about sorting clothes on wash day.

"Of course," I said, and held the receiver out so everyone could hear.

Aunt Sally cleared her throat and began:

"When scorching looks and angry words
Between you two have passed,
Just remember, ne'er forget
Each breath may be his last."

Les and I exchanged wide-eyed looks.

"Or you may die, and loving words
Are sealed inside your head.
They'll never reach his longing ears
Because your lips are dead."

Sylvia put one hand over her face.

"So cherish every kiss and touch
And welcome each new day,
For winter claims us, one by one,
And takes it all away."

I waited, wondering if there was more. When the pause lengthened, I said, "Aunt Sally, that . . . that's . . ."

"Awful!" Les whispered, holding back laughter.

"So . . . sad!" I said. "Uncle Milt isn't going to die!"

"But there were all these thoughts going through my head when we went to the hospital, Alice, and I wanted to write a poem about the guilt I was feeling for every argument we've ever had and how I'm pledging my life to just enjoying the good things and not nagging him about the little stuff."

"That's wonderful, Aunt Sally," I said, and handed the phone to Les.

Later, when Dad and Sylvia were watching a program, Les and I did the dishes.

"So what's the new girl's name, Les, and what's she like?" I asked.

"Name's Claire: two arms, two legs, brown hair, blue eyes. . . ."

"When do we get to meet her?" I asked.

"I'll have to give that some thought," he answered. "See if she's the family type."

"Is she at all like Tracy?" I asked. "Do you have a lot in common?"

"Oh, I wouldn't say we've made much progress in that department, but she's good . . . uh, very good . . . at other things."

I decided not to ask any more.

That evening, as I was searching for a slipper under the bed, I found a sheet of notepaper, scrunched and mauled, with tiny holes and tears in it. I fished it out and flattened the paper. It was the note that Liz had left on my bed the night we crept out to do the story. We must not have closed the door completely after us when we left my room, and Annabelle, coming in to sleep on my bed, had evidently found the note and toyed with it. I never appreciated her more.

We got my story in by the Monday deadline, took it to the printer, and the paper came out on Tuesday:

Edge Exclusive
This newspaper neither assigned this story nor gave its permission, but when it was submitted to us, we felt it deserved to be read. The photos accompanying the article are intentionally dark to protect the identity of the writer.

The City at Night
by Anonymous

Who has never felt, even for a moment, the urge to run away? To simply walk out of a bad situation and take a breather? To see what two girls might be up against on the streets of Silver Spring in the wee hours of the morning, a friend and I—followed at a distance by two guys to keep us safe—slipped out around midnight on a Friday night. . . .

That was the way my article began, and after telling all that had happened to us, I ended with:

What we learned was that anyone wanting to escape a bad situation at home needs to have moxie, moola, and—most of all—a plan and a place to go. Because streets can be mean after midnight, even in Silver Spring.

Wow! That story made a real splash. Did Liz and I want everyone to know we were the girls in the story? Does the sun rise in the east?

When Pamela read it in the cafeteria, her eyes grew wide and she immediately turned to me. "Who *were* they, Alice? You must know!"

Liz and I exchanged glances over our salads, and Pamela saw. She grabbed the copy of the newspaper again and studied the photos.

"That's *you*, Alice!" she said, pointing to the profile of me in the doorway of the gas station, trying to get the key. And to the others, she announced gleefully, "It was *Alice*! Wow! Alice! And you *wrote* this, I'll bet! Who was the other girl?"

"My lips are sealed," I said, grinning.

"Wait a minute," said Gwen. She took the newspaper out of Pamela's hands and her eyes traveled down the page. "Whoever it was knew a house where priests live, so she's probably Catholic."

All eyes turned to Elizabeth. Jill and Karen positively stared.

"*Elizabeth?*" cried Penny. "You and *Elizabeth*? Man, you guys could have been raped, you know that? You could have been killed!"

"Who were the guys?" asked Jill.

"Now, *that*," I said, just to savor the moment, "will remain forever a mystery."

It was raining that afternoon—a cold December rain—the kind that feels as though it could turn to sleet, but I didn't care. I was on cloud nine. All afternoon the news had traveled around school that Liz and I had been the girls in the story, and kids gave me high fives and hugs.

"You got a car?" Tony asked me. "I'll drive you home."

I was grateful for the offer, because the bus had long since left. Miss Ames had called the newspaper staff in for a conference with the principal, and they let us know that while the story was a good one and provided some useful information, we should not expect that we could publish whatever we wanted just by printing a disclaimer. All of us, but especially Scott, had to promise that we'd run the paper—the whole paper—by Miss Ames in the future before it went to press. We promised.

"Everybody's talking about the story," Tony said when he slid in beside me. "I think everyone knows now that it was you."

"Good!" I said, and laughed. "It probably took me as long to count the characters and lines as it did to write the piece. I don't know how you always get your sports write-ups in on time."

"Computer program," said Tony. "If you know the typeface, the number of characters needed per line, lines per column, and number of columns, you just feed in the information, click 'Enter,' and the computer takes your material and does the rest."

"Amazing," I said.

"We'll stop by my place, and I'll show it to you," Tony said. He turned left at the corner instead of right.

"Who's home?" I asked.

"Mom'll be there soon," he answered. He turned left again

farther on and finally into the driveway of a large house. "C'mon. I'll give you a demonstration."

I gave him my suspicious look, and he laughed. "Hey, this is *school*. This is *learning*. Jeez, does everything you do have to be an assignment? Don't you ever do anything just for fun?"

"Of course," I said, and old dry-as-dust Alice followed him into the house.

Tony lives in a more upscale neighborhood than we do. Actually, our house is, or used to be, the most modest house on the block. But Tony's ranch-style had a big lawn. The master suite and study were at one end, he showed me on a quick tour, with the family room and Tony's bedroom at the other. We said hello to the maid in the kitchen, then headed for Tony's end of the house.

I felt that warm flush at the sight of Tony's unmade bed—a pair of Jockey shorts on the floor. We went over to his computer.

Tony sat down and pushed a few keys. He found the article he'd written about our last football game against Churchill, then got up and told me to sit in his place.

"Click on 'Times New Roman,'" he said, and I did.

"Now specify thirty-four characters per line . . ."

I obeyed.

"Then fifty-one lines per column, and press 'Enter.'"

I did, and suddenly Tony's article disappeared, only to reappear in column form. He showed me how to add a heading and even wrap the type around photos.

"Oh, wow! I've got to get this!" I said.

He was standing behind my chair, hands on my shoulders, and he let them slide down my body until they reached my breasts. He bent over me, thumbs circling my nipples. Instantly, I felt the warm wetness between my legs.

"Tony . . . ," I said, laughing a little. He pulled me up out of the chair, turned me around, and kissed me. Without letting go of me, he reached out and slid a CD in his player, and a slow song began, a woman singing a love song.

"Just want to relive a little of the Snow Ball," he said, and started dancing with me, hands on my behind. We danced right over his Jockey shorts, in fact, and as we moved away from the bed, I relaxed a little and swayed to his rhythm.

We danced slowly around his room, our bodies together, and I could feel him getting hard.

I heard a voice from the hallway, a door closing. I startled and pushed away.

"It's the maid leaving," he whispered in my ear. We were alone in the house then.

"Your mom . . . ?" I questioned.

"Shhhh," he whispered, and we kissed again.

The next time we got near his bed, he nudged me down on it and lay beside me. "Oh, baby," he said.

I wanted to say, *Please don't call me that. I'm me. Alice.* But even thinking it, I sounded like Little Miss Sunday School.

My breasts again. He didn't try to unfasten my bra this time. Just reached up under my top and clumsily pushed my bra up over my breasts. It was sort of awkward, the way we were lying across his twin bed. Only our backs and hips were on it, our legs off the edge, feet on the floor. I thought of Aunt Sally's admonition to keep both feet on the floor and almost smiled when I thought of the trouble you could get in with feet firmly planted.

Now Tony was trying to get me to lie on the bed lengthwise, but I didn't like the thought of being pushed back against the wall, so I resisted. Then he was unzipping my jeans, tugging at the sides till they were down past my hips, and his hand was inside my underwear, finding my slippery place. I felt the swelling sensation in my vagina.

"Oh, baby, you're creaming for me," he said. "You want it as much as I do."

He didn't say he wanted *me*, I noticed. He wanted *it*. So did I, honestly, but not, I think, with Tony.

"Tony, your mom . . . ," I said again.

"She won't be home till six," he whispered. "Shhhh."

That was an hour away! I tensed but then gave in again and let his finger explore me. Then it was *in* me, and his other hand was tugging at my jeans, trying to get them all the way off. I was wildly excited.

"Baby . . . baby . . . ," he murmured breathily.

He reached over and yanked at the little drawer on his bedside table, pulling out a condom. "I'll put on a glove," he said, and unzipped his own jeans. Condoms at the ready, in his bedside drawer? Was I just one of his "babes" in a long succession of girls?

"Tony," I said, dislodging his finger and trying to pull up my jeans.

Another door opening somewhere. Closing. Footsteps in the house.

"Tony!" I said, panicking.

"It's only my dad, and he doesn't care," Tony said.

I edged away from him.

"He won't come in. He never does. Trust me," Tony said.

"No," I said, scooting back.

"Baby, don't leave me like this," Tony said, pulling me against him again and putting my hand on his penis. He squeezed my hand a couple of times, and a few seconds later he came.

"Oh, baby, oh, baby," he kept breathing in my ear. "We got a good thing going here. We could be so good together. . . ."

"Tony?" his dad called from out in the hall.

"Got company," Tony yelled back, still breathless.

I wasn't sure, but I think I heard his dad chuckle. "Just wanted to know if you were home," he said, and the footsteps went away.

I got up, pulled up my jeans, and zipped them. Reached under my shirt and pulled my bra back down over my breasts. "I've got to get home. I can't stay any longer," I said.

He wiped himself off with a corner of the sheet, then stood and zipped up, grinning at me.

I was embarrassed when we walked through the high-ceilinged living room.

"Alice, this is my dad," Tony said. "Dad, this is the girl I took to the Snow Ball."

"How you doing, Alice?" Mr. Osler said, and he went back to his newspaper.

Tony talked about his dad as he drove me home. How his dad had been big man on campus when he was in college. "A girl on each arm," his dad used to brag. And I began to get the picture—that if Tony couldn't be the sports hero his dad had wanted him to be, he'd try for big man on campus with the girls. Again I wondered, Who was he, really? Who was I?

When we got to my house, he said, "This was just a warm-up, baby. Next time I'll give you a taste of the real thing."

I smiled. "Your *next* girl, Tony," I said, and kissed him good-bye.

Back at home, while Sylvia was preparing dinner, I lay on my bed thinking about that scene with Tony. The awkwardness of the way we were lying, clothes half on, half off, my bra pulled up over my breasts. A narrow twin bed. I couldn't help thinking about Dad and Sylvia in their own bed, in their own room. Comfortable. Relaxed. Unhurried. Trusting, and in love.

Usually, I wanted to rush right to the phone and tell Pam or Liz or Gwen or all of them when something racy had happened to me. This time I didn't. Not for a while, anyway. Sometimes you don't tell your friends everything, either. I felt like there was a lot to settle in my own mind about what I wanted and what I didn't.

I liked sex, that's certain. I liked a boy to kiss my breasts, to run his hands up and down my sides, to thrust his tongue in my mouth, to explore my slippery place and finger me. I was eager, I'll admit, for whatever came next. But I was going to be choosy.

It wouldn't be lying sideways, with my bra yanked up like a rape scene. It wouldn't be in a guy's bedroom with his dad just down the hall. It wouldn't be with a guy who called me "baby" and was adding me to a long list of girls, condoms at the ready.

Why couldn't my hormones understand that? I wondered. Why couldn't they all stay quiet until I was with the right guy at the right time in the right place, and then go crazy? I was surprised to find myself smiling just a little. That would make a humorous subject to write about someday, but it sure wouldn't be for the school newspaper. Or maybe not for anywhere that my parents could read it.

There are things you keep from your parents. Some of them they should know, perhaps, like that night in Silver Spring, but you never tell them because you realize afterward just how dangerous they had been. And you know you won't repeat them. Each time something like that happens, you gain an experience, a little independence, but it's at a price. Growing up also means growing away, I discovered. After our night out on the town, I felt charged and elated that we had pulled it off. At the same time, there was a sort of homesickness inside me, like . . . well . . . that I was leaving a little girl behind. That I probably would never sit on my dad's lap again, as I had the other night. That there was a necessary distance between us now. Like, you can be excited and sad at the same time. And times like tonight, what happened between Tony and me—I wouldn't tell Dad at all.

15
WHAT HAPPENED NEXT

I still hadn't finished the assignment for Mrs. Cary and couldn't delay any longer. She was going to start calling on us to give our talks the next day and, as Les would say, I just had to "suck it up." But how could you give a persuasive speech about something you didn't believe in?

I'd done most of the research last week, starting with Google. No, to tell the truth, I'd started with Gwen. "Tell me one medical breakthrough that's come about through animal experimentation," I'd asked after explaining my assignment to her.

"The Rh factor in infants," she'd told me.

"What?" I asked.

"Blue babies. I learned about it at the hematology lab. A blood disease of newborn infants when they have a different blood type from their mothers. Doctors learned how to correct it by operating first on dogs. Go to Google and type in 'medical discoveries using animals in research.'"

The list of medical breakthroughs in front of me was long. By experimenting initially on dogs, for example, researchers had created the heart-lung machine that is used to keep patients alive during heart surgery. Operating on baboons, surgeons had learned how to remove cancer cells in bone marrow without destroying healthy cells. Pigs had played an important role in studying the healing process of burn victims. . . .

Of all the medical research involving animals, one article said, 92 percent of it was not painful. But what about the 8 percent that was? How could anyone stand by and watch a rabbit or a guinea pig suffer? And what about labs where the technicians were careless and needlessly let animals suffer?

I ran it past Dad at breakfast the next morning.

"There's no question that there should be stricter controls over laboratory experiments, Al," he said, considering it. "I've read some of those horror stories too. But if a critical experiment is needed, and it's a choice between a dog having to suffer or your uncle Milt dying, which would you choose?"

"Was Uncle Milt . . . ?" I began.

"Well, he's had heart surgery," said Dad.

I sat perfectly still. "Have they . . . have they ever discovered anything about . . . about leukemia from animals?" I asked.

"I don't know, Al. But if they had . . . if there was . . ."

I sighed. "I'd have wanted them to try whatever they could to save Mom. Or Molly."

Something dramatic happened in speech class that afternoon. I was the second one up, after a guy who argued against legalizing marijuana. I was halfway through my talk when I saw a woman slip through the door at the back of the room and quietly take an empty seat.

I saw Mrs. Cary crane her neck a little to see who it was, smile quizzically, then turn her attention back to me. I don't think any of the other kids noticed.

When I'd finished, but before the critique began, Mrs. Cary stood up and said to the woman, "I'm sorry, but I don't know your name."

Everyone turned to see whom she was talking to. The woman was short, a little stocky, dressed in a brown jacket and pants, with a bright-colored scarf around her neck.

"I'm Jennifer Shoates's mother," she said, rising from her chair, "and I'd like to talk to you about the completely irresponsible assignment you gave my daughter."

The quiet in the classroom was almost eerie. This was something I'd never seen before—well, not since second grade, anyway—a mom coming in to protest. Jennifer, the girl who had spoken against sex before marriage—sitting in the second row—turned as red as a cherry tomato.

We knew that Mrs. Shoates hadn't stopped at the office first because she wasn't wearing a visitor's pass. I'm not sure just how she got by security. All eyes were on Mrs. Cary now, to see how an experienced teacher would handle this.

"I'd be glad to discuss this in conference," Mrs. Cary said politely. "If you'd stop by the office, they can—"

"She's supposed to give her talk today, and you have no right to assign such a personal and irresponsible assignment," Jennifer's mom said.

"Mrs. Shoates, you're welcome to visit as a guest, but this *is* my classroom, and I'm afraid you need to follow my rules here," Mrs. Cary said. "We can put Jennifer's talk off for another day, if you prefer. . . ."

"Mo-*ther*!" Jennifer protested, and I wondered if a face could actually explode, her cheeks were so bright. "Just let me get this over with. *Please!*"

We held our breath. Mrs. Cary waited. Finally Mrs. Shoates sat back down.

It was strange, but I'd lost all stage fright, because I knew that everyone was thinking about the woman at the back of the room, not me.

"Okay, class. Comments on Alice's talk? How well did she do convincing us that animals are truly needed for research?" Mrs. Cary asked.

"I'm still not convinced that those experiments get the study they need before they're approved," one guy said. "I think she should have focused more on that."

"But that wasn't the point," another boy said. "The question is, if they *were* approved and monitored carefully, do the results justify using animals in that way?"

A girl said, "If *my* grandmother had cancer, wouldn't I want every possible study to be done that might save her?"

Mrs. Cary allowed another two minutes for discussion on my topic, and then it was Jennifer's turn. I took my seat, and Jennifer went to the front of the room.

If we hadn't felt sorry for Jennifer when she gave her first talk promoting chastity, we ached for her now. I did, anyway. If my dad ever came to school and threw a fit like that, I'd crawl under the desk. I mean, we're in high school now. How long is Jennifer's mom going to fight her battles for her? How can Jennifer become independent if her mom takes over when things get tough?

Jennifer's voice was a little too soft. Too shaky. She began by saying that she still felt that virginity before marriage was best. But there might be some situations where having sex would make sense. I stole a look at Mrs. Shoates, and she was shaking her head. Jennifer plowed on.

If a man or woman was physically disabled, she said, and they weren't sure they could have sex, maybe it was best to try first before they married. And if an elderly widow would lose her husband's annuity if she remarried, maybe it was forgivable if she had sex with another man without marriage if they had a loving relationship. But people who lived together before marriage had higher divorce rates than those who didn't.

Jennifer stood stiffly at the front of the room when she had finished, and I could tell she was purposely avoiding looking at her mother.

"Okay, class. Comments?" Mrs. Cary said.

"I thought she was supposed to be defending sex before marriage. How did those statistics about divorce rates help out there?" asked Brian.

"Yeah, what about couples who have sex but *don't* live together? What about that?" asked someone else. "Jennifer's argument was supposed to be about virginity, not just having sex."

The chair at the back of the room squeaked again. "I cannot believe I am listening to this discussion in a Maryland public high school," came Mrs. Shoates's voice.

"Mrs. Shoates, I'm going to ask you to use your guest manners and let my students do the talking," Mrs. Cary said. "I think your daughter can handle this herself, and it would be good to give her that opportunity."

I raised my hand. "I think Jennifer should be congratulated for examining another point of view under extremely difficult circumstances," I said.

Mrs. Cary nodded.

"But she only used extreme examples as opposing points of view," a girl said. "What about all the reasons two younger persons might want to have sex without it doing any harm?"

The chair at the back of the room squeaked again.

Jennifer said, "Maybe sometimes it's good to wait for the things that are most important to you. Maybe instant gratification shouldn't apply to *every*thing you want in life. I think maybe it makes it a little bit special to wait."

"That's also a good point, Jennifer, although you're back now to your original argument," Mrs. Cary said. "But I'm afraid our time is up, and we need to go on to our next speaker. Jay, your last talk was on teaching evolution, so let's see how persuasive you can be for creationism."

I realized then that Mrs. Shoates had left the room, and I felt quite sure she was on her way to the principal's office.

I was glad to see Lester hanging around at dinnertime that evening because I wanted to tell everyone what had happened in speech class.

"That Mrs. Cary is one brave gal," said Sylvia. "I'm not sure I'd take that on."

"You'd never come to school and embarrass me like that, would you, Dad?" I asked.

Dad grinned. "No. I just embarrass you in front of family."

"I remember when *you* came by school one day, Les, when I was being bullied on Seventh Grade Sing Day," I said. "But you didn't embarrass me, you *saved* me. Denise Whitlock said she'd stick my head in the toilet if I didn't sing all the verses to the school song."

"Yeah, I do sort of remember that," Les said. "Figured you needed a little help when I saw they'd backed you up against a car in the parking lot."

"That was one of the nicest things you ever did for me," I said. "Maybe someday I can return the favor."

"Doing what? Rescuing *me*?" he said.

"You never know," I told him.

When we got to speech class on Thursday, something wasn't quite right. Mrs. Cary's mouth. Her eyes, maybe.

"I've been informed that we have to suspend our assignment for the time being," she said.

"Whaaaaaat?" The exclamation came from all corners of the room.

"It's really all I can tell you right now," she said. "Someone will be doing an evaluation of it, and they'll make a decision."

All eyes turned to Jennifer Shoates, who sat like a stone, her face a pale pink.

"And so," Mrs. Cary said quickly, "we're going to do a reading of *Waiting for Godot*, by the Irish playwright Samuel Beckett. There are five roles, and we'll take turns reading the lines."

We didn't want *Waiting for Godot*. We didn't want an Irish playwright or reading lines. We had started the second part of an assignment we thought we were going to hate, and it was one of the most intense and thought-provoking assignments we'd ever had. We wanted to see it through. Jennifer must have been feeling our laser stares, because they seemed to pin her to her seat, keeping her motionless.

Mrs. Cary began the new assignment immediately, passing out paperback copies of the play and assigning the parts of Estragon and Vladimir and Lucky and Pozzo and the boy to various students. We were stunned.

When the bell rang at last, Jennifer was the first one out of the classroom, but some of the rest of us gathered outside in the hall.

"We know who's behind *this*, don't we?" Brian said.

"How can she do this?" I asked. "How can one parent decide what the rest of us can or can't do?"

"Look. My aunt has a friend who works in the school office," one of the guys said. "I'll find out what's going on and e-mail you guys. Give me your addresses." We did, then we walked off, grumbling among ourselves.

That evening the news traveled from one student to another by IM. Mrs. Shoates hadn't gone to see the principal the day before as we'd suspected. She'd gone home and called the superintendent, and he'd said that a supervisor would come out around noon on Friday to discuss the matter with Mrs. Cary, Mrs. Shoates, and the principal and that the assignment would be suspended for the time being.

One guy wrote:

Let's organize a walkout Friday when the super shows up.

Another said:

Hey, let's take the whole day off in protest!

But I suggested that we have a demonstration over the lunch hour when the supervisor was there, carrying signs saying how we felt. That seemed to go over well, and we set to work.

I told Dad and Sylvia about it, and I thought they'd try to talk me out of it. But Dad only said, "Don't try to stop the supervisor's car with your bodies, please."

And Sylvia said, "'Polite' and 'orderly' are the passwords, Alice. Don't give the principal any other reason to side with Mrs. Shoates."

I called Lester next and told him what we were going to do.

"Ah! A little civil disobedience, huh?" he said.

"If it's something I really care about, I can be as militant as anyone else," I said.

"You carrying an AK rifle or what?" he asked.

"*Signs*, Lester! Signs saying what we stand for," I told him.

"Go, Alice!" said Lester.

When lunchtime came on Friday, we took our homemade signs from one of the student's cars in the parking lot, where we'd stashed them before school that morning, and gathered on the sidewalk outside the front entrance. We'd told everyone to use thick black markers and print in big block letters. The pieces of cardboard were assorted sizes and colors, but they expressed what we felt: DARE TO THINK; SUPPORT CONTROVERSY; WHAT'S WRONG WITH DEBATE? WE LOVE CARY; DISCUSSION NEVER HURT ANYONE; WHO'S AFRAID OF LEARNING?

Somebody must have alerted the press, because a reporter showed up from the *Washington Post* and another from the *Gazette*. I had told Scott about it, and he made sure that Don was out there with his camera too, taking pictures for *The Edge*.

We were orderly. Polite. We didn't block the driveway or keep anyone from entering the school. When a car with a MONTGOMERY COUNTY PUBLIC SCHOOLS sticker on it pulled into the parking lot, we were pretty sure it was the supervisor and began to chant, "Keep our school . . . free to think! Keep our school . . . free to think!" The supervisor stared at us, at the signs, then she quickly parked and walked in a side entrance.

The principal came out on the steps and looked us over, seeming more puzzled than angry. "Anybody want to talk about this?" he called out, coming down the walk.

"We're just showing our support for a great teacher," somebody said.

"We want to show that we think the assignment Mrs. Cary gave us was a good one and that one person shouldn't be allowed to dictate what the rest of us can learn," I told him.

"I guess I'm a little surprised that an ordinary parent conference, which is an everyday occurrence at most schools, should become public knowledge," the principal said.

"Mrs. Cary doesn't know anything about this demonstration, but the Freedom of Information Act should apply to students too," a guy said. "We have a right to know what's happened to an assignment that involved us."

We stayed outside through the lunch period and through fourth period as well. We figured we'd get detention for that, but it was worth it. When the bell rang for fifth, though, we went back inside.

When we got to Mrs. Cary's sixth-period class, she simply

smiled, welcomed us back, and asked who was ready to give their three-minute persuasive talk. We cheered.

What we found out later was that the principal and supervisor felt the same way we did even before the protest, but they wanted to give Mrs. Shoates a chance to formally voice her concerns about the assignment.

Another thing we students agreed on—most of us, anyway—as we left the room after class was that Jennifer shouldn't have to suffer anymore. It wasn't her fault that her mom had caused a problem, and we shouldn't treat her like a freak. No girl should have to be accountable for the behavior of her mom. And I wondered if my own mother would have done anything like that to embarrass me. I think I would gladly have suffered what Jennifer went through, though, if only I could have *had* my mom.

Mark Stedmeister called me at the Melody Inn on Saturday and said that some of the kids were going to the old Steak House in Gaithersburg for dinner—our last get-together before the holidays. He wanted to know how many cars we could count on.

"Tonight?" I said. "Not mine. Dad's going to be working late here at the store, and Sylvia wants to do some shopping."

"Want to ride with me, then?" he asked. "I'm picking up Penny and Pamela. Liz can ride too if she wants."

It sounded like a good idea, and I told Dad where we were going. At seven that night, Liz and I got in Mark's car, and he set off for Penny's, then Pamela's. The Steak House restaurant was a sort of run-down place that was probably scheduled for demolition. The staff was mostly college kids who worked evenings, and though the food wasn't anything to rave about, it wasn't too expensive and the portions were huge.

Jill and Justin didn't show up, but Karen came with Keeno. Patrick didn't make it, and neither did Gwen. Brian and a few of his friends from school were holding a long table for us when we got there, so it was sort of the old gang and sort of not.

Pamela, Liz, and I shared the deep-fried onion rings, and we ordered steak sandwiches and Cokes. Mostly the talk at the table was about finals, the PSAT, what we were going to do over winter break, and who had already been out looking at colleges.

"Patrick, of course," I told them.

"Jill's waiting to see where Justin's going, and then she's going to apply," said Karen, who had the scoop. "Except that Justin's parents don't like her and want him to study in England or something."

"Really?" said Liz. "Why don't they like her?"

"Jill says they told Justin she just wanted to marry into money," Karen said. "I'll bet they don't realize that Jill and Justin have been going together almost longer than any couple in school, but that doesn't satisfy his folks. Jill said she and Justin have a plan, but I don't know what. It's all she'd tell me."

I noticed that down at the end of the table Brian was pouring beer into an empty glass, then slipping the bottle back in the gym bag on the seat beside him.

Pamela laughed. "That's the real reason the guys like to come out here. If you bring your own, the waiters look the other way."

I didn't know if Brian's folks knew he was raiding their beer supply or knew and didn't care. I figured they didn't care. Mark didn't appear to be drinking, though.

It was only nine when we finished at the Steak House, and Keeno said we were all invited to his cousin's birthday party in Germantown.

"How far is that?" I asked. "I have to be home by midnight."

"Only eight miles or so. We don't have to stay long," Keeno said. "I've got some gag gifts for him. His birthday was yesterday, but they're having a party for him tonight."

"So why weren't you there this evening?" Liz asked.

"Oh, I said I'd come by later with friends. He isn't really a cousin. Sort of a second or third cousin, actually. But he's a lot of fun."

Liz looked uncomfortable, but she had to be back by midnight too, so we were going to hold Mark to that. We followed the other cars.

Keeno's friend lived out beyond Germantown in a wooded rural area, and it took longer than I expected to get there. By the time our cars found the address and we made our way through the crush of people just inside the door, filling every room, it was after ten and had begun to snow. I figured I could stay until about eleven fifteen, and then I'd tell Mark we had to leave.

If there were any adults present, I didn't see them. Brian was goofing off, using a quart jar as a beer stein. There were as many beer bottles on the kitchen table as there were Coke and Sprite cans, and the floor was sticky.

Keeno had the usual gag gifts for the birthday boy—fly in a fake ice cube, plastic vomit, dog turds—but the guy was plastered and didn't appreciate them, so Keeno tried them out on us. It was when he put his hand up the back of my sweater, though, and pulled out a pair of black panties that he made me laugh.

"What are you? A professional magician?" I asked.

"Magic fingers," he said, letting them creep up under my sweater again, trying to unhook my bra. I laughed and slapped his hand away.

Several guys came up to me during the next hour and asked for my name and phone number. Liz's, too. I tried to think of a composer who sounded credible. J. S. Bach, maybe. I said I was "Janice Bach" and gave them the number of the Melody Inn. Liz thought it was hilarious. She gave them Jill's number.

Around eleven fifteen Liz and Pamela and I went looking for Mark. Some kids were going upstairs together, and I hoped I wouldn't have to look for him there, but Brian said he and Penny and Karen had headed out to a movie.

"What?" we cried.

"Relax!" he said, his voice a little too loud. "There are plenty of cars. Pu-len-ty!"

He told us to get in one of the cars out on the lawn—that those three were leaving now, taking kids home. Pamela and Liz and I went out on the porch. It was snowing lightly, and all the cars, bushes—everything—had been frosted with a quarter inch of white.

"C'mon, we've got room," someone called from one of the cars.

Liz was closest, so she ran over, bracing against the wind, and got inside. Some more girls ran past us and then some guys. I wasn't sure which of the cars Pam got in, but somebody yelled, "We can still squeeze in one more."

I stepped through the snow as the first car backed out into the street and crawled in the backseat of another just as Brian came around the hood to the driver's side.

"Whose car is this?" I asked in the darkness, as all the cars looked alike in the snow.

"Brian's," said a guy up front.

I got out. "No, I'm going with someone else," I said.

"Hey, Al, get *in*!" Brian yelled. "It's snowing! Close the fuck-ing door!"

"No . . . I've . . . I've got a ride," I said, and headed back to the porch, my heart pounding. *Damn Mark!* I was thinking. How could he drive us out here and then go off to a movie? I started looking for Keeno and went over to a window to see inside. Keeno was on the couch with a girl. Kissing. Very deep kissing, evidently. Great! *Now* what should I do?

Dad had said that if I was ever in a place I shouldn't be and needed a ride, I could call, no matter what time it was. But Germantown? *Should I call Les instead?* I wondered as I watched Brian's car go roaring off, snow flying out behind it.

It was coming down thicker now, and the noise was so loud in the house, I knew I'd better call from the porch. I fished in my bag for my cell phone. Some of the kids went down the steps and started a snowball fight.

Thunk! A snowball hit the front door.

Thwack! Another hit a post.

And then—a sound I will never forget—a high, horrible squeal of tires and then . . . *CRASH!* Metal against metal.

"Omigod!" someone yelled. "It's just down the road." And people began to run.

16

CONVERSATION

Someone dashed past me and jumped into another car out front. Then another. Motors raced, and two cars went speeding toward the sound of the crash. People on the porch held cell phones to their ears and everyone was asking, "Where are you? . . . Can you see anything? . . . Who's car was it? . . . Was it Sheryl's? Was it Brian's?"

I sank down on the steps and sat trancelike, unblinking, as the falling snow coated the part of me unprotected by the roof—my knees, my legs, my feet. *Which cars were Liz and Pam in? Were they together?* I felt as disconnected from this house, this party, the noise, the crash, as my shoulders were from my knees. Frozen solid.

"Yeah?" a guy behind me was saying, cell phone to his ear. "Oh, Christ! . . . Oh, man! . . . What about Sunny? . . . Yeah."

I jerked around. "What about Liz Price or Pamela Jones? Were either of them in that car? Who was hurt?"

"A kid, that's all I know," the guy told me.

"Has anyone called for an ambulance?" I screamed. And then we heard a siren.

"Oh, shit!" said the guy with the cell phone.

A guy out on the lawn, the one with the U OF MARYLAND sweatshirt, came racing back up the steps. "Get rid of all the bottles, man. The minute they know there was a party, they'll be breathing down our necks. Jeez! Where'd I leave my jacket?"

There was bedlam in the house. Someone came out the front door dragging a garbage bag full of bottles and cans and handed it to me.

"Take it over to the woods and leave it there," he said, pointing fifty yards off.

"Were Pam or Liz in that car?" I cried.

"I don't know! Take the damn cans, or we'll all be in trouble!" he yelled.

People were pushing past me out the door. We heard another siren, then another.

"Grab your stuff and let's get the hell out," somebody was saying from inside.

Car doors slammed. Engines started. People who had been to the crash came running back. People in the house were running out.

I dragged the bag through the snow, leaving a telltale trail behind it. Parking it behind a fir tree, I started back toward the house, pulling out my cell phone to call home, but was blinded by the light from a police cruiser as it careened around a bend in the road and pulled right up on the lawn.

"Stay right where you are, everyone!" an officer yelled, getting out the driver's side while the passenger door opened and a second policeman appeared. "We just want to ask some questions. Don't anyone take it in his head to go out the back door, 'cause we've got that covered too." The second officer was already going around the side of the house as another squad car pulled up.

I was shaking. Not just my hands, but my whole body. An officer came over to me, pulling out a notebook.

"Name?" he asked.

"A-Alice McKinley," I answered.

"Age?"

"Sixteen."

"Where do you live?"

I gave him my address.

"Do you know what just happened out there?" he asked me.

"We h-heard the crash," I said. "Were people hurt?"

"Yes, I'd say they were," the officer said. "How'd you get here tonight?"

"A friend brought me," I said.

"Know whose house this is?"

"N-No."

"Where's your friend?" asked the policeman.

"He left early with some others to go to the movies. I was looking for a ride home. I'm supposed to be home by midnight," I explained.

The officer looked at his watch. "Well, seeing as how it's two minutes after, you're not going to make it, are you?" He looked at the trail I'd made in the snow, my footprints beside it. "You been drinking?"

"No. Just Sprite."

"I want you to get in that car over there," he said. "Sit in the backseat. And hand me your cell phone, please. You'll get it back."

"I've got to call my dad!" I protested.

"We'll call him for you," he told me.

I felt sick. I knew right away that he didn't want me calling any of the other kids, all of us deciding on the same story to give the police—who was drinking and who wasn't, who was driving and who wasn't. I sat in the police car hugging myself, trying to stop the shaking, but it only got worse. I watched the police bring a guy over, the boy who had told me to drag the cans to the woods.

As he slid in beside me, I asked, "Do you know Pamela Jones or Liz Price? Were they in the car? Were they hurt?"

"I don't know anything, and you don't either, got it?" he murmured. Then, "I think Brian's killed somebody, so just be quiet."

I thought I was going to be sick. "I didn't know anything to begin with," I said, trembling. "I don't even know where I am."

A third cruiser pulled in, and more kids were rounded up. When we got to the police station, Keeno and a few others were already there, looking dazed and disoriented.

"Were Pam or Liz in the car?" I whispered to him as we came in.

"I don't know," he whispered back.

"Where's Brian?" I asked him.

"Rescue squad took him to the hospital," he said, but then a policeman interrupted. One by one we were taken to a desk and asked questions.

"Did you go anywhere else before you came to the party?" a policeman asked me.

I told him about the group of us who went to the old Steak House restaurant in Gaithersburg.

"Did anyone at the Steak House serve alcohol to Brian Brewster?" the policeman asked me.

"No," I said, knowing that was only half of the truth, but I decided to answer just what I was asked.

"Did anyone at the party serve alcohol to Brian Brewster?"

"I don't know," I said. "There were a lot of people there, and kids were helping themselves to whatever was on the table."

"Will you submit to a Breathalyzer test?" he asked me.

"Yes," I said.

They gave it to me. I passed. Then, at one fifteen, the awful phone call to Dad. When the officer hung up, he said, "Wait over there. Your father said he'd be here in about forty minutes."

* * *

When Dad got to the station, he didn't say a word. He hardly even looked at me. Just hugged me to him, so tight I could hardly breathe. On the way home I alternately cried and froze up, terrified of what might have happened to Liz or Pamela. Then Dad said he'd seen Liz come home, so I knew that at least she was okay, but I still worried about Pamela. I answered every question Dad asked me as to who, when, and where, but to all the whys, I had no answer. *Why* did I go someplace else when I'd only told him we'd be at the Steak House? *Why* would I go to a party at the home of someone I didn't even know? *Why* didn't I call him as soon as I saw they had alcohol and no adults were present?

I tried explaining, but there was no answer that satisfied him: I told him that when we left the restaurant, it was too early to go home; that we really thought it was Keeno's cousin; that we didn't know there wouldn't be adults in the house. . . .

I was exhausted and tight with tension when I finally walked inside the house.

"Oh, Alice," Sylvia said, her shoulders drooping with relief when she saw me. "You're okay!"

"Yes," I said.

"Was anyone else hurt, Alice? Are there other parents we should call?"

"I've been trying to find out about Pamela, but I don't even know what car she was in," I told her. "They said Brian was taken to a hospital. I don't know how bad he was hurt. . . . And I don't know who was in the other car, the one he hit. Somebody said he might have killed a kid."

"Oh my God!" said Dad.

I was numb with fatigue, and so was Dad. I curled up in one corner of the couch as he made calls to the police to see how badly Brian was hurt, but they wouldn't tell him anything and said all the parents had already been notified. It wasn't until we had called Pamela's house and found out she had been in another car and was safely home that we all went to bed, exhausted.

I slept until almost eleven the next morning, when the phone started to ring. While Dad and Sylvia were at church, I got all the news.

Brian had plowed into the side of another car at a rural junction only a quarter mile from where the party had been. The other car had gone through a stop sign. The air bags in Brian's car had protected him and his front-seat passenger, but Brian had two broken fingers and a dislocated shoulder, and the guy in the front seat with him had injured his knee. The three girls in the back were bruised and one had whiplash, but otherwise, they were all right. A little kid who had been asleep in the backseat of the other car was either seriously hurt or dead. That's all anyone knew.

Liz told me that my dad had called her house when he saw her come home, asking if I was there with her. She'd told him I was probably on my way home with someone else, that the car she got in was full.

At lunch the air was so thick with disappointment and disapproval that I felt smothered by it, even though Dad reached over once and patted my arm. Did they have any idea how scared I had been last night? I wondered. Did they think I had *wanted* this to happen?

"Well," I said finally, "what's the punishment? Am I grounded for the rest of the year?"

Dad looked at me helplessly. "How can I punish you when all I wanted last night was to hear that you were safe?" he asked. "I know you didn't plan it. But how many times have I asked you to call if . . . ?" He didn't finish.

"I know, I know," I said. "But if you'd been there, if you'd been in my place, you'd have been confused too. I thought I had a ride home. I didn't think . . ."

But that was it in a nutshell, of course. I didn't think.

It was the talk of the school on Monday. Brian wasn't there, and most of the kids at the party were from another school, so the rest of us were still guessing at what really happened. Pamela, Liz, and I just stood in the hall hugging each other. We didn't need words.

The construction workers were picking up for the day when I got home from school, putting away their tools, calling out to each other. Sylvia's car was out front. She rarely got home before four thirty or five, especially with all that pounding and clanking going on. I wondered if she'd taken the afternoon off.

I opened the door and started for the stairs, but she stopped me. "Alice," she said, "we need to talk."

I walked into the kitchen and dropped my backpack on the table. "What about?" I asked, knowing only too well.

"Sit down," she said, a teacher's tone in her voice.

I *almost* said, *I prefer to stand,* but something in her face told me I'd better sit. Sylvia remained standing in her pin-striped pants and rayon blouse, arms folded across her chest.

"I have something to say," she said, "and with Ben out of the house, it's a good time to say it."

I dreaded what was to come.

"I married your dad because I think he is one of the kindest, most intelligent, most wonderful men I've ever met," Sylvia said. "And when you love someone, you want to protect him from hurt. You want to be there for him when he's sick or worried or frightened. And in all the time I've known your father, Alice, I've never seen him as worried as he was Saturday night."

I swallowed. I wanted to look away, but there was something so intense in her face that I had to watch.

Sylvia went on: "I'd wanted to go to bed at eleven, but Ben said he'd wait up for you, so I decided to wait up with him. About eleven fifteen he said, 'If they just went to the Steak House, I'd think they'd be back by now.' I reminded him that you were allowed to stay out till midnight on weekends, that maybe you'd gone to a late show."

Sylvia didn't look away either. Our eyes were locked. Outside, I heard the construction guys driving away.

"He called Elizabeth's house when he saw her come home," Sylvia continued. "Liz told him you were getting a ride with someone else. He called Pamela's, but no one answered. She probably hadn't reached home yet. Then, about twelve thirty, someone called and asked if you were all right. Ben asked who it was—what they were talking about—but the person hung up."

Sylvia sighed and put her hands behind her, resting on the countertop. "Alice, it was like your father aged ten years after that last call. Every line in his face was deeper. He didn't want to use the phone in case you'd be calling, so I gave him my cell phone and he tried calling your cell several times, but there was no answer and he began calling police departments—in Gaithersburg, Silver Spring—to see if there had been any accidents. He called the Steak House, but it was closed, and I had to stop him from getting in his car and driving out there. I told him that if you *had* been in an accident, you could have been airlifted to a shock trauma unit in Bethesda or Baltimore—who knows where?—and that he should stay right here until someone called."

I felt an indescribable sadness rising up inside me.

"It was one fifteen when the phone rang and he heard someone say, 'Mr. McKinley, I'm calling about your daughter. . . .' His face went as gray as the ashes in the fireplace. All he could say was 'Is she all right?' and . . . the relief in that face when they said that you were . . . !"

A tear escaped from the rim of my eye and rolled down my cheek. I couldn't look at Sylvia anymore.

"I'm . . . I'm sorry," I wept. "I *told* him how sorry I was. I didn't realize . . ."

"I know you didn't know all of this, and your father would never tell you, so I am," Sylvia said. "I want you to know that last Saturday night was one of the worst nights ever for your dad. He was like a caged animal, wanting to get out and *do* something, and there was absolutely nothing to do, Alice, but wait."

She pulled a tissue out of her pants pocket and blew her nose.

I just went on sniffling. "The . . . the evening had started out so well," I said. "Just a bunch of us having dinner together. We've been to the Steak House a lot of times. And when Keeno said he just wanted us to stop by his cousin's house for a birthday party, it didn't seem so bad. It was only nine o'clock."

Sylvia handed me a tissue from the box on the counter, and I blew my nose too.

"But it took a long time to get there," I continued, "and it wasn't exactly a cousin's house. You're right. That's when I should have called."

Sylvia let out her breath and looked up at the ceiling a moment. I think we were both feeling exhausted. For probably a full minute we just remained there in silence, staring off into space.

"You know what?" she said finally. "Ben's working late tonight and I'm too tired to cook, but I'm hungry enough for popcorn. I'm going to make a big bowl of it. Let's kick off our shoes, go sit on the couch, and eat popcorn. And talk."

The last thing in this world I wanted just then was popcorn, but Sylvia opened the cupboard, pulled out a bag, and stuck it in the microwave. "Oh, heck," she said. "Let's put in two."

I sat silently at the table as Sylvia stuck in another bag, then stood watching the seconds go by on the clock, waiting for the popping to begin.

Strange, though, what just the aroma of popcorn will do for you. It reminds you of only good times in your life, because whoever heard of eating popcorn when you're sick or mad or grieving? Nobody eats popcorn at funerals.

As the corn began to pop, it sounded like an artillery range, and the expanding bags began taking up the whole space inside the microwave.

"Maybe you're not supposed to pop two bags at a time," Sylvia said. "You don't suppose they'll explode, do you?" We smiled.

"I'll get the bowls," I said, and took two large metal mixing bowls from the cabinet. When there had been no more pops for the recommended two seconds, Sylvia took the bags from the microwave, and we pulled at the tops to let the steam out, then poured the popcorn into the bowls. In the living room we kicked off our shoes and sat down on the sofa, bowls on our laps.

"Ah!" Sylvia said. "Supper!"

We chewed delicately, however. Politely. Finally Sylvia said, "I guess I was really, really angry at you Saturday night. I was furious, in fact, that you didn't call and tell us where you were or what had happened. Ben could only imagine the worst."

"I just . . . there was so much going on . . . I didn't think I could leave until I found out if Pamela or Liz were in that car. Then the police came and took my cell phone," I explained feebly.

Sylvia didn't say anything for a minute or two. Then she said,

"I just wish that every teenager could have the experience of one night—just *one* night—of the anxiety you put your dad through."

"You talk as though I did it on purpose!" I said.

"No. It wasn't purposeful, it was thoughtless. But, I suppose, if I put myself in your place . . ."

"I just wish you'd try to understand me more," I said.

"I suppose you do," said Sylvia. Her hands were motionless now on the sides of her bowl. "I guess I've not done a very good job of that. It's not easy coming into an already-formed household. I've found myself getting annoyed at small things. . . ."

"I guess I've been pretty mad at you too," I said. "I mean, now and then. Off and on."

"Yeah?" said Sylvia. She propped her feet up on the coffee table beside mine. "So . . . tell me about it."

"You're my analyst now?" I joked, and she laughed.

"The only thing I have to throw at you is popcorn, so you're safe," she said, and began to eat again.

I took a deep breath. "Well, like you said, it's hard for us, too—for me, anyway—to have someone come in and join the family. We just do some things differently from you, that's all. Sometimes you seem angry, and I can't figure out what I've done. Other times . . . other times you don't seem to be thinking of me at all. You just barrel on with your own plans—about the remodeling of the house, for example—like you . . . like you're taking over."

"Hmmmm," Sylvia said. "I guess I do get excited about things, and assume everyone else feels the same way. Ben's such a sweetheart that he doesn't usually object, and I just go sailing along." She looked over at me. "Anything else?"

"Yeah," I said. "Why haven't you ever yelled at me about riding that motorcycle?"

Sylvia looked startled for a moment. "Someone's been talking," she said.

"I wormed it out of Marilyn," I told her, "so I know you saw me that day. Why didn't you ever say anything?"

"Because later that day you told me that you had done something you wouldn't do again, and I guessed you were talking about that motorcycle ride. I wanted to give you the benefit of the doubt. And Ben's had so much on his mind lately, I didn't want to add that as well."

I told her then how it had happened.

"I guessed it was something like that," she said. "I think I know you *that* well. Anything else? Anything at all?"

"I can't think of anything at the moment," I answered. "But if I do, I'll let you know."

"Promise?" she asked.

"Promise."

She sighed contentedly and leaned her head back. "This is the best dinner I've had all week," she said. "I've got to remember this when I'm too tired to cook."

Our stocking feet were touching now, and Sylvia rubbed her toes against mine. "Let's think about dessert. What would taste good after eight cups of popcorn?"

"A caramel sundae?" I suggested. "With chocolate ice cream, of course."

"Of course," said Sylvia. "Whipped cream?"

"Naturally. And a maraschino cherry," I told her. "No nuts."

On Tuesday, I saw a small cluster of kids standing in front of the glassed-in bulletin board in the front hallway.

"Hey, Alice!" Sam called to me. "Come and look."

I walked over. He pointed to the story that had appeared in the *Washington Post* on Saturday, second page of the Metro section, with a picture of the demonstration outside the school. STUDENTS CHOOSE CONTROVERSY was the headline.

The reporter had written that fourteen students from Mrs. Cary's eleventh-grade speech class had demonstrated in support of her controversial assignment to examine both sides of an issue that affects them emotionally.

> "An irresponsible and dangerous precedent," said the objecting parent, Marsha Shoates, who is considering removing her daughter from the Montgomery County Public School System and enrolling her in homeschooling instead. "It's unfair to ask students to reveal some of their most deeply held beliefs and then demand that they challenge them."

The article mentioned some of our signs, quotes from us, and then one from our principal:

> "We're proud that our students take their assignments seriously," he said. "We're aware that it's difficult to examine

an issue one feels strongly about, but the object here is not to change an opinion necessarily, but to help students learn to study a controversial subject from many viewpoints—the hallmark of an educated person."

Scott came up to me then and gave me a hug. "Hey! You did it! You made the *Post*!" he said. "This gives me some ideas about a story on censorship when we get back from winter break. Don got some great photos."

I probably clung to him a nanosecond longer than he clung to me, and then . . . I couldn't resist. It was either now or never. I reached up and kissed him on the cheek. He looked down at me, puzzled, but only smiled and turned to someone else. Embarrassed, I bleated, "We *all* did it! The power of the press, huh?"

I'd thought he at least liked me, and I suppose he did. But it wasn't the way I liked him. I thought of going up to him sometime in private and saying, *How do you get over someone you're crushing on? Someone who doesn't feel the same way about you?* just to let him know what I was going through. But I couldn't. If I'd been at his house instead of Tony's? If it had been Scott who had nudged me onto the bed? Would I have resisted? Maybe not.

We got our PSAT scores that same day, but I didn't open mine till I got home because I wasn't sure what to expect. Dad has never pressured me to get all A's or worry about whether a grade has a plus or minus beside it. "Just do the best you can, Al," he always said, and I tried. I get more B's than A's, but I don't get many C's, except in math, so I guess you could say I'm a B+ student. Still, the PSAT sounded so *official*. Like, whatever I might have thought of myself before, the PSAT was the real McCoy. The PSAT was *truth*; it was my *future*. Pass or fail, sink or swim, what would it be?

My heart was actually racing as I opened the envelope. I read that the test measures three things: critical reading skills, math problem-solving skills, and writing skills, on a scale of 20 to 80, with 80 being the highest score you could get. The halfway point between those two numbers would be 50. I turned the page to see my scores:

```
Critical reading skills:    74
Math skills:                48
Writing skills:             77
```

I guess I did better than what I'd expected in reading and writing and about what I'd feared in math. The total of my three scores was 199 out of a possible 240, and the report said that the average for high school juniors was 147. I *wasn't* so dumb, then, except in math. I *would* go to college!

I *wouldn't* have to clean public restrooms or Porta-Johns. I put my report on the little stand beside Dad's chair and treated myself to a handful of M&M's.

Brian came back to school on Thursday, one hand bandaged up, a bruise on the left side of his face. His court date was three weeks away, and he wasn't supposed to talk about the accident, but he did. We gathered around him in the cafeteria.

"Yeah, I had a few more beers than I should have, but the thing is, the other guy had been drinking too, we found out! They said I was speeding, but he's the one who ran the stop sign."

"Brian, what about the people in the other car?" I asked. "Was anyone killed?"

"No. The driver's mostly okay, and the older sister didn't get hurt much. It was only the kid in the backseat who got thrown, and if she'd had her seat belt on, she'd probably be okay," he said.

"But how *is* she?" I demanded.

"You think they'd tell us anything?" he complained. "Dad finally called the hospital and got someone to give us the story, but it wasn't too bad. Broken pelvis or something. I feel bad about that, but she's going to be okay."

Gwen and I looked at each other in disbelief, then at Pamela and Liz.

"Brian, it's possible that the little girl is going to have some physical problems for the rest of her life," Gwen said.

"Maybe, but you don't know that!" Brian protested hotly. "Bones can heal. But if they take away my license for a year, what am *I* supposed to do?"

We could only stare.

"What you're supposed to do is suck it up," I said. "*That's* what you're supposed to do." I wadded up my sandwich wrapper, picked up my tray, and left the cafeteria.

Gwen and Pamela and Liz followed me outside. I felt so hot,

I literally had to cool off. I sat down on the stone wall, the same wall where I'd been watching Tony and his motorcycle friend when they'd called me over. I just felt . . . I don't know . . . like . . . like I was leaving something behind. But it was Liz who put it into words.

"The old gang just isn't the same anymore, is it?" she said.

I looked out over the street where cars were moving—the traffic pattern constantly changing. "Is that it?" I asked. "I'm feeling so . . . split! I'm just so furious at Brian and how he doesn't even seem to care! After all that, it's still all about him. *He's* changed."

"I don't know, has he really?" asked Pamela. "Or was he like this all along? Maybe we're the ones who have changed."

"It's not just Brian," I said. "I don't even like Jill and Karen anymore. They used to just puzzle me. Now . . . they don't like *me* either, and I'm not sure I care."

Gwen sat down on the wall and put her arm around me. "Hey, girlfriend," she said. "*We* still like you."

"You're one of the newer members of the group, Gwen. What do *you* think?" I asked. "How do we seem to you?"

She appeared to be thinking it over. "I guess I've never expected people to stay the same," she told me. "Sometimes we change for the worse, sometimes for the better. There were some things I liked about Brian, some things I didn't. But, hey! There were even things I didn't like about *you* after I got to know you."

"What?" I said, turning to face her. "Like what?"

I couldn't tell if she was laughing or frowning. "I don't quite know how to say this, Alice, but did anyone ever tell you that you can't sing worth a darn?"

We all broke into laughter. I bumped her with my elbow. "Hey, just because you sing in a church choir, you don't have to be so uppity about it," I said.

"Let's go," said Liz. "I'm freezing."

The bell sounded, and we went inside.

17
LESTER'S GOOF

Snow. Beautiful snow. Our last day of school before the holidays, and I woke to a four-inch snowfall. Schools were opening two hours late, so I ate a leisurely breakfast in my pajamas beside the kitchen window.

The blanket of white covered the piles of lumber, the bricks and cement blocks of the construction crew. It frosted every branch, every twig of the azalea bushes and the maple. I felt as though it buried all the mistakes and quarrels of the past few months and gave us all a fresh start. If only.

Pamela called and suggested we put on boots and hike the mile and a half to school, just for the fun of it. I called

Liz, and she said she'd do it. So forty minutes before school began, the three of us set out with wool caps pulled down over our ears, scarves whipping about in the wind. Other kids were doing the same, and we called to each other in the frosty air, the sun almost blinding as it reflected off the snow. It was intriguing to be the first to make an imprint in the soft white stuff, and yet, looking around, I felt guilty about mucking up the landscape. If only the mistakes we make could leave no imprints at all.

"What are you doing for Christmas, Alice?" Pamela asked.

"Not much," I told her. "Not with all this renovating going on."

"I suppose I'll spend Christmas with Mom and New Year's with Dad and Meredith. We'll probably go out to eat," Pamela said.

"Have they set a wedding date yet?" Liz asked, remembering that Pamela's dad and girlfriend had gotten engaged over the summer.

"No, I think maybe they get along better when they only see each other a couple of times a week," Pamela said. "It works, and that's fine with me. I hate quarreling. If I ever marry, we'll have to sign a prenup agreement saying that whichever one of us starts a fight has to apologize first."

"Yeah, right," I said.

"We're going to my aunt's house," said Liz. "She's got kidney disease and wants to have Christmas there while she can still do the cooking and decorating and stuff."

"I hate sickness and death and dying!" I said loudly. "I want it to *stop right now*!"

Liz laughed. "Me too. Throw in war and global warming while you're at it."

"I wonder what kind of Christmas Molly's going to have," I mused. "It'll probably be the worst Christmas of her life."

"Let's take her some snow!" said Liz.

"What?" I said.

"Snow. Let's go visit her tonight and fill a plastic container with snow, seeing as how she doesn't get out in it."

We laughed. "Deal!" I said.

It was a good day at school. The teachers were easy on us and didn't pile on a lot of work for the holidays. Most had given us long-term assignments in advance, and it was up to us whether we wanted to do them over Christmas.

The cafeteria was noisy—everyone talking about where they were going over the holidays. Tony and I were still politely avoiding each other, and that was fine with me. I was totally relieved that *that* was over. I heard from someone that Patrick had already left town with his parents for their usual skiing in Vermont and wouldn't be back until after New Year's. Gwen had a ton of relatives coming. Everyone had something fun to report except Brian, who didn't want to talk about the holidays. He was furious because the insurance company wouldn't go along with his claim that his car was totaled. Not only were they not paying him all he thought he should get for repairs, but they had upped his rates as well.

I made a point of searching out Amy Sheldon as the others

left the cafeteria, and I sat down with her as she was finishing her sandwich and a carton of milk, sucking noisily on her straw when she reached the bottom.

"You were mad at me the other day, weren't you?" she asked, staring right at me the way she does. It reminds me of a baby's stare—the way little kids stare at strangers with no self-consciousness at all.

"Not really," I said. "I was sort of mad at the world."

"How can you be mad at the whole world?" Amy asked.

"Easy," I told her. "I was just having a bad day. I'm sorry I was so rude."

"That's okay," Amy said. "I was just wondering why I haven't got my period yet, since I'm old enough and everything."

"You're small, Amy, that's probably it," I told her. "You just have a bit more developing to do, and your body will catch up. Everyone's different."

"Yeah, and some are more different than others," she said.

"Hey, Merry Christmas," I said.

"You too, Alice," she answered, and gave me a big smile.

We took the bucket of snow to Molly that evening. Gwen and Liz decided we should carol on her front porch, so Gwen drove us over in a brother's car. Liz, Gwen, and Pamela—all three— have good, strong singing voices, and I was sure my job would be to stand there holding the plastic container of snow with the big red ribbon on top. I was flabbergasted when Gwen handed me, instead, the metal triangle and stick from a kid's rhythm set and instructed me to make a loud *ping* after each phrase.

I stared at it. "How did you *know*?" I asked.

"Know what?"

"That this is what they gave me in grade school to make me shut up," I said.

The others stared at me, and Gwen looked conscience-stricken. I told them how the music teacher had made us sing a song a group at a time, then two at a time, to figure out who was singing so seriously off-key.

"I'm *sorry*!" Gwen said. "I only did it as a joke."

But suddenly all four of us burst out laughing.

"Hey, I'm over it now," I said. "I'll ping your little triangle. I'll even tap-dance if you want me to."

It was just growing dark as we gathered on the Brennans' porch. We had told Molly's mom we were coming so the TV wouldn't be on. Unless you've got a whole choir, it's hard to compete with a TV set.

> *"Silent night, holy night,*
> *All is calm, all is bright . . ."*

The girls sang, and I went *ping!*

We were halfway through the second verse when the porch light came on, and Molly's curious face appeared at the window. Then she broke into a smile and left to open the door.

"Oh, you guys! You're the best!" she said. "Come on in!"

Mr. and Mrs. Brennan were smiling in the background,

and two of Molly's sisters were watching from the stairs.

We came in, laughing, and handed Molly the plastic tub.

"What's *this*?" she exclaimed, sitting down on a chair in her jeans and sweatshirt. "Ooh, it's cold!" She lifted off the lid and shrieked. "You nuts! You're absolutely crazy!"

"We thought you'd like a little taste of the great outdoors," Liz said, and I went *ping* on the triangle.

The Brennans laughed as Molly playfully buried her face in the snow for a second and came up all frosted. "Put it in the downstairs freezer for me, Mom," she said.

"Yes, and when you're well, we'll have a snowball fight, no matter what month it is," said Pamela.

"I've been feeling a little better this week," Molly said. "My legs don't ache as much."

We had other small gifts to give her, and then we sat and talked for a while. She'd seen the story in the paper about the demonstration—about speech class and about Jennifer Shoates and all the different topics we'd discussed in class.

"I don't know, I sort of agree with Jennifer that it's a raw deal to tell you to choose something personal and then make you take the opposing point of view," Molly said.

"But if you knew at the beginning that you'd have to do that, you'd choose a subject you're only lukewarm about, and what would you learn from that?" I argued.

"Maybe you're right," said Molly. "But frankly, I think Jennifer was brave to stick it out. If my mom had come to school and made a scene, I'd have died of embarrassment."

"No, you wouldn't," said Pamela. "My mom embarrassed me in New York last spring, and I'm still here, aren't I?"

"How's she doing, Pamela?" I asked, knowing her mom was still bitter about Pamela's dad's engagement to someone else, even though they were divorced, and that it was Pamela's mom who had run off with a boyfriend in the first place.

"Better. At least we've both learned to listen. We're talking about stuff we couldn't before," Pamela told us.

"That's what you guys do for me," Molly said. "You listen. I'm glad you came over."

As soon as I got home from the Melody Inn the next day, Sylvia and I set to work decorating the house. We were probably the last ones on the block to get a tree up and the lights on—a wreath on the door and vases of holly on the mantel. There's not a lot of motivation to decorate a house surrounded by piles of bricks and lumber, but we got in the spirit and even fashioned a wreath to put on the Porta-John.

The cat sniffed warily at the Christmas tree and brushed her back along the lower branches.

"Drink it all in, Annabelle," I told her. "This is as close as you're going to get to Mother Nature. Thank goodness you're not a dog, or you'd probably pee on it."

I went to the Christmas Eve service with Dad and Sylvia a few nights later and loved walking out through the little woods surrounding the church to the parking lot afterward, in the darkness of the midnight hour, silently, softly, all of us holding lighted candles. I could see these little dabs of color moving through the trees, then each one going out as people got into their cars.

George Palamas and his fiancée were treating Les and his other roommate, Paul, to dinner at a fancy restaurant on Christmas Eve, so Les didn't come over to our place till Christmas Day.

Sylvia had made a wonderful brunch, and we helped ourselves throughout the long and happy present-opening time. We'd stop for coffee now and then, or for another piece of quiche, or perhaps some chocolate or melon. The snow had melted down a little, but a white Christmas is such a rarity in Maryland—southern Maryland, anyway, where we live—that we kept looking out the window, remarking on a blue jay that alit on a fence post or a cardinal, gorgeous against the snow.

One by one the presents were opened and admired, slipped on to check the size, passed around to enjoy, or set aside for further inspection later on. If we work at it, we can stretch the opening of presents out for an hour or two, with potty breaks now and then or recess for a round of cheesecake.

Les usually tucks his gifts to us at the very back of the tree, and he did the same this year. There was a joint present to Dad and Sylvia and a separate box for me. Dad opened his gift from Lester, and both he and Sylvia exclaimed over the digital camera he had bought for them, with a promise of four hours of instruction on how to use it.

"I don't know that four hours will do it, Les, but this is a great gift," said Dad.

"Now you!" said Les, reaching for the last box, which he handed to me.

It was a beautifully decorated Nordstrom box, all silvery and shiny with a huge, sparkling silver ribbon and bow.

"Wow!" I said, and slipped the ribbon off one side. Nordstrom is a really upscale store—not quite Saks or Neiman Marcus, but it has very nice stuff. I opened the lid and found a card on top of the tissue paper.

"'To heat up those cold winter nights,'" I read, and folded back the tissue paper.

"What?" Lester yelped, jerking forward. I startled as he lunged for the box, but it was too late. I found myself holding a red bikini trimmed in white rabbit fur.

"Wow!" I said again.

Les tipped back his head and howled. We stared.

"You got the wrong box!" he bellowed. "No! No!"

My jaw dropped. This was absolutely fantastic! Now I knew what he was giving his new girlfriend, and I tried not to laugh. But Lester was devastated. Dad and Sylvia looked amused too, but they were trying to look sympathetic.

"What time is it?" Les cried, looking around for a clock. And then, "Quick, Alice! You've got to come with me. Put on your shoes and bring the box. We've got to get somewhere before three."

I grabbed my shoes, pulled on my jacket, and followed Lester out to his car with the box, the lid, the tissue paper, the card, the ribbon, the bow, and the fur-trimmed bikini.

"Merry Christmas!" Dad called cheerfully from the porch.

18
KEEPING WARM ON WINTER NIGHTS

I slid into the bucket seat next to Les, and he backed out of the drive.

"Darn!" I said, looking at the fur bikini again. "I would have been a hit at sleepovers!" I had to press my lips together to keep from laughing out loud.

"It's not funny," Les muttered. "She's got your present instead!"

"Yeah? So what's so awful about *my* gift?" I asked.

"Nothing, but it's not right for Claire," he answered.

"So what am I supposed to do? Go grab it out of her hands and give her this one instead?" I asked, neatly placing the fur bikini back in the box, folding the tissue over it, and putting it all back together.

"She's been at her sister's house and said she'd be getting back around three or four," Lester explained. "I left her present—*your* present—outside her apartment door this morning. I'd *swear* the silver one was for you and the gold for Claire. The silver ribbon must have been for Claire and the gold for you. How could I have been so *stupid*?"

"What does she look like? Really?" I asked.

"She's got long brown hair. Straight. Sort of bangs. Medium height, weight. Maybe a little top-heavy."

"What's her apartment number?"

"Uh, 302."

"And you left the package at her door?"

"Right there on the mat, propped up against the doorframe. You can't miss it," Lester said.

Les was driving ten miles over the speed limit in a business area.

"Slow down, Lester! We don't need a ticket!" I said.

I just couldn't stop grinning, though. I kept thinking of that note—*To heat up those cold winter nights*—and it sent all kinds of images swirling through my head. I was beginning to think that Dad was right: that however mature Lester had seemed when he was dating Tracy, there was still a part of him that hadn't settled down yet, and that twenty-four for a man—well, for *some* men, maybe—was still a little young for marriage.

Les turned onto a street just over the D.C. line where there were several blocks of four-story brick apartment buildings. I looked at my watch.

"What time?" asked Les.

"Three seventeen," I told him.

"Oh, jeez," he breathed out. "If she's home, I'm toast."

He passed her building and pointed out the door. "Go inside," he said, "walk up to the third floor, and trade the boxes. Then come down. I'm going to park a block away so she won't recognize my car."

This was better than a spy movie!

We rode a block farther, and Les parked, then sank down low in the seat in case Claire drove by. I got out with the present under my arm, turned up my jacket collar, and started off.

Patches of ice had formed on the sidewalk where snow at the sides had melted, trickled down onto the concrete, then frozen. I had to make my way carefully to keep from falling, and I didn't want to step in the shoveled snow.

When I got to the right building, I tried to open the outer door, but it was locked. *Now* what was I supposed to do? Lester hadn't said anything about how I was supposed to get inside the building itself. I looked around. No one was coming up the walk. No one looked as though they were heading for this address. *Lester, you imbecile!* I thought.

Something moved beyond the door, and I could just make out a man coming down the stairs. He came up to the door, opened it, and looked at me curiously, waiting there on the steps.

"Thanks!" I said, smiling, and put one finger to my lips. "It's a surprise!" Then I slipped past him and went inside.

Up the stairs I went to the second floor, with its two apartments, one on each side. Up another flight to a landing, then on up to the third and the two apartments there: 302 and 304.

There on the mat was the present, the one wrapped in gold ribbon and bow. I reached down and replaced that box with mine and headed back down the stairs. One flight to the landing, another flight to the second floor. . . . As I was going down the last flight of stairs to the ground floor, I saw a woman come inside carrying a small overnight bag in one hand, a shopping bag full of presents in the other. She had long straight brown hair, wispy bangs, medium height. . . .

I slipped the present I was holding behind me and stared straight ahead as we passed.

"Hi," she said.

"Hi," I answered, and didn't stop till I was outside.

"Did you do it?" Les asked as I slid in the passenger seat beside him.

"Yes, you idiot!" I said, showing him the package. "But how was I supposed to get in the building? The front entrance was locked!"

"Oh, man, I forgot!" he said. "How'd you do it?"

"A man was coming out, and I squeezed by him."

"Clever girl!" Les said. "You're a winner!"

"And you know who I met coming out?" I asked him.

Les reached for the key in the ignition, but his hand dropped. "Claire?"

"Yep."

"Did she *see* you?"

"Of course she saw me. She didn't see the box, though. I kept it out of sight," I said.

"Did she *say* anything?"

"She said 'hi.'"

"What did *you* say?"

"I said, 'Oh, you're the one with the big boobs that my brother's so crazy about.'" I sighed impatiently. "I said 'hi' and kept going, Lester! What do you think?"

"Did she recognize you?"

"How could she? Not unless you carry around a picture of me in your wallet and show it to everyone you meet," I said.

"Fat chance," said Lester.

"Anyway," I said as he started the engine, "let's see what you bought for *me*. From Nordstrom too! And this better not be a mistake for *another* one of your girlfriends."

"I should be so lucky," said Lester.

It wasn't for a girlfriend, that's for sure. I took off the gold ribbon, folded back the tissue paper, and lifted out, not a fur-trimmed bikini, but a high-neck red flannel nightgown with a narrow white ruffle around the collar and cuffs.

To keep you warm on winter nights, the card read.

I could see why he wouldn't want to give this to a girlfriend, but I couldn't hide my disappointment, and Les could tell. He glanced over at me when I didn't react.

"You don't like it," he said.

"Last year, when I turned sixteen, you gave me a gorgeous silk robe," I said. "What am I doing? Regressing?"

"I just thought that with all the renovations going on, the house would probably be drafty and you'd be cold. A flannel gown would feel pretty nice then," said Lester.

"It would feel pretty nice if I were a virginal spinster living in Alaska with no prospects of marrying, ever," I told him.

"Hmmmm," said Les. "Now which of those descriptions doesn't fit? Let me guess—spinster, Alaskan. . . ."

I sure didn't want to have *that* discussion, so I said, "Would you mind very much if I exchanged it for something else?"

"Not at all," he said. "Get whatever you want."

"Thanks," I told him. "It'll be red, but it won't be a granny gown."

His cell phone rang just then. Les reached in his jacket pocket. "Don't you make a sound," he warned me. And then, into the phone, "Hello?" He immediately turned his head away from me. "Hi, baby," he said. "Merry Christmas."

I grinned and leaned back against the seat.

". . . Glad you like it," Les was saying. "Yeah . . . Yeah . . . Well, I can't wait to see you in it. Listen, my sister just came in, so let me call you back. . . . Sure thing. Bye."

"I don't know why whatever you had to say couldn't be said in front of your sister," I teased. "I mean, you'd think you were going to spend the night with her or something."

"Or something," said Les, and we laughed as he turned the car toward home.

I wondered if it was the same for Lester as it was for me—
that sometimes you know you're just treading water, passing the
time, and that your real self is just waiting for the right moment,
the right person, the right you.

We got our usual call that afternoon from Uncle Howard and
Uncle Harold down in Tennessee, wishing all us McKinleys
here in "Silver Sprangs" a Merry Christmas. They told us how
different it was not having Grandpa McKinley around anymore to supervise the decorating of the tree, as he always did
from his La-Z-Boy recliner, and we talked to my three aunts,
too, and wished them all a Merry Christmas and a Happy New
Year.

Sylvia called her sister Nancy in Albuquerque and her
brother in Seattle, and then we called Aunt Sally and Uncle Milt.
It was Uncle Milt who answered the phone.

"Milt, so good to hear your voice!" Dad said. "How *are* you,
and Merry Christmas!"

The rest of us couldn't hear Uncle Milt because his voice is
soft compared to Aunt Sally's, but we could tell from Dad's end
of the conversation that Uncle Milt was doing much better. Sylvia
talked to him next, then Les, and after I told my uncle how glad
I was to know he was feeling better, he handed the phone over
to Aunt Sally.

Aunt Sally wished me a Merry Christmas, like she always
does, but something was different. Something was wrong.

"Did *you* have a nice Christmas?" I asked her.

"Well, yes and no," she said. I heard Uncle Milt in the background saying, "Now, Sal, don't begin. . . ."

"What happened?" I asked.

"Well, Carol said she was having trouble with her telephone for a month now, which is why I couldn't reach her at her apartment, so I drove over there last week with some cookies and a mince pie, just so she'd have a little something to nibble on before Christmas, you know."

I knew what was coming even before she told me, and I realized I hadn't reported back to Aunt Sally after Thanksgiving as she would have liked.

"And I got the shock of my life, Alice," Aunt Sally said. "A woman came to the door whom I'd never seen before and told me that Carol doesn't live there anymore. My daughter has moved in with her boyfriend and didn't even tell her own mother! Why is the mother always the last to know?"

"Probably because she loves you the most and didn't want to hurt you," I said. Sometimes my answers positively amaze me.

"But . . . we were always so *close*!" Aunt Sally said, which wasn't exactly true, and now she was weeping a little.

"All the more reason not to hurt you," I said.

"You've met him, Alice," Aunt Sally went on. "They were there for Thanksgiving. What did you think of her boyfriend?"

"We liked him a lot," I said. "If Carol's happy, then you should be happy for her."

She sniffled. "Well, I'm going to try to do that. I'm going to try not to judge her."

"Good idea," I said.

"But you know what they say, dear," Aunt Sally said. "If you can get the milk for free, why buy the cow?"

"*What?*" I said.

"If a man can get sex for nothing, why should he bother to marry?" she explained.

"You're not suggesting she *charge*, are you?" I said, trying not to laugh.

Aunt Sally gasped. "No, no! I just think that if Carol has marriage in mind, she should hold out till then."

"You and Mrs. Shoates would get along great," I said.

"Who?" asked Aunt Sally.

"Never mind," I said. "It's not important. What's important, Aunt Sally, is that now you know, and now you and Carol can be close again."

"How did you get to be so wise, Alice?" Aunt Sally said. "My goodness, Marie would be so proud of you! She really would."

Maybe I'd make a good counselor after all, I thought. I pictured myself in my office at school. During Spirit Week. On Pajama Day during Spirit Week. In red. Red silk pajamas. And I knew what I was going to buy at Nordstrom when I took the granny gown back.

19
CALL FROM A FRIEND

The construction crew didn't work between Christmas and New Year's. The bricks lay undisturbed, the equipment untouched, the Porta-John standing alone in the front yard.

"Oh, the blessed quiet!" Sylvia said. "I was beginning to hear their constant hammering in my sleep."

"Enjoy," said Dad, "because the real noise begins when the men get back and start tearing down the back walls."

"At least these few days will give us time to move everything out of our bedroom and into Lester's," Sylvia said. "I still don't know how we'll do it. We'll practically be living on top of each other for a couple of months. I hope we can all keep a sense of humor."

"What about the downstairs?" I asked.

"The back walls in the kitchen and dining room come down too," said Dad. "All the dining room furniture has to be squeezed into the living room. The refrigerator needs to go there too, and a plumber's going to set up a temporary sink."

"Wow," I said. I wasn't sure whether this sounded adventurous or awful. We'd gotten used to the huge sheet of opaque plastic hanging beyond the back door of the kitchen and the windows of the dining room, and for now, anyway, there were walls in front of it that kept out the noise and the cold.

Sylvia grabbed my hand. "Come on. Let's go snoop while the workmen are gone," she said.

I got my jacket and followed her outside. We made our way around to the backyard, stepping over stray boards and bricks. The frame rose up two stories, with waterproof sheeting tacked to the outside. We got to the makeshift steps leading to a back entrance and stepped inside. It felt strange to be standing inside the skeleton of our new addition.

It was like a huge tent. There was a roof but no floors yet, neither upstairs nor down, waiting for the old walls to be torn down before flooring could be seamlessly added. There were only a few planks to walk on leading from front to back and side to side. Gingerly, we walked along one of the bottom boards.

"I'll bet this is where the new fireplace will be," Sylvia said, pointing to a large cement base.

"And I can see the layout of the closets—those little sections there and there," I said, walking a little farther. "This part's the family room, isn't it?"

"Yes. And over there's the study," Sylvia said. We turned slowly around, looking in all directions. "I suppose it will take some getting used to—all these changes."

"Oh, I don't think so," I said. "Having the old bathroom all to myself won't take any getting used to at all!" I grinned.

"In the meantime," said Sylvia as we walked back to the front of the house, "we're going to be very crowded. We'll practically be eating off each other's laps and sitting with our knees up to our chins."

"I'll probably spend a lot of time in my room," I said.

"Good thinking," said Sylvia. "But it will all be over in a couple of months, and then we're going to love it! Hope so, anyway."

As though a white Christmas weren't enough, Mother Nature gave us an encore. Two days after Christmas, we found not four, not six, not eight, but eleven inches of snow blanketing the area, with more to come.

"The weatherman's predicting thirteen inches," said Dad. "A good day to stay inside, I think. I'm not even going to open the store. Marilyn's already called to say she can't get her car out, the side streets are unplowed, and David's still out of town visiting his parents."

I didn't mind at all holing up with a good book—*The Color Purple*—and a cup of mint chocolate cocoa. Annabelle waited for me to finish the cup, then delicately licked the inside of it, and after that, she helped herself to my lap.

By afternoon we could hear snowplows in all directions, and by the following morning, roads at least were plowed and lawns were heaped with the sparkling white stuff, like meringue topping. I was debating whether to finish my book or drive to the mall and look for bargains when there was a loud *thunk* as something hit the storm door.

"What in the world was *that*?" said Sylvia.

"UPS maybe?" I guessed. Before I could even get out of my chair, there it was again: *thunk*. I went to the door and opened it.

"Roz!" I shrieked delightedly at my wonderful friend from grade school, who used to live near us in Takoma Park. "What the heck are you doing over here?" I walked to the porch railing.

"Come on out!" she yelled, packing another snowball and hurling it toward me. It hit a post and exploded, showering me with snow crystals. I yelped.

"Come on! Let's build something!" Rosalind called.

"Yeah? Remember what happened the last time we built something? Remember that snow cave that fell in on me when you kicked it?" I reminded her, laughing.

Another snowball hit my shoulder.

"Okay, okay, let me get some boots and stuff on," I said, and went back indoors.

I traded my flannel bottoms for heavy jeans, and by the time I got outside, Rosalind was already turning the Porta-John into an igloo.

It was one of the best ideas she'd ever had, and Roz was the original Idea Girl. We set to work rolling large orbs of snow up against the sides of the Porta-John, then medium-sized balls on top of them, and smaller balls on top of the medium. We filled all the spaces in between, packing it down well, until three sides of the blue metal structure were encased in snow. I got a stepladder, and we packed snow onto the roof. It was entirely covered now, all but the door, which still sported the wreath I had hung there at Christmas.

Neighbors driving by slowed and stared, then broke into smiles. Dad and Sylvia came out to admire it, and Sylvia even took a picture with the new digital camera Les had given them. Then Rosalind and I sat on the front steps, drinking hot tea, and I thought how wonderful it was that when everything else seemed to be changing, we had a friendship that went right on being the same.

I decided I wouldn't go out on New Year's Eve. Gwen's family was having a sort of open house, but it would be mostly family I didn't know, and Mark had planned to have a party, but it seems Brian was the only one who could come for sure, so Mark's parents scrapped the idea. Pamela had to help out at a party her dad was giving, and Liz was babysitting her brother. I could have invited myself to any one of their houses, but when I thought about what I really wanted to do, the answer was to stay home in my old scruffies and watch a movie on TV. I didn't really want to party. I didn't even want to watch the stupid silver ball descend at Times Square. Was I growing up, I won-dered, when I could admit I was content being very un-New-Year's-Eve-ish, and could even reply, if friends asked how I'd spent the evening, that I'd stayed home and watched a movie? Read a book?

That afternoon, however, something hugely embarrassing happened. The toilet stopped up, and though both Sylvia and I used the plunger, we couldn't get it unstuck. Dad was at work, so Sylvia had to call an emergency plumbing service to come out.

We stood by as the plumber tried his luck with the plunger. Then he went down in the basement with his machine and tools to shut off the water and open up the sewer pipe.

"Ma'am?" he called up to us later.

Sylvia went back downstairs, and I followed. We were afraid he'd tell us that he had to get a new part and that we'd have to go out in the yard in front of all the neighbors and use the Porta-John.

"Found the trouble," he said. "Now, I don't want to embar-rass anyone, but I'm going to have to remind you that sanitary things can't go down your toilet. A little two-inch item like that can cause a big problem." For one hundredth of a second he held up a pink plastic tampon applicator before dropping it in a bucket at his feet.

I could have died on the spot. I knew that, and I'm not sure why I'd been so careless with my tampon, but before I could even think, I heard Sylvia saying, "I'll certainly be more careful from now on."

The plumber went on lecturing us about what should and should not be flushed down the toilet, but all the while I stood there staring at the back of Sylvia's head. If ever I felt she loved me, it was then.

When the man had gone, I said, "I'm so embarrassed! You didn't have to take the rap for me, Sylvia. I should have fessed up."

And Sylvia said, "Well, I wouldn't want him to think I was *past* menstruating, now, would I?" And we laughed.

Dad built a fire that evening—the last chance we'd have to enjoy our living room as it was, and I sat on the floor as close to it as I could, Annabelle on my lap. She sat facing the flames, her eyes closing. Every so often a log snapped or popped, and her cat eyes opened momentarily, her ears twitched, and then she drifted off to sleep again.

"Her fur's getting warm," I said to Sylvia. "You don't think she'd self-ignite, do you?"

"Better scoot away before your socks catch fire," Dad said. He and Sylvia were on the couch, his arm around her shoulders.

"When we get the new addition, we'll have two fireplaces," said Sylvia. "I tried to persuade Ben to let me have one in our bedroom, too, but he put his foot down."

Dad just jostled her shoulder and grinned.

I sat watching the flames dance along the top of the log. "I could probably fit the whole gang in that new family room when it's done," I said. "It'll be a great place for parties."

"You can use it as often as you like," Sylvia told me.

More pops and crackles from the fire. Annabelle startled momentarily, extending her claws to keep her balance, then closed her eyes once again.

"She's like a hot water bottle on the legs," I said. "Too hot for me. Here." I handed her to Dad. "You wanted a cat on your legs in the winter, you got it."

"What more could a man ask?" said Dad, taking Annabelle. "A wife by his side, a daughter at his feet, and a cat on his lap. This is contentment."

New Year's Day was gray and cold and bleak. It was too cold to go outside and fool around, and there was school to get ready for the next day. The whole revolving wheel of life—school, supper, sleep . . . school, supper, sleep—would begin all over again.

But even the cycle seemed new somehow. Different, anyway. Like it was the new side of the old me. Like I was letting more of my real self show through.

I called Molly and wished her a happier new year; told her that when she felt up to it, I'd bring over a board game and beat the pants off her. I gathered all my papers and books and stuff for school and cleaned out my backpack. Did a load of wash so that my gym clothes and jeans would be fresh for a new semester.

The phone rang in the hall. Most of my friends call on my cell phone, so if the house phone rings, I let someone else answer. But Dad and Sylvia had gone next door to have drinks with a neighbor, so I padded out into the hall and picked up the phone.

"Hello?"

"Happy New Year," said Patrick.

"Hey! You're back!" I said. "Have a good time?"

"Yeah, we did. Snow was a little too soft, but I had some pretty good runs. How about you?"

"Well, I don't have the runs, if that's what you're asking," I joked, and he laughed.

"Anything exciting happen while I was away?" he wanted to know.

What I wanted to say was, *Patrick, a lot of things happen all the time that you never know about because you're always away. You're missing out on a lot of good times with the old gang.* But I didn't, because not all the stuff with the old gang is "good times." It's not even the same old gang anymore.

"Well," I said, "workmen are coming tomorrow to tear down the back walls of our house to build a new addition. And Rosalind came over a few days ago, and we turned the PortaJohn into an igloo. I can't wait to see the men's faces when they come tomorrow."

He laughed. "Now, that sounds like it was fun."

"It was." I brought the phone into my bedroom, Annabelle jumping after the cord as it dragged on the floor. When I climbed up on my bed, she jumped up too and began kneading my legs, my thighs, looking for a place to burrow down.

"So what's up with you?" I asked.

"Well, I made a decision and applied for early acceptance at the University of Chicago," he said.

"Hey! Good luck!" I told him. "What all did that involve?"

"For one thing, I did the Uncommon Application. It's online, and I had to answer the question 'If you could bridge a gap in the space-time continuum, what would you do?'"

"*What?*" I said. "I don't even understand the question."

He laughed. "It's just something to make you think. To get the creative juices flowing—give them a taste of how your mind works."

I knew right then I'd never apply to the University of Chicago. "Why did you choose that school?" I asked.

"Terrific political science program. Since I'm not sure of what I want to do later, I figured that might be better than international relations. Too much like my dad's field."

"Well, I hope you get in," I told him. "If you do, maybe I could see you sometime when I'm in Chicago visiting Aunt Sally and Uncle Milt."

"That'd be great!" said Patrick. "Actually, though, I'm calling to ask you to the prom."

I stared openmouthed at the wall. "The *prom*?" I said. "Patrick, that's six months away!"

"Five," he said. "It's in May. I figured I'd better ask before someone else snapped you up."

"I'd say five months is pretty early," I told him, still dazed. And then I realized I hadn't given him an answer. "I'd love to go with you, Patrick," I said. "I'll look forward to it all spring."

"I've been looking forward to it all year," he told me. "But I figured September might be a little too early to ask. I'll see you tomorrow, okay?"

"Tomorrow," I said, and gently, still smiling, put down the phone.

Almost Alice

To our granddaughter Tressa,

with love

Contents

1
THE TROUBLE WITH SADIE

It had to be in person, and they all had to be there.

Gwen was at a meeting over the lunch period, so I couldn't tell them then. I waited till we went to Starbucks after school before I made the announcement:

"Patrick asked me to the prom."

Two seconds of silence were followed by shrieks of disbelief and excitement:

"Five months in *advance*? *Patrick*?"

"You're *kidding* me!"

"*When*?"

"Yesterday." I was grinning uncontrollably and couldn't help myself. "He called. We talked."

"He called. You talked. What is this? Shorthand?" Gwen demanded. "Girl, we want *details*!"

"Wait! Hold it!" said Pamela. She jumped up, went to the counter, and bought a huge cup of whipped cream, then liberally doused each of our lattes to celebrate.

"Now *dish*!" she said.

"Well, I was just hanging out in my room, getting my stuff ready for school, when I heard the phone ring."

"He didn't call you on your cell?"

"I'm not sure he knows the number."

"I'd think he would have had it programmed in!"

"It's been *two years*," I told them, working hard to defend him. Defend whatever there was between us, though I didn't know myself.

Liz rested her chin in her hands. When she looks at you through half-closed eyes, you realize just how long and thick her eyelashes are—longer than any girl's lashes have a right to be. "Oh, Alice, you and Patrick!" She sighed. "I *knew* you'd get back together. It's in the stars."

Gwen, the scientist, rolled her eyes. She was looking especially attractive, her hair in a new style of cornrows that made a geometric pattern on top of her head. The gold rings on one brown finger matched the design of her earrings, and she was definitely the most sophisticated-looking of the four of us. She was also the only one who had visited three colleges so far and who had even picked up scholarship forms.

"How long did you guys go together, anyway?" she asked.

"I guess it was about eighth grade that I really started liking him. The summer before eighth through the fall of ninth grade." I was embarrassed suddenly that I remembered this so precisely, as though it were always there at the front of my consciousness. "We actually met in sixth, but sixth-grade boyfriends aren't much to brag about."

"He did have his goofy side," Pamela agreed. "Remember that hot day at Mark's pool when you fell asleep on the picnic table? And Patrick placed two lemon halves on your breasts for a minute?"

"What?" Gwen shrieked.

"Yes, and when I woke up, everyone was grinning and no one would tell me what happened. And I couldn't figure out what those two little wet spots were on the front of my T-shirt. Like I was nursing or something!"

We yelped with laughter.

I continued. "And the year he gave me an heirloom bracelet for my birthday that turned out to be his mom's, because she didn't wear it anymore."

"I never heard that one," said Liz.

"And Mrs. Long had to call me and ask for it back," I said. We laughed some more. I wondered if I was being disloyal, telling all this. That was the old Patrick. The kid. That was then, and this was now.

"So what attracted you to him in the first place?" asked Gwen. "Besides the fact that he's a tall, smart, broad-shouldered redhead? I wasn't in on that early history."

"Well, he wasn't always as tall or broad-shouldered," I said. "I guess it's because he's the most motivated, focused, organized person I ever met. His dad's a diplomat, and they've lived in Japan, Germany, Spain. . . . In some ways, he's a man of the world."

"And then he falls for Penny, the jerk," said Pamela. "I'm glad *that's* over."

I saw three pair of eyes dart in my direction to see how I was taking that, then look away. Wondering if I'd cry myself sick again if things didn't work out this time with Patrick. I remembered Elizabeth's organizing a suicide watch when Patrick and I broke up, so that a friend called every quarter of an hour to see if I was okay. I tried not to smile.

"Well," I said flippantly, "a lot can happen in the next five months. You know how everything else comes before fun where Patrick is concerned. And I didn't say we were back together. I just said we were going to the prom."

"But this is *his* prom, and then you can invite him back for *yours!*" said Liz excitedly, since Patrick's in an accelerated program that gets him through high school in three years.

"Yeah, and with *two* prom nights to make out, you know what *that* means," said Pamela.

"Will you *stop*?" I said.

To some girls, a prom means you're a serious couple. To some, it's the main event of high school. To some, it's the biggest chance in your life, next to getting married, to show off. And to some girls, it means going all the way.

"Well, I'm glad for you," said Gwen. "But I hope we don't have to talk prom for the next five months."

"Promise," I said.

"Some couples were just meant to be," Pamela said. "Jill and Justin, for example. They've been going out forever."

"What about you and Tim?" I asked. Tim had taken her to the Snow Ball last fall. A really nice guy.

"Could be!" said Pamela.

"So are you going to ask him to the Sadie Hawkins Day dance?" asked Gwen.

"I already have," Pamela told us, and grinned. Then she turned serious again. "Patrick better come through this time, Alice. He owes you big-time."

If my friends didn't quite know what to make of Patrick, neither did I. I'd always thought of him as special somehow, but . . . My first boyfriend? More than that. Patrick was someone with a future, and I didn't know if I was part of that or not. Or wanted to be.

But you can analyze a good thing to death, so I decided to take it at face value: He really, really liked me and couldn't think of anyone he'd rather take to the prom. *Now enjoy it,* I told myself.

Our house was a mess. Dad and Sylvia were having the place remodeled, with a new addition on the back. Their bedroom, the kitchen, and the dining room were sealed off with heavy vinyl sheets so that dust and cold wouldn't get through. Their bed had been taken apart and stood against one wall in the upstairs hallway. The rest of their furniture was pushed into Lester's old bedroom, where they were sleeping, and their clothes were piled all over the place in my room. Downstairs, the dining-room furniture had been moved into the living room along with the refrigerator and microwave, and the construction crew had fashioned a sink with hot and cold running water next to the fridge. We ate our meals on paper plates, sitting in the only available chairs, knees touching.

"Maybe it wasn't such a good idea to stay in the house during remodeling," Dad said that weekend when we didn't think we could swallow one more bite of Healthy Choice or Lean Cuisine.

"But think of all the money we're saving by not living in a hotel!" said Sylvia. "The foreman said that if we can put up with painters and carpenters doing the finishing touches, we might be able to move into the new addition by the middle of March."

Fortunately for us, the construction company had another contract for an expensive project starting April 1, and had doubled the workforce at our place to finish by then.

Dad was at the Melody Inn seven days a week, Sylvia was teaching, and I was at school, so we didn't have to listen to all the pounding.

Lester came over one night and took us out to dinner.

"Hey," I said over my crab cake, "why don't we move in with Lester for the duration?"

He gave me a look. "Don't even think it," he said. "I'm surviving on five hours of sleep a night while I finish my thesis."

"Oh, Les!" Sylvia said sympathetically.

"You need to get some exercise," Dad told him.

"I run to Starbucks and back," Les said.

"But . . . you're not seeing anyone at all?" I asked.

"Not much," said Les.

It was hard to imagine, but somehow I believed him. Les had made up his mind to graduate, and he was hitting the books.

"What about that girl you were going out with at Christmas?" I asked him.

"It's over," said Les.

"Already?" exclaimed Dad.

"Too high maintenance," Les told us. "All she wanted to do was party, and I can't afford the time. So I've sworn off women till after I graduate."

That was even more difficult to imagine, but I felt real sympathy for my twenty-four-year-old brother right then. I decided that somehow, sometime around Valentine's Day, I . . . or Liz and I . . . or Liz and Pamela and I . . . or Liz and Pam and Gwen and I were going to plan a surprise for Lester. I just didn't know what.

Patrick had called me twice since New Year's Day, when he invited me to the prom. He didn't call to chat, exactly. He either had something to tell me or a question to ask. You could say he's all business, but that wouldn't be true, because he has a good sense of humor and there's a gentleness that I like too. I just wish he were more accessible. He runs his life like a railroad—always busy, always going somewhere, *getting* somewhere.

But there was a lot more to think about during the second semester of my junior year. The SATs, for one. I decided that January would probably be my least hectic month, so I'd take the test on January 26, then take it again later if I bombed the first time. Getting my braces off was item number two. I also wanted to spend more time with our friend Molly Brennan, who's getting treated for leukemia, and to persuade Pamela, if possible, to audition for the spring musical, *Guys and Dolls*. I'd signed up for stage crew once again.

Tim Moss was doing a lot for Pamela's self-confidence. Pamela's pretty, she's got a good voice, and has a great body. But ever since her mom deserted the family a few years ago and ran off with a boyfriend, Pamela's self-esteem has been down in her socks. Lately, though, now that her mom's back and living in an apartment alone, Pamela's seemed a little more like her old self, and once she started going out with Tim, she really perked up.

Sylvia, my stepmom, said that one way to tell if a guy is right for you is if he wants what's best for you, encourages your talents, and—at the same time—has a good sense of self and where *his* life is going. She was speaking about my dad and her decision to marry him when she said that, but I think Tim Moss would just about get an A on all three.

"Go for it," Tim told Pamela when we were talking about the musical the other night.

"I'll think about it" was all she said, which is one step up from "No, I'd never make it," which is where she was last week.

And speaking of Sylvia, I'm getting along better with her.

Even Annabelle, her cat. *Our* cat. The cat I'd said such awful things about last year. Sylvia and I are both trying to communicate more. If she wants my help with some big household project, for example, she doesn't descend on me some weekend when I have a ton of homework or something else planned. And if I want to use her or Dad's car, I try to remember to tell them in advance, not just spring it on them.

I guess you could say that for me and my friends, cars and driving are a big part of our lives. They were sure a big part of Brian Brewster's, whose license was just suspended last week in court because he hit another car in December and badly injured a seven-year-old girl. She was in the hospital for three weeks with a broken pelvis and other injuries, but I think Brian would have to break his own pelvis before he'd worry more about her than about the fact that he can't drive for a year.

I don't hang around much anymore with Brian and his crowd. Patrick seems able to move in and out of a crowd whenever the spirit moves him; if there's one thing Patrick Long is not, it's a label. But mostly I go places with Pamela, Liz, and Gwen.

The four of us have different interests much of the time, but we still tell each other a lot of personal stuff. Liz and I used to go running together on summer mornings and sometimes after school. But I wasn't fast enough for her, so she joined the girls' track team this semester. Pamela was taking voice lessons; Gwen got a job as a receptionist in a clinic twice a week after school; and I promised my friend Lori that I'd join the

Gay/Straight Alliance at school to show my solidarity with her and her girlfriend, Leslie.

But there was one secret I hadn't told anyone: I had a crush on Scott Lynch, a senior, the editor in chief of *The Edge*. Last fall I'd done everything but beg him to take me to the Snow Ball, but he'd asked a girl from Holton-Arms. So when another senior, Tony Osler, asked me, I'd gone with him. And because Tony seemed more interested in getting into my pants than anything else, that didn't last very long. Now I was going to the prom in May with Patrick and was wildly excited about it, but Scott was still on my mind. Is life ever simple?

I have to say that Jacki Severn, features editor for *The Edge*, is not my favorite person. She's got an eye for copy layout and she's a good writer, but she isn't easy to work with. When I got to the staff meeting on Wednesday, she was on one of her rants.

"I think we ought to change the name!" she was saying. "It's historically inaccurate."

Now what? I wondered, exchanging glances with Don Spiro, one of our photographers. *Hissy fit,* he scribbled on a piece of paper and shoved it across the table.

"What's up?" I asked the others.

Scott was balancing a pencil between two fingers and offered an explanation: "Remember that last year the school decided to replace the Jack of Hearts dance in February with something more casual?"

I nodded. "Something fun and silly and utterly retro, like a Sadie Hawkins Day dance."

"Right. Well, the dance committee has scheduled it for February twenty-ninth, because the twenty-ninth happens only once every four years, sort of a nice kickoff for the first Sadie Hawkins Day dance. But Jacki wants to call it the 'Turnaround Dance.'"

I gave Jacki a puzzled look. "And if we call it 'Sadie Hawkins,' the world will end?" I asked, making Scott smile.

But Jacki sure didn't. "I've researched it, and Sadie Hawkins Day first appeared in a *Li'l Abner* comic strip in November 1937. If the whole rest of the country celebrates Sadie Hawkins Day in November, it's ludicrous to hold our dance in February unless we change the name."

"I doubt that the whole rest of the country even knows who Sadie Hawkins is," said Don.

"It doesn't matter!" said Jacki. "Besides, there's another SAT scheduled for March first, the day after."

"But not at our school," said Miss Ames, our sponsor. "And the newspaper has no authority to change the name of the dance. 'Sadie Hawkins' still lets people know that it's girls' choice."

"But—," Jacki began.

I was sitting at one of the computers and had Googled the term *Sadie Hawkins Day*. "Hey!" I interrupted. "Here's a West Virginia school that holds a Sadie Hawkins Day dance every February twenty-ninth."

Scott jokingly banged his notebook down on the tabletop. "Sold!" he said. "Next topic . . ."

Jacki gave me a long, hard look and angrily picked up her pen.

The topic may have been closed, but it sort of sealed the antagonism between Jacki and me. I guess I never quite forgave her for trying to do a story on Molly and her leukemia without any thought as to how Molly might feel about it. And Jacki probably never forgave me for being there with some of my friends, sitting on Molly's bed and eating a pizza with her—Molly in makeup, to be exact—when the photographer arrived to take a picture of a pale, limp girl in a lonely bed. Not exactly the story Jacki had in mind.

When I got home that night, I waited until I'd finished my homework before calling Patrick. I've always had the feeling he's out most evenings, because—in addition to his accelerated curriculum with all the extra homework—he's got band and track and probably other activities I don't even know about.

The phone rang three times before he answered.

"Hey!" he said.

"Hey, it's me. You busy?"

"Always, but I need a break. What's happening?" His voice was welcoming. Encouraging.

"We had a staff meeting after school—the newspaper," I explained, "and the big discussion was what to call the dance that's replacing the Jack of Hearts on February twenty-ninth."

"Pretty momentous. Right up there with the Mideast," said Patrick. Patrick always thinks global.

"Yeah. Jacki Severn's bummed because she says that most

places celebrate Sadie Hawkins Day in November, so she wants to change the name of the dance."

Patrick laughed. "A slugfest between the Sadies and the non-Sadies? Glad I won't be there."

I was quiet for a moment. "Where will you be?"

"The band's quintet is playing for a big Kiwanis Club charity dance. They hold it every leap year on February twenty-ninth, and Mr. Levinson asked us two months ago to play."

"So . . . you won't be able to go?" I said, sounding stupid.

"Unless I've got a clone," said Patrick. And then he must have sensed what I was thinking, because he said, "You don't have to sit at home, Alice. You could invite someone else."

I guess I didn't want to hear that, either. I wanted him to sound disappointed. Jealous, even, at the thought of me in someone else's arms.

But Patrick went on. "I don't want you to feel that because we're going to the prom, I've got a clamp on your social life." Now he sounded like a sociology professor. "I mean, I'm going to be away next year."

"I know," I said, feeling a heaviness in my chest.

"So I don't want you sitting around waiting for me."

When somebody tells you he doesn't want you sitting around waiting for him, it means he won't be sitting around in Chicago waiting for you. And maybe I wanted to hear that, maybe I didn't.

"Well," I said. "I just . . . wanted to make sure. You were my first choice."

"That's good to know," said Patrick, a chuckle in his voice, and I could just imagine his eyes laughing then. "I'll think of you at the Kiwanis Club that night."

I asked him what instruments made up the quintet, and he said a clarinet, a bass, a trumpet, a sax, and drums—the drummer, of course, being Patrick. But I didn't really care. I was thinking, *Sadie Hawkins*; I was thinking, *Girls' Choice*; I was thinking, *Scott Lynch*.

2
MAKING THE CALL

I knew I shouldn't wait. If I was going to invite Scott, I had to do it now. My guess was that he had already been asked. How could he *not* have been asked—Scott, with the topaz blue eyes and the squarest chin I've ever seen; the tall, slim guy—taller than Patrick, even—with that special Scott smile for everyone, not just me.

My heart began to pound, and I wiped my palms on my jeans. Maybe he hadn't been asked. The dance committee had only recently settled on the date. I think Jacki Severn likes him too, but after she was shooting daggers at everyone at the staff meeting, Scott included, I doubted he was her date.

I stood up and went to the bathroom, then made my way back through the disassembled furniture in the hallway and sat down again on my bed. I stared at my cell phone. It was the scariest thing around.

What if he just put me off? That was almost more frightening than if he said no. What if he said, *You're kidding, right?* Then I'd have to say, *Uh . . . no, I really mean it. Do you want to go?* And he'd say, *Alice, I'm sorry, but you're just not my type.*

I let out my breath and went over to the window, feeling perspiration trickling down from my armpits. How do guys stand this? How do they get up in the morning wanting to ask a girl out, then watch the minutes tick by all day, knowing that every hour they wait, the girl is that much closer to going with someone else?

The phone in the hallway rang, and I jumped. Maybe Scott was calling me! Maybe he was calling to say that if I was thinking of inviting him to the Sadie Hawkins Day dance, please don't embarrass myself.

It was Lester.

"Did I leave my scarf there when I came by the other night?" he asked.

"Oh, you scared me!" I said. "I thought you were somebody else."

"I sound different?"

"No. But listen, Lester, if a girl asked you out and you didn't want to go, how would you tell her?"

"What does this have to do with my scarf?" he said.

"Nothing. But I won't look for your scarf unless you tell me what to expect."

I heard him sigh. "Who are you asking out? What's the matter with Patrick?"

"He can't go to the Sadie Hawkins Day dance because his quintet is playing for a Kiwanis thing, and I want to ask somebody else, but I'm positive he'll turn me down."

"Well, if you're positive, then save yourself the trouble," said Les.

"You're not helping!" I bleated. "I want to ask Scott Lynch, and I don't know how he really feels about me. He's nice to everyone."

"Then he'll be nice to you, even if he turns you down," said Lester.

"But tell me how *you'd* do it," I said. "I want to be prepared. How do guys do it without hurting a girl's feelings? I don't want to hang up not knowing whether he said yes or no."

"It's impossible to do it without hurting somebody. It *always* hurts to be turned down," said Lester. "But if I had to say no to someone and didn't have a good excuse, I'd make up something."

"You'd lie?" I said.

"Yeah," said Lester. "Now, about my scarf . . ."

"But what if you wanted to make sure she never asked you again? What do guys say *then*?" I insisted.

"I suppose they could say, 'I'm not that into you,' but I'd probably say, 'I'm flattered, but I just don't think it would work out for us.'"

"*Oof,*" I said, feeling sick already. "I don't think I can take this, Les. What would I *do* if he says something like that?"

"I guess you could sue him for mental anguish, but it wouldn't make him like you any better," said Lester. "Hey, Al, where's your spunk? I thought you were braver than this."

"I'm not," I told him. "I'm terrified. And every minute I don't call him, some other girl probably will."

"Okay, then. Call the guy! But before you do, have you seen my scarf?"

"Is it cashmere? Extra long? Sort of creamy beige?"

"Yes. Exactly."

"It's in my locker."

"What?" he yelped. "That was a gift from Lauren."

"Lauren!" I exclaimed. "Les, you broke up with her two years ago."

"So I can't wear her scarf? I *like* that scarf. Why is it in your locker?"

"You left it here, and I thought I'd wear it to school the next time I drove Dad's car, then deliver it to your apartment afterward. But I forgot and left it in my locker."

"I want it back, Al. They're predicting snow for tomorrow."

"I'll *bring* it, Les! Calm down! I didn't lose it or anything," I told him.

After I went back in the bedroom, I picked up my cell phone and punched in Scott's number. A woman answered on the second ring.

No! No! What was his mom doing on his cell phone? Then

I realized I'd dialed the second number I'd scribbled in my staff notebook, his home number.

"I . . . I wonder if I could speak to Scott?" I said, wanting to die. I know you're supposed to identify yourself when you call, but I didn't want her announcing it.

"I'm sorry, but he's not in right now, and I see he left his cell phone here. I expect him back in twenty minutes, though," she said. "Should I have him call you?"

The phone felt clammy in my hand. I had to go through this a second time?

"Uh . . . no, that's okay. I'll call back," I told her, and went to the bathroom again. *Geez!* Why hadn't I just told Scott's mom to ask him to the dance for me? Then, when he said no, I wouldn't have to hear it from him.

Why are boyfriends' mothers so scary? I wondered. Mrs. Long always sounded so elegant and polite that I usually used the wrong words. Sam's mom was positively terrifying. Scott's mom sounded okay, but how did I know what she'd tell him?

Forty minutes later, though, at 9:50, I called his cell phone number.

"Hi, Alice," he said.

I was afraid I would faint. "H-how did you know it was me?" I asked.

"Um . . . caller ID?" he said, and I could almost see him smiling.

"Oh. Right," I said. "Hope I didn't interrupt anything."

"No. I just got back from the gas station. What's up?"

"About the Sadie Hawkins Day dance . . . ," I began.

"Not you too!" he said.

I was stunned. What? A dozen girls had called so far?

Then he said, "You want to change the name?"

"No!" I said. "Actually, I'm calling to see if you'd like to go with me."

Was it one second before he answered? Three? Five? "To the dance? Uh . . . sure," he said. "Sounds like fun! Thanks."

I was speechless.

"Alice?" he said.

"Oh, that's great!" I told him. "Great! I'll buy the tickets and everything."

"Okay. We can figure all that out later," said Scott.

"Great!" I said again. Was that my third *great*? "Okay, then, I'll see you at school tomorrow."

"Right," said Scott. "G'night."

"'Night," I said, and I think I actually wet my pants a little.

The first person I told was Liz, and I wished I hadn't. Wished I'd told her at a different time, maybe, or in a different way, and with less emotion.

Elizabeth Price is gorgeous. Of the four of us—Pamela, Liz, Gwen, and me—I think she's the beautiful one. Long dark hair, dark eyes, creamy skin. . . . But it's funny about Liz. She *must* know she's gorgeous, but she doesn't act as though she knows. In fact, Liz is definitely on the shy side.

She had a serious boyfriend, Ross, from the summer before

last when we were counselors at a kids' camp. They got together a few times after that, but Ross lives in Pennsylvania and we live in Maryland. It was just too hard, I guess, to keep a long-distance romance going. But she hasn't been out with anyone since, and she absolutely refuses to let us set her up with anyone.

One of the problems is that a lot of guys mistake her shyness as being stuck-up or something. They figure a girl as beautiful as Liz must have a dozen guys calling her every weekend. Little do they know that Liz would love to go out, but no one asks her.

So when I called and breathlessly told her that Scott Lynch—our senior newspaper editor, a great-looking guy everyone notices when he walks down the hall—would be my date for the Sadie Hawkins Day dance, I didn't get the squeal I thought would follow.

"You're going with someone else? Not Patrick?" she asked.

I explained where Patrick would be that night and how I'd secretly been crushing on Scott. But she still didn't sound too excited. "Well, gosh, Alice! You're doing okay," she said, and somehow her voice sounded flat. "*Two* guys."

And then I felt awful.

"Why don't you come with us?" I said. "*Ask* somebody."

"Oh, sure. I'll just pick a name out of the student directory," she said.

"No, but there must be *some* guy you've got your eye on, Liz. I was amazed that no one had asked Scott yet, so other guys must still be available."

"Well, I can make that decision myself," Liz said, and I

couldn't believe that this was Elizabeth Price, one of my best friends since sixth grade, sounding envious of me.

"Liz, are you mad or something?" I asked.

"Why should I be mad?"

"I don't know, but you don't sound like yourself," I said, feeling more uncomfortable by the second.

"I just don't need a cheerleader for my social life," she said.

"Liz, I—!"

"Anyway, I've got stuff to do," she said. "I'll see you tomorrow, okay?"

"*Not* okay!" I said. "If I said anything to upset you, Liz, I'm sorry!"

"I *said* I'm not upset."

"All right," I said, and we hung up.

I sat there staring out the window at the big white house across the street, wondering if she was over there looking out at me. Why did I think everyone should be as excited and happy for me as I was for myself? They'd already cooed and carried on when I said that Patrick had asked me to the prom, and now, a few weeks later, did I expect them to turn cartwheels because I had a second guy? It even surprised *me*. Yet, just because we were best friends, couldn't I understand that Liz might be a little jealous? *Tired* of me, even?

I have to say, I handled it pretty well the next day. I really tried to put myself in Elizabeth's place. If *I* hadn't gone out with a guy for a long time, and a friend called to tell me she had dates with *two* guys, and then apologized for upsetting me, how would I want her to treat me the next day?

I decided that another apology would only emphasize the fact that she didn't have a boyfriend. So I didn't even mention our phone conversation. She happened to be wearing a yellow sweater, and with her dark hair and lashes, she looked terrific.

"That's a great color on you," I said as I hung up my jacket in my locker.

"Thanks," she said.

At lunch I didn't mention the Sadie Hawkins Day dance. I think Liz was surprised that I talked about our cat instead, how she kept forgetting where her litter box was among all the stuff piled in our living room.

Someone eventually brought up the dance, and when I still didn't bite, Liz said, "Hey, did you know that Alice invited Scott Lynch?" and everyone turned toward me.

I casually explained that he was a friend from the newspaper staff, that I'd asked him because Patrick was busy that night.

"Well, hey!" said Pamela.

"Wow!" said Gwen.

But I was so offhand about it that the attention soon shifted to someone else. And when Liz asked me later if I had a tampon, I gave her the only one I had left. What are friends for?

I was nervous about seeing Scott at school. I mean, one day we're friends working on the newspaper together, and the next we've got a date for a dance. Did he realize I'd had a crush on him for a long time, or did he think it was just a spur-of-the-moment invitation? All the way to school that morning, I'd mentally practiced what I'd say if I met him in the hall. Had even stood in front of the mirror practicing a smile that wasn't too eager, not too strained, not too wide, not too narrow. . . . I was making myself sick.

And then, just before gym, I was putting some stuff in my locker when I heard a voice say, "Hi, Alice," and there was Scott, books tucked under one arm.

"Oh!" I tried to speak and swallow at the same time, and started coughing. He grinned and patted me on the back.

"You okay?" he asked, and I felt my face growing hot.

"Yeah," I said, trying to laugh it off. "I didn't know you were there."

"Sorry!" he said, and waited till the coughing was under control. "Well, look. About the dance . . ."

He's backing out! I thought, feeling weak in the knees.

". . . I don't want to disrupt your plans or anything, but Don e-mailed me last night and said a girl had invited him, and he wanted to know if we could double. I know that this is your party, but I was going to offer to drive and . . ."

I was so relieved, I almost choked again. "Of course! It's fine!" I said.

Don was the senior photographer for our newspaper, and he and Tony had been with Liz and me last semester when I'd researched my feature story "The City at Night." Don's a nice guy. Then I had another thought: What if the girl who had invited him was Jacki Severn? What if we were double-dating with Don and Jacki?

"Is Don taking anyone I know?" I asked.

"Another senior, Christy Levin," he said.

I smiled. "Great," I said. This was great. Scott was great. Life was great.

"I'll tell him, then," Scott said, and nodded down the corridor. "Gotta run. Chem's at the other end of the building."

"See you," I called out.

Pamela was out with Tim Moss on Saturday night, so Gwen and Liz and I went to Molly's to play Scrabble with her.

She wasn't wearing her old sweat suit this time, but had on jeans and a fleece pullover, a baseball cap on her head.

"You look like you're feeling better," I told her, and she did.

"It's been an okay week," she told us. "Either the chemo's helping or I'm just getting more used to it."

She had the board set up on a card table in one corner of the family room, and her mom brought in a high-calorie shake for her, Cokes and chips for the rest of us.

Q, of course, is the most difficult letter to play because you need a U to go along with it. All the tiles were drawn, and I got stuck with a Q at the end of the game, while Molly was stuck with two U's.

"Two!" I cried. "You've been holding out on me, Molly!"

But in the next game Molly played the word *quiz*, with the high-scoring Q and the Z.

"Who-eee!" she cried, and even her dad looked in and grinned.

"Hey, girl, you've got those tiles marked!" Gwen joked.

Molly held up the two letters to show that the backs of the tiles were clean. "X-ray vision," she said. "I can see through wood."

I wished I could see through things. Through people. I wished I could see through Molly and tell if the treatment protocol she was on was working. I wished I could read the fortunes of all four of us there at the card table: Molly, the sickest of the lot; Gwen, the smartest; Liz, the most beautiful; and me, the most ordinary. It would be interesting to know what each of us would be doing three years from now. Five years. Ten years. . . .

Then again, maybe not.

3
YO TE QUIERO

The SAT wasn't as bad as I'd expected. Maybe, having taken the PSAT last fall, I was better prepared or wasn't as nervous. I can't say I sailed through it, but I felt more confident than I had before. I'd been boning up on it every week since October and attended two Saturday workshops in January, and that helped. Liz took the test with me, and we both were relieved and hopeful when it was over. At last we could think about other things for a while.

Liz was really into track, but the school newspaper kept me busy, and I wanted to get back to working for Dad at the Melody Inn on Saturdays, to earn some cash. Then there was the Gay/

Straight Alliance, and on the first Thursday in February, I went to my first meeting.

It was good to know that Lori thought enough of me to invite me into the group and nice to see how much in love she and Leslie were with each other. The GSA had only been active in our school since last fall, though there were chapters in lots of high schools and colleges all over the country—just straight and gay friends, bonding together, offering support, so that gays didn't have to feel like a separate species and straights didn't have to feel they'd be labeled if they stood up for gay rights.

Everyone was sitting around in a loose circle when I came in, kidding with each other, sharing iPods, discussing new bands, showing off new jackets or hairstyles. I slid onto a chair next to Lori and listened to the chatter. Finally Mr. Morrison, the faculty sponsor, came in, said hello to the group, welcomed the new people, then started some sort of casual ritual, which everyone seemed to understand except me.

"My name is James," he said, smiling around the room, "and my socks are blue."

Whaaaaat? I thought. What did that have to do with anything? Especially because, glancing at his feet, I saw that his socks were definitely *not* blue, they were brown. Everyone was smiling, and I could tell that a lot of people were watching me, the new kid, to see *my* reaction.

Mr. Morrison turned to the person next to him, a large guy, one of the football players maybe, and this guy continued the ritual: "My name is Cary, and my socks are red."

His socks were *white!* What was going on? Were we talking in code or something? How did you play this game?

A girl was next. She grinned. "I'm Denisha, and my socks are pink." Yeah, they were. Well, coral maybe. It was hopeless.

As the strange ceremony continued, Lori leaned over and whispered, "The socks under your *pants*." And when I stared at her quizzically, she whispered, "Your underwear. But Morrison won't let us say that in case some parent goes berserk and tries to shut the group down."

What? Then it was Leslie's turn, then Lori's: "My name is Lori, and my socks are white."

What color underwear did I put on this morning? I thought desperately. But it was my turn, and all eyes were on me. All faces smiling.

"My name is Alice," I said, "and my socks are . . . are polka dot."

Everybody broke into laughter, and I was in. And I understood what the ritual was all about. In a way, it was a takeoff on Alcoholics Anonymous, where each person gives his first name and admits that he's an alcoholic. He says the words to own it— to make sure he recognizes that this is his problem.

But here, by describing our underwear, we were saying in effect that what we were didn't matter. We all wear underwear— well, except for one guy who said he wasn't wearing any socks at all. But who cared if they were red or blue? Who cared if you didn't *know?* Nobody had to answer that he or she was gay or straight or bisexual or transsexual because it wasn't considered a problem.

The next half hour was a sort of free-for-all. Anyone could share something that had happened during the past week—any problems, feelings, whatever.

"Somebody asked me how I felt about the word 'queer,'" one boy said. "And I thought, 'I don't know, man.' It seems okay when my friends and I use it, but if someone else calls me that . . . I'm not sure."

"Doesn't bother me," said another guy. "I look at it as a sort of status thing. You know, *Queer Eye for the Straight Guy*. Like we're the ones with style."

Somebody told a derogatory joke he'd heard in the locker room, and we talked about that for a while. This drifted into a joke-telling session, till we were so far off course that Mr. Morrison had to drag us back to business.

"We were planning to have a table at the Sadie Hawkins Day dance," he said. "Everybody okay with that?"

"No one expects trouble, do they?" asked Leslie.

"There wasn't any trouble at the Snow Ball, and there were at least three gay couples there," someone answered.

"Whose turn is it to table?" Morrison asked.

"Phil's and Lori's," said someone, checking a clipboard, and for the rest of the session there was a recap of coming events and distribution of new brochures describing GSA, and then the meeting was over and everyone left.

I felt pretty good as I drove home in Sylvia's car. I think that the more groups you join, the more you feel you belong. And to tell the truth, I felt very content at that moment—two guys, three best friends plus a bunch of others, a dad and a brother whom I loved, a stepmom I was beginning to love. . . .

And then, as always, I felt the wave of sadness that my real mom wasn't alive for me to talk with—that the last time she'd seen me, I was five years old. I wished she could have known me now.

It was time to do something for Lester. I asked Gwen and Liz and Pamela if they'd help me decorate his car for Valentine's Day to make him think he had a secret admirer. Then he wouldn't wonder if he was losing his appeal, and he could concentrate more on his studies and finish his master's thesis. Not that he *was* wondering, but then, people are always insecure after a breakup, aren't they? And hadn't he just broken up with the "party girl"?

Valentine's Day was on a Thursday. Gwen, Pamela, and Liz agreed to go with me around nine on Wednesday evening to lavishly decorate his car. Yolanda, Gwen's friend from church, wanted to go with us, so that made five. I just said I was going out with my gal pals, and Dad let me have his car. I told him I'd be back around ten.

We had ribbons and streamers and hearts and paper bouquets. We had valentine messages printed on hearts. We whooped and giggled all the way down Georgia Avenue and made the turnoff at last into Takoma Park.

Lester lives in the upstairs apartment of a big Victorian house owned by Otto Watts, who's elderly and lives in the rooms downstairs. Les has two roommates, Paul Sorenson and George Palamas, and our big worry was that one of them might come home late and catch us in the act. But when I pulled up in front of the house next door, we saw two cars in Mr. Watts's driveway and Lester's car parked at the curb.

"Are we lucky or are we lucky?" I whispered as we got out; we didn't even close the car doors, we were that quiet. Just reached in and took out all the stuff we'd prepared at home.

"Gwen, why don't you and Pamela and Yolanda do the rear windshield, and Liz and I will do the front," I suggested. "Then we'll drape streamers along both sides and take off."

Liz and I taped love messages against the front windshield so that the words could be read from the driver's seat. *Your secret crush*, read one. *Loving you from afar*, read another. There were bows and arrows, *X*'s and *O*'s, and *I love you* in three different languages.

We taped a large pair of open lips on a side window, cardboard "eyes" with fringed eyelashes over each headlight, a plastic cupid where a hood ornament might have gone. We tied a pair of black lace panties to the antenna.

Then the five of us unfurled the red and pink and white crepe paper streamers along each side of the car and around the bumpers. When I reached the door handle, I started to wrap the streamer twice around it to keep it from dragging, when suddenly the car erupted into a series of loud honks and beeps and sirens.

I jumped backward.

A theft alarm! When had Lester installed *that*?

"Omigod!" cried Pamela.

"Run!" I yelled. "Hide!"

We grabbed the rest of the streamers and started to run. Gwen lost her shoe, and we stopped to retrieve that, then barreled on, collapsing behind a panel truck parked two houses down.

Porch lights came on. A door opened. Then another.

"Alice, why didn't you *tell* us it was wired?" Gwen breathed on the back of my neck as we crouched practically on top of each other.

"It wasn't before! I didn't know!" I cried.

"They went that way!" a woman hollered. "I saw them running. I bet they're after the air bags!"

"Whose car is it?" we heard a man yell.

And another answered, "That one in front. Looks like somebody just got married."

I didn't realize anyone paid attention to those burglar alarms anymore. They're always going off, and nobody gets too excited. If we'd only had a minute longer . . .

We heard footsteps coming down the steps at the side of the house, and I knew in my bones it was someone from Lester's apartment.

"What the . . . ?" came a familiar voice.

A pause, then laughter.

"Hey, Les, somebody's got your number," another voice said.

The beeping stopped, and there was a long, plaintive yell from Lester: "Al-lice!"

"How did he know it was *me*?" I whispered to the other girls. "How? *How*?"

"Your dad's car," said Liz, and I crumpled.

"Al!" Lester bellowed again.

"Come on," said Gwen. "We've got to face the music."

Slowly we came out from behind the panel truck and walked sheepishly back toward Les and his two roommates, streamers trailing behind us. George Palamas, the shorter, dark-haired guy, was laughing, and Paul Sorenson was trying to read the messages on the rear window.

"That's them!" shouted the woman across the street on the front steps.

And at that very moment a squad car came rolling down the street, its light flashing.

"Al-lice!" Liz cried shakily.

The police car pulled over, and two officers got out.

"It's okay," called Les. "We've got 'em."

The policemen didn't respond, just came walking over, hands touching their belts. What they saw, of course, was three grown men with five young girls, and Les had his hand tightly on the back of my neck.

"Who called?" asked one officer.

"That's them!" screeched the woman across the street. "I saw 'em running."

"They were hiding behind that panel truck," yelled someone else.

"Oh, brother!" said George.

"So what's the problem here?" asked the second officer. And to Les, he said, "Put your hands down, please."

Les instantly released his grip on my neck.

"We didn't really do anything," I said quickly. "I'm his sister."

"We all did it together!" cried Liz.

"*Jeez!*" Les said through clenched teeth.

"The car!" Gwen said quickly, the only one of us who sounded intelligent just then. "All we did was decorate his car."

The policemen looked from us to the car and back again.

"Someone reported that there was an attempted car theft," said the first officer. "That didn't happen?"

"My sister here set off my car alarm, and someone must have seen them running," Les explained. "The neighborhood's had some air bags stolen recently, and we're sort of looking out for each other, that's all."

"We didn't take anything, honestly!" I said.

One of the officers gave us a weary smile, then turned to Les again. "You want the girls to undecorate your car?" he asked.

"Not until you've read the messages!" said Pamela. "We worked hard on this!"

"I'll handle it," Les told the policemen. "Thanks."

They got back in the cruiser and took off.

The people on their porches turned then and went back inside. Lester stared at his car, then at me. "Al—," he started.

But Pamela interrupted. "We're freezing, Lester. Can't we come in for something hot before we undecorate it?"

He sighed. "Come on," he said, and turned toward the steps.

* * *

Four of us squeezed together on the sofa, and Pamela sat on the floor, holding a coffee mug. Liz and Pam hadn't been in Lester's apartment since he'd let us help him move in, and Gwen and Yolanda hadn't seen it at all.

George sat across the room reading some of the heart messages he'd torn off the back windshield. Paul was rummaging around the kitchen for another cup.

"What *is* all this, Al?" Les asked. "What were you trying to do?"

"Haven't you ever heard of Valentine's Day?" I asked.

"And you figured I needed a heart?"

"She just wanted you to feel loved, Lester," said Pamela, smirking.

"Like a secret admirer or something," put in Liz.

"To keep you happy so you could concentrate on your studies," said Gwen, trying not to laugh.

Les stared at the five of us like we had just sprouted feathers. "Are you insane?" he asked, directing the question to me. "You figured that if I thought there was a woman secretly in love with me, I'd go happily back to my thesis and forget about her? Al, if there was a hot babe watching me from the bushes, I'd be out there *looking* for her; I'd be prowling the sidewalks, patrolling the streets, checking out every coffee shop in a five-mile radius from the U. Are you nuts?"

I leaned back against the cushions. "I guess I am," I said.

George was still reading the love messages. "*Io t'amo? Yo*

te quiero? Je vous aime? Who wrote these?" he asked.

"*The Berlitz Phrase Book for Travelers*," said Gwen, and that made us all laugh.

"So who's taken Spanish?" George asked.

"I have," said Yolanda and Liz both.

"And who wrote these?"

"I did," said Yolanda. "Well, sort of. My boyfriend did them for me."

"What's *Por favor, traigame otro tenedor*?" George asked, and I began to get the picture. George may be Greek or whatever, but he knew his Spanish.

"Uh . . . please . . . uh . . . ," Liz began.

"Please bring me another fork," said George. "What's *Tome izquierda despues del puente*?"

"Turn . . . ," Liz began again, then stopped.

"Turn left beyond the bridge. You girls flunk. Time to go home." He grinned.

The phone rang just then, and Mr. Watts, down below, wanted to know why that car out front was all dressed up like a birthday cake and whether the girls had brought over anything to eat. Les told him that no, unfortunately, no one was having a party, but Paul was going to get Chinese takeout on Friday, and Mr. Watts was invited.

Because Pamela had finally finished her tea, we put on our jackets, apologized once more to Les, and promised to take the stuff off his car before we left. He said he'd also settle for a wash job and vacuuming come spring.

"You and your bright ideas," Gwen said to me as we pulled the last heart off the windshield.

"But we got to see the inside of their apartment, didn't we?" said Pamela. And that made it all worthwhile.

Our high school doesn't allow students to have flowers or candy sent to the school office for pickup on Valentine's Day. In fact, Valentine's Day had gotten out of hand, with some of the more popular girls carrying around armloads of stuffed animals and chocolates and roses and stuff, while others—most of us, in fact—got nothing.

So the rule was that any Valentine's Day gifts arriving at the front office would be delivered to the nursing home down the street and that any Valentine's Day gift given privately from one student to another had to be kept in the locker till the end of the day.

We missed the Jack of Hearts dance, now that it was crossed off the calendar, but we had Sadie Hawkins to look forward to. And I was thinking of Scott as I walked to my locker after the last class.

I turned the dial on my lock and opened the door. Someone must have given out my locker combination, because there on my rumpled gym clothes at the bottom lay a single white rose. And a card beside it read *Patrick*.

You know how you can feel thrilled and horrified at the same time? Justified and guilty? It was almost as though I were cheating on Patrick.

Oh no! I thought. I hadn't given him anything! Didn't think we were . . . well, a couple. Not yet, anyway. Had he found out I'd asked Scott to the dance? Is that what this was about? Or did the rose mean he really cared?

I had a right to go with Scott. I knew that. Hey, who was it who once told me he wanted to go out with both Penny and me? Plus, Patrick had actually suggested I go to this dance with someone else. What I was keeping from him, though, was how big a crush I had on Scott.

I stood there staring down at the flower. Who was it who wrote, *A rose is a rose is a rose . . .* ? No, it wasn't. It was a little white bundle of ambiguities, and I wondered just how this semester was going to play out.

4
SUGGESTIONS

Pamela and Tim were getting to be about as close as any couple in high school, except for Jill and Justin maybe, who had been going out forever. Tim was considerate of Pamela, patient with her, and Pamela, in turn, liked to think of little ways to please him. She carried Tylenol in her bag for him when he had a headache, bought a refill for his pen, saved her dill pickle for him at lunch. . . . They really seemed to care for each other, and it was nice to see Pamela so happy.

I wish she could have told her mom about him. I was just getting to the place where I could confide in Sylvia now and then, and I liked that. But Pamela and her mom still fought much of the time.

Of the four of us—Pamela, Elizabeth, Gwen, and I—Pam was the only one right then with a bona fide boyfriend. I had two dates for two dances, but I couldn't call either one a boyfriend. Gwen was too wrapped up in AP courses to go out much, and Liz *wanted* a guy, but it just wasn't happening, and it was Liz I was thinking about.

What do you say to a girlfriend to make her a little more flirtatious? A little more friendly? A little more sexy or fun or approachable or *some*thing?

"It's your smile that turns guys on," I told her once.

"Joke around with the guys the way you do with us," Gwen said.

"When a guy follows you with his eyes, Liz, flirt *back*!" Pamela suggested.

We might as well have been trying to teach a cat to fly, I decided. Liz just didn't seem to have it in her. When the four of us were together, checking out a cute guy, or when we were around guys she *knew* were out of our league, she could play along. And obviously, when she and Ross fell for each other at camp two summers ago, she must have been more approachable then. In fact, I would have called her enthusiastic about guys. But when it came to boys at school, guys in our classes, guys who had *boy*friend potential, she shriveled up, like she didn't want to take the chance.

I think maybe part of the problem was that Liz took her romances a little too seriously. Her first boyfriend was Tom Perona, the summer before seventh grade, but he dumped her for a new girl at his school.

She had a crush on a teacher at the beginning of eighth, but of course that went nowhere. Then she fell for Justin Collier—before he started going out with Jill—but once he made a remark about her weight, it was over. Then there was Ross, and he was about as perfect for her as we could imagine, but the long-distance thing just didn't work out, and she didn't want to get hurt again.

But now it was like she'd forgotten how to try. It made me tired sometimes. Between trying to get Liz to be more friendly, Gwen to lighten up on her studies, and Pam to try out for the spring musical, I felt that I was using a lot of energy on my friends. And it made me wonder if there were things about *me* they'd like to change.

When I went to work at my Dad's music store on Saturday—I run the little Gift Shoppe in the alcove under the stairs—David asked me if I'd had a good Valentine's Day. David Reilly is one of Dad's part-time employees. He's about twenty and is thinking of becoming a priest.

"Define 'good,'" I said.

He smiled. "Okay. Something from a boyfriend maybe?"

"I don't have a particular boyfriend," I said. "But I did get a white rose, and I bought myself some M&M's on the way home."

He laughed. "Oh, too bad. I was hoping you had a stash of chocolates somewhere."

A woman came in the store just then wanting to sign her child up for trumpet lessons, and David took her to meet the instructor on the upper level. When he came down, I realized I hadn't asked him how things went in New Hampshire over Christmas. He'd told me he wanted to talk over things with his parents and his girlfriend—decide which he wanted more: the church or a wife. So I asked.

David leaned against the display case where I was polishing the glass top and stared down at the trays of novelty items. He's a really good-looking guy. Dark hair, square jaw, great clothes, great voice. He also sings in a men's choir. "I wish I could say I came back with a clear answer," he said. "My folks said they'd accept whatever decision I made. My girlfriend's the only one who's definite. She said she needed a decision by summer, that she won't wait for me after that. She doesn't want a half commitment."

I couldn't say I blamed her. "Did you talk it over with a priest?" I asked.

"Many times," he said. "They don't want a halfhearted commitment either. 'Finish college,' they say. 'Then think about seminary. Take a few courses and see if you know yourself better by then.' But that's too long for Connie."

"What's she like?" I asked as I rearranged the silver earrings and the necklaces made out of eighth notes.

He smiled. "Pretty. An inch taller than I am, and probably smarter, too. We broke up once already. But I'm down here taking courses at Georgetown, she's up in New Hampshire—I don't know. I think the church is winning."

"How do you ever know for sure?" I asked.

"You don't. You don't know anything for sure, Alice. Some of us take a leap of faith into religion, into marriage, and hope for the best. Some people embrace uncertainty and don't have any problems with doubt. It all depends on what you can live by, what makes you a better person."

"I have a lot of doubts about a lot of things," I told him.

"So do I," said David. "And people handle them differently, that's all."

I didn't have a chance to thank Patrick for the rose until the following Monday, because he was at some kind of a three-day science competition in Baltimore. If ever a person had too many interests, it was Patrick, but I didn't mind being one of his interests.

What I wanted to know was just where I was on the list—high priority or low? How many other things were ahead of me? I wondered sometimes if Patrick had any idea how much he'd hurt me when he'd said if he had to choose between Penny and me, it would be Penny. How does a girl ever get over a comment like that? But if she holds a ninth-grade mistake against a guy all the way up through eleventh, how mature is *that*?

"Elizabeth's gone out for track this semester," I told him after I'd mentioned the rose and we'd talked a few minutes.

"Yeah. I saw her running a couple days ago after school. Some of the other guys on the team noticed her too," Patrick said.

"Well, I wish one of them would ask her out," I said.

"You mean Liz can't get a guy?" asked Patrick.

Are all males this clueless? I wondered.

"Nobody asks her, Patrick!" I said.

"Well, I guess she *is* a little scary," he said.

"What do you mean, scary? Elizabeth?"

"Sort of perfectionistic. I mean, she *looks* so perfect that I guess if I asked her out, I'd worry that everything would have to go just right."

"Uh . . . *have* you ever thought of asking her out? Just curious."

"Maybe once or twice."

"Why didn't you?" I teased.

"Told you. I might order a hamburger and find out she'd turned vegan. I might wear sneakers and she was expecting loafers with tassels or something."

I laughed. "Patrick, I can't ever imagine you worrying about details. In fact, I can't imagine you worrying much about anything at all."

"You don't know me, Alice," he said.

"Really? What do you worry about, other than grades?"

"Life," he said, and then he laughed a little too. "Sometime when you've got six hours, I'll fill you in."

When we were laying out the next issue of *The Edge*, I asked Don about Christy Levin. "Someone I should know?"

"Probably not, but you'll like her. She's on the girls' basketball team. Brunette, kind of tall. . . . I took her to the Snow Ball."

"I'll probably recognize her when I see her," I said.

Scott came over. "What time do you want me to pick you up on the twenty-ninth?"

"Seven would be fine," I told him.

The dance committee had their work cut out for them, getting students familiar with the famous Al Capp comic strip *Li'l Abner*, most popular in the forties and fifties. They made poster-size reproductions of some of the strips and hung them in the hallways. There was handsome Abner, who had no idea that the full-lipped Daisy Mae was pining for him; Mammy Yokum and her pipe; luscious Moonbeam McSwine, who slept with the pigs—all those crazy characters.

It was all so dorky, so different, that it seemed to be catching on. Kids stood together in the halls, reading the strips and laughing, and some of them began imitating the characters—scratching their armpits, walking in Mammy's bowlegged stride, adopting Abner's clueless expression. Each day there was a new strip, and we heard girls talking about what they were going to wear.

And of course this was just what the school wanted—an informal dance that everyone could afford to attend. It would be an all-evening event, including a Dogpatch barbecue. The ticket price covered everything, so the girls didn't have to take the guys anywhere before the dance. No corsages. Just an evening in the high school gym.

I was getting excited now, and with Scott doing the driving, that made it simple. Still, Scott and Don and Christy were all seniors, and I wondered how I'd fit in.

"Directions to your place?" Scott asked.

He lived in Kensington, so I told him to take Connecticut to

University Boulevard, University to Georgia Avenue, Georgia to our street. . . .

"We're the house with the Porta-John in the front yard," I said.

He laughed. "You *really* go all out for Sadie Hawkins Day, don't you?"

I laughed too. "I'm serious. We're remodeling, and the workmen are still there."

"Okay, I'll find you," he said. "If no one answers the door, I'll try the Porta-John."

Why can't real life be more like the movies? Why couldn't the new addition be finished, the crew gone? Why couldn't Dad invite Scott inside and lead him back to our new family room, where a fire would be crackling in our big stone fireplace and Sylvia would be sitting beside it with Annabelle in her lap?

Now I didn't want him to come in! The dining-room furniture was squeezed into the living room, and there was only a narrow path leading to the stairs. The first thing Scott would see when he walked in the door was our refrigerator!

Then I thought of Molly and how she would probably give anything just to be well and going to the dance at all. The condition of her house would be the last thing on her mind.

I don't know exactly how she works it, but whenever Jacki Severn writes a feature article herself, she manages to make the front page. At least, her articles start there, along with her byline. We put out a paper every two weeks, and it's only eight pages long. Except for a controversial feature article I wrote last semester, "The City at Night," my articles have always appeared near the back. I wished that Scott would be a little more forceful.

The thing that really got to me—and some of the others, too—was that Jacki sometimes added little spot illustrations to her stories that she picked up off the Internet: a couple dancing, a girl with a book, a dog, a boat—whatever she was writing about. And if you counted up characters per line, one little piece of clip art took up three or four lines, but those never seemed to figure in *her* word count. She made the rest of us cut three or four lines when *we* went over, though.

When the paper came out this time, however, Jacki was steaming. As we were getting ready to distribute them to the homerooms before school on Tuesday morning, she marched over to Scott and said, "Okay, where are they?"

"They?" said Scott.

"The heart motifs."

"We had to take them out, Jacki—we got a new ad and needed the space. They took up too much room, and besides, Valentine's Day is over," he said.

"My article was about relationships!" she said.

"We need every ad we can get," Scott replied.

"You didn't even tell me!" Jacki said, her voice rising. "I *am* the features editor, you know!"

And now Scott's voice had an edge to it. Microscopic, maybe, but I could tell. "You weren't here when we did the final layout, remember? The ad came in just before our deadline, and removing that spot seemed the best way to get the space."

Yay, Scott! I was thinking.

"Well, next time I don't want anyone tinkering with my articles," Jacki said, and she included all of us in her sweeping glare.

Miss Ames had come in halfway through her tirade. "The thing is, Jacki," she said, "that clip art does take up space, and we needed to cut somewhere."

"I thought they added a lot to my articles! To the paper!" Jacki protested.

Miss Ames smiled. "In a perfect world, where we could put out as big a paper as we wanted, yes. But that's just not the case."

Jacki gave an indignant sigh, grabbed up her bundle of papers to distribute, and stormed out.

"Whew!" said Don. "Has the temperature gone up a couple degrees?"

The rest of us chuckled and picked up our bundles, and Scott and I exchanged smiles as I left for the homerooms in the west corridor.

Liz seemed to have forgotten that she'd been upset with me when I told her I had a date for the dance with Scott, as though I'd been bragging or something. On the morning of the dance, as we were riding to school, she asked what I'd be wearing.

"My good jeans with a big red patch on the butt," I said.

"And I sewed some patches on a peasant blouse. For a while I even thought about wearing a black bonnet with a corncob pipe in my mouth and going as Mammy Yokum."

"Now, *that* would be a hit!" Liz laughed.

When we walked inside the building, we heard laughing and shrieking up and down the halls, and we saw that someone had scattered straw here and there in the corridors. And then we saw the chickens—a dozen hens, maybe, all clucking and squawking and skittering down the tile floors.

"What *is* this?" we laughed, but nobody seemed to know, except that a big hand-lettered sign just inside the entrance read dogpatch tonight.

Some of the teachers thought it was funny, but the principal didn't, and the custodian liked it least of all. We were pretty sure the dance committee had pulled the stunt, but finally the senior class president got on the mike and announced that anyone who caught and delivered a chicken to the custodian's room would get free admission to the Sadie Hawkins Day dance. Within fifteen minutes, each of the dozen hens had been cornered in a stairwell or a classroom, and the school eventually settled down.

I doubt that anyone will forget the first Sadie Hawkins Day we ever had—the morning, anyway. And when I saw Don in the hall later, he said, "I got some great pictures for the yearbook!"

5
STUPEFYIN' JONES

I was ready to leave the minute Scott rang the bell that evening, because I didn't want him to have to be inside our messy house one second longer than necessary. He was grinning when I opened the door.

"Got any chickens you need rounding up, ma'am?" he asked.

"Scott, were you the one who let those loose at school?" I said, laughing.

"No, but I know who did. *The Edge* never reveals its sources, though."

I realized it would be impolite not to invite him in, so I said, "Want to come in for a sec?"

He stepped in the microscopic space just inside the door. "Wow! These *are* close quarters, aren't they?"

"*Told* you!" I said, and called, "Dad? Sylvia? We're leaving."

They came downstairs—Dad in his bulky knit sweater and Sylvia in a turquoise sweatpants set. She had her camera.

"Hello, Scott," said Dad genially, shaking his hand, and Sylvia gave him a nice smile.

"Great costumes, you guys," she said. "Sounds like a fun evening."

"A new experience, anyway," said Scott. "Nice to meet you both."

I didn't know if he meant that it was me or the dance that was a new experience, but he was dressed for it, all right. He was wearing overalls over a knit polo shirt with heavy work boots on his feet.

"Ready?" he asked.

"Let me snap a picture first, and then I'll let you go," Sylvia said.

We paused in the doorway for the flash. Then I threw on an old jacket with patches sewn on the sleeves, we said our good-byes, and we walked across the wood plank sidewalk on the front lawn. I guess I could be grateful I wasn't wearing a floor-length gown, trailing in the muddy snow, but it was still humiliating. Even more so when I opened the car door and heard a girl's voice saying, ". . . but in their front *yard*?" I knew that Christy Levin had spotted the Porta-John.

I couldn't see her face very well as I slid in the front seat.

The light went off again as Scott closed my door, but I did get a glimpse of a brunette with a topknot on her head, finely arched eyebrows, and a bright red mouth.

"Hey, Alice!" said Don.

"Hi, Don. Hi, Christy," I said, and immediately wondered why Scott had picked me up last.

As Scott started the car, he said, "They're in my neighborhood, so I picked them up first."

"Anyone heard of this band? The Yokum Hokem?" asked Christy.

Don laughed. "Probably just a bunch of guys who change their name for every event."

"Did you bring your camera, or are you off duty tonight?" Scott asked him.

"Off duty, man! Sam's going to take the pictures," Don said.

Great. I was going to this dance with my crush, Scott Lynch; my ex-boyfriend, Sam Mayer, was taking pictures; and I had a date to the prom with my former boyfriend, Patrick Long. Did I even have a clue about what was really going on inside my head?

It was a fun band, whether they had an official name or not: two fiddles, a guitar, drums, an accordion, and a harmonica player who also strummed a washboard with metal picks on his fingers.

There were no live chickens this time, but the art class had painted a large backdrop behind the band—a log cabin with a crooked chimney, a couple pigs in the foreground, and a winding path leading up into the mountains.

And around the edge of the gym were all sorts of fun stuff from the comic strip: a "Kickapoo Joy Juice" stand; a bowling alley with Schmoos for pins; a cave for Lonesome Polecat and Hairless Joe; a corner named Lower Slobbovia. Different members of the Drama Club wandered about the gym, dressed as Al Capp characters: Moonbeam McSwine, General Bullmoose, Pappy Yokum, Senator Phogbound, Joe Btfsplk, and Appassionata von Climax.

Most of the girls came in Daisy Mae Scragg's off-the-shoulder tops, paired with either tight jeans or short, tight skirts. A lot of the guys tried to look like Li'l Abner, with his big shock of hair in front. But nobody really cared. Any article of clothing with a patch on it would do.

Pamela and Tim came the closest to looking like the real thing. Somewhere Tim had got overalls with only one strap across the shoulder.

"Hey, Tim! Way to go!" I said, and we all clapped when they were declared the Best Dogpatch Look-Alikes—even better than Jill and Justin, who usually win the prize for any couples' event.

And then there was the dancing. Of all the times I'd worked with Scott on the newspaper, all the times we'd leaned over a layout or stacked bundles of newspapers in each other's arms or sat together in the sub shop waiting for the printed copies from next door—none of those times were we face-to-face, our bodies only an inch apart, hand in hand.

The first time he slid one hand behind my back and took my other hand in his, my heart leaped like a startled cricket. I was almost afraid he could feel it.

When we weren't dancing, we wandered around the gym, posed for photos with "Marryin' Sam" (Sam Mayer), me with a short little bridal veil on my head, Scott with a coonskin cap. Sam was still friendly with me, and I'm glad, because it would have been awkward working together on the paper if he wasn't. As long as Sam has a girlfriend, he's fine, and he was going out with a sophomore now, who adored him.

We watched the Jumping Frog contest and the Spittin' contest, and Christy and I sat down in a booth to listen to Mammy Yokum give a two-minute lecture called "Now That You've Got Your Man, What Are You Goin' to Do with 'im?"

Mammy Yokum was another member of the Drama Club, a short girl in a black bonnet, black fitted jacket, tight skirt, and striped stockings. She was really good. She talked with a corncob pipe dangling out one side of her mouth.

"This har's mah advice," she said. "Keep his stomach full, his hair cut, his toenails trimmed, his bed warm, and his dog fed, and ya'll won't have no trouble."

"And if he's out chasing other women?" Christy asked, to keep her going.

"Honey, he run so long and so fast afore you caught 'im, he's not about to go runnin' agin," Mammy Yokum said.

We paid her with the "Rasbuckniks" that were given out as we entered the gym. The sign said that one Rasbucknik was worth nothing, and a bunch was worth even less due to the trouble of carrying them around.

We were about to try on some "Wolf Gal" fashions when

Sean Murphy, chairman of the dance committee, took the mike, and a drumroll got the kids' attention.

"Hey, y'all," he shouted. "How ya doin'?" And after a few introductory jokes he said he was about to announce an unannounced event. We quieted down, and he continued: "As you know, Sadie Hawkins Day was established to help every gal get her man. Now, I don't know how many of you guys was roped and hog-tied into comin' or how many of you came willingly— *eagerly*, even. But it wouldn't be Sadie Hawkins Day without a bona fide, gen-u-ine, all-leather, one hundred percent natural Sadie Hawkins Day race!"

We all looked around, wondering if we were going to have to chase our dates.

"But relax, men," Sean continued. "You guys out there have already been caught. I want y'all to stand back now, clear a big open space—the whole basketball court, to be exact—'cause Earthquake McGoon here, the world's dirtiest wrassler . . ." He stepped aside as a rough-looking guy walked through the gym door behind him, holding his arms up in a victory salute. ". . . is going to be chased by the one and only, the most beautiful, most gorgeous *Stupefyin' Jones*!"

The gym door opened again, and in came a girl in a long black wig, sleekly curled, and a skimpy dress made of leaves or something. The plunging neckline exposed the top of her bulging breasts.

All the guys whistled and clapped.

I could only stare. Pamela, standing a few feet away, was staring too. Who *was* it? Somehow she looked familiar. . . .

And then Pamela gasped: "Omigod! It's *Elizabeth*!"

It was.

There are some things just too hard to believe. The breasts, for one! But there she stood, barefoot, one hand on her hip, looking seductively out over the crowd.

"Now, we all know that Stupefyin' Jones, according to Al Capp," Sean went on, "was so drop-dead gorgeous that she could literally freeze men in their tracks, just at the sight of her."

Here Earthquake McGoon glanced over at Liz and immediately stood motionless, mouth hanging open, eyes unblinking.

"So you might think," said Sean, as McGoon began to breathe again, "that she could have almost any man she wanted in Dogpatch. But sometimes there's a shortage of men, and even the most beautiful, the most voluptuous . . ."—here Liz let her fingers slide slowly down her body as Pamela and I shrieked with laughter—". . . is liable to get a little desperate." Liz's feet pawed at the ground, and she licked her lips as she leaned toward Earthquake McGoon.

"So this is it, folks. The big race! Earthquake McGoon, in a race for his life and his bachelorhood, versus the beautiful, the sexy, the fabulous Stupefyin' Jones! Let's hear it, everybody!"

We all cheered and whooped like mad, but . . . We still couldn't believe it. *Elizabeth?* Why? How? When? Who had persuaded her?

Everyone backed up a little and jockeyed for a good place to watch the race.

"Ready?" Sean said. "Take your places."

Earthquake McGoon scratched his belly and moved a couple yards in front of Liz.

"Set!" Sean called.

Both McGoon and Jones bent in the usual racer's stance.

"Go!" Sean yelled, and somebody fired a blank.

McGoon started running, Jones close behind, and it was obvious that this was a comedy act they had rehearsed. He would stumble, she'd almost catch him, he'd speed up, she'd be close behind. . . . Around the gym they went, Sean keeping up a commentator's rap: "And Jones is gaining, she's gaining, folks . . . around the bend and . . . Oops! Jones almost stumbles, but she's off again, and . . . Wait! Where's McGoon? Where the heck did he go?"

Detouring around the bleachers, McGoon was in and out of the crowd, everyone shrieking, urging them on. Once or twice Liz almost had him, but McGoon escaped her grasp. At long last, she caught him by the back of his pants, and down he went, yelping, braying, howling, pleading.

When he finally lay still, Stupefyin' Jones bent down to kiss him. Then—her face full of revulsion—she stood up again, holding her nose, and with a rejecting wave of her hand, walked away.

Everybody cheered again, whistling and clapping.

"Can you *believe* this?" I cried to Pamela. "Can you believe *her*?"

"She never said one word!" Pamela gasped.

"Isn't she the girl who went with you to do that feature story last year?" asked Scott.

"Yes!" I said. "I still can't believe this."

"A girl of many talents," said Scott.

"And she just joined the girls' track team!" I said in amazement.

"Not surprised," said Scott.

What was it like for Liz, out there in front of everybody, getting applause, everyone cheering? I wondered. For a moment I wished *I* were Liz, yet I hated to think I was jealous.

While the race had been going on, the buffet table opened behind us. Now people were moving toward the food, and I told Scott I'd join him in a minute. But first Pamela and I just had to find Liz, and we saw her, all right, with kids gathered around her, Liz all smiles.

All we could say when we grabbed her was "Liz!"

The three of us laughed, and her eyes just sparkled.

"You knew all the time you'd be here?" I asked.

"No, only a week ago," she said. Then she told us how Sean had called her and said they were looking for a girl from the track team to play Stupefyin' Jones, and someone had suggested her.

"But I just joined a month ago," she'd told him, and Sean had said never mind, he'd seen her picture. Would she do it? "My first thought was no, because I'd never heard of the character," Liz continued, "but when he said she was drop-dead gorgeous and all I had to do was run, I thought, 'I can do that!' So then we practiced, and I had a ball. It was so much fun! And it didn't matter if anyone laughed at me, because they were *supposed* to laugh."

"You were great!" Pam said.

"I was mostly afraid I'd fall, but they said that whatever happened, just make it part of the act, and it worked."

"Wow, Liz. What a part!" I told her. "You're a natural comedian! But . . ." My eyes dropped to her breasts. "How . . . ?"

She caught my arm and whispered, "Shhh. It's a push-up bra."

"Well, it . . . and *you* were fabulous," said Pamela.

Some guys were coming over to talk to Liz, so Pam went back to find Tim and I joined Scott in the buffet line. There were buffalo wings and smoked sausages, biscuits, corn, and blueberry pie. We sat on folding chairs along one side of the gym, and other kids crawled up in the bleachers. I hadn't had a chance to really talk much with Christy, so I took the chair next to hers. But she and Don were discussing a foreign film they'd seen, so I didn't have anything to add to the conversation.

Scott and I made another round of the gym, looking for things worth mentioning in a write-up. We stopped at the GSA table to look at the group's new brochure, and Scott talked with Phil and Lori about how many schools have a Gay/Straight Alliance.

Then the music started again and people began dancing. Christy and Don went back out on the floor. I went to the restroom and rinsed my mouth, put on fresh lip gloss, relined my eyes. When I went back upstairs, the music was slower, a bit more romantic. When Scott led me onto the floor, I waited for that little squeeze of the hand that meant he was enjoying himself, the tightening of his arm around my waist, an almost imperceptible tugging, pulling me toward him. . . .

It didn't happen, though. He smiled at me a lot, but it also seemed as though his eyes looked over my shoulder much of the time. He was polite, he was gallant, he was all the things a date should be. But I could tell he just wasn't all that excited by me.

A half hour before the dance was to end, he told me that Don and Christy wanted to leave, did I mind? I guess I didn't. I think I was ready for the evening to end. But it didn't.

"We're going for coffee, Alice. That okay?" Scott asked. "Starbucks is still open."

"Sure," I said. At least they had invited me. They could have taken me home first and gone out, just the three of them, and talked about what a drag I'd been, I suppose. So I put on my happy face and ordered a caramel latte with extra cream. Why did I get the feeling that somebody else was in control of the evening? That I was sort of here by default, because I'd paid for Scott's ticket?

I guess Christy's the type of girl you'd call handsome, not beautiful. An interesting face. Deep-set eyes topped by those carefully plucked eyebrows. A fine thin nose. Exceptionally white teeth. I wondered what she thought of me.

"Hope Sam got some good shots," Scott said to me over his triple mocha. "There were sure plenty of photo ops. We'll do a double-page spread on the dance."

"You write for the paper too?" Christy asked me, meaning that Scott had probably not talked about me at all on the way over. Maybe I wasn't worth mentioning. A byline wasn't exactly an attention-getter, nothing like running around the gym in a push-up bra.

Scott answered for me. "She sure does. Alice wrote that 'City at Night' piece last fall. Oops. We're supposed to keep that one anonymous."

"The article about two girls out on the town at night?" said Christy. "It was sort of . . . anticlimactic, wasn't it?"

"Well, it wasn't fiction, you know," said Scott.

"It had its moments," said Don. "Especially when that car full of guys stopped. . . ."

Christy just smiled at me indulgently. Then, turning to Scott, she said, "Any word from colleges yet?"

"Nope," he said. "I've applied to four, so we'll see what happens."

"I already know where I'm going," said Don. "Montgomery College. My dad says it doesn't really matter where you go the first two years as long as your grades are good. Get an associate degree, then transfer to a really good school, graduate from there. Save a heap of money."

"That's what my brother did, and he's getting his master's this spring," I volunteered, glad to be part of the conversation.

"Really," said Christy. "What's his major?"

"Philosophy," I told her.

"I'm impressed," said Don.

"So am I," I said, and everyone smiled.

But that was my last contribution for the evening, because the talk turned to student loans, where to get the best deals on used cars, then a film festival that all three of them had attended in Baltimore. Somehow the conversation always seemed about two steps ahead of me, just beyond my reach. Whatever I felt I had to add seemed ordinary, even juvenile, at times. So I kept quiet.

Was it just me feeling insecure? Or did one extra year of high school make that much difference? I wondered.

I'd have to describe the end of the evening as uneventful. Nobody said anything rude. I couldn't even say I was ignored. It was just that they could sort of take me or leave me, like it was okay if I was there and okay if I wasn't.

When it was time to leave at last, Scott helped me on with my jacket and kidded around a little with the girl at the counter who asked about our costumes.

"Fun evening, Alice," Scott said as he walked me up to our porch. "Thanks for the invitation."

"I'm glad you could come," I said. I didn't have to wonder if I should invite him in, because Don and Christy were waiting for him out in the car. "Good night, Scott," I said, looking up at him.

"G'night," he said, and kissed me on the forehead. The forehead! Like I was eleven years old or something. He squeezed my hand, then trotted back down the steps, across the board sidewalk to the street, and as he opened his door, I opened mine. They closed at exactly the same time.

6
INTIMATE CONVERSATION

The best part of having a new adventure is telling your friends. Even a bummer can have the makings of a good story. For Elizabeth, the Sadie Hawkins Day dance was a terrific tale she could tell again and again. But for me, the dance was a sort of nonevent. There was no romance to report, no huge embarrassment to share.

At the Melody Inn the next morning, I wished I hadn't told anyone I was going to the dance. Both Marilyn, Dad's assistant manager, and David were watching for me, anticipation in their eyes.

"No," I said, giving them what I hoped was a wry smile as I slipped my bag under the counter.

"Oh?" said Marilyn.

"Neither good nor bad."

"Okay," she said, and knew enough not to ask more.

"A blah sort of evening," I told David. "Nothing spectacular either way."

"It happens," he said.

Dad and Sylvia had been curious, of course, but mostly I talked about Liz and how funny and fabulous she had been. They laughed at my description of the big race. When I told them that Scott and Don and Christy and I had gone to Starbucks later, and that Scott brought me home first, that seemed to answer whatever else Dad needed to know. But I could tell from Sylvia's eyes that being brought home first, when your date is doing the driving, is not a good thing.

"Well," she said, in a confidential whisper, "you have the prom to look forward to, don't you?"

"Yes!" I said. She understood.

Pamela invited Liz and me to her house for a sleepover that evening so we could talk about the dance. I figured we'd chill out in Pamela's bedroom, but when I got there, Mr. Jones and Meredith—the woman he's engaged to—said they were going into D.C. for dinner and a show, and Meredith had left taco fixings for us. So we sprawled out on the living-room rug instead.

"I can't wait until our remodeling is finished and I can invite you over," I told them.

"Neither can we!" said Pamela. "It's been ages since I've been inside your house. When will they be finished?"

"A couple of weeks, they're telling us. At least, that's when the plastic sheets come down and we can start moving our stuff into the new addition."

"Did you invite Scott to come in?" asked Liz.

"Are you kidding? I was ready to go the minute he came to the door," I joked, and immediately changed the subject. "Liz, when did you get to the dance? What did they do—keep you hidden until the big moment? And why didn't you *tell* us?"

She giggled. "I waited until they called, and then Dad drove me over. They told me not to tell *any*one about the race, so I didn't."

"Well, you sure had a crowd around you the last time I checked," said Pamela, grinning. "Mostly guys, too!"

Liz was positively radiant. "You know what one boy said to me? 'I never would have suspected.' I asked what he meant by that, and he looked embarrassed. He just mumbled something about how funny I was, but later—when the music started again—he came back and we danced."

"Well! Liz!" I said, smiling. "Who was he?"

"I didn't even get his name. Another guy came over, and then I danced with him."

Pamela and I beamed at her like proud mamas. The next best thing to having a great evening yourself is seeing one of your friends, who really needs it, having a good time. And then we noticed that Liz looked a bit—well, more than a bit—fuller under her crewneck T-shirt.

"Keeping a little reminder of the Sadie Hawkins Day dance?" I said, nodding toward her chest.

She laughed. "Yeah. I thought I'd try out the push-up bra, get a little more use out of it. Unless it's false advertising."

"Hey, guys will like you for more than that," I said.

"Let's hope," said Elizabeth.

Pamela turned her attention to me. "Soooo," she said, dumping another spoonful of meat in a taco shell, then heaping on the cheese. She took a crunchy bite and chewed for a minute. "How'd it go with Scott?"

I didn't want to prolong the pain. "It was just an okay evening," I said. "We went to Starbucks afterward with Don and Christy, then he brought me home. *Before* he took them home."

Pamela winced. "Ouch," she said.

"I know." I idly ran my finger over my plate, picking up the odd bits of cheese.

"No . . . sparks?" asked Liz.

"Not really. We danced. He was sweet. Attentive. Friendly. How's that? No cheek-to-cheek dancing. No hand squeezes."

"What happened when he got you home?" asked Pamela, as though if she kept at it long enough, she could extract *something*.

I sighed. "He kissed me on the forehead."

Pam and Liz both groaned.

"But it's a *start*, maybe," Liz said encouragingly.

"Well, if he had to start somewhere, I'd suggest farther down," said Pamela, and at least that made us laugh. If you can laugh with your girlfriends, you don't feel all that bad.

"Did he at least have a good time?" Liz asked.

"I think so. He liked all the stuff connected to Sadie Hawkins—we all did. The Schmoo bowling alley and stuff. The food was good. He liked the conversation with Don and Christy about colleges and student loans and stuff, but I was more or less a bystander. I mean, what do I know?"

"So there just wasn't any . . . guy/girl sort of feeling? On his part, I mean? Nothing sexy?" asked Pamela.

"I'd say it was more just friends," I said ruefully.

We sat quietly for a few moments.

"I saw him stop at the GSA table," said Pamela. "Maybe he's gay."

"Maybe he's *not!*" I said. "He took a girl to the Snow Ball. Maybe it's *me*. Why is it that whenever a guy doesn't pay attention to a girl, some girls assume he must be gay?"

"I didn't say there was anything wrong with it," Pamela said.

"Of course there isn't, but why can't it be that he's just not that into me? Period."

"Then why did he agree to go?" asked Liz.

"Maybe he wasn't sure how he felt about me. Maybe he was just curious. Maybe he hoped bells would ring and violins would play, and it didn't happen. Who knows?"

"But . . . what's not to like, Alice? You looked wonderful!" said Pamela.

That made me laugh in spite of myself. "So did a hundred other girls. You don't fall for every guy just because he looks good and is interested in you, do you?" My eyes narrowed. "*Do* you?"

"Is that a trick question?" Pamela asked, and we laughed.

She settled back against the cushions we'd propped against the couch. "I think I'm just plain lucky to have Tim, because it's not just looks that matter to us. We talk a lot. I've never liked a guy as much as I like Tim, you know?"

I grinned. "I know it. If you'd been dancing any closer, you'd have been joined by osmosis."

Pamela glanced at me quickly and there was something about her face, her smile. . . .

"Pamela?" I said.

She pretended to wipe her mouth, but I think she was trying to disguise her smile. "Yeah, we're close," she said.

I studied her. "How close is *close*?"

"Close," said Pamela.

Liz looked as though she were holding her breath. "*Close* close?" she asked.

"*Close* close," said Pamela. Anyone listening to our conversation would have thought we were insane.

"You . . . you . . . did *it*?" I asked, and I'm not sure why I was surprised, but I was. I mean, we had promised each other once, the three of us, that whoever had sex first—intercourse, I mean—would tell the others what it was like.

"Oh . . . my . . . God!" Liz gasped.

"Wow!" I said.

"And you didn't *tell* us?" Liz cried.

Pamela laughed. "I wasn't about to ask your permission."

"*When?*" I said. "For how long?"

"Two months ago," Pamela told us, smiling down at her hands. "And six or seven times since."

"Whew!" I said, trying hard to take it all in.

Liz was still astonished. "*Where?*"

"Here. Dad works until six, you know. Tim's house sometimes. And, yes, Liz, quit looking at me like that. We do use condoms, if that's what you were about to ask."

Liz giggled.

What to ask? Man, oh, man, this was important. This was education. This was . . . *Pamela!*

"Okay, tell all," I said. "What was it like?"

There was a sparkle in her eyes. "Well, imagine waves crashing against the shore and fireworks going off and an avalanche," she said.

"*That's* what it's like?" asked Liz.

"No," said Pamela, and we giggled some more. "It isn't like any of that. But it's exciting and it feels good and it's a little frustrating and you don't want it to stop. And just thinking about doing it makes you want to do it again."

I was trying to put those pieces together and come out with an "experience," but I was having a hard time of it. I began to wonder if we should be asking all these personal questions. I wanted details, but it also seemed very private. I was sure it was private when Pamela said, "I figure it gets better with time. We're still exploring . . ."—she broke into a smile again—". . . and that's the fun part."

We knew then that the question period was over, but Liz

had one more: "Just tell me this: The first time, does it hurt?"

"Yeah. Enough that I made him stop. I was bleeding a little. We tried again later. Once you heal, though, after a couple of days, you're fine. It's sort of like a little cut down there."

Liz pushed back against the pillows and thrust both hands between her legs. "That's it. I'm going to be a nun," she said.

"No, you're not. You'll love it. Choose a gentle guy, though. Don't let it be someone like Brian."

We both looked at her. "Brian Brewster? Did he ever . . . ?"

"No, but he wanted to. I can't imagine Brian being gentle with anyone."

We thought about that a moment.

"You know, I thought he might change after the accident," said Liz. "I really thought that he'd think about that little girl and what the accident might mean for the rest of her life, but he's just been a cranky bore. All he does is complain because he can't drive for a year."

"It's like he goes around with a big 'Me' sign on his shirt," I added. "If Brian was religious, he'd worship himself. It's as though that little girl is an obstacle to his career. 'Man, I've got things to do!' he says. 'This is my junior year. It's not like I purposely tried to hurt someone.'"

We groaned.

"You know what I heard?" said Pamela. "Keeno told me that Brian's dad promised him a new car if he'd just wait out the year without getting in any more trouble. A *new car*!"

Keeno, a friend of Brian's from another school, probably

knows him better than anyone else. Sometimes he goes to the movies with us. But I think maybe he's getting a little sick of Brian too.

"Oh, man!" I said.

"Anyone ever meet his dad? Maybe he's just as self-centered as Brian," said Liz. "I've heard that if you want to know what your future husband will be like in twenty years, take a look at his dad. I suppose that goes for a girl, too—she'll be like her mother. Which means that any guy who is serious about me should study my mom. Now *there's* a sobering thought."

Pamela rolled her eyes. "God forbid! Or *mine!*"

I was the only one who didn't say anything. I couldn't even understand the feeling. I would give anything in this world to be like my mother. To *see* my mother. To know what she had really been like.

By the time I went to school on Monday, I began to feel that my crush on Scott was fading. There's something about knowing for sure that you aren't special to somebody that both breaks your heart and frees you. Or maybe I'm just the kind of girl who doesn't go after the unattainable. I've never been nuts over a celebrity—guys I know I'll never have or perhaps wouldn't even like if I got to know them.

If Scott had loved me madly once and now he didn't, that would be one thing. If I had rejected him and now I wanted him back, that would be different too. But when I saw him at his locker Monday and stopped by to say hello, and he smiled that same friendly, platonic smile as before, I didn't feel my pulse speed up the way I used to. Just a little ache.

The romance wasn't over, because it had never really begun. What I mean is, *I* was over it. I no longer imagined that his smile meant something personal. And when we had our next staff meeting for *The Edge* on Wednesday, I didn't get the familiar *ting* when we worked side by side and our arms touched. I *had* been crushing on him, but there was also a wisp of a thought that I'd wanted to go out with him at least once to compare him to Patrick—to see what kind of guy I preferred. No, I was definitely over him. I think. . . .

Two months ago, I thought I had a handle on who I was. Now I wasn't so sure.

Lester called that night and I was trying to explain it to him. He'd wanted to ask Dad about something, but Dad wasn't home, and he got me instead.

"I used to think I knew the real Alice," I told him. "'Almost Alice' is more like it. I'm not absolutely positive I'm over Scott; I'm not completely sure that Patrick and I are right for each other, and if we are, how serious we should get; I wish I could do something wild and funny like Liz did at the dance, but I don't know if it's really me. . . ."

"Why do you have to have the answers to any of this right now?" Les asked me.

"I just want to be sure of *something*, Lester! If I can't be sure about a guy, can't I at least be sure of myself?"

"But *why*?" he asked. "Why do you have to have your future

all wrapped up like a Christmas present, ready for you to open when you're twenty-five or something? Why can't you just relax and let things happen?"

"I don't know," I answered. "I just can't."

7
PUSHING PAMELA

When you can't figure yourself out, you concentrate on friends, and that's why I now focused on Pamela. Liz and Gwen and I were determined that she try out for a part in the spring musical, *Guys and Dolls*, to be performed the last two weekends in April. A sign-up sheet for auditions was posted outside the choir room, and anyone could ask to borrow a copy of the songs and to try out between March 10 and 12. The cast would be posted on Friday, March 14.

It's weird about Pamela. In elementary school she was a real show-off and loved being the center of attention. She always said she wanted to be an actress or a model, and she got the lead in our sixth-grade play. In high school she joined the Drama Club in her freshman year, then dropped out the second semester. She said she couldn't possibly compete with all those talented people. I finally persuaded her to sign up again last year— just for stage crew along with me—and she did. But even though she's been taking voice lessons, she still doesn't feel she's "good enough" to try for anything more.

Liz and Gwen and I decided to change all that.

First, I called Tim. "We need your help," I said. "We want to persuade Pamela to try out for *Guys and Dolls*, but she really needs a push. Do you think you could talk her into it?"

"I suggested it myself," he said. "She sings when she's around me. She sings around you guys. She sings along with the car radio. But when I try to get her to—you know—really perform, she clams up. I'll see what I can do."

Next, Liz invited Pamela and Tim and Gwen and me to her house on Friday night just to hang out—watch a DVD or something, she said. Gwen had signed out a book of songs from *Guys and Dolls* and brought it along with her.

"One guy and four girls?" Pamela had asked when Liz told her who was coming.

"I'll let my little brother hang with us," Liz joked.

It was Tim who brought the video of *Guys and Dolls*, starring Frank Sinatra, Jean Simmons, Vivian Blaine, and Marlon Brando, who, would you believe, sang "Luck Be a Lady."

"Hey! What *is* this?" Pamela asked suspiciously as the credits rolled on the screen and we passed the popcorn around.

"Stage crew's supposed to watch it, remember?" I said. "Get some idea of what we'll be dealing with." We watched the singers and dancers converge on Times Square. The story, of course, is about a gambler who bets another that he can't get a date with the pretty Salvation Army–type sergeant, Sarah Brown.

"We just want to get you interested, Pamela, that's all," Liz said. "You can sing! You can dance! You can act! You're a natural!"

Pamela only laughed and answered in a Brooklyn accent, just like the character Adelaide: "Aw, youse guiys, quit ya kiddin'." We laughed.

To tell the truth, we were only thinking about Pamela being in the chorus line when the movie began.

"Hey, Pamela, you can do that!" Liz would say when a dancer kicked up one leg.

"And don't tell us you can't sing like that," Gwen said when Sister Sarah began "Follow the Fold."

We shrieked and cried, "Oh, Pamela, that's you!" when the chorus girls, dressed like sexy cats, sang "Pet Me, Poppa," even though we didn't know how much of the movie version or even the Broadway performance would make it into the script of a high school musical.

But we got quieter as the movie went on, and I think we all began to realize that not only was Pamela right for the chorus, but she would be great for the part of Adelaide, Nathan Detroit's girlfriend, who's been trying for fourteen years to get him to marry her.

Pamela has short blond hair like Adelaide's; she's cute, like

Adelaide; and—like Adelaide—Pamela can sing up a storm. If she didn't chicken out, that is.

When Gwen finally put it into words—"Pamela, Adelaide is *you*!"—we all began talking at once. Every time Pamela raised an objection, we threw popcorn at her. Liz's three-year-old brother heard the commotion and ran in to join the fun.

We watched the movie through to the end, of course, but whenever the ditzy Adelaide sang another song, especially "Adelaide's Lament," we knew just how right the whole musical was for our beloved, ditzy, risk-taking, act-without-thinking Pamela.

"All right already! I'll sign up for the chorus!" she said finally, and at least that was a start.

When Monday came, we all escorted her down to the sign-up sheet to witness her signature for the chorus. It wasn't till the next day that Pamela discovered Tim had signed her up to audition for Adelaide, too.

Patrick didn't think we ought to have done that.

We've talked once since he got home from that thing in Baltimore. He asked how the dance went and—can you believe this?—whether Scott was a good dancer, and I said it went fine and I had no complaints about Scott's dancing. That's all he wanted to know, which was disappointing. I was still smarting from that.

"I didn't sign Pamela up for the Adelaide audition," I said. "It was Tim."

"But you're all pushing her. I think that when she's ready to try out for a part, she'll do it," Patrick said.

Sometimes he really gets on my nerves. I'd been lying on my back on the bed, but now I propped myself up on one elbow, holding the phone to my ear. "Patrick, you've probably never had to be pushed to do anything in your life except eat broccoli," I said. "You're so motivated, you could move a mountain, but not everyone is like you. Right now Pamela needs all the support she can get."

"Have you ever thought that maybe the more you reassure her, the more she might feel she needs it?" Patrick said. "If you just said, 'Pamela, you know you can do it, and it's up to you whether or not you audition,' it might make her feel more confident?"

I wasn't sure of anything except that I wanted Patrick to be a little bit jealous that I went to the dance with Scott, and if he couldn't be jealous, couldn't he at least be curious? Didn't he even wonder if Scott held me close when we danced? Kissed me? I should be the topic of conversation here, not Pamela.

"Maybe you're right," I said flatly. What did I mean to him, anyway? Maybe he just asked me to the prom because he was afraid if he put it off, he'd forget. Maybe he just wanted to make sure he had a date. Old reliable Alice.

"Anyway," Patrick went on, "the orchestra got the music for *Guys and Dolls* last week. I'll be doing percussion."

I forgot momentarily that Patrick plays the drums for both the band and the orchestra—Patrick, the master of all trades: orchestra, band, track, Chess Club, debate team. . . . Why the heck didn't he run for class president while he was at it?

"Good for you," I said.

There were a few seconds of silence, and then he asked, "Alice? Something wrong?"

"Yes," I said. "Life is so easy for you, Patrick. You succeed in everything you do while—"

"Whoa! Whoa!" he said. "Where did you get that idea?"

"But isn't it true?"

"Not by a long shot. You don't know the half of it."

I felt a little foolish then. "When will I know the other half?"

"Oh, when the time's right," said Patrick.

I didn't ask when that might be, because with Patrick, there's never enough time. But he made it sound as though he might *make* time for me somewhere down the line. I guess I'd wait.

He did have a point about Pamela. The way we kept pushing and persuading her must have made her feel as though she couldn't do it on her own. So when she called me that Tuesday night and said she was furious at Tim for putting her name on the list for Adelaide and she wasn't going to audition tomorrow, I said, "You're right, Pamela. He shouldn't have done that. And I apologize for all of us for trying to make you do something you don't want. I think you know you can sing and dance better than most of us, and we know it, but it's entirely up to you."

We didn't see her before school on Wednesday. Gwen said she checked the sign-up list, and Pamela hadn't crossed out her name for either the chorus or for Adelaide, but we didn't know if she was going to audition or not. No one else could attend the auditions—only the names on the sign-up sheet. Mr. Gage (the choir director), Mr. Ellis (the drama coach), and Miss Ortega (the dance teacher), along with a piano player, would be the only other people in the room during tryouts. They said they didn't want any cheering sections watching from the wings.

I got all this from Charlene Verona, the girl who drove everyone nuts back in ninth grade when she got the part of Tzeitel in *Fiddler on the Roof*. I hoped she wasn't trying out for the part of Adelaide and was glad when she said she auditioned to play the role of Sarah Brown.

Pamela didn't call me Wednesday night, and we didn't call her. Gwen and Liz and I made a vow we wouldn't even bring up the topic at lunch the next day. It was a struggle, though. It was Charlene, of course, who spilled the beans. She breezed by our table as we were finishing our sandwiches and said breathlessly, "We both got callbacks, Pamela! Wouldn't it be great if I played Sister Sarah and you played Adelaide?"

We looked at Pamela and began to grin.

"Way to go, girl!" said Gwen.

Gwen and I went to visit Molly after school on Thursday. She was up in her room, working at the computer, baseball cap tipped at an angle on her head.

"Hey!" Gwen said. "How you doing?"

"Busy!" Molly answered, giving us a smile.

We threw our jackets on the bed. "Homework?" I asked.

"Stage crew," said Molly. "Mr. Ellis put me in charge of props." We stared. "He called last week and asked if I wanted to be part of stage crew again this year, and I said yes. So he e-mailed me a list of all the props, and I'm seeing how many I can find for him."

"Great!" I said, sending Mr. Ellis a hug by mental telepathy. "What have you got so far?"

Molly read off some things from her screen. "The print shop's working with the auto shop to make a Times Square street sign; an art class is doing the lettering for the Save-a-Soul Mission; the band's supplying a bass drum; a church is supplying the hymnbooks; a thrift shop is loaning us some fifties dresses; and a restaurant says we can borrow two fake palm trees for the scene in Havana."

Gwen and I hooted with laughter. "Oh, Molly, you're amazing!" Gwen said.

She grinned. "That's what my doctor said."

"Really?"

"So far so good," said Molly.

"Wonderful!" we told her.

"So who's trying out?" she wanted to know. "Pamela would be so good with that music."

"Actually, she tried out for the part of Adelaide, but the cast hasn't been posted yet," I said.

"Adelaide?" shrieked Molly. "The ditzy girlfriend? The one who sings 'Take Back Your Mink'? She'd be great!"

"Yeah, but there are lots of girls trying out, and they always cast seniors when possible," I said. "But drink the rest of your

milk shake and I'll show you the photos we're using in the newspaper of the Sadie Hawkins Day dance."

Molly made a face, picked up her half-full glass, and dutifully drank the rest of her shake. Then we sat together on the
cushioned window seat in her bedroom and I showed her the
first photo.

"Omigod!" She gasped. "Is that . . . is that Liz?"

"Stupefyin' Jones in the flesh," I said.

Gwen hadn't seen the photos yet either—they'd be coming
out in the next issue of *The Edge*—so we had some laughs. I wondered after a while whether this was helping or hurting . . . if I
wasn't just reminding Molly of all the things she was missing. But
she genuinely looked as though she were having a good time. And
when we put the last photo back in the envelope, she said, "I plan
on coming to one of the performances of *Guys and Dolls* and going
onstage for a curtain call with the rest of the crew."

"Yay, Molly!" I said.

We were waiting for the official cast to be posted on Friday,
the last day before spring vacation. Callbacks had been the day
before, and those who were on the final list today were to pick
up their scripts and music to study over the break. After we
came back, there would be four weeks of rehearsals, with performances the next two weekends.

A little crowd had gathered just before homeroom, but the
list wasn't up yet. I went by after first period, and it still wasn't
there. Tim was checking too.

"Fingers crossed," he said.

Just before lunch, we heard that the list was up. Pamela wouldn't come. Gwen and Liz and I rushed down to the choir room and strained to see over the heads of the others. The hall was already filled now with squeals and cheers as well as murmurs of disappointment. All the big parts had gone to seniors, and a girl named Kelsey Reeves would play Adelaide. But Pamela was listed as her understudy, and she made the chorus, too.

"Do we cheer or console each other?" I asked Gwen.

"Cheer," said Gwen. "This might be just what she needed. It will give her confidence without scaring her to death."

What I was thinking, though, was that this had been Pamela's chance to shine. The school alternates each year between plays and musicals. During our freshman year, the musical was *Fiddler on the Roof*. During sophomore year, the play was *Father of the Bride*. Now it was time for a musical again, and in our senior year, it would be a play.

But I think Gwen was right about Pamela. We cheered when we saw her, and I think she was both happy and relieved. The casting group had recognized her talent without making her the center of attention.

"I've got to learn the whole thing, just like Kelsey Reeves," she said excitedly. "Same costumes and everything, except I'm in the chorus too, so I have to learn all their songs! And dance! I have to do some of the dances!"

"Say good-bye to Tim for the duration," I joked. But I was ashamed that I'd managed to stick a little needle in the celebration.

* * *

The fact was, none of us would have a lot of time over spring break. Dad asked me to work at the Melody Inn—the store was having a spring clearance sale; Pamela was memorizing Adelaide's lines and learning the songs; Liz was putting in applications for a summer job; and Gwen was working five afternoons instead of two at the health clinic.

Some kids were going on trips with their families. Karen and her mom, for instance, were going to New York, and Justin's folks were virtually kidnapping him for a trip to the Bahamas because, as Jill said, they were doing everything possible to separate her from Justin. Charlene Verona said she didn't have time to be in the musical after all (now that she didn't get a lead part) because she was getting ready for a ballet recital, and Patrick was working again part-time for the landscaper he'd worked for last summer. That left Mark Stedmeister, who was repairing an old car he was buying from his dad. I didn't know what Brian Brewster was doing, and I didn't care.

I'd promised myself I'd start looking at prom dresses over spring break, but to be honest, I dreaded it. Neither Liz nor Pam nor Gwen had been invited to this prom yet, so if we went shopping together, it would be all for me.

I'm just one of those girls who doesn't especially like to shop. I want to be gorgeous and have nice clothes; I just don't like to go looking for them and trying stuff on.

When I went to work on Saturday, I asked Marilyn what I

should do. Dad's assistant manager was looking more beautiful by the day. I figured marriage had something to do with it.

"Where should I start looking?" I asked.

"Depends," said Marilyn. "What did you have in mind? Long or short? Full or slinky?"

"Long," I said. "I want to feel like I'm at a prom, not a cocktail party. I love the halter-top dress I wore to the Snow Ball, but I don't want to wear that with Patrick. But then, I don't want to spend a fortune, either."

"Maybe . . . a creamy aqua? Say . . . a form-fitting dress, simple top, spaghetti straps, three overlapping layers at the bottom, each with a two-inch satin border?"

I didn't know how anyone could mentally design a dress so fast, and I tried to visualize it. Marilyn even drew it on the back of a cash register receipt—the first layer of the skirt ending below the knee, the second layer ending mid-calf, and the third just below the ankle.

"Sold," I said. "Who sells it and how much?"

She laughed. "A friend loaned it to me, and you and I are about the same size. You can wear it if you'll dry-clean it after."

My eyes opened wide. "Marilyn! Really? I didn't think you ever dressed up!"

"I didn't think I did either, but a girlfriend of mine—a *wealthy* girlfriend—invited us to a charity ball. She told me if I'd come, she'd even loan me a dress, and the ball was last week. She's in no hurry to have the dress back. I'll ask her if you can borrow it for one night, but I'm sure it's okay."

"You're like a fairy godmother!" I squealed, hugging her.

"Hey. Try it on first. *Then* you can thank me," she said.

I told Sylvia about it when I got home, and she said we could go to Marilyn's some evening and see how it fit.

"Do you think I'm weird that I don't like to shop?" I asked her.

"No," said Sylvia. "I think your dad and I are lucky, that's what!"

We had brunch at a restaurant on Sunday and invited Les along. He happily reported that he was nearing the finish line on his thesis and would probably graduate in May. Dad was overjoyed, and we all raised our glasses to toast Lester's MA in philosophy.

I had to rib him a little, though: "That's great, Les, but can you say 'self-sup-port-ing'?"

He grinned. "Don't rush me. First things first. George Palamas is getting married in the fall, so we'll be looking for another guy to share the apartment. Meanwhile, we'd like to take off for a week if we can find someone to look after Mr. Watts."

The three men have had an agreement with old Mr. Watts, who owns the house—that they can live upstairs rent-free if they'll do odd jobs around the place and that one of them will always be there in the evenings in case Mr. Watts has an emergency. He has a nursing aide during the day.

"So where would you like to go?" asked Sylvia.

"We're looking into flying to Moab and taking a mountain bike tour," said Les.

"Moab?" I said. "Where's that? Arabia?"

Les leaned over the table. "Can you say 'U-tah,' Al?"

Frankly, my knowledge of geography really sucks. I knew there were mountains in Wyoming and Colorado, but Utah was a blank.

"I think I've failed you there," Dad said apologetically. "We didn't do much traveling as a family, did we?"

"*Much?*" said Lester. And then, realizing, I suppose, that Dad felt guilty enough, he said, "We drove from Illinois to Maryland when we moved, didn't we?"

"And we've been to Tennessee," I said, remembering the trip we made last fall just before Grandpa McKinley died. "I've been to New York and to the ocean a couple of times."

"I hope that both of you will see a lot more of the world than I have," said Dad.

Sylvia laid one hand on his arm. "We've been to England, remember."

He winked. "I was so fascinated by you that I don't even remember the rest."

"You old romantic!" she said. "Someday we're going to Paris."

That afternoon when we got home, I went to my computer and e-mailed Pamela, Liz, and Gwen:

The summer we graduate from college, i want the 4 of us 2 drive 2 california and back. Deal?

Deal, Liz e-mailed back.

Deal, agreed Pamela.

Unless I'm accepted at medical school, wrote Gwen.

8
MURDER IN THE MANSION

Wonder of wonders, Patrick called me Monday night.

"Hi. What's happening?" he asked.

"Well, it's St. Patrick's Day, so I made some lime Jell-O. I mean, we really live it up around here," I told him. "So how are *you* celebrating? It's not everyone who has a holiday named after him."

"I'll be loading fertilizer all week," he said, "but I'd like to do at least one fun thing before spring break is over. How about going to a mystery dinner on Thursday?"

"You mean I won't know what I'm eating until I've swallowed?"

He laughed. "No, it's part of the entertainment. The waiters are part-time actors, and there's a mystery to be solved somewhere during the evening. Customers get to help solve it."

Only Patrick could think of a kitschy idea like that and not be embarrassed about it. But it sounded like fun. "Sure!" I said.

When I went to work the next day, I told Marilyn I was going out with Patrick on Thursday.

"Aha! So it's *not* just the prom! I *knew* you'd get back together!" she said.

I thought about that. "Patrick's a complex person," I said.

"Aren't we all?" said Marilyn.

Dad told us that if we'd be willing to work a couple hours overtime that night, he'd treat us to lunch at the new restaurant next door. David went with me to place the order, and we brought back Cobb salads, with cheesecake for dessert.

"Have you heard from your girlfriend lately?" I asked him back in the break room. "Or shouldn't I ask?"

"No harm in asking," said David. "I may go up there for Easter. Father Bennett asked me to be a reader at mass."

"And . . . Connie?"

"Well, I'd see her too, of course." He smiled. "She sent me a valentine last month."

"David, when you guys go out, what do you do for fun? What is there to do in New Hampshire?"

"What is there to *do*?" he exclaimed, putting down his fork in mock horror. "You never heard of the White Mountains? Never heard of the Atlantic Ocean?"

"*Ocean?* New Hampshire's squeezed between Vermont and Maine! How can there be ocean?" I asked.

"Look at a map, Alice. We've got thirteen miles of beaches at the southern tip."

I was embarrassed. "I'm a geographic imbecile, David. I didn't know it had ocean; I didn't know it had mountains! I didn't even know there were mountains in Utah!"

"You're kidding!" said David. "Utah's one of my favorite states. You haven't seen the U.S. till you've been to Canyonlands, Arches National Park. . . . Utah's gorgeous!"

"So, back in New Hampshire, you and Connie . . . ?"

"We hike. Swim. Canoe. Camp out sometimes."

"Uh . . . separate tents?" I was pushing it, I knew.

He grinned. "Separate sleeping bags. We like old movies, classical music, Brahms. . . . We both love the church. Love poetry. Crossword puzzles. Sailing. . . ."

I studied his face. "If you give her up, won't you be lonely?"

He smiled again. "Some of the time, probably. No, absolutely, I'll miss her. But it's not as though I won't have anything to do. I'll have the whole parish. And I'll be with other priests who love the church."

I sighed and took another bite of dessert. "I guess I've never loved anyone that much. Well, my dad maybe. . . . But I can't even imagine loving a *church* so much that I'd give up all that."

"What about loving God?"

"If I ever get to that place, I'd want human love too, David."

"Many people make that choice, and it's a fine choice. But I don't just want to love, I want to be close to God . . . in a totally committed way."

I thought of David's girlfriend back in New Hampshire, waiting for his decision. Of David and Connie lying out under the stars. Canoeing, sailing, reading poetry . . . And David, okay with being alone.

"You know what I think?" I said at last. "I think you've already made up your mind, and somehow I think Connie knows it."

He was nodding his head before I'd even finished. "I think so too."

But I still couldn't understand it. Would I ever feel that absolutely committed to anything? Anyone? "I just wonder how long it takes a person to really, *really* know herself," I said.

"Forever," said David. "You'll discover new things about yourself as long as you live."

"Well, that's discouraging. Every time I think I've got a handle on who I really am and what I really feel, something happens and I'm back to square one," I told him.

"That's called 'life,' Alice. You have to live with"—his fork flashed, and he swiped my last bite of cheesecake—"risk," he said.

On Wednesday evening Sylvia and I drove over to Marilyn and Jack's. Marilyn's husband is a folk guitarist, and he was putting on a children's program somewhere, so we had their little two-bedroom house in Rockville to ourselves.

Marilyn was one of Lester's first serious girlfriends, and I'd always hoped he'd marry her, but that wasn't meant to be. The original "nature girl," Marilyn usually wore cotton and sandals, and I couldn't imagine her in a long crepe dress, but there it was, all laid out on the bed.

"It's beautiful," said Sylvia. "Whoever this friend was, she had taste."

"I figure maybe I'll borrow it again for my twenty-fifth wedding anniversary or something," said Marilyn.

I'd worn my strapless bra, so I took off my shirt and jeans, and Sylvia lowered the dress over my head and let it fall gently around my hips. The dress skimmed my legs as it fell. She zipped me up, and I turned toward the mirror.

"It's . . . gorgeous!" I breathed.

I could tell by Marilyn's and Sylvia's smiles that they thought so too.

"The straps need shortening just a bit, but I can do that without hurting the dress or making it permanent," Sylvia said. "We'll lower them again before we return it. What do you think, Marilyn?"

"I think my friend must have known somehow that I'd be generous with this dress, because she told me to keep it as long as I like," said Marilyn. "And I can't think of anyone I'd rather share it with."

I didn't dress up for the Murder Mystery Dinner Theater on Thursday, but I looked good. I was wearing the same tight jeans

I'd worn to the Sadie Hawkins Day dance, minus the patches, and a cream-colored shirt.

When Patrick came to pick me up, I was still getting dressed. From down below, I heard Dad answer the door. "Well, Patrick! Good to see you! Come in, come in!" he said.

"Hi, Mr. McKinley." Patrick's voice.

A shiver of excitement went through me. How long had it been since Patrick was in our house? I wondered. Was the last time he had stepped on our porch the night we broke up? The night we walked around the neighborhood and, when I realized we were only going to make it one block, I knew it was over?

I heard Sylvia's footsteps then, and she said, "My gosh, let me get a good look at you! Patrick, you *can't* have grown a foot since you were in my class! And don't you hate it when adults talk this way?"

Patrick laughed. "Actually, I sort of like it. Not bad, looking *down* on everybody for a change."

Dad chuckled.

"Hey, *this* place has changed too," Patrick said. "New addition, huh?"

"And it's almost done," said Sylvia. "Tomorrow the men will be here to take down these horrid plastic walls, and we can move all this stuff back where it belongs."

"Sweet!" said Patrick. And here's the reason my dad likes him so much: The next thing Patrick said was, "I'm working tomorrow, but I could stop by afterward if you need any help."

"We just might," said Dad, "or we may be all moved in by then. I'm taking the day off. Saturday, too. Stop by anyway and see what we've done to the place."

I came down then and found both Dad and Sylvia beaming. Did they really think that Patrick and I were back together again, as a couple? Didn't they know—*surely* they knew—how complicated relationships are and how little time Patrick had for me? The fact that in a few months he'd be going to the University of Chicago, a thousand miles away?

Patrick was wearing a dark red shirt, a black sweater thrown over one shoulder. I must say, we made a great-looking couple. We walked out to the car, Patrick with his hand lightly touching my waist as if to guide me along the boards that served as our sidewalk.

"Well, I guess *this* has been fun," he joked, nodding toward the Porta-John.

"Everybody makes cracks about that," I told him. "No, we didn't have to use it, thank God."

The night was gorgeous—clear sky with a three-quarters moon. Even above the lights of Silver Spring, we could see stars.

Patrick was driving his mom's car—a silver Olds. He opened the door for me and waited till I'd found the seat belt, then came around to the other side.

"Are you taking a car to Chicago?" I asked.

"Naw. I won't have a car there. I'll take Metra or grab a bus to the El if I want to go downtown. And I'll have my bike around the university."

"You're officially accepted, then?"

"Yep. Start the summer quarter. I don't even have to wait till fall," Patrick said.

That meant we wouldn't be together over the summer! But I might have known. Whenever Patrick saw a chance to get ahead, he took it. I was determined, though, that nothing would spoil the evening.

"Then tonight we're going to celebrate your going to the University of Chicago?" I asked cheerfully.

He smiled as he started the engine. "We'll celebrate whatever you want," he said.

The Blakely Mansion was a huge old brick house on the border between Silver Spring and Takoma Park. It had balconies and turrets and high narrow windows with black shutters, some of them closed.

Patrick and I walked up the steps and were greeted by a man who looked like something out of a Victorian melodrama— dark slick-backed hair, mustache, heavily painted eyebrows. He checked our reservation.

"Please follow," he said, barely smiling, and pointed to a smaller man with a stubby beard and an eye patch. We were led to a table covered by a purple cloth, a purple candle in the center. Heavy black drapes obscured the walls and windows, and at times they rustled as though there were open doorways behind them.

Stuffed crows looked down on us from a high ledge, their steely yellow eyes seeming to catch every movement, and a thin woman in a black dress somberly plucked a harp in one corner, her black lip gloss matching her nails.

"Creepy!" I said to Patrick. "Have you been here before?"

"No, but I've heard about it. Something a little different," he said. Same thing Scott had said about going to the dance with me.

It wasn't the sort of restaurant where you gaze into each other's eyes by candlelight exactly. In elaborate script above a doorway were the words *Expect the Unexpected.* Patrick smiled at me from across the table. "Soooo?"

I smiled back. "So? Are we going to give each other an account of what we've been doing for the past week or past month or past year?"

"All of those, if you want," said Patrick.

"Well, let's see. I've grown another half inch, gained a couple pounds. I'm letting my hair grow longer, I *may* get my braces off this spring, I'm taking an accelerated course in English, and I'm running three times a week before school."

Patrick grinned. "And you're looking great," he said.

"Thank you," I told him.

A man with a Van Gogh beard and a bandaged ear brought us our menus and a black olive appetizer. We laughed at the menu. The steak was "hoary beef," the salad "plucked shoots," the dessert "black raspberries with clotted cream. . . ."

I studied Patrick as he studied the menu. His hair wasn't as fiery red as it had been back in grade school, but he had the complexion of a redhead, and his eyebrows were orange as well.

The biggest change I saw in him, though, was that he didn't

talk about himself the whole time. It wasn't that he had been conceited before. It was just—well, there was always so much to tell! He was involved in so many things. But this time he was interested in Les getting his master's degree; he asked what colleges I was planning to apply to and what it was like having my seventh-grade English teacher for a mom. He even asked about Aunt Sally. I was surprised he remembered her. I started to fill him in on my relatives in Chicago when the harpist stopped playing and a man wearing a long black cape took the microphone.

In a low raspy voice he said that his name was Edgar (yes, as in Edgar Allan Poe), he welcomed us to his house, to his banquet, and asked us to please make ourselves at home. He must, however, ask us to confine ourselves to the dining room, the library, and the restrooms, for there were portions of the house, unfortunately, that were unsafe.

"I regret to inform you," he said, "that my brother, Allan"—everyone laughed—"of a somewhat deranged mentality, has escaped his quarters in the upper story and may possibly be roaming the halls. He is quite harmless unless cornered, but let me assure you that his keepers are searching for him even now. I don't wish to disturb your meal in any way, so please, please continue. . . ." And with a flourish of his cape, he disappeared behind a curtain to the applause and laughter of the guests.

As we ate our dinner, I finished telling Patrick all the news about my family—Uncle Milt's heart attack and recovery, my cousin Carol moving in with her boyfriend, and how Aunt Sally found out. Every so often we would hear muffled shouts or exclamations, and there would be movement behind one of the curtains. Once a figure darted through the dining room, chased by the cook, and somebody said, "Allan's on the loose again."

For dessert we shared a slice of devil's food cake, slathered with whipped cream. We each started at one side of the dish and smiled when our forks touched in the middle.

"The mystery starts after dinner, I think," Patrick said.

"Then I'm going to the restroom first," I told him, and picking up my purse, I asked a waiter directions to the ladies' room, then followed as he ushered me to a long hallway, with only dim lighting overhead.

I groped my way along, pausing at each closed door, looking for a LADIES sign, and finally saw it down near the end. Inside, I wished that Patrick could have seen it. There was an old bathtub on one side shaped like a coffin, and both of the sinks were empty skulls. When I sat down on the toilet seat, a groan came from beneath me, and I jumped to discover an electronic monitor that had triggered the moan of a man being crushed. I laughed out loud.

When I came out of the stall, one of the black-clad waitresses was reapplying her lip gloss. Her face was chalky white, and her eyes were heavily outlined in mascara.

"Hi," I said as I approached one of the sinks.

"*Au revoir,*" she murmured, and slunk out the door.

I put on fresh lip gloss, gave my hair a few swipes, then opened the door and started back down the hallway toward the dining room.

Suddenly a hand clamped tightly over my mouth, my arms were pinned to my sides, and before I could think, I was lifted off my feet and carried up a flight of stairs.

"Shhh," a male voice whispered. "Relax. You're part of the show. One more flight, please." And two men hustled me on up to the third floor.

All I could think about was how glad I was they had kidnapped me *after* I'd peed.

We entered a large room, a parlor of some kind, only slightly more lit than the hallway and stairs. I couldn't make out the men's faces exactly, but the guys were dressed like two of the waiters. They walked me over to a large painting on the opposite wall. One of the men pushed against it, and the painting swung open. The men hurried me through into another hallway and, from there, into another old-fashioned bathroom, with one dim light above a cracked mirror.

"Sorry about this," one of the men said, smiling apologetically, "but you worked so perfectly into the plot that we just had to make use of you. Georgene, our scullery maid, was waiting in the bathroom to see who showed up first, and we were so happy it wasn't a three-hundred-pound woman."

"What am I supposed to do?" I asked, my heart still pounding.

"Nothing at all. When it's time for you to reappear, we'll come get you," said the second waiter.

"But please don't come out before then," the first man said. "It would ruin everything."

"Can you at least tell me the plot?" I asked.

"It changes each night," he said. "But they'll start searching for you in about twenty minutes."

"The customers, you mean?" I asked.

"Yeah, but unless someone leans against that painting, they won't find you here," he said. "Try not to make any noise." He grinned again. "If you use the john, don't flush." And putting their fingers to their lips, they slipped back out again, closing the door behind them.

I looked around. The toilet was so old-fashioned, its tank was high on the wall. The claw-footed bathtub had a ring of rust around the drain, and there were little pieces of chipped plaster in the sink. I had my purse with me, but no cell phone.

And suddenly I thought of Patrick. They said I needed to be here for twenty minutes! What were they telling Patrick? Were they telling him anything at all? What if he thought I'd called a cab and gone home?

My mind raced with possibilities. What if he called my dad? What if he called the police?

Oh, sit down and enjoy it, I told myself. Except that there were only two places to sit—the edge of the tub or the toilet seat. I chose the seat. Ten minutes went by. Fifteen.

"Alice!"

It was a faraway voice. My eyes opened wide. It seemed to be coming from outdoors, but I had to crank open the window and stand on tiptoe to see the ground.

There, walking back and forth in the parking area, was

Patrick, looking all around him. "Alice?" he called again. They *hadn't* told him! A few other people were milling about the veranda.

I looked around the bathroom. There were no towels to wave, no shower curtain to use as a flag. Nothing but a half roll of toilet paper sitting on the floor.

I picked it up, went back to the window again, unfurled it six or eight feet, and let it dangle. Back and forth, back and forth I moved it, but Patrick didn't look up.

"Pssst!" I whispered loudly, but of course he didn't hear. I didn't dare call out to him, because others would have heard it too, and it would have ruined the mystery.

Patrick started back inside, heading to the door beneath the window. I had to let him know I was okay. Holding the roll out as far as I could, I let it drop.

Peering down below, I saw Patrick stop, stare at the toilet paper, then up toward the second floor.

Up here! Up here! I wanted to call. He looked down at the toilet paper again, then tipped his head way back and looked up. This time he saw me and stepped backward a foot or two. I held my finger to my lips, ducking back as another couple looked up at the same time, then peeped out again after they'd walked on. Patrick was grinning now. He gave me the OK sign and went on inside.

Now there were voices and laughter from below. The search party had begun. The sound of footsteps going up and down the stairs; voices calling out to each other from the next room.

It was another twenty minutes before the two men came

back, and this time they had two more men with them, carrying a plywood box painted like a casket.

"I've got to lie in that?" I said.

"Only until we tap on the lid, then you push open the top and crawl out. We'll take it from there. Thanks for being such a good sport and helping the plot along."

"But what *is* the plot?" I insisted. Even if I had no lines, I wanted to play the part.

"The story tonight is that the host has persuaded the guests that not only is one of their number missing, but that his criminally insane twin has escaped his quarters and is roaming the mansion. Edgar pretends to fear for the safety of the missing girl and has promised his guests that whoever finds her will get his dinner on the house. But all the while, Edgar and his brother, Allan, not deranged at all, have been quietly picking the pockets of their guests as they grope about looking for the missing girl—which is, of course, you."

"And when do I get to come back in?"

"Edgar has stolen you away himself and locked you in an upstairs room, supposedly. But unbeknownst to him and his thieving brother, two detectives have infiltrated the dinner party. They have rescued you, retrieved the bag of stolen wallets and jewelry, and at the critical moment—shortly after Edgar reports to his guests that he had no choice but to shoot his brother . . ."

A shot rang out from below.

"Our cue," the man noted, then continued, ". . . the detectives enter the room carrying a coffin—not of the brother, who faked his death, but of the missing girl, very much alive—and the bag of jewels."

It would have been a grade-D movie, and the plot would never have made it beyond fifth-grade English, but it was fun.

When we got downstairs, just outside the dining room, I climbed into the coffin and we listened as Edgar dramatically gave the account of finding his brother in an upstairs room, about to strangle the missing girl. There was a swell of recorded organ music, and the men carried me into the dining room, the lid of the coffin closed.

"What's this?" I heard the host exclaim. "This isn't part of the plot!"

Laughter from the audience, and I tried to hear Patrick's laughter in it.

There was more protracted conversation between Edgar and the detectives, and then I realized that someone was tapping repeatedly on the coffin. I rose up, hands folded over my chest, and climbed out of the coffin and onto the floor.

The detectives announced that the plan was foiled, that they had retrieved all the wallets and jewels, and different actors scattered among the guests cried out in fake surprise when pearls and money clips and wallets were returned to them. Everyone hooted and clapped as the host was led out of the room in handcuffs, protesting all the way.

Patrick and I laughed about it on the way home, and he was especially pleased that we got our dinner free, not because he had found me—no one had—but because I had played along.

"So was it worth the loss of my companionship?" I asked, glancing over at him as he drove back down Georgia Avenue.

"Oh, *nothing* could compensate me for that," he said, "but if I had to eat hoary beef again, I don't think I'd do it."

"Well, I had a good time," I said.

"So did I," said Patrick. And when we got up on the porch, he said we should end the evening with a flourish. At that, he swooped me up in his arms, bent me over backward, and gave me such a movie-star kiss that I expected us both to fall over, but we didn't.

And then he was gone and I was grinning. *Grinning.* It was not exactly the way I imagined our evening would end, but I think it erased forever the kiss on the forehead from Scott.

9
MOVING ON

I woke up smiling, thinking about that kiss. About the fact that the food was forgettable, the performance was awful, and yet we'd managed to have fun.

Snuggling down under my blanket, I wanted to imagine what it might have been like if I could have invited Patrick inside. If there had been *space* to squeeze him inside. If he could have sat down in Dad's armchair, me on his lap, Patrick's hand on my . . .

I heard voices coming from somewhere, the slam of a car or truck door, footsteps, more voices, and suddenly I remembered that this was the day we could move into our new addition.

I sprang out of bed and bounded to the bathroom before the workmen came upstairs. I was as excited as a kid at Christmas.

My first thought, of course, was that this bathroom would be all mine now, except for the times Les spent the night. My second thought was that I could cozy up to a guy in the family room—Patrick or someone else—while Dad and Sylvia stayed back in the living room. I did a quick washup, tied my hair in a ponytail, brushed my teeth, and slipped on my old jeans and a T-shirt.

"Today's the day!" Sylvia said happily as she came up the stairs. "Just wanted to see if you were decent before I let the workmen come up."

"Bring 'em on!" I said. "I can't wait."

I made myself a piece of toast and trailed along after the burly workmen like a five-year-old. They started upstairs, untaping the thick blue wall of plastic that sealed off Dad and Sylvia's old bedroom. Yesterday we'd heard the sound of sweeping and vacuuming coming from the new addition, and now, foot by foot, the plastic was peeled away, exposing the windows of the bright new master bedroom, sunlight streaming through. There were the two doors to the walk-in closets and another door leading to the master bath, with its double-sink vanity and Jacuzzi tub.

I didn't even have to ask.

"Yes, Alice, you may use it whenever you like," Sylvia said, smiling as she studied my face.

"It's all beautiful!" I said. "How did you stand that old cramped bedroom for so long?"

"I wonder that myself," Dad said.

But the workmen were rolling up the blue plastic and heading downstairs, so I trotted along after them. They started at the wall between the kitchen and the hallway, and when the new cabinets came into view, then the new stainless steel sink, I had to be the first to go through, because beyond the kitchen was the family room, with its big stone fireplace all the way to the ceiling.

"I can fit *everyone* in this room!" I said, thinking about the newspaper staff, the GSA, stage crew, and whoever was left of the gang that used to gather at Mark Stedmeister's.

"I could invite the teachers from school!" said Sylvia.

"We could even hold the Melody Inn Christmas party here," said Dad.

But this wasn't all. There was a screened porch beyond the family room, and then, coming back inside, I entered the door that led to the new study, and a door from the study to the revamped dining room, and when the workmen pulled off the last of the plastic sheets, I was back in our old living room and then the hallway again. It was as though we had moved into a brand-new house, and I loved it.

There was no furniture yet for the family room or study. The workmen moved Dad and Sylvia's bedroom set into their new bedroom. They put the appliances back in the kitchen and disconnected the temporary sink they had hooked up in the living room. They moved the dining room table and chairs back where they belonged, and Dad's computer and table into the study.

"It'll be another couple weeks before we take care of all the small stuff, but you folks go ahead and put your things where you want them, and we'll work around you," the foreman said before the men left. And then it was just the three of us, exclaiming over each room, pointing out little details, opening cupboards, eager to put things back on shelves and in drawers, to spread out and *breathe* again. Annabelle moved cautiously through the rooms, sniffing at all the new scents, her tail straight up in the air.

Back upstairs, I moved all of Dad and Sylvia's clothes out of my room and into their new closets. Then I tackled the bathroom, helpfully taking all their stuff out of the medicine cabinet and from under the sinks and transferring it to their new bathroom. I moved their towels as well, and when I was done, I wiped off the shelves and rearranged my own shampoo and conditioner and cosmetics. Was I lucky or was I lucky?

We ordered pizza for dinner and ate it in lawn chairs we'd moved up from the basement into our new family room. It was hardly cold enough for a fire in the fireplace, but we built one anyway. I felt as though we were the richest people in the world, to have a stone fireplace that reached the ceiling.

"I can hardly believe it's finished," said Sylvia. "Oh, Ben, I'm so happy with the way it's turned out."

Dad put an arm around her on the aluminum love seat they were sharing. "So am I," he said. "How about a bearskin rug, right here by the fire?"

Sylvia's smile disappeared. "You don't mean that."

"Of course I mean it! A large brown rug. . . . No, maybe a polar bear skin—with the head and paws still attached. And a buck's head and antlers on the wall between the windows."

She knew he was teasing then, and we started to laugh. The doorbell rang, and I was still smiling when I went to answer.

"Patrick!" I couldn't believe I'd forgotten he might come by.

"Just your friendly neighborhood moving man!" he said. "Am I too late?"

"Not for pizza, you're not. We've still got a couple slices left," I said. "Come on in."

We gave him the official tour, and even though Patrick's family has a bigger house than we do, even with our addition, Patrick said all the right things. He especially liked the fireplace.

We *didn't* exactly have everything moved, because when Patrick asked Dad if there was anything he could do, Dad asked if he'd move the boxes of books he'd left up in Lester's room, as well as Sylvia's three-drawer file cabinet.

After the fifth box of books, Patrick stripped down to his T-shirt. I was amazed at the broad range of his shoulders, the muscular back, the wide chest.

"Sure that's not too heavy for you?" Dad asked as Patrick lifted out one of the drawers of the file cabinet, holding Sylvia's records and lesson plans.

"Not any heavier than the mulch I've been unloading all week," Patrick said.

"That landscaping job obviously agrees with you, Patrick," Sylvia said.

"Yeah," Patrick said. "That's what all the girls say."

Dad and Sylvia went upstairs at last to organize their new closets, and Patrick and I had the family room to ourselves. We were sitting side by side on two aluminum chairs.

"Well, the *fire's* nice, anyway," he said, glancing over at me. "Can't say much for the chairs."

"Wait," I said.

I ran upstairs to my bedroom and lugged down the old beanbag chair I've had for as long as I can remember, plus all the pillows off my bed. We propped the pillows against the wall, put my beanbag chair in front of them. Then Patrick sank down in the chair and I sat on his lap, just as I had imagined. We turned out the lights and watched the fire.

And . . . little by little . . . memories, feelings came winging back. Some came at me sideways, sneaking in at an angle. Others came head-on, and still others came as a pair. The scent of his skin, the texture of his hair, the way he nestled his chin against my shoulder, stroked my side, just at the edge of my breast. I loved the way he pressed his lips against my cheek or my arm or my neck—not a kiss exactly, as though just touching me with his lips was all he needed.

I let myself be vulnerable. "It's nice to have you back," I said, trust overriding caution.

"Nice to be back," he whispered.

I didn't say it was nice to be a couple again, because—well, who knows?

* * *

Saturday morning, since I didn't have to go to the Melody Inn with Dad, I was working on a special article for *The Edge*. This year April 25 would be observed as the Day of Silence by Gay/ Straight Alliances in high schools and colleges all over the country. But because it was new to our school, and because that date would coincide with the final weekend of our spring musical, we decided to hold our Day of Silence two weeks earlier, on Friday, April 11. To emphasize how gays and lesbians have had to keep their sexual orientation hidden, those of us in the GSA were going all day long wearing armbands and staying silent as a way of demonstrating what gays have had to do.

Since I was a member, Miss Ames had asked me to write an article explaining what it meant and how any student who wanted to show solidarity was welcome to join in. We didn't want kids to think that the GSA was some kind of cult or that we were using the silence as a way of not having to answer questions in class.

My final draft of the article was half done when Sylvia came to the door of my bedroom.

"Ben and I are going shopping for family room furniture," she said. "Do you want to come along and help choose?"

I looked up. "Well . . . sure!" I said. "I thought it was a done deal."

"We've only looked. Haven't decided on anything," she told me.

I changed my shirt, put on my shoes, and we were out the door.

"Saw some furniture we liked at Scan in Rockville," Dad said. "Let's swing by there first."

I sat happily in the backseat, thrilled to have been asked along. I had a new CD in my bag and would have loved to hear it again on the car player, but I wasn't going to press my luck. Traffic was awful and I didn't want to make Dad tense.

Somehow I knew when we walked into Scan, with its sleek modern furniture, that this was probably the place, and I was right. A rosewood desk for the study, bookcase to match, a lamp.

But when it came time to buy the couch and chairs for the family room, nothing really said *Comfortable* to me. Nothing said, *Welcome* or *Hanging out* or *Put up your feet*.

Dad and Sylvia studied my face.

"I don't know . . . ," I said.

"We don't have to buy everything from one store," said Sylvia. "Let's try Marlo's."

That store was huge. There were whole sets of furniture, whole room displays, one after another.

"Hey, look at this!" said Dad. He liked a high-backed sofa in tweed, with masculine-looking chairs. "Price is right," he said, checking the tags.

"Possibly," said Sylvia, which probably meant *Ugh*. "Let's keep looking."

Sylvia liked color, and she longingly fingered an Ultrasuede sofa in soft peach, with matching armchairs. It was okay, but . . . could I see myself hanging out with peach? I gave a little shrug.

"Well, there's more," Sylvia said, lingering a minute longer, and then we moved on.

The sofa that caught my eye was an L-shaped sectional that

you could take apart and rearrange. It came with a huge otto-man on which at least four people could rest their feet, and the whole set was marine blue.

"Hey, what about *this*?" I said. "This is neat!"

Dad and Sylvia stopped to look at it. Their expressions were engraved in granite, and because I couldn't tell one way or the other how they felt, that should have told me something.

"Well, it's interesting," said Dad.

"I don't know about the color," said Sylvia. "We were sort of sticking to cinnamon or beige or something that would blend with—" She stopped. "It's certainly a possibility," she said.

I tried it out and sank down five inches. I leaned back and put my feet on the ottoman. "It's really comfortable," I told them.

A salesman standing by came over.

"Does this set come in any other colors?" Sylvia asked him.

"I'm afraid not. This is a one of a kind," he told her. "We got it from another store, half price."

Dad sat down on the sofa. He tried tipping his head, but the back wasn't high enough to support him.

And suddenly I realized that I would be out of the house in a year, away at college, but they would be in the house for a long time yet. The rest of their lives, maybe. Once I started college, I'd probably be home just for the summers, and after that I'd drop in only now and then, like Les.

"I'm willing to look around some more," I said, and saw the relief on their faces.

We ended up with an apricot-colored couch with thick

cushions and a high back, along with two matching chairs and a rocker. Then we drove back to Scan and bought a perfectly gorgeous area rug to go with it, in apricot, ginger, and olive. And finally a new rug for my bedroom, in a sort of African print. I loved it.

We were so pleased with our shopping expedition that we went to Gifford's and ordered Swiss chocolate sundaes with Swiss chocolate sauce. When the clerk asked if we wanted whipped cream, nuts, and cherries, Dad said, "Why not?"

Molly called me on Monday and said she was having trouble finding costumes for Adelaide's chorus girls. Mr. Ellis had told her to get everything she possibly could free of charge from merchants who would be glad to have their companies or stores listed as sponsors in the program. Community service always got the attention of parents and teachers.

"He said we'd rent whatever we absolutely had to, but I'd love to get practically everything we need without having to pay a cent," she said.

"What don't you have yet?" I asked.

"Black net stockings and short sexy costumes that would look okay with a cat's ears and tail," said Molly.

"Oh, wow!" I said.

"I can buy cheap stockings on the Internet, but if we could find the right kind of costumes locally, they'd probably come with the stockings," said Molly.

"What sizes do you need?" I asked, and she read off the sizes of the girls who were playing Adelaide's "alley kittens" in the chorus, Pamela included.

"I'll see what I can do," I promised. I spent the evening looking through the Yellow Pages, then called Elizabeth.

Tuesday after school, Liz and I drove to a place just over the D.C. line called Nighttime Fantasies. They'd advertised "costumes for every taste and occasion." Liz insisted on wearing dark glasses when we parked and walked down the block, but when we got in front of the store window, I said, "Better take them off so you can see better. You don't want to miss this."

Elizabeth took off the glasses and looked at the display window. She stared for a minute and popped her glasses back on.

"I'm leaving," she said.

I laughed. "No, you're not. We got this far."

"But . . ." She was staring some more. "Do people really *use* this stuff? I mean, this part goes in, and that . . ."

"Don't ask," I said, but I was trying to figure the gadgets out too. Trying to figure out how couples climbed in bed with a bunch of sex toys and kept the mood while they figured out how to use them.

"Maybe they practice ahead of time," said Liz.

We went inside, and a little bell tinkled. A woman with obviously dyed red hair and a very low neckline got up from a stool behind a counter and put down the magazine she was reading. She smiled knowingly as we came in.

"May I help you?" she asked.

"Just looking," said Liz.

We were looking, all right. There were crotchless panties and curved appliances, about the size of a cell phone, "to increase feminine satisfaction." There were black leather hip-length boots, and whips and ostrich feather "ticklers," and condoms flavored raspberry, chocolate, and cinnamon. Oils to put in secret places, satin sheets, bras with no cups, navel jewels, penis enlargers, and racks of sexy nightwear, for him and for her.

"We're here from the high school newspaper *The Edge*," I said, and immediately the woman's expression changed. Her eyes grew cold, lips pressed into a straight line. I could tell that she thought we were going to do an exposé of students coming in to buy stuff, but when I told her what we wanted and what they were for, her eyes twinkled and she began to smile again.

"And my store will be included in the list of donors?" she asked.

"Absolutely," I said. "We'll send you two free tickets, and will include a program when we bring back your costumes, all dry-cleaned of course."

So who would have thought that someone's sexual fantasy was to be a kitten! We smiled all the way back to the car, a shopping bag in my hand. Wait till I told Molly that the program for *Guys and Dolls* would express our gratitude not only to Giant, CVS, the Mercy Mission, and the Department of Motor Vehicles, but to Nighttime Fantasies as well.

10

PROMOTION

All during spring break, I had worked really hard on that article about the Day of Silence. I found out how the first observance began. I described the way many gays and lesbians were ostracized, not only at school and by former friends, but in their own families. I wrote about methods people have used to try to change sexual orientation. Most of this I got from articles Mr. Morrison had given me, but I also interviewed some of the members of the GSA.

I think it was one of my best articles. I'd quoted Lori and Leslie on how it had been for them and recounted the time back in middle school when some girls cornered them in a restroom and kept taunting them with "Kiss her! Kiss her!" I ended the article by saying that the GSA wasn't trying to change anyone's sexual orientation; it existed to help people accept others' sexuality as much as to feel good about their own.

At the first staff meeting after spring break, I arrived early, and both Miss Ames and Scott read my piece and commented on it. Tony Osler just sat off to one side with a knowing smile, like, *Is that what's wrong with you, Alice? Why you wouldn't let me go all the way?* I know what Tony's thinking even when his lips are sealed.

"It's really excellent, Alice," Miss Ames said.

"It's great!" said Scott. "So what other ideas do you have for us?"

"Well . . . we do a lot of student interviews, polls and stuff," I said. "Why not do something called 'Teachers' Secrets'?"

"Whoa!" said Tony. "Report on who's sleeping with whom?"

I gave him a look. "No. I thought of asking fifteen or twenty teachers to tell us something about themselves that their students probably don't know—anything they want to share. See what we come up with."

Miss Ames smiled a little. "Could be interesting."

"We could start with you," said Scott, warming to the idea. "How about it?"

"We have to be sure we don't print anything that's said off the record," she said. "But . . . well, let me think. I guess one thing students don't know about my past is that I once won a hot dog eating contest at the beach."

"*You?*" said the sophomore roving reporter. "You're so thin!"

"Well, thin girls have stomachs too." Miss Ames laughed.

"How many did you eat?" I asked.

"Eleven and a half. They almost disqualified me because I threw up before they announced the winner, but the judge said I got it all down, and that's what counts."

Everybody cheered.

Jacki Severn breezed in just then and apologized for being late, but she said she had just got this great idea for the next issue:

"It's our first issue in April—you know, April showers and stuff. I remembered this photo from last year when there was all that rain and the parking lot flooded. Remember? Mom took this picture when she came to pick me up. . . ." And Jacki pulled out a picture of herself, laughing as she waded ankle-deep in water, holding her books over her head. A couple of friends were behind her, but obviously, Jacki was the main attraction. "I thought we could title it 'April! Will It Happen Again?' And I'll interview other kids to see how they got home that day."

Scott looked at the picture, smiled a little, and passed it on. "I don't know, Jacki. It's old news. We should have used it last year," he said.

"All the more reason to use it now!" Jacki said emphatically. She always speaks louder when she wants to make a point. "It would make a great story! One of the teachers said that the water came up so fast that the physics teacher was stranded at the end of the parking lot!"

"Our freshman class wasn't even here last year," said Miss Ames. "It wouldn't mean much to them."

"It doesn't make any difference!" Jacki argued. "The tie-in is April! Spring! Rain! I think it would get a lot of attention on the front page."

"Well, that's not going to happen," said Scott. "The school board's ruling on sex ed is the top story. And the bottom half of the first page will be the Day of Silence."

Jacki stared incredulously around the room. "Day of *Silence*? The gay thing? That doesn't have to be front page, for God's sake! It's not like it affects the whole school."

"Well, perhaps it should," said Miss Ames. "That's our point."

"I thought *I* was the features editor!" Jacki fumed.

Everyone was staring now. Sam Mayer had come in with the sports photos for the next edition, and he immediately sat down on a desk near the door, out of the line of fire.

"Jacki, we discussed the Day of Silence piece at the last meeting, and you didn't say a word about a feature on rain, much less a photo," said Scott.

"Well, *I* thought a newspaper could be spontaneous!" cried Jacki. "*I* thought we were supposed to be current, and what could be more current than the month of the year! If we have a big rain between now and next week when the paper comes out, we'll be right on top of the news."

Tony had been reading the Metro section of the *Washington Post*, and he turned to the weather report on the back page. "Five-day forecast," he said aloud. "Fair and breezy."

"Well, I won't insist on the front page, but there's no way I'm going to settle for putting my feature on the *last* page," said Jacki.

"I've got the basketball scores, and Sam's got photos," said Tony. "Those have to go somewhere."

"What about news from the roving reporters?" asked another guy.

"And we're printing the cast for *Guys and Dolls*. We've got to start publicizing that," said Scott.

"Jacki, since this is the first year we've had a GSA in our school, it's important that students understand its purpose," Miss Ames explained. "And because we're holding our Day of Silence two weeks before the national observance, it's especially important that this feature make the coming issue."

"Then we can take out something else!" Jacki said hotly. "If we put my feature off, April will be half over by the time it comes out."

"Then I'm sorry," Miss Ames said, "but there just isn't room for it."

I hadn't said a word. I wasn't even certain I was breathing. Jacki's cheeks flamed. I'd never seen those large red blotches on her face before, but there they were, as though she'd been out in the wind.

"In that case, I quit!" she said, and threw down the features editor's notebook. Papers sailed across the floor. She strode past me, her arm brushing mine, and plowed on out the door, almost knocking down the freshman roving reporter who was just coming in.

For a moment no one spoke.

"Wow!" said Tony finally.

Scott sucked in his breath. "Whew!"

"Oh, she'll get over it," said Sam, ever the conciliator.

But Miss Ames quietly picked up the notebook, and the rest of us began gathering up the scattered pages.

"Alice," Miss Ames said, "would you be features editor for the rest of the year?" She looked at Scott. "Is that okay with you?"

"More than okay," he answered.

I didn't know what to say. My God, taking over for Jacki! She'd kill me.

"Sure," I said.

"She left the room like a tornado!" I told Sylvia later when we were sharing a bagel in the kitchen. We both like ours lightly toasted. She uses butter, I like cream cheese.

"Sure sounds like an overreaction to me. Maybe she thought they'd go after her and beg her to come back," said Sylvia.

"Fat chance," I said. "If I had to describe the atmosphere after she left, I'd call it relief. But, Sylvia, she'll *hate* me! She never did like me very much."

"Do you care?" asked Sylvia. "She's a senior, you said. Do you have any classes with her?"

"No. . . ."

"She probably expects the paper to fall apart if she's not on it. Prove that it won't. Do you have any plans for the next issue?"

"That's all wrapped up. But I was thinking about the next few issues on my way home. Like, now that the school year's almost over, maybe the freshman roving reporter could do a little piece on fears that freshmen have when they start high school, and how things really turned out."

"Possibility," said Sylvia.

"Or maybe that would be better for fall," I went on. "We could also interview Molly on the ingenious ways she's getting all the props for *Guys and Dolls*. We wouldn't even have to say she's doing all this from home. Help her feel more connected to school."

"I like that idea," said Sylvia.

"And we could also assign the senior roving reporter to do an article on what kids who aren't going to college are going to do—like travel or help out at home or get a job. . . ."

"You're full of ideas, you know it?" Sylvia said. "And you know why I think you'll make a better features editor than Jacki? Because your focus is on broadening the scope of the paper, getting other kids involved, not just on what kind of article you could fashion around yourself."

"Thanks," I said, pleased.

"But *also*," Sylvia added, "I've read the features you've written, and you're not afraid to let your emotions show. It helps the reader connect with you."

I wondered if she knew what she was saying— if she'd forgotten that fight we had last November over her car. I'd let my emotions show then, all right—the worst ones. I'd wondered then if Sylvia and I would ever be friends again. And obviously, we were.

"It took me a while to learn that," she said.

"Learn what?"

"To express my feelings. My family was sort of formal when I was growing up. Reserved, I mean. Consequently, when anyone was really angry or sad, it was kind of scary."

"How . . . *did* you act when you were angry?" I asked.

"When we had arguments, it was more like a debate society. I even thought I was more mature than other girls simply because I could hold in my feelings. What a mistake!"

"Really?"

She nodded. "It was Mom's funeral that turned me around. Dad didn't cry, so I didn't. When I felt tears welling up, I learned to stop them before my eyes brimmed over. And everyone commented on how brave I was, how well I held up." Sylvia shook her head. "For months after that, I'd do my crying in private, and I never allowed myself to cry in front of friends. And then I began to wonder: Why is this good? Why is it important? Why do I have to be a 'real trouper,' as the neighbors called me?

"And then, when Dad died—and I'll always believe it was from all the sorrow he'd kept inside—I sort of went to pieces. I cried all over the place. At school, at the mall . . . I cried out of grief and anger both, that Dad had held his feelings in and passed that legacy on to me and my sister and brother."

I thought about that awhile. "Can you really die of a broken heart?"

"A lot less likely if you can share your feelings with some-one. It's amazing, really, what a good listener can do—no solutions necessary." She blinked suddenly. "How did we get started on this?"

"You were talking about expressing emotion."

"Right. And because you can express yours, you're going to be a good features editor, I can tell."

"It's only for the next couple of months," I told her.

But it wasn't. When the first April issue came out with my article about the meaning of the Day of Silence, the principal told Miss Ames that it was one of our best.

"Alice," she said, "I don't usually appoint the new staff until fall, but you've already got your feet wet as features editor. If you plan on being on the newspaper next year, I'd like to keep you in that spot."

"I'd love it!" I said, thrilled, and everyone came over to give me a hug, Scott and Sam and Don and Tony included.

Jacki Severn had passed by me that morning as I was delivering my bundle of papers to homerooms, and her glare was as cold as the frost on a soda can.

By lunchtime some of her choice phrases were making the rounds: "They don't recognize the importance of a good photo on the front page" and "Alice as features editor is a laugh and a half."

A half hour before school let out that day, the office made an announcement: "We're sorry for the interruption, but due to an electronic glitch, the yearbook needs new photos of the following: the senior class officers, the Sadie Hawkins Day dance committee, and the newspaper staff for *The Edge*. As you know, the deadline for the yearbook has passed, but we're holding up production until we get these three photos. Will all students who belong in those photos please report to the auditorium immediately after the close of school. . . ."

I needed a haircut and wished I'd worn a different shirt. I especially wished my braces were off. But after the last bell I went down to the auditorium, where the photographer was already lining up the dance committee.

The senior class officers were sitting on the steps of the stage eating doughnuts, and members of the newspaper staff were milling around at the back of the auditorium.

"I hope he makes this quick, because I'm supposed to drive my brother to the dentist," Scott said, glancing at his watch.

"I'll ask if he can take our picture next," Miss Ames said. "I've got an appointment too."

At that very moment Jacki Severn came through the double doors and smiled as though we were her best and only friends.

"Miss Ames," she said, in a voice as phony as it was poignant, "I was really having a bad day last Wednesday, and I apologize. I still think I had a good idea, but . . . well, I can't win them all. So anyway, I want to be a good sport. I heard the announcement about a new photo, so I'm reporting for duty."

No one said a word—just looked toward Miss Ames.

"Oh, I'm sorry, Jacki," the teacher said. "But Alice is now

features editor, so you're excused. Thanks for coming by."

Jacki blanched. "There are only two months left of school," she said. "I've been features editor for almost the whole year!"

Miss Ames nodded. "Until last Wednesday. But you resigned, and I've appointed Alice."

Jacki looked almost numb with astonishment. "But I'm a senior! And this is *my* yearbook, not Alice's!"

"I know, and that's really a shame. But a newspaper can't run with unpredictable people on the staff. If you'd like to be listed as coeditor of features, along with Alice, you may stay for the photo if you like."

"But I . . ." Jacki looked at her pleadingly. "I've already listed this on my college applications! I'll be using it on my résumé when I look for a job! I didn't say I was a coeditor."

"That's fine, Jacki. You can tell anyone you like that you were a member of the staff, and you were. But you can't be listed any other way than coeditor for the photo, because you're no longer features editor."

I think that Jacki was on the verge of throwing her whole armful of books on the floor, and she probably does that at home, who knows? But she must have thought better of it, because she gave us all a hateful look, spun round, and marched back through the double doors, thundering on.

Miss Ames said nothing. The rest of us gave each other secret smiles as we followed her down the aisle and tried to look professional as the photographer lined us up for the picture.

I wasn't sure how the photo would come out, but I was

standing sleeve to sleeve between Scott and Tony, and Don and Sam were on either side of them, along with the roving reporters and our layout coordinator. I was pleased as anything when Miss Ames read off my part of the caption: "Alice McKinley, Features Editor and Junior Class Roving Reporter."

Sometimes the bad guys *don't* win!

11

THE PERFORMING ARTS

Pamela was getting impossible. She sang every chance she got. It wasn't like she was showing off. She was just trying to memorize Adelaide's songs. All of Adelaide's lines. She had to memorize the songs the chorus sang as well, plus do her homework and still squeeze time out of all that for her boyfriend.

"I *almost* wish she hadn't gotten a part," Tim said as we sat together in the auditorium after school, watching another rehearsal. "Almost, but not quite. I'm glad for her, sure, but it's like she's turned into this . . . robot. Press a button and she sings. Press another and she eats. Press another and she—"

"Never mind," I said quickly. "It'll all be over in three more weeks."

There had been rehearsals every day, often well into the evening. Since I'd volunteered to help paint some of the sets, most of my work would be done ahead of time. I didn't have to adjust the lighting or tweak the sound. Molly had enlisted so many volunteers—*every*one wanted to help Molly—that the props were well taken care of, so some of the time I was able to go home pretty early while Pamela had another hour or two of practice yet to go.

If Tim hadn't been at a restaurant celebrating his mom's birthday on Saturday, I don't know when we would have had Pamela to ourselves. The minute Gwen found out she had a free Saturday night, she invited Pamela, Liz, and me to sleep over.

"I really should be studying for that French test," Pamela told me as I drove to Gwen's in Dad's car, Liz in the backseat.

"Pam, you've got to relax a little! You're so tight, you're going to snap a string!" Liz told her. "You're starting to get lines on your forehead."

Pamela reached for her bag and pulled out a mirror, trying to see herself in the dark interior of the car. When we got to the Wheelers', we told Gwen not to let her in until she smiled, and Pamela finally got the message.

Gwen's mom had made paella and a salad, and we heaped our plates with shrimp and sausage and mussels and took over the family room. Mrs. Wheeler stood in the doorway in jeans and a T-shirt. She works at the Justice Department and puts in long hours on weekdays—sometimes Saturdays, too—so I don't usually see her in anything but a suit.

"There's some mint chocolate chip in the freezer, but I can only guarantee it till eleven or so, when the guys get home," she said. "They went to a movie."

"Great paella!" I told her. "Seconds?"

"As long as it lasts," she said, laughing. "When those boys get home, everything that's not nailed down gets devoured. Be careful they don't fall over you. Bill's idea of indoor lighting is to turn on the TV."

Gwen's grandmother—"Granny," Gwen calls her—was watching TV in her own little apartment at the back of the house, and we took some ice cream in to her before we settled down for the evening.

"You remember my friends?" Gwen asked her. "Elizabeth, Pamela, and Alice?"

Granny looked up from the *TV Guide* for a moment, pointed to the screen, and said, "*That* program should never be on TV. I don't like it."

On the screen a drunken couple had just taken off in a car they had hijacked.

"Then don't watch it, Granny. Turn it off," said Gwen.

"If I turn it off, someone else will watch it," said the little woman in the pink sweater and the glasses at the end of her nose. She studied us over the rims. "You girls don't watch this, do you?"

"What is it?" asked Liz.

Granny looked at the *TV Guide* again. "*Prime Crime*," she said. "If you run out of bad things to do, you just turn on this program. I never saw such trash."

Gwen picked up the remote and changed the channel, but Granny grabbed for it. "It's only the ending that's good," she said. "The villains always get it in the end, but what they've been doing in the meantime is something we don't need to know a thing about."

Gwen leaned down and kissed her on the cheek as she set the ice cream on the little stand beside her. "Well, if you insist on watching it, don't come crying to me if you have nightmares," she teased.

Granny thought that over for a moment or two, then smiled. "Nice to meet you, girls," she said, wanting to get back to her program. "And, Gwen, say a prayer for your Uncle Albert. He's got himself a new car, and you know how he drives."

We were smiling too as we left Granny's apartment.

We hunkered back down in the family room with our ice cream, and the first hour was filled with gossip—who went where and said what—then boyfriend biz, mostly about Tim. I sort of wanted to keep my feelings about Patrick to myself for a while, and though Liz had gone out with a couple guys since the Sadie Hawkins dance, she didn't have a boyfriend, and Gwen had sworn off guys till summer.

"The problem," Gwen said, "is that I want a guy around when it's convenient for me, and I *don't* want him around when I'm studying or doing family stuff. No guy's going to put up with that."

"A guy who's as serious as you are, maybe," I told her.

"Gwen, if you could choose any guy you wanted, what would he be like?" Liz asked.

"Hmmm." Gwen leaned back against the couch, palms resting beside her on the rug. "He would absolutely have to have a goal. I wouldn't want any guy who doesn't have a picture of where he wants to be ten years from now."

"Really?" said Pamela. "I want to be on Broadway, but that doesn't mean I'll get there."

"I'm not interested in guys who are content to just let life happen," said Gwen. "I want a guy with plans."

"Then you should be dating Patrick," I said.

"Don't think I haven't considered it," she said, and laughed.

I was curious. "Did he ever ask you out?"

"No, but I was tempted to ask *him* out a time or two. Back when you were going out with Sam. But Patrick was never around long enough to ask, it seemed. Dad thinks I ought to stick to guys my own race—less hassle—while Mom says go with your heart. But don't worry." She nudged me. "Everyone knows that Patrick belongs to you."

"What do you mean, everyone knows?" I asked. "He was going with Marcie for a while, remember? And with Penny? What's this 'he belongs to me' business?"

Gwen took another swallow of her Pepsi to hide a smile. "Oh, it's just that he has 'Alice' engraved on his forehead or something. Anyway . . ." She got up. "Let's do something different." There was a computer at one end of the family room, and she slipped in a software program that invited you to sing along to an accompaniment—words on the screen—then it would rate your performance. If you got a good score, you'd hear applause; the higher the score, the louder the applause. If you bombed, you'd get boos.

"Let's each try it," said Pamela, adding, "Not you, Alice. You're excused."

I was grateful for that, because they know I can't sing. But it was a blast listening to the three of them. Gwen went first. She chose country music. The guitar accompaniment played "She's Stolen My Man," and Gwen was awful. She's got a good voice—she sings with her church choir—but this time she gave the words a nasal twang and let her voice slide from note to note till we were hooting with laughter. She also purposely sang off-key, Pamela told me. I wouldn't know. Pamela says that's even more difficult to do than singing the right way. Gwen got a chorus of boos at the end, and that encouraged Liz to do a love song to violins. She put a lot of drama into it and got a good score, so we clapped and cheered along with the canned applause.

Finally Pamela got up to sing one of Adelaide's songs, "Pet Me, Poppa," and she did it up royally, the original sex kitten. We were all really into it by now, and we were shouting and cheering as she moved suggestively about the floor. Then she got down on her hands and knees, mewing like a cat, wiggling her hind end, and suddenly, out in the hall, we heard a male voice say, "What is it?" And one of Gwen's brothers walked in.

Pamela rolled herself into a ball of embarrassment and

wouldn't uncurl even though the song was over and the computer audience was cheering.

"Hey, Jerry!" Gwen laughed. "I want you to meet Adelaide. Adelaide, this is my brother Jerome."

And then Pamela, with the Brooklyn accent that only she can imitate, uncoiled herself, held out one limp hand, fingers down, as though offering it to be kissed, and said, "Hello, big guiiy. Pleased t'meetcha."

Jerry laughed.

"Where's Bill?" Gwen asked.

"Deena came along, so he's with her," said Jerry. Both of Gwen's brothers are in college, though they're not as old as Lester. "Anything left from dinner?"

"Paella for one," Gwen said, and Jerry disappeared.

Gwen's folks had gone to bed, so we settled down about midnight and got into our sleeping bags. Pam was the first one asleep. She's a noisy sleeper and hates it when we tell her she snores. I could tell that Gwen fell asleep next, because I could hear her slow, steady breathing a few feet away from me.

I lay there feeling a little sad that I couldn't sing. It must have been fun hamming it up like that. Performing in front of your friends. I've missed some good times because of it—Christmas carols, joining in on "Happy Birthday," high school musicals, chorus. . . . The thing is, I'm so bad, so tone-deaf, I can't even tell the difference. I'd get a chorus of boos, but it wouldn't be funny.

My mind wandered back to the early embarrassment in grade school when I sang and was terrible but didn't know it. Kids stared at me at parties when the birthday song came around, and a music teacher once tried to figure out who was ruining "America the Beautiful."

I was on the verge of sleep when I heard soft voices coming from the hallway and the almost imperceptible close of a door.

My eyes popped open, and I remembered I was on the floor of the Wheelers' family room. Somebody was coming in. Any minute the light would come on, and I braced myself.

The murmurs continued, but there was no light.

"They don't know I'm here, Bill."

"So? I'm not going to wake them up to tell them."

"What if your dad comes down?"

"He won't. He sleeps like the dead."

"Your mom?"

"I'll turn on the TV. So we're watching TV. . . ."

A girl's giggle. "At one in the morning? What are we supposed to be watching?"

"The Weather Channel?"

More giggles. Murmurs.

Omigod! I thought. Bill was here with his girlfriend, and any second now I was going to get a foot in the face.

I coughed.

"What . . . ?" Bill's voice.

"Somebody's here!" The girl's frantic whisper.

"Mom?" Bill said tentatively.

I lowered my voice. "Go to bed," I said.

Silence.

"Bill! Your mom's on the sofa! Come *on*! Let's go!"

"Uh . . . I'm just taking Deena home," said Bill.

"Good," I answered.

There were hurried footsteps in the hallway. The soft open-ing and closing of the front door. Then I heard Liz's giggle from the other side of me.

"Alice, you were great!" she said. We rolled into each other, suppressing our laughter, and didn't tell the others till morning.

When we went in for breakfast around eleven, Mr. Wheeler was in his robe scrambling eggs for us.

"Your mother upset with me or something?" he asked Gwen as he set a plate of sausages on the table.

"You're asking *me*?" Gwen said. "Not that I know of."

"Well, I passed Bill in the hall this morning, and he mur-mured something about her sleeping on the couch last night. I thought she was in bed with me the whole time."

It was all we could do to keep our faces straight.

"Guess you'll have to talk that over with Mom," Gwen said.

On Monday, long-awaited Monday, after a year and a half of waiting for this Monday, I went to the orthodontist after school, and he removed my braces.

Eighteen months of Metal Mouth. Five hundred and forty days of catching spinach, corn, chicken—every edible thing—in my braces, of feeling that pull on my teeth, the soreness of my gums, the intrusion of wire when I kissed.

"Now," said Dr. Wiley when the last wire was removed, "look at that smile!" He handed me a mirror.

I grinned like the Cheshire cat, but to tell the truth, I didn't see that much of a difference. A straighter tooth here, maybe. A little less space between teeth there. But he said I now had a healthier mouth, a perfect alignment, a better bite, and my teeth could grow as God intended. And I wondered why God didn't make them grow right in the first place. But the orthodontist was happy, so I was happy. And I half regretted some of the remarks I'd made to him when I was most miserable. I especially regretted bleeding on his chair once during my period.

"Now, here's the thing," he told me, and his face was serious. "You *must* wear your retainer at least twelve hours a day, Alice, or your teeth will grow back like they used to be. Wear it at night, wear it at school, but you can take it out when you eat and for special occasions."

That's really all I wanted to hear—that I didn't have to wear my retainer to the prom.

"Gorgeous!" Sylvia told me when I got home. "Now you can do a full frontal smile."

I gave my full frontal smile to everyone I met the next day. I laughed at every joke, ran my tongue over my teeth for emphasis, ate an apple, and only one person noticed.

"What's so funny?" Patrick asked when he caught me grinning uncontrollably, and I guessed then that it was time to stop.

12

911

On April 11 the GSA had members stationed at all the school entrances to pass out armbands to anyone who wanted to show support for gays and lesbians to be who they are without having to hide it. There were also printed sheets explaining what the Day of Silence was all about in case anyone had missed my article. A few of the kids in the GSA wore tape over their mouths to emphasize their presence.

It was sort of a relief to go all day without talking, I discovered. Gwen wore an armband, but neither Liz nor Pamela took one, I noticed. I didn't ask them about it, but Pamela volunteered that it might be confusing to friends who knew she was going out with Tim. Liz simply said that if she couldn't answer questions in class, it might affect her grades. I guess all of us can think of excuses when we don't want to do something, but I know that this was an issue they would have to decide on personally; the GSA wasn't out to change people's minds with a wrench.

The teachers noticed which of us were wearing armbands and didn't ask us questions, and at lunch a bunch of GSA members sat together, so we wouldn't be tempted to talk to other friends.

What would it be like, I'd asked in my article, to have a secret so basic about who you really are and to feel you had to hide that part of yourself? What if I felt like a fraud, a phony? That I was pretending to be something I wasn't? What if I suddenly found myself on a planet where lesbians were the norm, and everyone kept trying to hook me up with a girl? How would I feel?

Most of the kids got it, I think. A couple of the guys who wore tape over their mouths got grins and a few jeers, but several people gave me the thumbs-up sign in the halls because of my article, and I found a note in my locker saying it was a good piece.

There was a little "breaking of silence" ceremony at the end of the day in the auditorium. Probably half the kids ditched and went to Ben & Jerry's, but the other half listened to Mr. Morrison explain how this would be an annual observance at our school, how it was intended to end bullying and harassment of gay students. He thanked us for participating and said that we were part of a national movement to send the message that hate would not be tolerated.

I looked forward to talking again when I got home, and the first conversation I had was with Aunt Sally, who called to ask if we had moved into our new addition yet. I described the rooms in detail.

"They sound lovely! I'll bet you're almost too busy to enjoy them, though, with all those extra things going on at school," she said.

"But guess what?" I told her. "I'm the new features editor for our school paper!" And I explained how Jacki Severn had quit and how Miss Ames wouldn't take her back. "The features editor plans the more in-depth articles we publish in each issue," I said.

"Features editor! Think of it!" said Aunt Sally. "Oh, your mother would have been so proud of you, dear! Those features are the best part of any newspaper! Of course, some features go a little deeper than they have to, but then, that's what newspapers do, I guess."

"Well, if you have any good ideas, let me know," I said.

"Why, I've got a good idea already," Aunt Sally said. "I think that every newspaper should have a column called 'The Answer Woman,' and that could be you."

I didn't know how to tell her that columns weren't considered features and that the last thing anyone would call me, least of all myself, was "The Answer Woman."

"Um . . . what do you mean?" I asked.

"Anybody could write in and ask a question; the Answer Woman would research it, and then she'd answer in the next issue," Aunt Sally explained. "And these would have to be the kinds of answers you couldn't always find on the Internet."

"Like what?" I asked.

"Like why is it that you can buy canned apricots with seeds only if they're peeled? If you want them unpeeled, they're cut in half and missing the seeds, and seeds give them flavor," Aunt Sally said.

"Huh?" I said.

"Why do you never see dead rabbits in the street? That's another question. You see dead squirrels, but when did you ever see a run-over rabbit?"

"Well, I . . ."

"And speaking of squirrels, did you ever see a baby squirrel? You see baby rabbits hopping through the tiger lilies in your yard, but when did you ever see a tiny squirrel skittering down a tree? Never."

She was right about that.

"Why can you say 'A girl whose clothes . . . ,' but you can't say 'A house whose windows . . .'? Did an English teacher ever explain why there's no word like 'whose' for an inanimate object? And don't get me started on sex. . . ."

"I wasn't about to," I murmured.

"Here's the question: Why do the parts of your body you make love with—well, not you, Alice, I mean married people's parts—have to be down *there*, for goodness' sake, right between those other parts we don't even *talk* about?"

"Well, the last time I looked, mine were down there too," I said.

"But *why*?" said Aunt Sally. "Why couldn't they be somewhere else . . . between the shoulder blades, maybe? Think how much neater it would be!"

I tried to imagine a man and woman rubbing their backs together.

"I don't know, Aunt Sally. Just doesn't do it for me, I guess. But I could do a feature story on *you* sometime," I told her.

Lester came over Sunday when we were sitting out on our new screened porch behind the family room. It was April at its best—birds everywhere, scouting out their territory—and Sylvia was talking about putting a bird feeder and bath out in the backyard . . . well, what was left of it, now that we'd put in the new addition. The air was balmy, breezy, totally perfect.

We heard a car door slam out front and, a little later, footsteps coming through the kitchen.

"Lester, I'll bet," Dad said, smiling.

We hadn't seen Les for several weeks and were sure he'd have come by when the renovations were complete. But his master's coursework wasn't over until the second week of April, so we knew he was too busy earlier this month to take time off.

"Anybody home?" Les called.

"Hey, Les!" Dad called. "Out here!"

I jumped up and ran inside. "Isn't this gorgeous?"

Lester walked into the family room. "Wow!" he said, looking around. "The Porta-John's gone! There's sod on the front yard! I can't believe it's finished!"

"Believe it," said Sylvia, coming in to give him a hug. "We're just loving this house, Lester. Come see the porch."

I followed him around like a puppy as we gave him a tour, wanting to see his reaction to everything.

"Now I wish we'd done it sooner," Dad told him. "All this space!"

"The fireplace! The windows! Man, oh, man!" Les said, then stepped out on the porch to look around there.

We moved from room to room, back to the hallway again and on upstairs. Lester gave a breathy whistle at each stop. "Fantastic job!" he said. "Great colors! If we'd had this addition when I was back in high school, think how I could have impressed the girls."

"Not up here in our bedroom, I hope," Dad said.

"And I don't have to share the bathroom with anyone, Lester!" I said, scrunching up my face at him. "Just think! The whole medicine cabinet! The entire countertop, just for me and my stuff!"

"Didn't I tell you I was moving back home for the summer?" he asked, and then, when all three of us looked at him in dismay, he burst out laughing.

We went downstairs again and sat around the table in our newly expanded kitchen. The coffeepot was still plugged in from breakfast, and Sylvia brought out a plate of lemon bars. As Dad set cups on the table, he asked, "So how are things with you, Les? Everything squared away?"

When Lester didn't answer immediately, just reached for the sugar, I could tell somehow that the news wasn't good.

"Well, could be better," he said. "I just found out that I can't present my thesis by the eleventh."

"Oh, Les!" said Sylvia. "What a disappointment for you!"

"They found something that major?" asked Dad.

"Afraid so. One of the philosophers I'm working on just had a new book come out that says pretty much exactly what I'm arguing."

"But does this invalidate your entire thesis?" Dad wanted to know.

"No, in a way, it's reassuring, but now I need to clarify exactly how my view is different from his and contributes something new to the debate. And it does, actually, but I haven't emphasized that as much, and an entire section needs an overhaul. I'm wiped out. I need a break."

Since I didn't understand much of anything they were talking about—and because his thesis had something to do with utilitarianism, I remembered that much—I just sat and tried to read their faces.

"So what's the plan?" asked Sylvia.

"I'll graduate in December, not May. Not what I'd hoped, but at least I know what I have to do," Lester said.

I'm embarrassed to say that my first thought was for myself.

I'd already bought his graduation present—a beautiful expensive pen that looked like green marble and wrote so effortlessly that you hardly felt it touch the paper. And I'd found a funny little wire figure of a graduate in cap and gown, holding a diploma in one hand, a beer stein in the other. I'd even found a card! In fact, I'd imagined myself at his graduation ceremony yelling *Go, Les!* when he crossed the stage!

Graduation in December? The month reserved for Christmas? It just didn't compute.

Dad was concerned about finances. "Will your fellowship cover the next six months, Les?"

"Well, there is *some* good news," Lester said, putting down his cup and smiling a little. "The fellowship ends in June, but I've been hired to work in the admissions office full-time—just a low-level job, but it'll buy the food and gas and haircuts till I get my degree."

"Full-time?" I asked, because, as far as I knew, Les has never worked full-time in his life.

"Yeah. Hard to imagine, isn't it?" he joked.

"Well, it'll all turn out, Les," Sylvia said.

"And I sure can't complain about my living arrangements," said Les.

The windows were open all over the house, and a light breeze blew my paper napkin off the table. A lawn mower was going somewhere down the street, and off in the distance a siren sounded, seeming to grow louder. As it grew louder still, we paused in our conversation, expecting it to wane as it passed by on Georgia Avenue, but instead, it became earsplitting, with a honking and urgency that made us get up from the table. It sounded as though it were going to come right through the house.

I ran to the front door.

"It's Elizabeth's!" I yelled. "The fire truck's stopped right in front of their house!"

A second truck followed the first. We rushed outside. Smoke was coming out their opened front door. Mr. Price was standing on the porch, directing the firefighters inside. Mrs. Price was out on the lawn with Nathan, who pointed excitedly at a rescue vehicle just rounding the corner. Elizabeth stood a few feet away, her eyes huge, hand over her mouth.

Already one fireman was running up the steps to the porch with an ax, and a second was uncoiling the long hose and dragging it to the hydrant two doors down.

We carefully made our way across the street, as neighbors gathered on porches and sidewalks.

"Janet," Dad said, going up to Mrs. Price. "Is there any way we can help?"

"Oh, I don't know!" she said. "Isn't this *some*thing? We're not even sure where it's coming from. We started smelling smoke, and when Fred opened the basement door, it just rolled out! We can't tell what's on fire, and the dispatcher told us to get out of the house."

I looked at Liz and wondered if she was going to throw up. Her face was pale.

There was the sound of crashing glass, and immediately smoke came pouring out of a basement window.

I put one arm around her. "Don't worry," I said. "They'll have it under control in a minute."

"I was in the basement just ten minutes ago!" she said.

"Well, the firemen know what to look for," I told her.

An ambulance pulled up.

"No pets in there, are there?" Lester asked, coming over. Liz shook her head.

Nathan was jumping up and down. "Will they put up the ladder?" he kept asking. "I want to see them put up the ladder!" He tugged at his mother's hand.

"Nathan, *stop* it!" Mrs. Price said.

Sylvia came over and took Nathan's hand. "Here, Nathan. Let's go get a better look at that ladder," she said, and Mrs. Price gratefully turned him over to her care.

There seemed to be a lot of coming and going. We couldn't hear any more crashing of glass or banging. One fireman stood by the fire hydrant, waiting for an order to attach the hose. But the minutes ticked by, and the man who had run up the steps with an ax was replaced by a man with a clipboard. More discussion on the front porch with Elizabeth's dad.

Liz turned away, biting her bottom lip.

Finally the fireman on the porch gave a "roll-'em-up" sign to the man at the hydrant, who dragged the hose back to the truck.

"Oh, thank goodness!" Mrs. Price said. "They must have found the trouble. I'm afraid to look inside."

"Most likely smoke damage, but nothing major, I'll bet," said Les.

The smoke coming out the front door had stopped entirely, and smoke from the basement was growing weaker.

"I just can't imagine what it could have been!" Mrs. Price went on. "Elizabeth was doing the laundry for me, but we haven't had any trouble with the washer and dryer before."

The firemen were putting things away. The ambulance drove off. So did the rescue truck.

The first fireman came down the steps and across the lawn toward us. Perhaps, because I still had one arm around Liz, he thought we were part of the family.

"Everything's under control, ma'am," he said to Liz's mom. "You had a fire in the dryer, and I'm afraid you'll need a new one. But it only scorched the wall. Maybe have to scrub down a room or two upstairs."

"But what caused it?" Mrs. Price asked. "I cleaned out the lint trap only last week."

"Think it was this," the man said, reaching into the big pocket of his yellow fireproof jacket and handing something charred and black to Elizabeth's mom.

"What is it?" she said, and then, slowly pulling it apart, she stared down at the remains of a bra.

Liz's face turned pink with embarrassment. Her Stupefyin' Jones push-up bra!

"Probably shouldn't put those things in the dryer. Anything with rubber padding's likely to overheat," the fireman said. And with a quick nod to Dad, he walked back to the truck.

Mrs. Price looked at Elizabeth. "Whose *is* this?" she asked. Then she saw Elizabeth's embarrassment, and crumpled it up in her hand as Dad and Lester turned discreetly away.

"I got it at a costume shop," Liz said miserably. "It was just a cheap thing, but I've been wearing it a little. . . ."

Neighbors were coming over now to talk with Mrs. Price.

"What happened?" they asked. And Les, as usual, came to the rescue.

"Just a stuffed toy that caught fire in the dryer," he told them.

Mrs. Price nodded gratefully. "Some things just weren't meant to be washed," she said.

Les and Dad and Sylvia went inside with the Prices to look at the damage, but Liz and I sat down on the porch steps as the neighbors dispersed.

"Oh, Alice, I'm mortified!" she said. "I should have just thrown it out. I'd got it all sweaty running around the gym but it's kinda fun to wear, and . . ." She rested her arms across her knees and her head on her arms. "I'll never be able to face Lester again."

"Why? He knows you have *breasts*, Elizabeth!"

"It was a push-up bra, Alice, for girls who *don't*."

"But Les doesn't know that."

"Les knows everything about women," said Liz. "He can tell a push-up bra at twenty paces, I'll bet." She tipped back her head and wailed, "Why does this have to happen to *me*?"

"Embarrassing stuff happens to all of us," I told her.

"Not like this! Not with a fire department announcing it to every neighbor on the block." And then she said, "I can remember every year of my life by something utterly humiliating that happened to me. Eleventh grade, the flammable bra; tenth grade, buying the Trojans; ninth grade. . . ."

"Liz, lighten up," I said. "*Nobody's* going to remember this except you. And Nathan, maybe, because of the fire trucks."

"Lester will."

"He won't. He's probably forgotten it already. He's got his mind on school and his thesis and graduation and—"

The screen door slammed behind us, and Lester came out on the porch.

"Gotta take off, Al," he said. "Take care." And as he went on down the sidewalk, he said over his shoulder, "Hey, Liz, the next time you decide to burn your bra, do it for a cause, huh?"

And then he was gone.

13
OUT ON THE TOWN

On Monday a special assembly was called at school for twelve forty-five. All students were to attend, and names would be checked off at the doors to the auditorium.

"Well, I'll miss the first half of English lit, but it takes fifteen minutes off our lunch period," said Liz. "It's raining out, though, so we can't do much anyway. Save me a seat in the cafeteria."

We hate it when anything intrudes on our lunch period or when we all have to eat inside. I was halfway down the hall to geometry when I heard Amy Sheldon call my name. She used to be in special ed, but this year she's attending regular classes. I don't know quite what it is about Amy that rubs people the wrong way. She's small for her age, and her features are a bit out of alignment, but she looks essentially like everyone else. I guess it's her social awkwardness that makes her the butt of jokes. "Amy Clueless," some of the kids call her.

I had to rescue her at the Snow Ball last winter when she came to the dance alone and some girls were trying to humiliate her. She makes a good target, evidently, because you're never quite sure whether it affects her or not—if she even knows it's a joke. I've asked her before not to call out my name in the halls like she does, but it hasn't stopped her.

"Alice! Alice! Guess what?" she was yelling.

Kids started laughing and turning around, rolling their eyes. *Should I just keep going?* I wondered. *Duck into a classroom to shut her up?* I stopped and turned, frowning.

But she came on like a spinning top.

"Guess what?" she cried again. "I got my period yesterday! I really did!"

There were loud guffaws all around me, kids slowing down to listen in.

"Hey, Amy!" one girl called, fishing in her bag. "Want a tampon?"

"Yeah, Amy. Want a pad?" called another, and boys laughed.

Before I could get to her, Amy answered back, "I can't wear tampons yet, 'cause I'm a virgin, but I always carry them in case somebody else needs them."

The hall erupted in loud laughter, and Amy's comment was

passed along from one group to another. You could hear laughter coming down the corridor, wave after wave, like dominoes falling.

I took her arm and hustled her on down the hall away from the catcalls. "Amy, that's something you don't talk about so everyone can hear," I said. "You don't want people laughing at you like that."

She looked at me blankly. "What's funny? I'm *glad* I got my period. I've been waiting and waiting!"

"I know, but it's bathroom stuff, so you just talk about it softly to other girls. Okay?"

"Okay. Mom says I'm a woman now and I have to be careful," she told me with satisfaction.

"She's right. You can never be too careful, Amy," I said. *Especially you*, I thought sadly, and gave her a little congratulatory pat on the back as I let her go.

"What do you suppose the assembly's about?" asked Liz as we found seats in the auditorium. "Some kind of compulsory sex ed, I'll bet."

"Nope. I'm guessing it's about discipline," said Gwen. "Whenever all students have to attend, you know it's discipline. A new set of rules."

Jill and Justin were sitting in front of us, and they thought so too.

"If we leave a book in our car, we'll probably need a pass to go back out and get it," said Justin.

Karen, sitting next to Jill, said, "Clothes. The principal will probably explain why we can't wear thongs."

"Who says we can't?" Gwen joked, and we laughed.

"See-through backpacks," said Sam, behind us.

But my thought was that the school was about to take away the open lunch period and make us stay on school property. Why else would they be taking up part of our lunch period for this?

Finally the principal came onstage. The *principal*, not the vice principal, so I figured it must be serious. Gradually the chatter died down, and when he said, "Good afternoon, students," everyone clammed up to see what the new restriction would be.

I was looking around for Pamela, because we always sit together at assemblies, but I couldn't see her, so I just assumed she was with Tim.

"Thank you all for attending," the principal continued, "especially those of you who are missing part of your lunch period. But we have two items of interest on the program. As you know, the faculty chooses one of our top seniors to be valedictorian at graduation. That has not been announced yet, but we have decided to honor three of our top students from each grade and to do this each year in a spring assembly. When I read the names, we would like the following students to come up onstage."

Well, *this* was a surprise. I think we were all relieved, and certainly curious. The principal read off three names from the freshman class, and there were cheers and applause after each one, as surprised students, somewhere in the auditorium, got awkwardly to their feet and made their way past the legs in their rows to get to the aisle.

The sophomore list.

Then the juniors. We whooped and cheered when Gwen was named, and we gave her backside slaps all the way down the row as she squeezed past us.

But what about Patrick? I wondered. Everyone knows he's a brain. And then I heard the principal announcing his name as one of the seniors. That's right. Patrick was a senior now. He was sitting down in the first row—something Patrick doesn't usually do, and I wondered if he'd gotten advance notice.

When all twelve students had been recognized, the principal gave their grade point averages and mentioned some of the activities they'd been involved in. Then he gave each of them a gold pin and a handshake, and when Gwen came back to sit with us, we passed the pin along so that we could all admire it and congratulate her again.

"And now," the principal said, "for the second part of this program we have a special treat. For the next two weekends, as you know, our music and drama departments will be giving performances of a great musical, *Guys and Dolls* . . ."

What? I thought. This assembly was going to be *fun*?

". . . And we're hoping that all of you will attend and bring your friends and families. To give you a taste of the music, we've asked the understudies of the four major parts to sing a few songs for you . . ."

Cheers and clapping. The understudies? That means Pamela!

". . . So may I present, *Guys and Dolls*!"

There was a drumroll, and I realized that Patrick and the other orchestra members had taken their places just below the stage. Mr. Kleingold, the conductor, brought down his baton, and the music began. The guy who was playing the gambler, Sky Masterson, came out first in his slick suit and shoes, and he sang "Luck Be a Lady." He didn't have quite the voice of the guy who had been chosen number one for the part, but he'd do in a pinch, and he got a hearty round of applause. The understudy for Sister Sarah Brown came next and sang "If I Were a Bell." Then the crap game operator, Nathan Detroit, sang "Sue Me."

But it was Pamela who got the cheers when she came out from behind the curtain in a chorus girl's cat costume, complete with whiskers, ears, and a tail, and sang "Pet Me, Poppa" in her Brooklyn accent.

Guys stomped their feet and whistled, and just before she left the stage, she flirtatiously twirled her tail at the audience.

The principal said he'd see us all at the musical. The assembly was over, and Gwen and Liz and I rushed backstage to tell Pamela just how great she was. But Tim had got there first and was hugging a happy, glowing Pamela.

"You were fabulous!" we told her, and I think she actually began to believe us.

I did have a lot of fun with my feature on teachers' secrets, except that I changed the title to "Would You Ever Guess That . . . ?"

The first line was: *Would you ever guess that journalism teacher*

Shirley Ames once ate eleven and a half hot dogs to win a contest?

I'd spent the whole week going to classes early to ask teachers for contributions, stayed late, stopped teachers in the hallways, interviewed them in the faculty lounge. . . . Some said they'd think it over and get back to me but never did. Others called me at home after I'd given them my number.

Would you ever guess that . . .
Bud Tolliver plays the ukulele?
Linda Jackson can belly dance?
Corina Galt owns a Model T?
Ernie Shepherd survived an avalanche?
Myra Bork raises ferrets?

"Kids are going to love this," Miss Ames said. "They'll never think of us in quite the same way. Every time they look at me, they'll think, 'Mustard and ketchup.'"

"Except there's so much more to each teacher than this," I said. "Next year maybe we could feature different teachers each month—every other issue—and tell about their backgrounds, families, hobbies. . . ."

"Yeah. I want to know how that sexy French teacher spends her Saturday nights," said Tony.

"Let's put that feature—no, not the French teacher—on the agenda for next year, Alice," Miss Ames said. "You'll have to help us remember, though, because all our seniors will be gone."

"Just my luck," said Tony.

* * *

The last week of rehearsals was wild. School in the morning, rehearsals each afternoon till eight or nine at night, stuff to write for the newspaper, leftovers to eat when I got home, then homework till midnight or later, and I was up again at six.

"You're trying to do too much," Dad told me one morning when I appeared zombielike at breakfast and knocked over my orange juice.

To tell the truth, I had one of the better jobs on stage crew. The art department had pitched in on most of the sets, and we'd rented a couple backdrops for select scenes, so all I had left to do was a little more painting: a lamppost here, a few bricks there, a table—things like that—extending a set or filling one in.

I didn't have to be one of Molly's prop girls who dashed onstage between scenes and moved stuff around, and being careful not to leave out something important, something a character needed in one of the scenes.

But I was supposed to help out as needed, so I made myself Pamela's personal costume changer between scenes. I had copies of Adelaide's costumes at the ready in case the original Adelaide broke an arm or something and Pamela had to go on. A lot of the time, though, I sat far back in the auditorium and did homework during rehearsals, waiting to see if I was needed.

I was actually glad not to be spending more time with Patrick right then, seeing what Pamela was going through. Tim hung around some of the rehearsals, and the minute Mr. Kleingold or Mr. Ellis called it quits for the night, he would whisk Pamela away and drive her home. Or they'd go somewhere to eat.

If I'd still been going out with Sam Mayer, for instance, his hovering would have driven me over the edge. It's nice to get a back rub when you're tired or a kiss when you're discouraged, but sometimes you just need time to get stuff done, and the less demands on you, the better.

Everyone on stage crew was allowed to take off one of the six performances to watch the show from the audience, as long as he had someone cover for him. One of the prop girls said she'd look after Pamela's costumes for me, so I decided to attend the musical on the first Saturday night, which would be the third performance. I wanted to sit with Liz and Gwen, and that was the night Molly was going to be included in the curtain call; she had chemo again the following week, so she wanted to attend when she felt her best.

Dad had let us put up one of the *Guys and Dolls* posters in the window of the Melody Inn, and I mentioned it to every customer who came in that day.

David, I noticed, was unusually quiet and seemed absorbed in some order sheets that Dad had asked him to tally. Except that when I stopped by the office on my ten-minute break, he didn't seem to be looking at the papers in front of him at all—he was just sliding his thumbnail up and down the edge of the account book.

I knew then.

"David?" I said. "You ended it with Connie, didn't you?"

He slowly raised his head and looked in my direction. "Yes," he said.

"Is that what you're thinking about? Whether you did the right thing?"

He smiled and shook his head. "No. I'm at peace with that. I'm just wondering if I did it the right way, and I'm sorry she's taking it so hard. And sorry that when we broke up the first time, I didn't make it stick, so she wouldn't have to go through it again. But this time I'm sure."

I waited. How do you know what to ask? How do you know when to just listen? Your gut feeling, that's all. But I let my curiosity get the better of me. "Did you go camping together? Is that when you told her?"

"You guessed it," he said.

"Only because you told me you probably would. Go camping, I mean." And I thought about David and his girlfriend sitting out under the stars on a romantic night and then David telling her it was over.

"You told her *that night*, or the next morning?"

"Actually, we talked all night long," he said.

"I don't understand love," I said after a moment.

"Neither do I. Human love, anyway," said David. "But I understand love of God, and that's why I'm at peace."

"I don't think I'd ever be able to make that choice."

"You don't have to. Not everyone is called to be a priest or a nun, and you're not even Catholic."

"But if the pope changes his mind and says it's okay for priests to marry, won't you be mad?"

"No, because if Connie was the right girl for me, maybe I would have decided differently," he said.

This wasn't making any sense, because how did David know that he just hadn't found the right girl yet, that she wasn't still out there somewhere, just waiting to be discovered?

"Listen, David," I said suddenly. "Does the fact that you're going into the priesthood mean that you can't have any fun?"

"Of course not!"

"Then what are you doing tonight?" I asked.

"What?"

"Tonight. Do you have any plans?"

"I hadn't thought much about it, actually."

"Then how about going to see *Guys and Dolls* with me and my friends? We'll pick you up around seven, and I'll even pay for your ticket."

He looked surprised. "Well, hey! How can I refuse? That had a long run on Broadway, didn't it?"

"Yes, and it'll be a blast tonight because one of our friends is in it. Where do you live?"

"In the District. I think I'll stay here at the store, though, and put in some overtime. Pick me up at seven. I'll be ready," he said.

14
THE DINER WITH DAVID

"You did *what*?" asked Liz.

"I invited a priest to go with us tonight. Well, a priest-to-be, and we're picking him up at seven," I said. "He's cool. I already told Gwen. She'll get him after she picks up Molly."

"This is wild!" Liz said. "You're not trying to tempt him, are you?"

"No, Liz. I'm saving him from another night of beer with the boys, that's all."

Liz and I were on the porch when Gwen pulled up, and David slid over in the backseat to make room. He was wearing jeans, cowboy boots, a black turtleneck, and a jean jacket.

"Hi, Molly! Hi, Gwen!" I said. "Liz, this is David, and tonight he's our guest for . . . Yay! The high school musical!"

"Bet it's been a while since you've seen one of those," said Liz.

"*Seen* one? I've *been* in one, and not so long ago, either," David told us. "You may not believe this, but I was the Royal Canadian Mountie in *Rose Marie*."

"What's that?" asked Molly.

"A musical so old that nobody does it anymore. We did it in a sort of camp style. The year before we had done *Hair*, and several of our more conservative citizens were upset, so we did the revival of *Rose Marie* to placate them."

"And you sang?" asked Gwen.

"Did I *sing*? You bet'cha. In full uniform. I was even in *The Mikado* in community theater."

"The Secret Life of David Reilly," I said, and we were on our way to the school.

Molly refused to wear a wig. She had on her trademark baseball cap, but she chose one with sparkles and spangles for this night. She'd even glued some sparkles on her sneakers. She had no eyebrows or eyelashes—those fall out temporarily too from chemo—but she wore makeup and had glitter on her cheeks that made her eyes dance.

"I want a good look at those lampposts—see if they got them right," she said. "And the low curtain in the Save-a-Soul Mission. I told them it's got to look faded. I found a storefront church in D.C. that said we could use theirs."

At the school Molly went backstage to sit with the crew while Gwen and Liz and David and I found ninth-row seats. The full orchestra was in place, and the auditorium was packed. The assembly had been good advertising for it. David seemed as eager for the curtain to rise as we did.

The overture began. I didn't have a good view of the orchestra pit, but my ears were tuned to percussion—I'm better at that than the melody—and I knew that Patrick was there. Finally the curtain went up, and the scene was New York City, with actors and actresses parading around Times Square. Pamela, as a member of the chorus, looked great.

There were no big mishaps that I could see—the girl who played Adelaide didn't break a leg or anything that would have given Pamela the role—and the enthusiasm of the audience made the singers perform even better. At the curtain call, after the whole cast had taken their bows, Mr. Ellis called the crew onstage, and I felt tears in my eyes when Molly was introduced as the prop manager. When she stepped out from behind the curtain, I grabbed David's hands and made him clap extra loud. Everyone stood and gave her a standing ovation.

Pamela was going out with Tim after the show, and we didn't want to keep Molly up too late, so as soon as we could collect her from backstage, we got in the car. David said, "Molly, when's curfew for you?"

"No curfew," she said, "but I fold around eleven."

"Then how about some food? My favorite place, and it's on me," David told us.

"Great!" said Gwen. "Just give me the directions."

Twenty minutes later, after many twists and turns, we pulled up in front of the Tastee Diner in Bethesda and piled out.

It was one of the old original diners, modeled after a dining car on a train. A backboard of shiny fan-shaped aluminum stood behind the stacks of plates and saucers, and the short-order cook expertly tended to fried eggs, burgers, sausages, and fries, all cooking at once on the grill.

"Hi, David!" the grill man said. "How's it goin'?" Then he looked at us and said, with a wink, "Pretty good, huh?"

"David!" called the waitress who was holding the coffeepot and filling a customer's cup. "Nice to see ya!"

"You must come here pretty often, huh?" I asked as we took a corner booth, all five of us squeezing in.

"As often as I can," David said. "Some friends introduced me to the Tastee Diner last year, and I'll take any excuse I can get to come out here."

It was popular with everyone else as well. Teen couples on first dates, apparently—a little too polite and self-conscious; gangs of girls in hooded sweatshirts, with private school logos on the front; guys and girls back from a game; a homeless man or two with matted hair and just enough money for some coffee and bacon; an off-duty bus driver ordering the turkey dinner, with extra gravy; and a small seventy-ish woman eating chipped beef on toast.

We eyed the menu and the coconut layer cake there on a pedestal beside the cash register. The middle-aged waitress was smiling as she came over. "Well, I knew you must have a love life, David, but I never suspected *four* girlfriends," she joked. "Coffee's on us tonight. Where y'all been?"

We told her about the musical.

"Oh, I loved that show!" she said. "And who would have thought that Marlon Brando could sing?"

Gwen was checking out the menu, and I could tell by the funny rise of an eyebrow that everything on it was a caloric disaster. *Pork chops and gravy, ribs and fries, macaroni and cheese, fried chicken and biscuits.* . . . "David, how do you stay so thin?" she asked. "Wow, but it looks good."

We settled for a club sandwich, two burgers, a couple of chocolate malteds, and a short stack for David. When the food arrived, miraculously fast considering that the waitress gave the order in code, it was exactly right.

During a lull, the cook came over to chat. "What's the occasion?" he asked David. "Night on the town?"

"Went to see *Guys and Dolls* at their high school," David answered. "Lots of fun."

"What's it about? Gangstas?"

"Deceit, deception, redemption . . ."

"And the Salvation Army," Molly added.

"Huh," said the cook, puzzled. "No accounting for taste."

When the cook went back to his grill and we were savoring our malteds, I noticed how skillfully David kept the conversation on the present. He seemed to be taking his cues from Molly. If she talked about what courses she was going to take next year, then he talked about next year. If she focused on school productions in the past, David went with that. He was usually future oriented, and if Molly hadn't been with us, he would probably have asked about Liz's plans for college, what Gwen hoped to become. He had the ability to look straight into your eyes when he talked to you, as though you were the most important person in the world.

He'll make a good priest, I thought. At the same time, *He'd make a good husband and father.*

We watched the parade of night owls come in—an old man wanting a plate of bacon and toast; father and son for cheeseburgers; a slightly drunk woman for coffee; three college girls back from a movie.

"A microcosm of humanity," said David.

Molly smiled with satisfaction and took one last swallow of her malted. "Whatever," she said. "It's been a fun evening."

When I got home at last around midnight, Dad and Sylvia had gone to bed. I'd turned my cell phone off during the performance, so I checked it just before I went to sleep. Only one call. From Patrick. No message.

I slept until noon the next day. Dad and Sylvia were at church. I toasted an English muffin, buttered it, set the saucer on the floor when I was through so that Annabelle could lick the remaining butter. Then I read the comics and finally picked up *Heart of Darkness* to finish before class on Monday.

By mid-afternoon, when Patrick still hadn't called, I punched in his number.

"Hi," I said when he answered. "What's up?"

"Oh," said Patrick. "Hi. What'd you think of the performance? Not that you haven't watched it a dozen times."

"Not from out front, though—not all the way through," I said. "I thought it went pretty well. Pamela looked so natural up there, I think she was born for the stage."

"You didn't see me wave at you?" Patrick asked.

I paused. "When? From the orchestra pit? No, I guess not. It was sort of dark in there."

"Oh," said Patrick. "Thought you saw me."

"I didn't see you wave," I said.

"My mistake."

Where was this conversation going? I wondered.

"I guess I thought you'd be hanging out after—with Pamela and everything," Patrick went on.

"No. She went out with Tim. We'd brought Molly."

"Well, I'd thought maybe we could go somewhere after, but I guess you had other plans."

"Sorry, Patrick! I didn't know you wanted to! I'm not a mind reader."

"Yeah. Well, we were both at the same place at the same time. . . ."

Are guys especially programmed to drive you nuts or what? "Patrick, we're both at the same place at the same time when we're at school, and we don't wait for each other after," I said.

"Good point. So . . . where *did* you go?" he asked.

"We had a full car. Gwen was driving."

"Yeah?"

"I was so glad Molly could go up onstage. And everyone gave her a standing ovation. I almost cried."

"Yeah, I gave her a little drumroll. Did you notice? You didn't tell me where you went after, though."

"We went to the Tastee Diner."

"And who was the guy?"

The guy? Aha! So this was it! "David?" I said innocently.

"You're asking me? I don't know. Was that his name?"

"Yes! David! He works part-time at the Melody Inn."

"And the rest of the time?"

"A student at Georgetown."

"Really? I didn't know you knew anyone at Georgetown," said Patrick.

"Only because he works for Dad." I hoped Patrick couldn't hear the smile in my voice.

"So . . . he's a college man, right?"

Oh wow! Was Patrick ever jealous!

"Yes, he's a college man." I couldn't help myself from adding, "He just broke up with his girlfriend, Patrick, and I was trying to cheer him up."

There was silence. "And . . . *did* you cheer him up? When I looked, you had your hands all over him."

I remembered that I'd grabbed David's hands and made him clap extra hard for Molly. "We *all* cheered him up, Patrick. Gwen and Liz and Molly and I. We had a good time and so did he." Then I decided to take pity on him. "Patrick, do you know *why* he broke up with his girlfriend?"

"Do I want to know this?"

"Yes. He's going to become a priest."

"Oh!" said Patrick.

"I don't understand you," I said, still hoping he wouldn't detect the smile in my voice. "You didn't seem to care when I went to the dance with Scott."

"Scott I can understand," said Patrick. "But College Man . . ."

"You're going to be a college guy yourself pretty soon."

"Then maybe you'll invite *me* out with your girlfriends?" said Patrick, and we laughed.

We talked a little more about school, about homework, about Patrick's dad retiring from the foreign service, and finally he said he had to study for a test and we said good-bye.

I turned off my cell phone. Then I stood up and looked at myself in the mirror. I looked pretty good. I was grinning.

He's jealous! He's jealous! I said to myself as I danced around and around the room. I never thought it would happen.

The following week everyone connected to the show was a zombie. We were trying to catch up on all the assignments we had missed the week before, and we still had three more performances to get through the coming weekend, with more rehearsals every day after school. Some teachers were understanding about it, some weren't. But finally it was the weekend, and I was able to give Pamela my full attention backstage.

Adelaide's chorus girls had to change costumes the most, and Pamela was afraid she'd get her period and leak through her satin pants. But every show went off without a hitch, and on the final night, as I watched Pamela onstage, I felt a little down. Envious again. Jealous, even, and it bothered me. She'd dash backstage with the other chorus girls, and all I had to do was have her costume ready. Help yank off the pink top and pull on the blue. Unzip the satin shorts and help her step into a skirt. Zip her up, put on the headpiece, give her an encouraging pat, and send her off again.

What was I, anyway? A mother hen? I got to write a feature story about the musical, of course, but was that it? Was I just a byline? A shoulder to lean on? Was it so much to ask that just once in my life, I'd get to walk onstage in front of a zillion people in an auditorium with crystal chandeliers and receive a prestigious award to the wild applause of admirers?

Well, okay. Without the chandeliers, maybe.

And maybe not a *zillion* people.

And maybe not *wild* applause.

But when would *I* get a little public appreciation and recognition, just for me? For something important? When would I get to say, *Thank you very much*?

Not this night, evidently, because Pamela rushed back to tell me I had handed her the wrong shoes, and she barely made it onstage in time.

* * *

What I really did feel bad about was that Pamela didn't invite her mom to the show. Didn't even tell her she was in it. Her dad came, bringing Meredith, and they came backstage with a little bouquet from the grocery store, like many of the other parents did. But I couldn't understand why Mrs. Jones couldn't have come to a performance. She would have loved it, loved seeing Pamela up there.

"Why *didn't* you invite her, Pamela?" I'd asked.

"Are you kidding?" she'd answered. "She would have embarrassed me! She'd be trying to outdo all the other moms by cheering and carrying on. She's breaking her neck trying to be 'The Good Mom,' and the harder she tries, the more it turns me off."

Pamela brought Tim to the cast party on the second Saturday night, of course, and I could tell he was relieved that the musical was finally over and he'd have Pamela to himself. I'd missed the cast party last year because I was sick, but this time I rode over with Patrick. Orchestra members hadn't been invited, but cast and crew were allowed to bring dates.

The guy who played Sky Masterson was having the party at his house—a big house in Kensington—and his folks even had caterers in the kitchen, serving up Coney Island hot dogs and Junior's cheesecake from New York. Patrick was wearing a black shirt with his jeans, and stage crew wore black too, so we wouldn't be so visible in the wings.

At the party the main characters got to perform all over again. They put on little skits—dance routines and parodies of songs that they'd obviously cooked up in advance for the party. The senior who played Adelaide, Kelsey Reeves, did a really funny takeoff of a stripper, except that just when you thought she was down to bare skin—and I could tell that Mr. Ellis was looking nervous—we saw that she was wearing a body stocking with signatures of the entire cast written all over it.

Pamela, as her understudy, did a tap dance with a top hat twirling on one finger, and Sky Masterson and Sarah Brown sang a duet.

The funniest act, though, was the one the three directors—Mr. Ellis, Mr. Gage, and Miss Ortega—put on. The two men played guitars, and Miss Ortega wore a long silky tunic and a blond wig with bangs. They pretended to be the folksinger trio Peter, Paul, and Mary, popular back in the sixties. They sang "Puff, the Magic Dragon" but completely overacted, which made us howl with laughter.

Mostly we stage crew members just watched and applauded, and I thought to myself, *Well, if it weren't for the audience, there wouldn't be anyone to perform for, would there?* Besides, I was content just to be there with Patrick, even though he had a headache from three nights of staying up late and playing the drums. We kissed in the car when he took me home, but I know it's not easy to be romantic when you have a headache—or a cold, a sore throat, cramps. So I told him to go home and get some sleep, and he seemed grateful.

But I was feeling dissatisfied, not with Patrick, but with myself. Looking over the past few months, I couldn't help thinking that Liz got to chase a cute guy around the school gym to a cheering crowd; Pamela got to tap dance; Gwen got an award in front of the whole school; but the only applause I'd received so far was for climbing out of a coffin, and I'd almost missed my cue to do *that*. I *had* to be good at *something*, but it was taking me a long time to find out what.

15
WAITING

There was only one more full month left of school, and it made us crazy. Seniors could more or less coast—they had their colleges nailed down, their jobs for the summer; that was my theory, anyway. I guess we always think that seniors have it made.

My SAT results had come back, and they were better than my PSAT scores—not fabulous, but pretty darn respectable, and I decided I'd let them stand. It tired me out to keep comparing them against everyone else's scores, especially Gwen's or Patrick's. I kept thinking about the way I compare myself to others, to my friends. Why I couldn't seem to be content to just be *me*. On the whole, it had been a pretty good year, and I thought of all the people for whom it had been bad. Molly, for example. Brian Brewster, for another, though I wasn't sorry for him in the least. Amy Sheldon, for whom every year, it seemed, was a bad year.

I was thinking about what I might propose for *The Edge* when I went to our planning session on Wednesday. My feature story on the Day of Silence had been well received, though it hadn't made the huge buzz I'd hoped for. Hadn't stirred up much controversy, and perhaps that was good. It would be great if we didn't even *need* a Day of Silence to remind us what gays go through. Didn't need a GSA. But still, it would have been nice to get a *little* more attention.

A lot of kids liked the article about teachers' secrets, and everyone liked the photos of *Guys and Dolls*, thanks to our photographers, Don and Sam.

"What do we have for our last two issues?" Miss Ames asked.

"We already decided to delay the final issue until we get some pics of the prom," Scott said. "And we always do a farewell piece for any teacher who's leaving."

He went around the table, asking each of us in turn what we had for the next issue. "What about features, Alice?" he asked.

I read off the list of ideas I'd been keeping in a notebook: a story on favorite hangouts, an article on the school parking lot situation, the current policy on suspensions and expulsions, summer footwear with photos, student representation at school board meetings. . . .

"All good," said Scott. "Let's see what you work up first."

After the meeting I was all the way down to my locker before

I realized I'd left my jacket in Room 17. I turned around and went back, and just as I reached the journalism classroom, I heard Don say, "We're good for Saturday night, then—you and Kendra and Christy and me?"

"Yeah, we're on," Scott answered.

Then Don: "You and Kendra are really tight, huh?"

And Scott: "I guess so. She's even talking about switching colleges and coming to mine."

"No kidding?"

I took three steps backward as they came out the door and bent quickly over the drinking fountain as they started down the hall. Rising up, I swallowed the gulp of water and said, "Forgot my jacket. See ya!"

"See ya," said Scott.

"Take care," said Don.

I went inside the empty classroom and slowly put on my jacket. I guess a lot had happened in the last two months since the Sadie Hawkins Day dance. Maybe Scott had agreed to go with me because he wasn't sure of Kendra. Maybe Kendra hadn't been sure of him. And maybe I had invited Scott because I wasn't sure of my feelings for Patrick.

In any case, the crush was definitely over, and I was almost relieved to hear that Scott and Kendra were "together," and he was out of my dreams for good.

The first week of May was spent on catch-up. Catching up on all the homework I'd let slide, the papers that were late, the feature story I was writing for *The Edge*, straightening my messy room, doing my wash, answering e-mails. . . .

I took time out to give Sylvia a hand in the garden after work on Saturday, though—the first Saturday of May—and it helped chill me out. The lawn had been so torn up during the renovation that we had all new shrubs planted along one side, and Sylvia splurged on tulips and daffodils, already in bloom when we replanted them: purples and yellows in one place, reds and yellows in another.

"If you hadn't become a teacher, would you be a gardener?" I asked, seeing how much pleasure she took in it.

She chuckled. "Gardening's one of the things I enjoy part-time, but I'm not sure I'd want to make it my life's work."

"Did you ever want to be anything else? Like a . . . Shakespearian actress or something?"

"I don't know that the stage can support too many Shake-spearian actresses, Alice, though it might be fun to work at it for a summer. No, I think I'd miss the interaction with students. An audience doesn't give that much feedback. And I'd probably be bored with so much attention to myself," she said.

That was a strange thought, I decided. I didn't think per-formers ever got tired of themselves. But maybe they had to be constantly fed by an audience in order to feel good about it. Still, could you really get tired of a life of applause and adulation?

"Where should we put these?" I asked, lifting up the last pot of white tulips—SNOW WHITES, the little tag read.

Sylvia thought for a minute. "You know, I think they deserve a spot all to themselves. They're not as showy as the reds, but they're beautiful in another way. Let's give them a green backdrop—right over here—and let them have center stage."

Dad and Sylvia were going out that night, and I was tired from all the gardening. I didn't really want to go anywhere, but I didn't want to spend the evening alone, either. I called Liz.

"You doing anything tonight?" I asked. Liz has gone out with a guy three times since the Sadie Hawkins Day dance—not the same guy, either—and probably had a waiting list, but I asked anyway.

"A guy in my biology class said he'd call, but a girl told me he's a 'hands-on' type of guy, so I was going to make some excuse if he did," she said.

Every time Liz has a date, I want to call out the cheering section, but then I remember what Patrick said about how a lot of reassurance can make somebody insecure. So I just played it cool, like, *Of course guys like you! Why would they not?*

"Want to sleep over, then?" I said. "Eight o'clock? Earlier, if you want. I imagine Pamela's out with Tim, but I'll call anyway. Gwen, I know, is at her aunt's for the weekend."

I called Pamela on her cell phone, and it was a while before she answered.

"Hello?" she said finally.

"How you doing? I thought maybe you were out with Tim," I said. "Liz is going to sleep over."

"He's got a really bad cold," Pamela told me. "I suppose I'll catch it next."

"Then you want to come? Dad and Sylvia are out."

There was an uncharacteristic pause. "Yeah," she said finally. "I guess so."

"Don't let me twist your arm."

"No, I'll come," she said. "Will Gwen be there?"

"She's at her aunt's. Come about eight, okay?"

"See you," she said.

The usual letdown after a performance, I thought. The stage crew feels it, but it's worse for the cast. All that attention, the footlights, the spotlight, the costumes, the makeup . . . For six weeks or so, you're part of a group, a family, a team, a production. You're all involved in the same thing—the excitement, the inside jokes, the sharing—and then . . . poof! It's over. *Fini.* I checked the freezer for Pamela's favorite ice cream, coffee. *Perfecto.*

Liz arrived first and brought some brownies she'd made. "Everything cleaned up at your place?" I asked her, realizing I hadn't seen cleaning crews outside her house for a while.

"We were able to wash down some of the walls, but the hall had to be repainted," she said. "And of course we had to replace the dryer. Dad's getting over it now, but he was so mad at me! I don't think he'll be buying me a car anytime soon."

Pamela didn't realize she'd forgotten her sleeping bag until she walked in. "I'll go back," she said.

"Never mind," I said. "You can sleep on the couch. Come on. Liz brought brownies."

I brought out the whole half gallon of ice cream, and we carried our bowls into the family room, making brownie sundaes. Pamela settled down with a little sigh and spooned ice cream into her mouth.

"Post-performance letdown?" I said.

"I guess. Everything happens at once."

"I know what you mean. How's Tim?"

"He sounded awful on the phone. Temperature, too. He says he's probably contagious, so he's staying in this weekend."

"Lucky for us!" said Liz. "Girlfriend time! I wish Gwen were here, but she's got so much family, somebody's always celebrating something."

"That must be nice," I said. "I've got to go all the way to Chicago or Tennessee to see my relatives."

We rehashed old news, new news, tidbits, gossip. . . .

"You heard about Jill and Justin, didn't you?" asked Liz.

"They didn't break up, did they?" I asked.

"Are you kidding? They're plastered together with industrial-strength glue!"

"Yeah, I heard that Justin's parents took them both to the Bahamas over spring break," said Pamela. "First they were going to take Justin alone to get him away from her; then they ended up taking them both."

"Well, that's not quite the way it happened," Liz confided. "I got it straight from Karen. Mr. and Mrs. Collier took Justin to the Bahamas, all right, to get him away from Jill, whom they consider to be a grade-A gold digger. But guess who showed up at the hotel next door? Justin sent her the money, and Jill flew in. His folks were furious."

"Omigod!" I said. "Why didn't we hear about this before?"

"We don't move in the same circles, I guess. I don't have any classes with them, do you?" said Liz.

"No. I think his parents better give in," I said. "It's a losing battle. They've been together a long time."

"Karen says the Colliers are hoping that college will put a brake on the romance. Get them as far away from each other as possible."

"Unless she follows him there," I said, thinking about Scott and Kendra.

"And she probably will," said Liz.

We all sat pondering that a minute.

Then Pamela said, "I'm two weeks late."

I had just reached for a pillow. Then I paused. Looked at Pamela. "What?"

Pamela's voice was softer now. "My period's two weeks late."

I think I stopped breathing. Elizabeth was staring.

"You think . . . you're *pregnant*?" Liz asked.

"I . . . I don't know." Pamela swallowed.

I let go of the pillow and leaned back, studying her face. "But . . . but you said you were using condoms!" My heart was pounding.

"We were. Well, most of the time."

I didn't want to hear this. "Most of the time?"

"Well, except for a couple of times during rehearsals. I'd hardly had any time for Tim, and he was feeling left out. . . ."

But it was still five days from the middle of my period!"

"Five days!" I exclaimed. "But, Pamela, sometimes your period isn't regular!"

She sucked in her breath and it sounded shaky. "Don't make me feel worse," she pleaded.

I wanted to grab her and shake her. I wanted to hug her. I wasn't sure what I wanted to do.

"Maybe it's just all the tension and everything from the musical," Liz said quickly. "You *have* been under a lot of stress, Pamela. And all that strenuous dancing. My periods are off sometimes when I'm upset."

"That's what I keep telling myself," Pamela said. "But . . . two weeks?"

I couldn't take my eyes off her. She seemed so tiny all of a sudden, like a little girl. How could a little girl be having a little baby? It was as though we were back in sixth grade when I'd first met Pamela Jones, and she had blond hair so long she could sit on it. She could sing and dance and got to play Rosebud, the leading role, in the class play. All I got to be was a "bramble bush with branches thick," and I was so jealous. I sure wasn't jealous now.

"Have you said anything to Tim?" I asked.

"Not yet. He's miserable enough with that cold. I don't want to worry him about this."

"You're right," I said. "You could start getting it at any time, and it would be all this worry for nothing." But even I didn't believe it.

"If . . . what if I *am* . . . ?" She stopped as though she couldn't even say the word. Her voice was even softer than before.

"Well, it won't change anything between you and me and Liz, you know that. Gwen, either."

"Don't tell Gwen," said Pamela.

"Why not?" I asked. "We're not telling anybody, but if we did, why not Gwen?"

"Just because." Pamela fidgeted with a hole in the knee of her jeans. "She's so smart and . . ."

"But she's had intercourse!" Elizabeth said. I always laugh when Liz says *intercourse* instead of *sex*. But it didn't seem funny now.

"I don't want Gwen to know because she's too smart to get pregnant," said Pamela.

"Stupidity and carelessness aren't necessarily the same," I told her. "But even if you *are* pregnant, and that's a big 'if,' Pamela, it's your story to tell, not ours."

"Thanks," said Pamela, and her voice was shaky again.

"Listen." I studied her for a moment. "Why don't you just buy a pregnancy test kit and . . ."

"No!" cried Pamela. "I'm not *ready* for that!"

"Let's watch a movie," said Liz.

We put in a DVD and moved to the couch, sitting side by side, Pamela between us. I don't know if any of us really watched or what. All I could think about was Pamela, and I felt sick to my stomach.

* * *

For the next week I felt as though I wanted to call Pamela every fifteen minutes to see if her period had started yet. I thought about her when I was supposed to be studying for an exam. I worried about her when I should have been writing a feature story.

I e-mailed her about trivial things so that if she'd happened to have started her period and forgotten to tell me, she'd think of it then. Nothing.

At school Pamela went around with a drawn look on her face. She wasn't throwing up. She didn't say she was nauseated. She just looked thinner, was quieter at lunch, distracted when we went to Starbucks after school. Every once in a while she would laugh loudly at something somebody said, as though she were just tuning in occasionally and had to let us know. She even seemed more distant from Tim, I noticed, when they were together.

On Saturday she called.

"I told Tim last night," she said.

"Told him that . . . ?"

"That I'm over three weeks late. He wanted to have sex, and I just didn't feel like it, so I . . . I told him."

"What did he say, Pamela?"

"What *could* he say? All the right things, of course. That maybe it was just stress, but that if I *was* pregnant, he'd be here for me. But what does it really mean, Alice—'I'll be here for you'? For what, exactly? He can't have the baby for me, can he?"

"He's trying to be supportive, Pamela." I didn't even like to hear the word *baby*.

She was crying now. "I know. I could tell he was upset. Shocked, even. Oh, he kissed me and told me not to worry, that he loved me no matter what, but . . . we're both scared. Why did this have to happen to *us*, Alice? Jill and Justin have been having sex forever, and *she's* not pregnant!"

"Don't you think it's time to take a pregnancy test? Do you know how soon it would tell?" I asked.

There was a tremulous little sigh at the other end of the line. "I'm too scared to find out."

"But if you're not pregnant, Pamela, you could stop all this worrying and waiting!"

"Will you come with me to buy one? You and Liz?" she asked.

"Of course," I said.

Ironic that we celebrated Mother's Day that Sunday. Next year, maybe, I'd be sending a *Happy Mother's Day to a Friend* card to Pamela, and I couldn't bear to think about it.

I'd already bought a gift for Sylvia, though, and when Dad said we were going to take her to a buffet brunch at the Crowne Plaza, I tucked it in my bag and climbed into the backseat with Les.

It's impossible to be serious and moody if Les isn't. First of all, Sylvia still wasn't "mom" to us, but here we were, celebrating Mother's Day. And second, it felt weird to be sitting in the backseat with Lester, like young kids on an outing with their parents.

And suddenly Lester whined, "Are we there yet?"

Sylvia's tinkling laughter filled the car, and I could see Dad's grin in the rearview mirror. But before either of them could respond, Les said, "Alice is making faces at me, Dad!"

I jumped in with, "He started it!"

"She's over on my side! Make her move, Dad!" Les continued.

"Huh-*uh*!" I croaked. "Here's the line, and you're way over where you're not supposed to be!"

"One more word out of either of you, and it's no dessert, and that's final," Dad said.

We were still laughing when we entered the restaurant.

I liked that we looked like a family, though. Liked that I was beginning to feel that Sylvia was family too. At the buffet table Sylvia asked for sour cream, then got distracted and walked on. When the server came back with the little container, he gave it to me and I liked that he said, "Would you give this to your mom?"

After the meal, when we were having coffee, I slipped a card across the table. "Happy Mama's Day," I said.

Sylvia gave me a surprised smile. "Well, *thank* you, Alice!" she said, and opened it. Inside was a gift certificate for one pet grooming session at *Fur and Feathers* for Annabelle: hair trimmed, coat brushed, claws filed, teeth brushed, ears cleaned—the works.

If Sylvia remembered the bitter words I'd spoken last November about her cat—*our* cat—she didn't show it. She just gave me a full smile, and her eyes were warm and friendly. "This means a lot," she said. And it did.

16
TEARS

On Monday, two days before my birthday, Pamela, Liz, and I went to the CVS store after school, moving woodenly down the aisle of sanitary products, condoms, lubricants, ointments, and finally—pregnancy test kits.

I didn't want to be doing this! We should be looking at college catalogs! Summer sandals! At sunscreen and sunglasses! We should be planning parties and raft trips and bike rides and picnics, not thinking about baby clothes in nine months. *Eight* months!

But it was hard not to think about babies. The end of each aisle had a little bouquet of spring flowers on it. The gift wrap featured baby chicks and bunnies. Advertising signs placed here and there were done up in yellow, pink, and blue.

When we found the test kits, Pamela said, "Keep an eye out at each end of the row, will you? All I need is for someone from school to see me. Or for a neighbor to tell Dad."

I moved to one end of the aisle and stared at remedies for yeast infections. Liz moved to tampons at the other end.

It took longer than we thought, because Pamela wanted to read the directions for each test kit before she finally chose one. We covered for her at the cash register, too, to make sure no one we knew was around. But when we got outside and I asked Pamela where she wanted to take the test, she said, "I'm not going to do it yet, because maybe I just didn't ovulate this month, with all the tension. Maybe I've just skipped a period. I'll wait one more week, and then I'll do it."

"Any morning sickness or anything?" I asked.

"No, just a little queasy sometimes, but I think that's because I'm not sleeping very well."

Isn't that the same as nausea? I wondered, but I didn't push it. We left her at the corner of her street, then Liz and I walked slowly home.

I thought of all the times we'd taken this same walk, on this same sidewalk, with no other worries than whether or not you were supposed to close your eyes when you kissed. When the future stretched endlessly before us—high school, college, on and on. And now, for one of us, maybe, this huge detour. . . .

Finally Liz said, "If, like we promised, we don't tell anyone . . . and something happens to Pamela . . ."

"Don't even *think* it!" I said.

By Tuesday morning I thought *I* was going to be sick. Scenes kept running through my head: Pamela telling her dad and Meredith; Tim facing his folks; the accusations, the tears, the lectures, the anger. . . . It wasn't just Pamela and Tim's lives that would be disrupted, but their families' as well.

But maybe Pamela *wasn't* pregnant! Maybe she was . . . maybe she wasn't . . . maybe she was. . . .

"What's with you?" Gwen asked Pam at lunch when she didn't finish her turkey wrap. "You usually eat yours and bum a pickle off me too!"

Pamela faked a laugh. "Watching my weight," she said.

"Yeah. Right, skinny gal. You don't want that oatmeal cookie? I'll take it."

I changed the subject. "How's Molly? Anyone check on her lately?"

"Looking good, as far as I can tell," said Gwen. "Her mom said her blood tests definitely showed improvement. New combination of drugs, I guess."

"Well, at least something's going right for one of us," Pamela said as the bell rang, and I saw Gwen studying her closely.

After school Liz and I sat out on the new screened porch behind our family room. The azalea bushes were in bloom, the grass was thick and green, the first bumblebee of the season was buzzing slowly around outside the screen, and a light breeze blew through from the southeast, hypnotically caressing our faces.

"Do you think . . . if she *is* pregnant . . . she's eating okay?" Liz asked me. "Have you noticed if she drinks milk with lunch?"

I shook my head.

"I mean, is she supposed to be taking vitamins or anything?"

"You're asking *me*?" I said.

We were quiet some more.

"Is it possible she's already taken the test and just doesn't want to tell us?" I said aloud. And then, answering my own question, "With Pamela, anything's possible."

"Maybe we should set up a doctor's appointment and just take her there by force," Liz said.

"Yeah. Right."

"We could tell her there's someone we want her to meet."

"And then he tells her to climb up on the table and put her feet in the stirrups?" I turned my head suddenly and listened. "Was that the doorbell?"

I got up and went back through the family room, the kitchen, the hallway, and opened the front door. There was Pamela, holding the test kit.

"Are you alone?" she asked as I pulled her inside.

"Liz is here, that's all," I told her.

"I guess . . . I'm ready," said Pamela.

I got Liz, and the three of us went upstairs. We sat together in my bedroom—Pamela and me on the bed, Liz on the desk chair.

"Do you have a paper cup?" Pamela asked.

I went to the bathroom and brought one back. Pamela went over the instructions again: "I'm supposed to pee in this cup, then put this dipstick in for five to ten seconds. . . ." She suddenly handed the instruction sheet to me. "I'm too nervous. You read it."

"'Immerse the dipstick in the collected urine for five to ten seconds,'" I read. "'A minute or two later you will see "pregnant" or "not pregnant" on the stick.'"

"I'll time it," said Liz, looking at her watch.

For fifteen seconds or so Pamela just sat on the bed holding the cup. But finally she squared her shoulders, took a deep breath, and went into the bathroom.

It seemed to be taking too long.

"Think we should go in there?" Liz asked.

Then we heard the door open and Pamela's footsteps in the hall. She was holding the half cup of urine, and she carefully placed it on my desk, a tissue beside it. "I'll do it in here," she said. "I want you guys to be with me."

She unwrapped the dipstick, then stuck it in the urine. "Count," she said.

"One . . . two . . . three . . . ," Liz began, looking again at her watch. At the count of ten Pamela took out the stick and laid it on the tissue. We gathered around.

"How long did it say, Alice?" Pamela asked.

I looked at the instructions again. "A minute or two."

I tried to remember when I had been this nervous, this

uncomfortable, this terrified. We were staring at the dipstick as though it were some alien life-form that would suddenly start pulsating or breathing or beeping.

"It's starting to show," said Liz, and we all leaned forward as the letters became more visible.

And finally there it was. *Pregnant*, it read.

Pamela sat down on the bed again and cried.

I couldn't take my eyes off the stick. Maybe we had just missed it. Maybe the *not* was yet to come. But it didn't.

We sat down on either side of Pamela and let her cry. Babies were supposed to be happy occasions! How did this get so mixed up?

"H-he even said he'd marry m-me if it happened," Pamela wept.

Liz couldn't help herself. "But you guys are only *seventeen!*" she said.

Pamela violently shook her head. "I didn't want it to be like this. I don't want a guy marrying me because I'm pregnant. I'm not sure I even want to marry at all. I *know* I don't want this baby. And yet . . ." Her face screwed up again. "It . . . it's *T-Tim's!*"

We just sat there and stroked her hand. Her back.

When the tears stopped a second time, Pamela said, "Sometimes tests are wrong, you know! This could be a false positive. Maybe I should go back and buy a kit that just shows a plus or a minus. Or changes color or something. I mean, shouldn't you always get a second opinion?"

The doorbell rang and we all froze.

"It couldn't be Dad or Sylvia," I said. "Unless they lost their key." I stood up and went to the window. "It must be Gwen! It's her brother's car."

I was afraid that Pamela would tell me not to let her in, but Pamela just sat there on the bed like a wad of wet tissue, so I went downstairs and opened the door.

Gwen's good at reading faces. She just cocked her head and studied me. "I called Pamela's and no one answered," she said. "I called Liz's and her mom said she was over here. So I decided to drive Bill's car over and see what the heck is going on."

"Pamela's upstairs. Come on up," I told her.

As Gwen followed behind, she asked, "Is this something I'm not supposed to know?"

"Yeah," I said, and smiled a little over my shoulder. "Because you're too perfect and too smart to ever let this happen to you. But I think Pamela's accepting visitors now."

Gwen still looked puzzled. But when she entered my bedroom, she took it all in—the opened test kit on the floor, the cup of urine on my desk, the dipstick. And Pamela, forlorn and tearstained on the bed.

"Oh, girl!" Gwen said, and put an arm around her.

And then, Gwen the Practical took over. She pulled up the desk chair and sat facing Pamela. "Okay, what's the plan?" she asked.

"Go to a convent, what else?" Pamela said grimly.

"Have you told Tim?"

"Yes. He knows I'm late. But he doesn't know this."

"What about your dad? Have you said anything to him or Meredith?"

"They'd kill me."

"Now listen, Pamela," said Gwen, taking her hand and gripping it hard. "You've got choices, you know. You don't have to decide anything right now. Got that? You don't even have to decide anything this week. Promise me—*promise* me—you won't do something stupid, like eat a whole box of Ex-Lax or jump off a roof or swallow a bottle of pills."

"I'm too tired to do anything but sleep," said Pamela.

"You *will* tell Tim, though, won't you? He needs to know."

"Yes."

"How did you get over here?"

"Walked. I just want to take a nap."

"Then c'mon, I'll drive you home," Gwen told her.

We all hugged Pamela, and then they left.

I looked at Liz. "I don't want Pamela there by herself," I said. "I'm calling Tim."

When he answered—and *fortunately*, he answered—I said, "Pamela needs you, Tim. She's at home." And I didn't have to explain.

It was a rather somber seventeenth birthday for me the next day. I'd already told my family I didn't want a party, and I didn't. I was getting too old for a lot of fuss, and I was too wiped out worrying about Pamela to enjoy it much. I let Dad and Sylvia think I was just tired from studying for my finals.

I went to the newspaper staff meeting after school, and when I got home, Lester was there, and Sylvia was frosting the cake she'd baked the night before.

Lester blew on the little paper horn he'd stuck in one pocket, and I decided I was going to be cheerful no matter what. If I couldn't tell my family what the matter was, then I owed it to them not to play Guess Why I'm Grumpy.

"Looks delicious!" I told Sylvia of the German chocolate cake.

"Do you realize you were born in one of the most beautiful months of the year?" she said. "Just look at our yard. Everything that can bloom has blossomed."

"The flowers that bloom in the spring, tra la!" sang Lester, and even I recognized the song from *The Mikado*. The words, anyway.

What was really a surprise was that Dad came home bringing David, Marilyn, and her husband, Jack, along with him.

"Now, this isn't a party, Alice," Sylvia said quickly. "We just invited a few friends in for dinner."

I laughed and was grateful that there was *some* kind of a celebration after all—grateful for family. And I tried to keep Pamela out of my mind for the present.

Jack had brought his guitar, Marilyn brought flowers, and at seven sharp a delivery man from Levante's brought shish kebabs and tabbouleh and lemon rice soup. We had a feast.

"So this is the age when magical things happen, huh?" said Lester.

"Magical how?" asked Marilyn.

"Well, every time I pass a newsstand, I see that magazine,

Seventeen. It's been in print forever, but it never says *Eighteen*. It's as though seventeen is the age a girl wants to be forever."

"Oh, no," said Marilyn. "Twenty-one. Definitely twenty-one."

"I say whatever age I am right now," said Sylvia. "Whatever age I get to be, that's the best."

"Live in the moment," said David.

"So what's the magical age for a guy?" I asked Lester.

"Easy," he said. "The age he graduates."

"Amen to that," said Dad.

After dinner Jack played "Happy Birthday" for me on his guitar. Then he and Marilyn sang some duets they'd been performing at folk music concerts, their own arrangements. We'd had so much food that we sent some of it home with them when they left, and I gave them both a hug at the door.

I *really* appreciated my family that night. But of course the evening could not be complete without a phone call from Aunt Sally and Uncle Milt in Chicago.

"Happy birthday, honey," said Uncle Milt. "Wish we could be there to give you a hug."

"I wish you could too," I said, and thinking about his heart operation last fall, I asked, "How *are* you?"

"Fit as a fiddle," he said. "Taking good care of myself. But the big news here is that Carol is getting married in July to that Swenson boy. We like him a lot."

"Oh, we do too!" I said. "That's wonderful." And I told the others.

"Well, you'll all get invitations," said Aunt Sally on their speakerphone. "But I'm writing poetry now as my hobby, Alice, and I've composed a poem for your birthday. I mailed it to you with a card, but I'm afraid it won't get there until the weekend. So I'd like to read it to you."

"I can't wait to hear it," I said. "I'm going to hold the phone away from my ear so everyone can hear, Aunt Sally. Is that okay?"

"Of course!" she said. "And I'll speak louder." She cleared her throat and began:

> "When you were born a little girl,
> As pure as driven snow,
> We knew that you'd be tempted to
> Say 'yes' instead of 'no.'
>
> Your mother left our earthly home
> And asked me to take care
> That you would lead a virtuous life
> In thought and deed and prayer.
>
> We've watched you grow up straight and tall,
> So beautiful of face.
> And hoped that you would keep yourself
> In innocence and grace.
>
> But whether you are pure or not,
> Or somewhere in between,
> You'll always have our deepest love,
> So, Happy Seventeen."

I hardly knew what to say. Aunt Sally has been worried about my virginity for almost as long as I can remember, but her preaching always comes at me sideways, and she thinks she's being subtle.

This time, though—maybe because I'm almost grown up— it didn't bother me a lot. I was moved that she cared for me so much, and I wished that Pamela had a mother she could talk to. Even an Aunt Sally.

"Thank you, Aunt Sally," I said. "It's an honor to have a poem composed just for me on my birthday."

After we'd talked a little about Carol's coming wedding and how the reception would be held in the hotel where the groom is manager, we said good-bye and I gently put down the phone.

"Only Aunt Sally!" Lester said, grinning. Turning to Dad, he asked, "Do you remember the article she sent me on my thirteenth birthday, warning me of the dangers of smoking? And the newspaper clipping on my eighteenth birthday about teenage drinking? Oh yeah. And the story of the man who fathered eleven illegitimate children, and once they learned to trace DNA, they tracked him down and made him pay eleven mothers for child support? And Aunt Sally would always write at the bottom of each article, 'But we know this would never happen to you.'"

"What would we do without Sally?" Dad said. "She got us through some rough times when Marie died. Ah, yes. Sal and her poetry. Now, this one's a keeper."

17

THE BUS TO SOMEWHERE

I put on my pajamas at about ten thirty and was reading one more chapter in my sociology book when my phone rang. I glanced at the clock, puzzled, then reached down for my bag on the floor and took out my cell. Pamela.

"Pam?" I said, holding the phone to my ear.

"I feel horrible that I forgot your birthday," she said. Her nose sounded clogged.

"Hey, there's a lot on your mind," I said.

"How was it?"

"My birthday? Fun. Les came over, and Dad brought Marilyn and Jack and David from work. Jack played his guitar."

"What'd you get?"

"Money, mostly. Everybody's been asking what I wanted. My feet have grown a half size, I think, and I need new heels for the prom, among other things."

"Did Patrick give you anything?"

"A kiss. Before school."

"That's all?"

"It was a pretty good kiss."

"Who are you doubling with?"

"No one that I've heard. I think we're going alone."

"Uh-oh," said Pamela knowingly. Then, "I'm not keeping you from anything, am I?"

"Only sleep," I said. "Do you know what time it is?"

"Oh, I'm sorry," she said. But she didn't say good-bye. "Just wondering . . . do you and Sylvia have good talks? I mean, after that last quarrel over the car, can you tell her stuff?"

"Not entirely. Some. We're working on it."

"Lucky," said Pamela. And when she didn't say anything for so long that I started to ask about it, she interrupted and said, "Alice, I'm scared."

"I know you are," I told her. "How long are you going to keep this secret? You've got to talk with someone. An adult."

"Yeah? Like who?"

I couldn't tell if she was crying or not.

"I think you ought to tell your mom."

"Are you crazy?" she said. "Why would I listen to her?"

"She's still your mom."

"And hear her tell me all the mistakes *she's* made?"

"You'll have to take that chance," I said. "She didn't ask to be put in this position, remember. But you won't tell your dad or Meredith, and *someone's* got to know, Pamela. You need to start seeing a doctor."

She *was* crying now. "I don't *want* to go through this! I don't *want* this baby!"

"What does Tim want you to do?" I tried to be as gentle as I could.

"He said he's not ready to be a father, but he will if he has to. I don't want him to *have* to. I don't want *me* to have to. I just don't want to *be* in this mess!"

I thought of all the times Pamela had slept over—all the good times we'd had in my bedroom. The phone conversations. The laughter and jokes and music and movies and scrapbooks and bulletin boards and . . . We weren't even in college yet! How could Pamela be a mother? How would she act? What would she do?

We'd had this same conversation several times already. And each time Pamela said she didn't *want* to be pregnant, as though if she said it enough, it wouldn't happen. And the conversation always ended with Pamela in tears.

I think we were on the phone until around eleven thirty. My battery was going, and Pamela's voice was fading in and out. I told her we'd talk again the next day after school. We'd go somewhere and get ice cream, I said. Make a list of all the things she was worried most would happen, and we'd go over them one by one.

* * *

I dragged through the next morning. Probably no one except Gwen and Liz and Tim and I noticed that Pamela laughed too loud, sat too quiet, walked too fast, ate too slow. . . . It was as though none of these usual activities was familiar to her. Like she was playacting her life, trying to fit in, with a future so uncertain.

She fell asleep in sociology.

"Miss Jones, if you *please*?" the teacher said. "The musical's over now. . . ."

Tim, too, looked distracted, worried. How did a guy tell his parents that he was going to be a father? That eight months from now, he'd either be moving out to set up housekeeping or that a baby would be moving in? How did he ask his mom if she could babysit five days a week until the kid was in school? If he could bring a wife home to live in his bedroom? How did he give up plans for college and settle for bagging groceries at Giant? It wasn't just Pamela and Tim whose lives would change; it was everyone's.

I was on my way to sixth period that afternoon when I saw Pamela, tears streaming down her face, walking rapidly toward the south exit.

"Pamela?" I called.

She kept going. There was something about her face that was frightening. I ran after her, ignoring the bell. She ran down the steps and out toward the soccer field.

"Pamela, stop!" I yelled again. "Wait up."

When I finally caught up with her, she was breathing in

little gasps and spurts, and her eyes were so teary that she'd walked right into the fence.

I put my arms around her. "Talk to me," I said. "Tell me."

She kept crying. "Tim w-walked away," she said.

"When? What do you mean?"

"I w-was heading for his locker, and . . . I *know* he saw me! But he turned and walked away! Like he didn't even want to *talk* to me!"

I just held her. "Well, maybe he didn't want to talk right then. He's still trying to deal with all this too. And maybe he's mad at himself."

Pamela just sobbed into my shoulder. "Alice," she wept, "I w-want to call M-Mom."

By the time we got back to the street, she'd changed her mind. I guided her into Ben & Jerry's and bought her a dish of chocolate raspberry.

"Call her," I said.

"She won't be home," Pamela said. "She works on Thursdays."

"Then we'll go over there when she gets home."

Pamela took a bite of ice cream, then wiped her eyes with her sleeve. "She's probably going out tonight."

"You don't know that."

"I can guess."

"We'll call her at work," I said. I knew if we didn't call right then, Pamela might not do it at all. "Finish your ice cream, Pam, and then we'll call."

She ate slowly, stirring the ice cream around until it became soup.

"You know what she'll say," she said.

"No, and neither do you."

"She'll say, 'How did you get yourself in this mess?'"

"And if she does?"

"I'll say, 'How did you get into the mess *you* made for yourself?' And then we'll fight."

"Give me your cell phone, Pamela." She didn't move, so I reached for her bag and retrieved it myself.

I knew that last period would be over soon, that kids would be leaving school. I'd been waiting for Pamela to finish her ice cream, but now I saw that she was crying again. Any minute crowds would be dropping by. The warm days of May were great for Ben & Jerry's.

"What's the number?" I asked Pamela, holding the cell phone out in front of me. "Do you have it programmed?"

She shook her head. "I don't know it."

I called information. "Nordstrom, Montgomery Mall, Bethesda, Maryland," I said. The operator gave me the number and connected me.

"What department?" I asked Pamela.

"Career wear," she said.

I repeated it into the phone, and when the extension started ringing, I handed the phone to Pamela.

Pamela waited until she heard her mother's greeting, and then, in a voice like a kitten's mew, she said, "Mom? I . . . I . . .

I need to talk to you. Could I come over, m-maybe tonight?"

Please say she can come! I whispered in my head. *Please don't tell her you're going out.*

She must have been telling Pamela something, because Pam was quiet, listening. "All right, then," she said, and my heart sank. She ended the call and sat there staring at the cell in her hand, then at me.

"She's leaving for home. She said to come right over."

I think we had just missed a bus, because we waited twenty minutes for another. Then it was a twenty-five-minute ride to Glenmont Apartments.

Pamela's eyes were red, and she looked as though she hadn't slept for a while. I wondered if I should be coming along and told Pamela I could sit out on the steps or over in the kiddie playground while she and her mom talked. But Pamela said she wouldn't go inside unless I went with her.

"This is about the hardest thing I've ever had to do," she said. "You know what Dad would say if I told him I was pregnant? That I was growing up just like mom. What he'd mean is, a slut."

"He may have told you that once, Pamela, but has he said that recently?"

She thought about it. "No. I guess he's mellowed some since he met Meredith. But I don't think he's ever going to forgive Mom for walking out on us. I don't think he ever can."

"People change," I said.

"And sometimes for the worse."

"Sometimes."

Mrs. Jones must have gotten there just before we did, because she was still wearing heels and a silk top over her dark skirt. When she opened the door, she barely saw me at all. Just took one look at Pamela and opened her arms.

I sat in one corner of the living room, Pamela and her mom on the couch across from me. I think Mrs. Jones knew, even before Pamela opened her mouth, that she was pregnant.

"I . . . I'm going to have a baby, Mom," Pamela wept. "And I'm s-scared."

The grief on her mother's face turned to sympathy in moments. "Oh my God!" she breathed. "When, sweetheart?"

"I don't know. January, maybe."

Mrs. Jones was holding one of Pamela's hands in hers. "And . . . the father?"

"My boyfriend, Tim. He's a really nice guy, Mom. But I don't think he wants to be a father. . . ."

"Of course not." Mrs. Jones kept stroking the back of Pamela's hand. "Have you told your dad?"

"I'm not suicidal," Pamela said, making me smile a little.

"Or Meredith, either, I suppose. . . ."

"No."

"Oh God!" Mrs. Jones said again, shakily. She pressed her lips tightly together, studying her daughter some more. "Are you sure about this?"

"Yeah. I took a test."

"How late are you?"

"Four weeks."

"But you haven't seen a doctor?"

"No."

Mrs. Jones nodded. "Do you want to keep it, Pamela? Have you thought about what you want to do?"

Want to keep it? The words chilled me. Imagining Pamela with a baby chilled me. How do you ever decide what's best for everybody?

"I don't *know!*" Pamela wept. "I don't want a baby, Mom, but . . . it's T-Tim's baby!"

"And yours," her mother said.

"What do *you* think I should do, Mom?"

"Pamela," said Mrs. Jones, "this is a decision you're going to have to make yourself, and it's one of the biggest decisions a woman could ever face." She didn't say *girl*, she said *woman*. "I don't think you should decide anything right this minute, but I want to take you to a doctor so we can talk about it and see what the choices are."

I sat silently through the long conversation. Mrs. Jones was saying all the right things, it seemed—that whatever Pamela decided to do about the baby, she'd support her. That Pamela hadn't ruined her life—she had to believe that—but she was taking a detour. And that somehow they would get through this together. She told Pamela that they would get all the information they could about her choices—abortion, keeping the baby, or giving it up for adoption—that it was a situation none of them wanted to be in, but they were. People made mistakes in their lives, and this was a big one. But she knew what it was like to make a mistake.

I excused myself to go to the bathroom, then purposely stalled to give them some time alone. I'd taken my bag and cell phone with me, and I tried to call Sylvia to tell her I'd be late for dinner, but I hadn't recharged the battery and couldn't get through.

When I finally went back in the living room, Pamela was standing by the door, hugging her mom. And as we left, Mrs. Jones said, "Thank you for coming, Alice," and hugged me, too. Her eyes were so sad.

Pamela was quiet on the way back to the bus stop. She looked drained. Relieved, maybe, but sad. Everything about this was sad. But just before the bus came, she leaned against me, hugging my arm, and said, "Thank you, Alice. I'm glad I talked with Mom. I'm glad you made me do it."

"I didn't make you. Encouraged you, maybe," I told her. "But I'm glad you gave her the chance to act like a mother."

We got on board and took a seat near the back. "It's good that it's almost summer," Pamela said. "I won't have to answer a lot of questions at school if I've got morning sickness. Maybe I'll go live at Mom's after I start to show. For a while, anyway. First, I guess, I have to decide if I'm going to keep the baby."

"And you have time to think about it, Pamela," I said, and glanced over at her. "You won't do anything impulsive, will you?"

"Like a clothes hanger, you mean?"

"Like *any*thing that isn't safe."

"I won't," she promised.

I could have gotten a transfer to another bus that would have taken me to Georgia Avenue, but I was tense and needed to walk off some anxiety. So I said good-bye to Pamela and got off at a corner where I had seven blocks yet to go. After a while, I thought, you have to stop telling yourself that it can't be happening and realize that it can. That it is. And that somebody you've known since sixth grade, someone you love, is an expectant mom and has to deal with it.

I was a block from home when I realized it was almost seven, and I still hadn't called Sylvia. I could hardly believe it was so late! I should have used Pam's cell.

When I got in the house, I called, "I'm home! Sorry I'm late."

I could smell Sylvia's homemade spaghetti sauce. Dad's special garlic bread.

"We put some dinner aside for you, Alice. Help yourself," Sylvia called from the family room.

I was glad I could eat alone and would do it later, because I wasn't hungry. I went upstairs and dropped my bag on the rug, realizing that I'd left not only my sweater at school, but my books, my homework, my assignments. . . . Suddenly I felt exhausted. I lay down on my bed and closed my eyes, one arm across my forehead.

I'd probably been there about ten minutes when there was a light tap on the door.

"Al?" Dad said. "Can I come in?"

"Sure," I said, but didn't get up.

He stood looking at me a minute, then pulled a chair over.

I could barely see his face from where I was lying, but I still felt too tired to get up.

"Anything wrong?" he asked.

"I'm okay," I said, begging the question.

"When Sylvia got home, she checked the voice messages," Dad said. "There was an automated call from the attendance office saying that you skipped sixth period."

Damn! I thought. Why did they have to be so darn efficient? Skip a class, it's transmitted immediately to the school office, and the phone call gets made.

"What was that all about?" Dad asked.

"Something really important came up," I said. "There was something I had to do, that's all."

Silence. I hate silence almost more than anything. More than quarreling.

"I'm worried about you," Dad said finally. "Is there anything you want to tell me?"

"No. Why are you worried?"

"Because . . . I was emptying the wastebaskets before dinner— for the trash pickup tomorrow—and I found this."

I looked over and saw that he was holding something in one hand, and I sat up. There was the wrapper from the pregnancy test kit.

"It's not mine," I said quickly, which sounded totally ridiculous, because it had been in *my* wastebasket.

"Al," Dad said. "All these years I've tried to keep an open relationship with you and Les. And I know that at seventeen you tell me only a small percentage of what goes on in your life, and that's only natural. I don't have to know everything. But when it's something serious, I hope you'll tell me."

"I will," I said. "But I wasn't the one who took that test, Dad. I can't tell you more than that. Not yet. But I'm sorry that it got you worried about me. Really."

Dad was so relieved that I could see the crease lines disappearing on his forehead, the little smile crinkles at the corners of his eyes growing deeper.

"Okay, honey. I won't ask. Except . . . where were you this afternoon? Can you at least tell me that?"

I smiled a little. "We weren't doing anything illegal or dangerous. Just having a talk with somebody's mom."

He didn't say anything. Just sat there smiling at me. Finally he said, "Did I ever tell you I think you're great?"

I smiled a little too. "I don't remember those exact words."

"I never said you were fantastic?"

"Nope. Not that, either."

He was grinning now. "Trustworthy, loyal, helpful, friendly, courteous, kind . . . ?"

"Keep talking," I said.

"Come on down and I'll heat up that garlic bread for you," he told me, and I followed him downstairs.

18
FINALE

I hadn't asked Patrick for the details of prom night, because that kind of thing bores him. He isn't much for stuff like clothes and flowers and photos and such. But it was *his* senior prom, *his* invitation, so I would go along with whatever he had planned. Or hadn't planned. All he'd told me was that he'd pick me up at six and to bring a change of clothes for the after-prom party at school. But I'd go with Patrick if he wore a Hawaiian shirt and rode up to our house on a bicycle.

Because Marilyn had loaned me a dress and Dad and Sylvia didn't need to help me buy a new one, Sylvia said she'd pay for my hair appointment—I wanted it piled high on top of my head, with curls in back. Then Dad said he'd pay for a manicure, which was their way of telling me they were glad that Patrick was back in the picture and that I wasn't going out with guys like Tony.

"Hey," I told them, "you'd think I was getting married or something."

But I really did want to look different for Patrick's prom. Blend in with the seniors. I wanted to look older, mysterious. Seductive, even. I hate fake nails, though—hate what they do to your natural ones—and only a professional manicurist could make my old nails look glamorous.

Liz came over to give me a pedicure. The guys she'd dated this semester were all juniors, so she hadn't been invited to the prom. But she knew I'd be wearing my new beige strappy sandals and wanted to make sure that my toes were gorgeous.

"Patrick doesn't notice toes," I said, but willingly rested one foot in her lap.

"How do you know?" She massaged lotion into my heels. "He could have a secret fetish and go nuts over women's shoes. But frankly, I think he's more of a butt man."

My eyes opened wide. "A *what*?"

"Hey. Men are divided into three groups, you know: breasts, legs, and butts. And I've seen Patrick's eyes following you out of a room, so I think he's a butt guy."

I laughed. "Those are all brain-dead guys, Liz. Isn't there a category for guys who take in the whole girl?"

"I'm still looking," she said.

I loved the Burnished Copper color the manicurist had used on my nails, so I'd bought a bottle of it, and now Liz was using it on my toenails.

"Remember when Pamela painted—," she said, and then stopped. I think we were both remembering the time in eighth grade when Pamela had inked J-U-I-C-Y on each foot—one letter on each toenail—and the gym teacher gave her polish remover and made her take it off.

I figured that Liz didn't want to ruin my evening by bringing up Pamela, so that's why she didn't finish the sentence. But I don't think either of us could stop thinking about her, not really.

"Sorry," Liz said. "I didn't mean to remind you of that."

"She's on our minds no matter what," I said.

Liz sighed and carefully brushed Dry Kwik over the polish of each toenail. "And it will never be like we planned, will it? I mean, we'll never go to the same college or drive to California like we wanted. Everything changes in the blink of an eye."

"That's life, I guess," I told her. "Or, as David would say, that's what makes life so 'terrifyingly wonderful.'"

We did my makeup last. I'd bought a bronze blush with glitter in it, and after I did my foundation and powder, Liz did my brows, my mascara, and my eyeliner, then topped it off with the bronze blush on my cheekbones.

We'd told Sylvia we'd invite her up for a final inspection, but I didn't want to put on my heels till I had to; I'd be on my feet all evening as it was. Forty minutes before Patrick was to pick me up, my cell phone rang.

Liz and I looked at each other.

"If Patrick tells you he can't make it, tell him you'll never speak to him again, *ever!*" Liz said. "Remember how he got mono the night of the eighth-grade semi-formal?"

"As though it was his fault!" I said, reaching for the phone. But it wasn't Patrick's number. "It's Pamela," I told Liz.

We both stared at the phone. I was afraid to answer. What if Pamela was crying? What if she was threatening to do something awful? What if she really, desperately needed to see me again? What if . . . ?

"Should I answer for you? Tell her you're just about ready to leave? That you've left?" Liz asked.

I shook my head and picked up my cell.

Pamela was breathless. Again. I couldn't tell if she'd been crying or not. "Listen, Alice, I know you're getting ready for prom, and I didn't want to upset you and I'll only take a minute and you don't have to come over, but . . . I don't think I'm pregnant anymore."

"*What?*" I cried, and Liz looked stricken.

"About an hour ago I felt like I had to go, and I went to the toilet and passed these really big clumps of blood. I was cramping and there was blood in the toilet, and I think . . . I think everything came out."

I didn't know what to say.

"Could you . . . could you tell . . . by looking?" I asked finally.

"Just big clumps of blood."

"But . . . are you *okay*?"

Liz was trying to read my face, and I made a sweeping motion between my legs. She understood and sat with her lips apart, waiting.

"I called Mom," Pamela said, "and she called her gynecologist, and he said if I wasn't cramping anymore and the bleeding had stopped, it was probably a complete miscarriage."

"Oh, Pamela!" I said. "I'm . . . I'm . . ."

"Glad," she answered for me.

"You didn't . . . ?"

"No. No coat hangers or Ex-Lax or jumping or anything. Mom said that somehow I lucked out, but I couldn't count on that ever happening again. The doctor wants to see me tomorrow, and we've got an appointment at the clinic. If I start bleeding or cramping again, Mom will take me to the emergency room."

I was doubtful. "You're not just making up this story so I'll have a good time tonight and won't worry about you?"

"Honest. I called Tim before I called you, and you know what he said? He said that the last couple of weeks have been the worst of his life. I told him, me too. But listen, have a great time, okay?"

"Are you alone now?" I asked.

"Yeah. Meredith's out somewhere, and Dad's watching a baseball game. He doesn't have a clue. Mom's coming over later to get me. I'm going to spend the night with her."

Liz was motioning to herself, then pointing in the direction of Pamela's house. "Do you want Liz to come over? She just gave me a pedicure," I said.

"Oh no, Alice! She's there to help on your big night!"

"Hey. She's volunteering." I handed the phone to Liz.

"Pamela," she said, "I'm through here. And I'll be right over." She handed the phone back to me.

"Alice?" said Pamela. And now her voice sounded choked. "You're the best, you know it?"

"And you're the bravest," I told her.

I ended the call, and Liz said, "She had a miscarriage, right?"

"Yeah, and we're celebrating. It's weird, isn't it? If she was married and wanting a baby, we'd all be in tears. Her mom said to consider herself lucky but not to count on it happening again."

"Oh, man! It'll be nice having the old Pamela back, won't it?" Liz said, gathering up her bag.

"You can't go through something like this and not be changed a little," I said. "And maybe that's a good thing."

Patrick didn't come in a limo, and he didn't come in his dad's car. He and fifteen other couples came in an old school bus they had hired for the evening, with a big banner stretched along one side reading PROM OR BUST. All the windows were dropped down, and as soon as I opened our front door, we could hear all the laughing and chatter coming from inside it.

"Wow!" I said, partly for the bus, partly for Patrick, who was dressed in a white tuxedo, white vest, and white tie, a handsome contrast to his face, still lightly tanned from his week of landscaping work during spring break. "Patrick, you look terrific!"

"And you're gorgeous," he said, kissing me lightly on the lips when he handed me a wrist corsage of white baby roses, tied with an aqua ribbon. He must have called Sylvia at some point about my dress.

I put a boutonniere in his lapel, and we posed for pictures for Dad and Sylvia in front of the stone fireplace in our family room. They even got a picture of us on the porch, with the bus in the background.

Then we were climbing aboard with my after-prom bag under a seat, and Patrick introduced me to some of the other seniors. I didn't really know any of them. I'm sure I'd seen them around school, but it's hard to recognize people who are all dressed up in glitter and tulle and fancy tuxedos with bow ties.

The ones Patrick knew best were a Latino couple, Mario and Ana, and his Asian friend, Ron Yen, and his date, Melinda. One of the many things you can say for Patrick is that he's international, and he speaks four languages. But if I ever thought that Patrick was all work and no play, that he didn't know how to have fun, prom proved me wrong.

The bus took us to Clyde's, where we sat at long tables, guys across from their dates, and we feasted on crab cakes and steak and chocolate mousse. Ron and Mario kept us laughing, telling how they had asked their dates to prom. Mario said he printed the question on a big sheet of poster board and planted it in Ana's front yard. Great idea, he said, except that her dad came out and told him to stay off the lawn, he'd just planted grass seed, and to bring the sign inside.

"So here I am, walking in their living room, holding this huge sign on a stick, and I knocked a picture off the wall," said Mario.

Then Ron said he'd been thinking for weeks of a creative way to ask Melinda to go with him, and finally he invited her out to dinner and persuaded the waiter to bring her a piece of cake with *Prom?* written in frosting. But either the waiter couldn't spell or the *o* looked like an *a*, because it came to the table reading *Pram?*

And Melinda said, "I looked at it and said, 'Pram? A baby carriage? What is this, a proposal or a proposition?'" We shrieked with laughter.

No one asked if Patrick had invited me in some creative way; he had simply phoned and asked. But I'll bet none of the other girls had been asked five months in advance, on New Year's Day. Patrick and I just smiled at each other across the table.

We got to the prom at the Holiday Inn about nine and took our bags in with us so we could change in the restrooms later. The ballroom ceiling was dark, studded with pinpoints of light, as though we were dancing outside under the stars. Potted plants along the sides of the room gave the feel of an island veranda, and as we passed a mirrored wall, I caught a glimpse of my face and my hair—Marilyn's dress with its satin-trimmed layers—and I looked good. No, I looked great. My dress was different from all the other dresses—very elegant and sophisticated and chic.

I didn't *feel* especially chic or sophisticated or elegant—just good. Just me. Like I was *almost* comfortable with who I was right then. I liked Patrick's friends. I liked the way he *made* friends—the way he could be different and still be funny, be smart, be Patrick.

"Hey, babe," he said, putting his hands on my waist and moving me out onto the dance floor.

"Hey, guy," I said, and put my head against his chest as we slow-danced along the edge of the ballroom.

I was having a wonderful time, and yet not a single one of my close friends—other than Patrick—was here. I could be part of the senior crowd and no one looked at me as though I didn't belong. I caught a glimpse of Don and Christy having their picture taken, and we danced by Scott and his date. I just smiled in his direction as Patrick turned me around and we moved on across the floor.

At some point in the evening, when I went out on a balcony with Patrick, I *almost* told him that Pamela had miscarried. Then I caught myself, realizing it was Pamela's secret—or story—to tell, not mine. Another one of those things you just "hold in your heart," as they say, and learn to keep to yourself.

So I just stood on the balcony with Patrick, my arms around his neck, the breeze in my hair.

"You surprise me, Patrick," I said after we'd kissed. "You look so good tonight. I mean, I figured you as a black tuxedo man, if you wore a tux at all."

"Symbol of my purity." He grinned.

When the couple who had been occupying the one bench went inside, Patrick and I took it over. He had his arm around me and pulled me closer.

"Having a good time?" he asked.

"Yes," I said. "I like watching you enjoy yourself. You usually seem so . . . so busy. Like you're running your life on a railroad timetable or something."

"That's not a compliment, right?"

"Just an observation. I like to see you having fun. Sometimes you seem so driven. Do you ever feel that way? Driven?"

He appeared to be thinking it over. "Just the way I'm wired, I guess. Only child syndrome, I suppose."

"Your parents push you, you mean?"

"No. They've never really pushed me at all. But then, no brothers or sisters to compete with, so . . . I don't know. I've always looked up to Dad—being a diplomat, the diplomatic license plate and all . . . the dinners, the parties—and Mom used to be a college administrator . . . Ph.D. When there's just the three of you, you don't want to be the only flunky."

"Flunky! Patrick, you're good at *everything*!"

"No way."

"Name one thing you're not good at."

"Uh . . . let's see." I could tell by his voice that he was smiling. "Conversation?"

"You could talk the wind out of the whole debate team."

"Clothes? Style?"

"No complaints there."

"Well, let's see. Kissing?"

"You *could* use more practice," I said.

He cupped one hand under my chin, turned my face around, and we kissed, both of us smiling.

Then he backed away a little and looked down at me, and this time his face was serious. For several seconds he just studied me, like his eyes were conversing with mine. And then he leaned slowly toward me, kissed me lightly on the lips, and then he gave me a full, forceful kiss that almost sucked the breath out of me. After that he just held me close, my lips against his neck, and I drank in that wonderful, familiar Patrick scent.

We went back inside as other couples came out to get away from the music for a while. Teachers must hate prom duty. At the beginning of the evening they're all smiles and compliments, joking around with us, telling us how great we look. But by eleven thirty or so, you can tell they're waiting for that last slow dance of the evening, signaling that the end is in sight, so that they can get home and go to bed.

But for us, the night was still young. We were waiting for midnight too, and soon the restrooms were filled with girls exchanging their satin slip dresses and their lavender tulle for jeans and shorts and T's.

We filed back out to the bus, our dresses thrown over our arms, our strappy heels, strapless bras, dangly earrings, and wrist corsages tucked away in our travel bags. When we reached the school gym, we piled out and got in line at the door for the post-prom party.

* * *

I'd never been to one before, but I'd heard kids talk about those parties as even more fun than the prom. And though all the work was done by parents—it was *run* by parents—it was definitely *the* place to go from one until six in the morning.

The parties change from year to year, but we walked into the school to find that the hallway had been transformed into a Wild West set, and we felt as though we were walking down an unpaved street, with saloons and bawdy houses and cigar stores and saddle shops on either side of us. From a hidden speaker, a honky-tonk piano played a ragtime tune, and there was laughter and raucous talk in the background.

"Wow!" said Patrick, handsome now in jeans and a T-shirt. We didn't know what to try first, so we followed Ron and Melinda along a huge obstacle course that took us up close to the ceiling of the basketball court—through tunnels, across bridges, climbing over nets and going down slides.

When we came down to floor level again, Ron and Melinda went off to rock climb while Mario and Ana and Patrick and I went to the "casino" to play the roulette wheel, using fake money. I stopped and stared, because there at the next table, the blackjack table, was Mr. Long! Patrick's dad! The redheaded man with graying hair and the trim mustache! The diplomat! Dealing blackjack! He pretended not to know us, but he was hiding a smile.

Patrick laughed.

"I knew they were helping out, but I didn't know how," he said.

"You mean your mom's here too?" I asked, and then there she was. The slim, elegant woman—the Ph.D., the college administrator—in a Western shirt and jeans, pouring drinks (sparkling cider) at the saloon.

"Hi, Alice!" she called, and made a point of not acting like Patrick's mom, for which I'm sure he was grateful.

We walked along "streets" lined with cowboy boots and cactus ornaments, our feet crunching on peanut shells, craning our necks to see what the crowd was watching at one end of the gym. Then we howled at the sight of Mario and another guy slipping into enormous padded sumo wrestling bodysuits and helmets covered with fake sumo-style hair. Outfitted with the mock fat of four-hundred-pound wrestlers, the two of them crashed their stuffed bellies into each other until one of them fell over.

Then we had to try the game where we were blindfolded one by one and ushered into a tent with see-through vinyl sides. There we tried to grab one-dollar bills and gift certificates that were swirling about in the air.

"Alice," said Ana, grabbing my arm, "you gotta try this with me." And with the guys looking on, she dragged me over to these crazy oversized toilet bowls that went whizzing around a track. I don't know what they had to do with a Western theme, but like providing sumo wrestlers, parents try to squeeze in every possible gimmick they think would appeal to us. I gamely climbed on one, Ana on the other, and someone pressed the starter button.

With kids cheering us on, the motorized toilet bowls raced around in a circle, but at some point I fell in—no water, of course—and I couldn't get out while the bowl was moving. With only my arms and legs dangling over the sides, the toilet bowl continued to whiz, with everyone shrieking and clapping. When they finally pulled me out, Patrick was laughing so hard, he was doubled over. Somebody even took a picture.

It was silly, it was meaningless, and it was about the most fun I'd ever had in my life. I couldn't wait to tell my friends about it. Couldn't wait to see Pamela's face—relaxed, for a change—and hear her funny laugh.

But I especially wanted to tell them how Patrick looked riding the mechanical bull, thighs gripping the leather, and how—one hand clutching the cord, the other hand in the air—he held on for twenty-two seconds, beating the night's record. Who would have thought?

Students weren't allowed to come back to the party once they left, but there were places we could go when we needed a break. So about four o'clock, with country music playing, Patrick and I sat down on the floor at one end of the gym, our backs against a dune made of sandbags, and shared a Coke.

Patrick's legs were sprawled out in front of him, and he leaned against my shoulder, one hand on my leg. I caressed his arm and nuzzled the top of his head.

"Patrick," I asked, "when do you leave for the U?"

"Three weeks," he murmured.

"Three *weeks*?" I said.

"Classes start in June," he reminded me.

"I'm going to miss you." I sighed. Somehow I thought we'd have more time.

"I'll miss *you*," he said.

"What, exactly?" I asked. "Tell me what you'll miss the most. My sultry smile? My bedroom eyes? My legs? My backside? *What?*"

"Hmmm," Patrick said sleepily. "You've got a great shoulder, you know."

"Shoulder?"

"To lean on."

I tipped back my head and smiled. I sort of liked that. I guess I *did*. And maybe it was enough.

"Yeah," I said. "Maybe I do."

Intensely Alice

To Matt Zakosek,

undercover agent extraordinaire

Contents

1
PLANNING AHEAD

"We've got to do something wild this summer."

Pamela extended her toes, checking the polish, then leaned back in the deck chair and pulled the bill of her cap down a little farther over her forehead.

"Define 'wild,'" said Gwen, eyes closed, hands resting on her stomach.

It was a Sunday afternoon. The Stedmeisters had opened their pool two weeks ago, and Mark had invited the old crew back again for a swim. Not the whole crew, because Patrick had left for summer courses at the University of Chicago and Karen was visiting her grandmother in Maine.

Everyone else had gathered at the picnic table except Liz, Gwen, Pamela, and me. The four of us seemed too lazy to move. We'd played badminton for an hour and a half, then took a swim, and now there was a wonderful breeze that played with my hair. I thought of Patrick.

"I don't mean *dangerous* wild," said Pamela. "I just want to do something spectacular. If not spectacular, then unusual. I want at least one good story to tell when we go back to school."

"Such as?" asked Elizabeth, reaching for her glass of iced tea.

"I don't know. That we visited a nudist colony or something?"

Liz almost dropped her glass. "You're joking."

"Why? Nudity's a natural thing. Don't you want to know what it feels like to play badminton with a breeze touching every square inch of your body?"

Gwen opened her eyes and gave Pam the once-over. "Girl, in the bathing suit you're wearing, the only parts of your body the breeze can't touch are the private parts of your privates."

We laughed.

"You guys want any crab dip before it's gone?" Mark called.

Even if we're not hungry, we make a point of tasting whatever Mrs. Stedmeister puts out for us. She and Mark's dad have been so great all these years about letting us hang out at their pool. They're older than most of the other parents, and I guess they figure that since Mark doesn't have any siblings, they'll do whatever they can to keep his friends around.

We'd filled up on hamburgers earlier, but Gwen padded

over to the picnic table, her brown feet pointing outward like a dancer's, her short, shapely legs bringing her back again, dip in one hand, a basket of crackers in the other.

"Well," she said to Pamela, offering the crackers, "you could always get yourself arrested. That would be a first."

"For what?" Pamela asked, considering it.

"Don't encourage her," I said, but who was I kidding? I wouldn't refuse a little excitement, especially with Patrick gone and nothing more for me to do all summer except work at Dad's music store. My cousin's wedding was coming up soon, though, and that would make life more interesting.

"Here's something you all could do," Gwen suggested. "If you're going to be around the third week of July, you could volunteer from four to nine in a soup kitchen. Montgomery County's asking for high school students to take over that week and give the regular volunteers a break."

Jill and some of the others had followed the crab dip back to where the four of us were sitting.

"Whoop-de-doo. Now, that's a fun idea," Jill said, rolling her eyes.

"What kind of help do they want?" I asked, ignoring Jill.

"Whatever they need: scrape veggies, set tables, serve food, clean up. We wouldn't have to plan the actual cooking. There will be one adult at each place to supervise that. I'm volunteering for the soup kitchen in Silver Spring."

Brian, all 170 pounds of him, sat perched on a deck stool, Coke in hand. "Why don't they make the homeless cook for themselves?" he asked. "I work hard at Safeway. Why should I spend my evenings waiting on people who don't even work at all?"

"Because most of them would trade places with you in a minute if they could," Gwen told him.

"I'll volunteer," I offered.

"Me too," said Liz. "Come on, Pam. It's only for a week."

"I suppose," said Pamela.

Justin said he would if he could get off work early. Penny said she'd be away. But Mark said we could count on him, and he'd call his friend Keeno to see if he wanted to come.

I think Gwen was pleased with the response. It was about what I expected from Brian. And even if Justin could get off work, it was up for grabs whether or not Jill would let him come. For the rest of us, it was altruism mixed with the fact that since we weren't going to be in London or Paris or even the beach that week in July, we might as well make ourselves useful. But it wasn't exactly what Pamela had in mind.

Later, Pamela and I walked slowly back with Liz to her house. I hadn't seen Tim around for weeks, and Pamela confirmed what I'd suspected.

"We broke up," she said. "It wasn't so much a breakup as . . . I don't know. Just scared off, I guess."

Getting pregnant last spring, she meant. Scared all of us. Even after Pam had a miscarriage, it was too much for Tim.

"I'm really sorry," I said, and Liz slipped one arm around her.

"It was mutual," Pamela told us. "Things just weren't the same after that. The only good that came of it is that I'm closer to Mom." Pamela's mom had been surprisingly understanding when Pam had told her about the pregnancy—something Pam couldn't ever have told her dad.

How could it be, I wondered, that Pam and her dad could live in the same house together, and Mr. Jones didn't have a clue? But then, how much do Dad and my stepmom really know about me? How much do I tell them? They know where I am most of the time, but they don't always know what I'm doing or how I feel. Certainly not what I'm thinking.

Natural? Or not?

Les, the moocher, came over for dinner that night. Now that his master's thesis has been held up, he won't graduate till December. He's a little more relaxed, though, and we see him more often, especially at mealtime. But Sylvia never cares.

"Got it all planned," he said, telling us about a mountain bike tour he and his two roommates were taking in Utah the first week of August. "A guy from school's going to stay in our apartment and look after Mr. Watts in case he needs anything."

My brother and his roomies live in the upstairs apartment of an old Victorian house in Takoma Park. They get it rent-free in exchange for odd jobs around the place and the assurance that one of them will always be there in the evenings in case old Mr. Watts has an emergency.

"How long a trip is it?" asked Dad. "Sounds spectacular."

"We fly out on a Friday, stay a week, fly back the next Sunday. Can't wait."

I took a bite of chicken diablo. "You ride around looking at monuments or something? Mount Rushmore and Custer's Last Stand?"

"We *ride*, Al, we *ride*," Les said.

"But if you don't see anything . . ."

"Of course we see things. The mountains! The sky! The naked babes lining the trails, waving us on!"

"Seriously, Les. Describe your day."

"Well, you wake up in a tent. You pull on your jeans, crawl out, take a leak—"

"Where?"

"Depends where we're camping. A Porta-John. An outhouse. On some tours you're simply given a shovel and some toilet paper."

"Eeeuuu! Do you all sleep in one tent?"

"No, they're small. People usually bring their own."

I dangled a bit of tomato on my fork and studied my twenty-four-year-old brother. Dark hair, dark eyes, stubble on his cheeks and chin. "Any women on the trip?"

"A few, usually. If they can take the pace. Tours are rated by difficulty, and this one's pretty rugged."

"Where do you take a bath?"

"Shower. River. Creek. Whatever's handy."

I tried to imagine myself going on a mountain bike trip with a bunch of guys. I could imagine everything except using a field for a toilet. And not brushing my teeth before breakfast. And getting dusty and muddy. And pedaling up steep inclines. And . . .

"Well, I'm glad you're getting away for a while," Dad told Les. "You've had your nose to the grindstone lately."

"But what about you and Sylvia?" Les asked him. "When do you guys get a break?"

"We're going to New York for a weekend," Dad said. "Sylvia wants to see a new exhibit at the Met, and there's supposed to be a fabulous new Asian-fusion-something restaurant at Columbus Circle."

Life is so unfair. No one mentioned me. Nobody even looked in my direction, though Sylvia did say, "We've also got to get plane tickets to Chicago soon. Carol's wedding is July eleventh. If you're flying with us, Les, we'll pick up tickets for four."

"I'd better make my own arrangements," Lester said. "I probably won't be staying as long as you are."

"Yeah, we'll probably stick around a few days to visit with Milt and Sally," said Dad.

I took the plunge.

"Oh, by the way, Patrick's invited me to visit the university while I'm there. Get a taste of college life."

Now all heads turned in my direction.

"That's a good idea," said Sylvia. "Did he say what day?"

"Well . . . I thought a couple of days, actually. I mean, there's a lot to see."

I noticed a pause before Dad spoke. "Did he mention where you'd be staying?"

"Oh, he'll work something out," I said, my heart beating wildly.

"When did you decide all this?" asked Dad.

I looked around incredulously at the three of them. "Whoa? Les is going on a mountain bike trip, you and Sylvia are going to New York, and . . . oh, yeah, I'm working at the Melody Inn this summer, as usual. I thought maybe I was entitled to a *couple* days of vacation."

"Of course you are," said Sylvia.

"We just want to know the details," said Dad.

That was a yes if I ever heard one. Now all I had to do was tell Patrick.

I called Elizabeth.

"You did *what*?" she said. "Without checking with Patrick?"

"Yep. It was then or never."

"Alice, what if he has other plans for that weekend? What if he's not even there?"

"Then I'll have his roommate all to myself," I joked, feeling sort of sweaty.

When I told Pamela, she said, "Maybe we should all go with you. We're looking for something wild, remember."

Actually, my even visiting the University of Chicago was wild, because it's so far out of my league, I'd never get admitted. My IQ would probably go up two points just breathing that rarefied air, I told Gwen when I called her next, but she doesn't like me to talk like that.

"You're always putting yourself down when it comes to

Patrick," she said. "It's always, 'He's brilliant. He's motivated. He's persistent. He's original,' and what are you? A doorknob? There are all kinds of smarts, you know. Why do you suppose he likes you?"

"Opposites attract?"

"He likes you because you're real. Maybe you help keep him grounded. Ever think of that?"

"No, because we're never around each other long enough for me to have that effect," I said. "But I *am* excited about seeing him. I can't believe Dad's letting me go. I can't believe I pulled this off."

"You haven't yet. You still have to talk to Patrick," she said.

It's exciting thinking about visiting your boyfriend at college. Well, kind of my boyfriend. I'm more serious about Patrick than I've ever been about anyone else, but I'm here, he's there, and most long-distance things don't work out. Still . . .

A lot of things raced through my mind, the first being privacy. A dorm. A room. A night. Two nights? I mean, I was inviting myself. It's not as though he had asked me to come and said he had the whole weekend planned.

Carol was getting married on a Saturday, and Dad said we could stay over till Monday. We couldn't stay longer than that.

I began to feel as nervous as I'd been last spring when I'd called Scott Lynch to invite him to the Sadie Hawkins Day dance. What if Patrick said, *Hey, great, Al! Where're you staying?* And then I'd have to rent a hotel room or go back and forth from one side of Chicago to the other.

Maybe I shouldn't even tell him I was coming, I thought, so as not to make a big deal out of it. Maybe I should just stuff some things in a tote bag, take a bus or the El to the South Side, look up his address, and walk in.

I liked imagining that. Liked thinking about the look on his face. His smile. Patrick jumping up and hugging me in front of his roomie. I also imagined his not being there and my carrying the tote bag all the way back to Aunt Sally's.

I drank a glass of water and went back in my room, closed the door, and called Patrick's cell phone number.

It rang six times, and I expected to get a message that he was out, but then I heard his voice, faint-sounding, with lots of background noise.

"Hey!" he said. "Alice?"

"Hi, Patrick. Is this a bad time?"

"I can barely hear you," he said. "I'm at a White Sox game."

"Oh, wow! Listen, I'll call tomorrow," I said.

"No, it's okay. What's up?"

I raised my voice. "I just wanted to tell you that Dad says I can visit you . . . for a couple days, maybe . . . after Carol's wedding on July eleventh."

"When? Sorry, the crowd's noisy. Bases are loaded."

"July eleventh?" I said loudly.

"Seventh?"

"No. The eleventh!" I was practically shouting. "I could come see you on the twelfth."

"Sounds good! I'll have to check!" he shouted back. "I'll

figure out something. Call you later this week, okay?"

"All right," I said. "Later, then."

I ended the call and sat on the edge of my bed, clutching my cell phone. My heart was pounding. What exactly had I agreed to? Only visit him, right? And Patrick had said, "I'll figure out something," so the next step was up to him.

But I had to be honest. I wanted to stay with him. All night.

2

COMPANY

Dad and Sylvia were able to get tickets to an off-Broadway show the following Friday, so they decided to go to New York sooner than they'd planned.

I didn't say a word about having the house to myself for that weekend. Each time I sat down to dinner, I expected Sylvia to tell me that one of her friends was going to stay with me to "keep an eye on the house" or Dad to say that he'd talked to Elizabeth's mom, and she'd invited me to stay over there. Nothing. Dad busied himself checking hotel rates on the Internet, and Sylvia scoured their closets, deciding what they should wear.

I began to worry that the doorbell would ring and Aunt Sally would come in, all the way from Chicago. And when Friday came and there were still no instructions from Dad or Sylvia, I wondered if they knew what they were doing. They'd never left me alone overnight in the house before.

What if I threw a big party? What if a bunch of kids crashed it? What if I forgot to lock the door and someone broke in? Or I left something on the stove and burned the place down? What if I was kidnapped? Didn't they care?

Evidently not, because they were packing when I left for the Melody Inn that morning, and all they said was that there was food in the fridge and good-bye.

Maybe I was more mature than I'd thought. I mean, maybe they thought I was more mature than I am! Whatever, I started a mental list of girls I wanted to invite over. A sleepover, of course. But then I thought, *Hey! What about guys?* Forget the sleepover and throw a spaghetti party, maybe. Tell everyone to bring either salad or drinks. Play music. Dance. Talk. Invite some of the guys from stage crew.

We were really busy at the store that day. The clarinet instructor was sick, and Marilyn, the assistant manager, was trying to find a substitute. David, our clerk, had to leave early for a dental appointment, and of course I had the Gift Shoppe to handle alone.

I'd never been so glad for closing time, and as I drove home, I set my mind on the party I was going to have the following night. This was even better than I'd thought. Not only did I have the house to myself, I had Dad's car. I could go anywhere

I wanted—to Bethesda! Baltimore, even! So this was what it felt like to be single and on my own. I looked at the gas gauge. Well, if I had the money, that is.

When I pulled in our driveway, I was mentally counting the number of guys who might come, and as I crossed the porch, I counted the number of girls.

I opened the front door, then stopped. There was a noise from upstairs. Then two soft footsteps. I turned quickly to see if Sylvia's car was out front, if she hadn't driven it to the Metro as they'd planned and they'd canceled their trip to New York. The curb was vacant. Only a couple of neighbors' cars lined the street.

I took another step inside and stopped again, listening for the slightest sound. No sign of a forced entry. Then a floorboard squeaked somewhere over my head. Somebody was definitely up there.

"Aunt Sally?" I called hesitantly.

Suddenly there were rapid footsteps, and then two feet appeared at the top of the stairs. I turned to run, my hand on the screen, when I heard Les say, "Hey! What's up?"

"Lester!" I screamed. "Where's your car?"

He stopped halfway down. "You only love me for my car?"

"I didn't know you were here! You scared me half to death!"

"It's getting a brake job. George drove me over," Les explained.

I let my shoulders drop and began to breathe normally again. "No one told me you were coming. I thought the place was being robbed."

"Sorry. Just dropping my stuff in my old bedroom," he said.

"Are you here for the whole weekend?" I asked, unable to disguise the disappointment in my voice.

"Till Sunday afternoon. Didn't they tell you? I *did* used to live here, you know."

"Did Dad ask you to babysit me?"

"No, he asked me to make sure you didn't invite a hundred kids over, get stoned, and have wild sex in the bedrooms," Les said.

"What?"

He laughed. "Relax! We'll make Kraft dinner! We'll watch *Sesame Street*! We'll play old maid!"

I sprawled onto a chair. "Why didn't they tell me you'd be here?"

"I don't know." Les sat down on the couch and thumbed through a magazine. "What difference would it make? Who'd you invite that you have to cancel?"

I hoped he couldn't read my expression. "Nobody." And then I added, "Yet."

He shrugged and turned a page. "No one said you couldn't invite a few friends over."

I sighed. "What if I don't want to invite anyone over? What if I want to go someplace myself?"

"Depends."

"You mean I have to run my life by *you*?"

"Hey, you can go anywhere you want as long as I approve."

"Forget it," I said.

"Lighten up," Lester said. "C'mon, Al. Let's make dinner."

* * *

It *was* sort of nice to set the table for two, grate the cheese, and listen to Lester's take on things.

"What are you going to do after George gets married and moves out?" I asked when he crowed some more about the mountain bike trip he'd be taking.

"We'll have to get someone else," he said. "We've still got utility bills to pay, car payments, gas. . . . We'll get the word out when it's time, but we're picky."

"How picky?"

"Has to be a nonsmoking grad student who picks up after himself."

I almost fell over. "I can't believe I'm hearing this from you."

"Hey, once you've lived through piles of dirty laundry and rotting food in the sink, your standards go up a notch or two."

"But how do you ever know for sure how someone will turn out?" I asked.

"You don't. You just look for clues, listen for vibes, take a chance."

We sat down. Les opened a beer and I poured myself a glass of iced tea. We hadn't fixed anything but tacos—a big platter of them in the middle of the table.

"My kind of meal," Les said.

"I guess you never know anything for certain, except math," I said.

"Not even that," said Les.

"But don't guys have an easier time making decisions than girls?"

"About what?"

"About anything. Like . . ." My mind was racing on ahead of me. "Well, when they go out with someone, do they decide in advance how far they'll go, or do they just let it happen?"

Les grinned. "I don't know any guy who puts the details in his daily planner."

I'd made an opening in a conversation I didn't know we were going to have, and I wondered if I'd ever have the chance again. Just Les and me at the table together. I didn't even have to look at him. I made a pretense of picking up all the little bits of meat and cheese and stuffing them back in the taco shell as I continued: "I mean, I think most girls would admit that even though they're curious, even though they want it, they're scared half out of their minds when they have sex for the first time. Are guys?"

"Is this a general question?"

"Of course."

"More nervous than scared, I'd say. The guy's the one who has to perform." Les paused, and I could tell he was looking at me even though my eyes were still on my plate. "Any particular reason you're asking? Nothing to do with a particular city and visiting a particular friend in July?"

"Just curious, that's all," I told him.

"Right," said Lester.

None of my friends had any great ideas about what to do that evening, so we just said we'd get together on Saturday. Now that Les and I had finished dinner, I sort of liked the idea of staying home with him, even though I was sure he'd rather be with somebody else. I figured this was payback time for all the meals he'd mooched off Sylvia, all the times he'd borrowed Dad's car.

Since he'd made the tacos, I did the dishes while he watched the news, and then we took some ice cream out on the back porch and sat together on the glider.

"Just like old married people, huh?" I joked. He grunted. "Do you think you'll ever get married, Les?"

"Oh, maybe when I'm thirty-five," he said.

"That's years off!"

"I know. Lucky me."

I pushed my feet against the floor, and the glider moved back and forth. "When you think about it, though, it's sort of scary, isn't it? I mean, spending your whole life with one person?"

"Yep. No guarantees."

"How do you suppose people do it? The ones who stay together?"

"Well, back when I was dating Tracy—when I thought she was the one—I knew that when I took my vows, I'd have to be as committed to the marriage as I was to Tracy."

"Meaning what, exactly?"

"That I'd need to protect the marriage from anything that might harm it, just as I'd protect her."

"You know who you sound like? David Reilly. At work. The guy who gave up his girlfriend to become a priest. Can you imagine doing that?"

"No, but I'm not David."

"He's giving up romance and sex and everything for God. And he's *happy*! But his girlfriend's not."

"I wouldn't think so."

We rocked back and forth, the squeak of the glider competing with crickets.

"Do you think a lot about God, Les? I mean, is religion something that ever crosses your mind?"

"You can't major in philosophy without thinking about religion, Al."

"I thought philosophy was a bunch of old men sitting around discussing how many angels could dance on the head of a pin. Give me an *interesting* philosophical question, then. And I'm not interested in angels."

"A religious philosophical question? Let's see. Here's one: If you consider all the suffering in the world, is God all-powerful but evil? Or compassionate but not all-powerful?"

"And the answer is . . . ?"

"Oh, that's up to you. Philosophy provides the questions, not necessarily the answers. It just gives you different ways to think about them."

"Well, that sucks," I said.

Les laughed. "*Some* people would say that's great—you get to discover the answers for yourself. Others say it's awful, because they want somebody else to make the decisions."

"Which are you, Lester?"

"I like to question. Which are *you*?"

I stared out over the backyard. A firefly flickered somewhere above the tiger lilies. Then another. "I don't know. Sometimes I just want answers. I hate having to think, 'Should I do this?' 'Am I ready?' 'It is time?' 'Is it—?'"

I stopped suddenly and wondered if my cheeks were blushing—if Les could see. What was I *saying*?

"Want some more ice cream?" I asked quickly.

"No, but *you* look like you need to cool off a bit," he said.

The question of how to spend Saturday night was solved when I got a call from Keeno. He goes to St. John's, but we know him through Brian. He started hanging around with us last summer, and now he comes over to Mark's sometimes even when Brian's not along.

"Mark and I are going to a movie tonight. Any of you girls want to come along?" he asked.

"What movie?"

"That spy thing—*Midnight Black*. Mark said he'd drive, but if there're more than five, I'll take my car too."

I called Gwen.

"I saw it with Yolanda last week," she said.

Liz and Pamela said they'd go, however, and I was relieved to have the decision made for me. Still, this was my one big weekend with my parents away, and all I was doing was going to the movies?

Keeno's cute, though. Very blond. Next to Brian, he's probably got the best physique of any of our guy friends, and he has a dolphin tattoo on his butt that he showed us once. He's also crazy and fun to be around.

The five of us got to the mall a half hour early, but the nine o'clock show had already sold out, and there were only three seats left for the eleven o'clock.

"Crap," said Keeno. "Let's see something else."

We scanned the movie lineup on the board behind the cashier. A movie titled *Heathen Born* had started five minutes earlier, and two others were still an hour away. We made a quick decision and headed for *Heathen*.

In the darkened theater the previews were still running. Keeno went back out and returned with two giant-size buckets of popcorn just as the feature movie came on the screen.

We could tell from the music and the scenes that flashed in strobelike fashion behind the credits that this was a screamer. Faces of women gasping . . . of feet stalking . . . fingers clutching.

"Oh, man, Keeno, if this is another chainsaw-massacre movie . . . ," said Pamela.

"Probably machetes," said Mark.

"I'm going to be sick," said Liz.

"No, you're not. We're going to study it from a sociological angle," said Keeno. "What kind of people would go to a movie like this?"

"Brain-dead people who can't think of anything else to do on a Saturday night," said Pamela.

We were sitting in the last row, and the guys rested their feet on the backs of the empty seats in front of us. The theater was only half full, another bad sign.

The story opened with a young couple, obviously in love, walking along a neighborhood sidewalk at night. They stopped to kiss under a streetlight, then walked on, now and then waving away the mosquitoes. Or what they thought were mosquitoes. Actually, the flying insects laid eggs under their skin, and an hour or so later, when the couple was about to make love in the park, they realized they had huge boils on their arms and faces, and then the boils popped, and from each one a greenish blob leaped out and, with slimy fingers, strangled the man, then the woman.

"Way to go!" said Mark, laughing, as he dug his hand in the popcorn again.

Soon boils were breaking out on everyone in town, and people were getting strangled, and the populace was walking around wearing insect gear and inspecting their kids before bedtime. . . .

"I paid nine dollars for *this*?" I said to Mark.

"We'll get some pizza after," he told me.

Keeno, with Mark and me on one side of him, Liz and Pam on the other, said, "Approach it scientifically. What needs does this movie fulfill? What is its socially redeeming feature? What—?"

"Will you guys shut up back there?" a man five rows down yelled at us, half rising out of his seat.

We quieted down then, but after the first forty minutes we'd had enough, and left.

"Any more ideas?" I asked Keeno as we settled for a basket of buffalo wings and fries next door. Pamela and Liz were going to sleep over when we got home, but I wanted my big evening in a parentless house to be a bit more memorable than this. Keeno and Mark, I knew, would probably be content just to cruise around in the old Chevy Mark had bought from his dad and had spent so much time and work fixing up.

"What? You want *more*?" Keeno asked, in mock pain. "All right." He slammed one palm down flat on the table. "Cemetery Tag."

"What?" asked Liz.

Mark took the last of the buffalo wings while Keeno looked thoughtful. "Where's the nearest cemetery?" Keeno asked.

And we were off. Pamela, Liz, and I sat in the backseat, singing a song we'd all sung back in grade school. I mostly recited the words while the others sang:

> *Did you ever dream when the hearse goes by*
> *That one of these days you're going to die?*
> *They wrap you up in a long white shirt,*
> *And cover you over with six feet of dirt. . . .*

Keeno seemed not to know it, because he turned around in the passenger seat to watch us, so we put even more drama into our performance:

> *All goes well for a couple of weeks,*
> *And then your coffin begins to leak. . . .*

At this point Mark remembered the words and joined in the last part:

> *The worms crawl in, the worms crawl out,*
> *The worms play pinochle on your snout,*
> *The pus runs out, as thick as cream,*
> *And then you're as green as a lima bean.*
> *And when they get through with you,*
> *There's nothing left of you*
> *but a mem-o-ry.*

"And you guys were complaining about the movie?" Keeno said.

Funny how you can sing the song when you're in third grade and it's so unreal, it doesn't even give you pause.

The traffic had thinned out some since we began the evening, but there were still a lot of cars on Colesville Road. When we stopped for the next light, Keeno yelled suddenly, "First-Grade Fire Drill!"

Mark yanked the emergency brake, and both he and Keeno opened their doors and leaped out at the same time.

"Get out! Get out!" Mark yelled.

"What?" we cried, but—afraid the car was on fire or something—Pamela and I both shoved our doors open and spilled out onto the concrete, Liz behind me.

"Run around the car! Change places!" Keeno yelled, now over on the driver's side.

I had no idea what was going on, but I tore around the car, Liz at my heels. While Pamela climbed in our side, we climbed in hers, the light changed, and Keeno was at the wheel.

"What was *that* all about?" I gasped, fumbling for the seat belt.

Mark was laughing. "Haven't played First-Grade Fire Drill before?" he said. "The driver calls it. And when he does, you all have to change places."

"We're out with a couple of wackos," I told the girls, but two stoplights later, they did it again, and I realized that half the fun was looking at the astonished faces of adults in the cars beside us at the light.

"Okay," said Mark, after we'd driven fifteen minutes and were halfway to Rockville. He turned off onto a side road. "Here's one."

It was a large cemetery with only an iron gate in front, for effect. No fence along the sides. We opened the car doors and piled out.

3
CEMETERY TAG

"This is crazy, Keeno," I told him.

Across the road from the cemetery, cornfields separated the few small houses in the area. There was an almost full moon, and the gravestones stood out white against the dark of the grass. Crickets and katydids chorused off and on as we ambled around.

"Now what?" asked Pamela.

"Here's the deal," said Keeno. "You can't touch a gravestone, can't step on a grave. And as soon as you're tagged, you have to howl at the moon so we'll know who's It." He reached out suddenly and slapped Elizabeth's arm. "Gotcha."

We scattered in all directions as Liz gave a feeble howl and came after us. We ran into each other making right-angle turns to avoid the graves. When Mark was tagged, he imitated a werewolf's howl, and we yelped at him to be quieter as we spread out farther still. The cemetery was longer than it was wide and ended far back at a ditch.

Liz, on the track team at school, was better at chasing down the guys than Pamela and I, and could outrun both Mark and Keeno. But when Pamela or I was tagged, the guys made the mistake of hanging around to taunt us, and sometimes we caught them then.

A car drove slowly by on the side road, so we quieted down and took a break, watching as its taillights disappeared out on the highway.

We played for another ten minutes, and then Keeno said, "This is too easy. Let's have a race. The Tombstone Trot."

"What were you in your previous life, Keeno? A playground supervisor?" I asked.

"Yeah, they still have recess at St. John's?" asked Pamela.

"You wanted action, didn't you?" said Keeno. "Stop your bitchin'. Everybody move back to the ditch."

We obeyed, and Keeno put us all in a row. He pointed to the gravestones closest to us. "Pick a stone, any stone," he said, "and when I say go, head back to the entrance, jumping over every tombstone in your path. The one who jumps over the most in the shortest time wins."

"Wins what?" asked Mark.

"Uh . . . the ski cap my aunt gave me for Christmas?" Keeno said. We laughed.

If I was going to play this silly game, I'd better choose a short stone, I decided, but of course I couldn't see all the stones ahead of me. The other kids spread out down the line.

"On your mark, get set . . . ," Keeno said. "Go!"

With shrieks and grunts, we each leaped over the gravestone we had chosen and ran to the next. The tombstones, of course, weren't quite in the neat rows Keeno imagined, and every so often we collided with each other or tried to jump over the same stone.

We went galloping on down the cemetery, where the ground dipped into a slight gulley, and had just started up the slope ahead of us when we saw the beams of two flashlights and, behind the flashlights, two police officers.

"Oh, crap!" Mark said under his breath.

I came to a stop so suddenly, I almost went sprawling, but managed to grasp the large wing of a stone angel.

"Oh, God!" Elizabeth whispered.

"Good evening," one of the officers said sarcastically, and both men moved forward.

This was the second time in a year that I was involved in something that brought the police, the first being when Pam and Liz and Gwen and Yolanda and I were decorating Lester's car for Valentine's Day.

We squinted in the flashlight beams as the officers scanned each of our faces in turn, then the area around us to see who else was there.

"Just the five of you? Anyone missing?" the second officer said.

"Just five," said Keeno. "And it was my idea." That put him two points up in my book.

"What exactly was your idea?" asked the policeman.

"Cemetery Tag," said Keeno.

"Tag?"

"Well, and a race. We were jumping over tombstones to get back to the car."

It sounded even more stupid than it was.

"Whose car?" the first officer asked, pointing the flashlight toward Mark's car, then back again.

"Mine," said Mark.

"Would you open the trunk, please? The rest of you stay where you are."

I glanced at Keeno. I had no idea what the police were looking for or what they'd find in the trunk.

"What do they suspect we were doing?" I whispered to Pamela.

"Probably drugs. Shhhh," she said. I glanced at my watch and tried to read the dial. It was about a quarter of one.

We watched as Mark went over to his car, fished the keys from his pocket, and opened the trunk. The policeman shone the light around inside, moving things, checking under the spare.

"License?" the policeman said.

Mark handed it over. "Want to check inside the car?" he asked the officer.

"We already have," the policeman said, and motioned Mark back to where the rest of us were standing. "Clean," he murmured to the other man, and I was double-triple grateful that Brian wasn't along. I wouldn't swear to anything in the car if Brian had been in it.

The policemen faced us again, and this time they turned off their flashlights. "We've had two episodes of vandalism in this cemetery in the last five months, and the neighbors are pretty watchful. Any of you been here before?"

We told them no.

"We'd just been to a movie and were letting off steam," Mark said. I was glad Liz didn't pipe up and tell them we'd also been playing First-Grade Fire Drill. Were we seniors or not?

"Going right home?" they asked us.

"We are now," I said. "I was due home at one."

"Okay. Don't show up here again," the officer instructed.

We trooped back to the car.

"Oh, man, lucky they didn't find the crack under the seat," Keeno murmured after he'd closed the door.

"What?" I cried.

"I'm kidding! I'm kidding!" he said.

"Well, *don't!*" Liz told him.

Mark turned the car around, and we went back to the main road, heading for Silver Spring.

"Jeez!" Mark said after a minute or two. "They're right behind us."

And they were. Mark obeyed every speed limit, every stop

sign, every light. When he made a turn, they turned. And when we finally pulled up in front of my house, so did they.

Liz gave a little cry. "I sure hope Mom and Dad aren't watching out the window," she said, glancing at the big white house across the street. But all the windows over there were dark. As we got out of the car, however, I saw the front door of my house open, and Lester appeared in the doorway, one arm resting against the frame.

"I'm dead," I said.

"G'night," we told the guys.

"Call us if you need bail," said Pamela.

Mark's car moved slowly up the street, the cruiser tailing it. I started up the walk to the house.

"It's after one, Al," Les said when we reached the porch. "Thirty minutes after, to be exact."

"I know," I told him.

"Why didn't you call?"

"I thought maybe you'd be asleep."

"You know better than this. What have you been doing?" he asked.

"You're worse than Dad!" I said.

"Why the police escort?"

"You're not going to believe this, Lester," Pamela told him, "but we were playing tag."

"In a cemetery," added Liz.

"Playing tag in a cemetery and the police brought you home? What, you have all your clothes off or something?"

"Don't you wish!" said Pamela, who's always had a crush on Les, but he ignored her.

"It was just another one of Keeno's crazy ideas," I told him. "We couldn't get in the movie we wanted to see, the movie we *did* see was awful, Keeno tried to think of something to salvage the evening, and Mark drove us to a cemetery to play tag. You jump over tombstones and stuff. That's when the police showed up because they'd had some vandalism there."

"So what happened?" asked Les. I don't think he believed us.

"They gave us the third degree and searched Mark's car, I don't know why."

"Probably looking for shovels and crowbars," Lester said. "Nice of them to see that you got home safely. I should have gone out and thanked them."

"Lester, listen to you! You've metamorphosed into Dad!" I cried. Was this really my brother—the guy who had given a girl a fur bikini last Christmas? I almost said that out loud, but caught myself in time. If I gave away his secrets, I'd never find out any more.

"Anyway, you're home, and I'm going back upstairs," Les said. "And, Al, I'd like to get up early tomorrow and go hiking with a couple guys. Could you please not do anything that'll involve the police for a few hours on Sunday morning?"

"Am I allowed to go to Mass?" Liz joked.

"Am I allowed to stay home?" asked Pamela.

"Am I allowed to sleep in?" I added in a whiny voice.

Les gave us a half smile. "Sleep tight," he said. "If the cops come back for any reason at all, you guys are toast."

I gave him a military salute and he went upstairs.

We took over the family room, spreading our sleeping bags into one giant mattress. Sylvia had put a large wrought-iron candelabra in the fireplace opening for the summer, so I lit all thirteen candles. The slight draft that came down the chimney, even with the flue closed, kept them flickering.

We rehashed the evening, and it was even funnier in the telling. But then they asked about Patrick.

"Have you called him yet?" Pamela asked.

"Yep. He knows I'm coming."

"Overnight?" asked Liz.

"Yes."

"And . . . ?"

"He said he'd work something out."

Pamela settled back in a chair as though she were about to enjoy a delicious dessert. "O-*kay*!" she said. "That probably means he'll get rid of his roommate."

"How? Just ask him to leave?"

Pamela shrugged. "Ask him to go sleep somewhere else, probably."

"For the whole night?"

"Patrick would do the same for him, I'll bet."

"Maybe the roommate could just stay and pull the covers up over his head," said Liz.

We stared at her.

"That's what girls do sometimes, I heard. If your roommate

brings a guy in after you've gone to bed and you hear them making out, you're supposed to pull the covers over your head."

"Liz, you can be my roommate *any*time!" Pamela said, laughing.

"I can't even *imagine* doing it with someone else in the room," I said. "Besides, I didn't tell him I was coming to sleep with him. I just said *visit*."

"Yeah, like maybe you wanted to apply for admission?" said Liz.

"No. Like I just wanted to see my boyfriend."

"You've already *seen* him, Alice! You've been looking at him since sixth grade," said Pamela. Then she grew quiet all of a sudden and slowly examined one fingernail. "Just don't forget to use protection. I don't ever want you guys to go through what I did last spring."

"What's a girl supposed to do? Carry a condom around in her purse? Like she carries tampons, just in case?" Liz asked.

"Technically, the guy's supposed to do it," I said.

"Technically, the guy's not the one who gets pregnant," said Pamela. "My motto is: Be prepared."

Liz leaned back and closed her eyes. "I almost wish we were in sixth grade again. Life seemed so much simpler then."

"Yeah, no makeup to worry about," said Pamela.

"No periods," said Liz.

"No breasts," I added.

My cell phone rang, and I answered. It was Mark.

"What happened?" I asked him. "Did the police follow you home?"

"Yeah. I figured that when Keeno got out and climbed in his car, they'd follow, but they drove off after that," Mark said. "Guess they figured we weren't vandals after all. You get any grief?"

"Not much. Lester's here for the weekend, and he's playing daddy. Thanks anyway for driving tonight," I told him.

"See you around," said Mark.

After the girls went home on Sunday, I realized just how lucky I was that Dad and Sylvia weren't here to see the police escort. Les could always squeal on me, of course, but I didn't think he would. Still, I had to be really careful. I had to be completely mature and reliable between now and July eleventh. If there was any hint that I couldn't be responsible, Dad would veto my overnight with Patrick.

I straightened up the family room, picked up the pages of the Sunday paper, baked some cookies, and made a cold salad of tomatoes, onion, macaroni, and hard-boiled eggs. I picked some flowers and made an arrangement for the coffee table. I watered the azalea bushes at the side of the house, did the laundry, and drove Les back to his apartment in Takoma Park. I had just made a pitcher of iced tea when Dad and Sylvia came home about seven.

"Oh, the place looks beautiful, and you even made a bouquet, Alice! What a nice welcome!" Sylvia said.

Dad beamed and gave me a hug.

"Did you have a good time?" I asked.

"The best!" said Sylvia. "The play closes next week, so we were lucky to get tickets. How did things go here?"

"Fine," I said. "Les and I ate together on Friday and just spent the evening talking and hanging out. His car was in the shop—George brought him over, so I drove him home a little while ago." They didn't ask about Saturday night, so I didn't tell.

"Well, it's good to know that Sylvia and I can get away now and then and that everything's under control back here at the house," said Dad.

"Totally," I said.

"We went to the Metropolitan Museum; we took a Circle Line cruise," Sylvia went on. "I can't believe we squeezed so much into one weekend, but we had such good weather. The last time we were in Central Park, everyone was riding bikes or scooters. Now, it seems, everyone's on Rollerblades."

"You both certainly look relaxed," I told them.

"Next stop, Chicago!" Dad said. "I'm feeling very good about the fellow Carol's going to marry."

"Yeah, me too," I said, and wanted to change the subject as soon as possible. I didn't want any more talk about Chicago and my visiting Patrick until we were there and it seemed like a done deal, too late for Dad to change his mind. "There's a pasta salad in the fridge," I said, "and I made some cookies."

"Perfect," said Sylvia, and wandered out to the kitchen.

I had just started up to my room when Dad said, "Any word from Patrick?"

I turned halfway around. "Patrick? He's going to call me this week."

"Does he know yet where you'll be staying?"

My throat felt dry and my forehead hot. "I think I can stay with a friend of his in the girls' dorm," I answered.

"Good plan," said Dad.

I went into my room and sat down on the bed, my heart thumping painfully. It was the first time I could remember telling Dad an outright lie. But maybe it wasn't a lie exactly. I didn't say I *was* staying in the girls' dorm, did I? I didn't say that Patrick had *said* that I would. Heck, I didn't even know if the University of Chicago *had* a girls' dorm. All I said was I thought I could stay with a friend of his. I thought it might be in a girls' dorm.

I mean, that's often the way it's done, isn't it? Didn't Pamela say that maybe Patrick's roommate could sleep somewhere else? People moving around, giving up beds? Wouldn't a person naturally *think* it might happen? And if I got there and found out that Patrick hadn't planned that at all, or there wasn't a girls' dorm, or he didn't have a friend I could stay with, well, I didn't know that yet, did I?

Liz was right. Things were simpler back in sixth grade. A lot simpler.

4
CHANGE OF PLANS

I got a phone call the next day at the Melody Inn, and it wasn't from Patrick.

"Alice!" came Carol's voice. "Am I ever glad to talk to you!"

My mind wouldn't compute why my cousin needed to talk to me. She was getting married in two and a half weeks! She should have a million things on her mind, the least of which was her seventeen-year-old relative out in Maryland.

"What's wrong?" I asked, wondering if Aunt Sally had suddenly vetoed the wedding plans.

"You sound just like Mom whenever I'd call her long-distance," Carol said, laughing. "Nothing's wrong, unless you say no. One of my bridesmaids is five weeks pregnant, and she's been having morning sickness that lasts all day. She doesn't think she would make it through the ceremony and wants me to get someone else. You're about her size, and we already have the dress. Alice, could you possibly . . . ?"

"Are you *kidding*?" I shrieked. "I'd *love* to be a bridesmaid."

"I was hoping you'd say that," Carol told me. "We tried to work it so that everyone in the wedding party was local and no one would have to travel from out of town to be fitted for anything. But Joan just doesn't think she can handle it. This is her first baby, so we're all happy for her, minus the morning sickness."

"When would you need me to come?" I asked. "The wedding's on a Saturday, right? I think we were planning to fly in on Friday."

"Could you change your reservation to Wednesday, Alice? It will give us a chance to get any alterations on the dress if we need them. And besides, you'd get to go to my bachelorette party."

"I love it!" I said. "What should I bring? What color is the dress?"

"I'll surprise you," Carol said, "but I think you'll like it. Bring a strapless bra—nude, if you have one. I'm not fussy about shoes, but they should be light and airy—strappy beige heels would be perfect as long as they're comfortable. And don't worry about your hair. We'll have someone do it for you."

As soon as I hung up, I rushed into Dad's office, where he

was working on the payroll. "Dad, I've got to go to Chicago two days early!" I said. "Someone's pregnant!"

Dad stared at me, pen poised above the papers.

"I've got to take her place!" I panted. "One of the bridesmaids is having morning sickness. Carol just called."

Dad's face finally relaxed. "Well, thank goodness it's not Carol. Call Sylvia and see if she can change your reservation. She and I can't leave before Friday, but you can go early."

I threw my arms around him, then picked up the phone and called Sylvia.

Patrick called that evening.

"Still on for Chicago?" he asked. "My parents were in town for the weekend and we were at the game when I took your call. The crowd was pretty raucous."

"Who won?" I asked.

"White Sox. Extra inning."

"Must have been fun! Listen, I'm coming two days early because I'm taking the place of one of Carol's bridesmaids. She's pregnant and having morning sickness, so I'm coming the Wednesday before to try on the gown. I also get to go to Carol's bachelorette party."

Patrick laughed. "Cool. Hope it's wild. When will you be free?"

"The wedding's on Saturday, the eleventh, so I probably could meet you somewhere Sunday at noon. Would that work?"

"Sure."

"We fly out again late Monday afternoon, so I'll only be at the university one night." When Patrick didn't say anything, I added casually, "Hope you've found a place for me to crash."

"I'm working on it," Patrick said. "I've only been here a couple of weeks myself, but we'll find something."

How do you come right out and say, *Patrick, I'd hoped I could stay with you?* How do you say it and not say it? I mean, if you aren't really sure? How do you show you want to without saying you're ready, especially if you don't know if you're ready or not?

So I said, "Whatever," and then hated that I'd said it. Like anything would be okay. Like I didn't care one way or another. And then, with my heart pounding, I added, "Not too far from you, though, I hope. I . . . I mean, I don't know the neighborhood at all." *Argggghhh!* That sounded so stupid.

"Hey, don't worry," Patrick said. "It's not every day my girlfriend comes for a visit."

The tingly feeling came back and made me warm.

"Let's plan to meet somewhere downtown," he said. "We can take a bus back to the university. Maybe you'll meet a couple of my friends."

"I can't wait," I said. "But I really want you all to myself, at least some of the time."

"That can be arranged," Patrick said, and it sounded as though he might be smiling. "Be sure to think of things you'd like to do while you're here."

"Mostly I want to see where you have classes, where you hang out, where you sleep. . . ."

"Okay. What if we meet at Water Tower Place on Michigan Avenue—anyone can tell you where that is—and we'll take things from there. Noon at the Water Tower."

"Sounds like a good title for a movie. You know, *Sleepless in Seattle, Noon at the Water Tower . . .*"

He laughed, and I love to make Patrick laugh.

"Can't wait," he said.

Neither could I.

On Friday, after cashing my paycheck at the bank over my lunch hour, I passed a small lingerie shop with a new display in the window: red pants, blue bras, and white bikinis, guaranteed to set off fireworks on the Fourth of July. And suddenly I thought about what I should wear when I spent the night with Patrick.

My Jockey fems just wouldn't do. Neither would my cotton briefs with the little hearts all over them. I wanted to wear something more special than Vanity Fair but not as obvious as Victoria's Secret. This lingerie shop had its own brands of stuff that you didn't see in shopping malls all over the Washington area. I went inside.

"Just browsing," I said to the thirty-something saleswoman who was folding lacy bras at the counter and putting them in a tray.

"Take your time," she said, smiling, and immediately turned away to give me privacy.

I made a quick check of the price tag on a sapphire blue bra and discovered right away I couldn't afford a matching set.

I'd settle for one really special pair of pants, and I walked over to the far wall, where row after row of silky underwear was arranged by color.

Pink was definitely out. Too innocent-looking. White, too virginal. I imagined standing in front of Patrick in a pair of red, white, and blue underpants with stars across the bottom, and nixed that in a hurry. A pair of red tap pants with little slits up the sides intrigued me, but it made me think of a toreador, which wasn't quite what I had in mind.

I wanted to look casual but alluring. Surprising but not shocking. Sexy but not slutty.

The saleswoman glanced my way. "All the prints there on the left are on sale, if you're interested in those," she said, and busied herself arranging a gown on a mannequin.

I looked at the prints. One had red ants all over it. Another had the word *juicy* on each cheek. There were pants with *love* in six languages, sailboats, top hats, teddy bears. . . . I imagined Patrick slowly undressing me to find a pair of pants with yellow smiley faces all over them.

I turned back to the wall again and finally chose a bikini of stretchy black lace with a nude-colored lining, so it would look as though skin were showing through. I settled on size small. I could have bought six pair of my usual cotton pants for what this cost, but I took the bikini over to the counter and got out my wallet.

The saleswoman said, "Lovely," and carefully folded it in tissue paper and put it in a little lavender bag with a ribbon handle.

"Please come again," she said after I'd paid.

Maybe I will, I thought. *We'll see how things go with Patrick.*

For the Fourth of July, a bunch of us had planned to take the Metro down to the concert on the Mall and stay for fireworks after, but it absolutely poured. The rain let up a little around three, and we thought of taking rain gear and chancing it. But then the rain started again and the wind was even stronger. We knew that the ground would be like a sponge and gave up the idea altogether. Mrs. Stedmeister, being her usual generous self, told Mark that we could all come over for hot dogs and to watch the fireworks, if there were any, on TV.

We sat around listening to Jill complain about the designer jeans she had to return; to Keeno moan about needing more money to buy the old car that he and Mark wanted to fix up and sell; to Karen telling about the boredom of visiting her grandmother; to Penny saying she was getting fat, which she wasn't—maybe a pound or two. And as I watched the rain pour down the windows, I thought how this Fourth of July really sucked. On TV the people at the concert were huddled under umbrellas, and you could tell that some of the musicians in the band shell were getting wet. But halfway through, the rain stopped, and the emcee announced that the fireworks would go on at the Monument at nine. It was right then that Mark's mom brought in her homemade strawberry shortcake.

"Let me help," I said, jumping up and lifting some of the

dishes off her tray. Mr. Stedmeister, beaming, followed her in with an extra bowl of whipped cream.

"Heeey!" said Justin. "Looks great!"

They were little monuments themselves, the shortcakes—halves of biscuits stacked on top of each other, drizzled with berries and juice and whipped cream.

"Wow! Thank you!"

"What a treat!"

"This is fabulous!"

The exclamations came from all corners of the room. If the Stedmeisters had been wallpaper in the past, staying on the sidelines when Mark had the gang over, they were suddenly the focus of our attention, and Mark grinned as he watched us dig into our dessert.

"She makes this every year, one of her specialties," he said, and his mom flushed as she put another spoonful of strawberry juice on Pamela's shortcake.

"Stay and eat with us," Liz said, scooting over to make room on the sofa.

"No, no, we're fine right here," Mr. Stedmeister said from his chair in the dining room, his bowl of strawberries in his lap.

When the fireworks began, however, and Mark said that his dad liked fireworks more than Christmas, we cleared the couch and insisted that Mr. and Mrs. Stedmeister have the best seats in the place.

"Come on, Mom," Mark coaxed, and shy Mrs. Stedmeister finally came into the room with her husband and sat down in front of the TV while we stacked the plates and took them out to the kitchen.

The celebration at the Mall is always special, with its view of the Washington Monument in the background, the Capitol, and the National Symphony Orchestra onstage. Each year the fireworks include something new, and this year, when two rockets went up side by side in two twin explosions of tiny jewels, Mark looked toward his parents and said, "That one was for you guys." And then, to us, he explained, "They were married on the Fourth of July."

We clapped and cheered.

"Twenty-seven years!" Mark added, smiling at his parents.

"Congratulations!" we said.

Mr. Stedmeister grinned back at Mark. "And we had to wait eleven years for this kid to come along."

"Just wanted to make sure you guys were ready," Mark joked back, and we laughed.

Later, when Gwen and I were drying the dessert plates and putting them in the cupboard, I told Mrs. Stedmeister that Mark was lucky to have her for a mom.

"Well, thank you, but we're the lucky ones, because he's certainly brightened our lives," she said, then added, "He's talking about going to Clemson, you know. . . ."

"Yeah?" I looked over at her, and she gave a little laugh.

"If he's accepted, I know I should be grateful that he's here on the East Coast, but . . . Well, we'll go right on having the crowd here on college breaks. That's one thing we can look forward to."

"We'd *love* that," I told her.

* * *

"Can you think of *any*thing else you might need in Chicago?" Sylvia asked me as we eyed my suitcase, open on top of my bed. "What about a shoulder wrap, Alice? You never know about the air-conditioning in some of these hotels. You could use one of mine. . . ."

I wouldn't use a shoulder wrap if goose bumps as big as baseballs popped up on my skin. "Not for me," I said. "I'll be dancing, Sylvia. I'm always warm."

"Jewelry? String of pearls?"

"Carol said she's giving each bridesmaid a pair of earrings to wear at the wedding, and we won't need necklaces."

"Then I guess you're all set."

Sylvia had asked if I could take along the set of Irish linens— tablecloth, place mats, and napkins—we were giving Carol and Larry, along with a check. It took up more room in my suitcase than we'd thought, but I had a small carry-on bag as well and got everything in.

Mentally, I went over the clothes I had packed for my time with Patrick. The cutoff shorts, the jeans, the halter top, the sweatshirt . . . and, in a pocket of my suitcase, the lacy pants and . . . a package of condoms.

Dad drove me to the airport, and I tried not to think of the last time I was in a plane, when we went to Tennessee to see Grandpa McKinley before he died. But this was a happy occasion. A thought kept coming back to me again and again: Would I sleep with Patrick? My breathing had become more shallow and Dad looked over. "Not nervous about this plane trip, are you?"

"Not really," I told him. "I'm just excited. I hope I don't do anything too embarrassing at the wedding."

"Hey, there has to be at least *one* embarrassing incident at every wedding, or what's there to talk about afterward?" he joked.

I smiled. "Well, I'm going to go with the expectation of enjoying myself, even the plane ride."

"That's my girl." Dad turned off the parkway and headed for the terminal. "And where will you be staying at the university?"

"Patrick says he has it all arranged," I lied, and hated lying just before I went away. What if the plane crashed and the last thing I'd told my dad was a lie? But by now, I figured, Patrick *must* have arranged something, so it probably wasn't a lie at all.

Traffic was circling in front of the terminal, and Dad's attention was diverted as we looked for United. A cop blew his whistle to hurry us along, and we finally found a passenger drop-off place.

We hurriedly got my bags out of the trunk, and Dad pointed to the check-in desk beyond the door.

"Three items," he said, as though I couldn't count. "Your purse, your carry-on, and the bag you're going to check. Always count the number of things you're responsible for and keep that in your head."

He sounded like Aunt Sally.

"Good-bye, Pops," I said, giving him a kiss on the cheek. "See you Friday. Love ya." *That* wasn't a lie.

"Have fun," he said. "You've got good weather, so the flight should be easy."

I gave him a final wave as I rolled the larger bag through the double doors and into the terminal.

Free at last, I thought, and could feel my pulse throbbing in my temples as I took my place in line.

5
WINDOW SEAT

The plane had three seats on each side of the aisle. First-class passengers, the elderly, the handicapped, and parents with small children had all boarded first, and I slipped past the white-haired Asian man who was sitting in the aisle seat of my row and noticed, after I sat down, that he was already dozing.

Seat number 9A was by the window. I was glad of that because I was too excited to read the magazine I'd brought. It was a short flight, about two and a half hours, nonstop. I welcomed the time just to be alone with my thoughts—the busy tangled ball of thoughts—to see if I could sort anything out before we got to O'Hare, especially the "just see what happens" thoughts. My large bag had been checked, my carry-on stowed in the compartment overhead, and I had a package of cheese crackers in my purse if I got hungry. I settled in and watched the workers outside on the tarmac.

The slow parade of passengers in the aisle seemed endless as bags were stuffed into overhead bins, jackets removed, magazines retrieved, and seats exchanged. As the crowd thinned out, I saw that not all the seats were occupied, and I began to hope that the seat between me and the dozing man on the aisle would stay vacant so I could put my stuff there.

A few minutes later, however, a couple more passengers got on, and a forty-something man, balding and slightly on the chunky side, thrust his suit coat in the overhead bin and excused himself as he wedged past the Asian man and sat down heavily in the middle seat.

"Sorry," he said as his elbow bumped mine. "Taxis! Didn't know if I'd make it or not."

I gave him a sympathetic smile and turned again to the window. The cargo doors were being shut, and a man with headphones was backing away from the plane, signaling the pilots. The engine noise grew louder, and I folded my hands in my lap and closed my eyes as the plane began its turn toward a runway.

"First flight?"

I opened my eyes and saw the middle-aged man studying me.

"No," I said. "I've flown before." I was glad I was wearing my long pendant earrings, though, and my slinky tangerine-colored shirt, to give me a more sophisticated look. I didn't want anyone treating me like a nervous ten-year-old, explaining all the different engine noises I was going to hear.

"Douglas," the man said. I thought he was giving me the name of the plane's manufacturer. Then he added, "Doug Carpenter."

"Oh," I said. "Alice McKinley."

"Very pleased to meet you," he said, and nodded toward the sunlight now flooding through my window. "I think this will be a very pleasant flight."

"Hope so," I said.

He opened his briefcase and took out a paperback book. I turned toward the window again. We were at the end of a runway, and I watched another plane taking off on a course perpendicular to ours. The long silver body pointed upward, reflecting the sun, leaving a muffled roar in its wake. Then it was gone. Our plane began to move, turned, and the engines revved up louder and louder as we picked up speed.

I pressed my lips together. Faster and faster we went, and then the world outside the window began to slant and we were off the ground.

Stay up, stay up! I silently begged the pilot. A clunking sound beneath the plane told me the landing gear was up. I also realized that my hands were now gripping the armrests so hard that my knuckles were white.

Doug was smiling at me. "Could I buy you something to drink?" he asked.

"Oh, no, I'm fine," I said. "I just don't like takeoffs." As though I had flown a dozen times before.

"I guess if you fly as much as I do, they're as common as taking your shoes off," he said. "Where you going?"

"My cousin's wedding in Chicago. One of the bridesmaids is sick—well, pregnant, really—so I'm taking her place. All sort of last minute."

"You'll make a beautiful bridesmaid," said Douglas. And when I didn't respond—turned toward the window, in fact—he opened his book and began reading. Ten minutes later, though, when I faced forward again, he turned his book upside down on his lap and said, "Bridesmaid, huh? Seen the dress?"

"No, but Carol has great taste, so it's probably elegant."

"Even more so with you in it," said Douglas, and seemed to be studying my face. "You're . . . let me guess . . . college freshman?"

"Almost," I said, leaving it open as to whether I was starting this fall.

"Those were great years—high school, college," said Doug. He leaned toward me confidentially, and I expected to hear that he'd been the high school quarterback. "I was one of those guys who was into everything—sports, student council, yearbook, girls . . . whatever there was, bring it on."

His elbow was resting against mine on the armrest, and I discreetly moved mine and let it rest in my lap. Then I closed my eyes and settled back, as though I wanted to sleep.

"How about you?" he asked after a few minutes. "How involved are you?"

"Excuse me?"

"At school. Extracurricular stuff."

"Oh. Just a few things. Drama Club and features editor of our paper."

"*Features* editor? That's great. What are some of the stories you've done?"

"Well, I did one last year about what goes on in our town after midnight. My girlfriend went with me to research it. We wanted to see where two runaway girls might find food and a place to sleep—how hard it would be to survive on our own."

"That was crazy," Doug said. "Two girls out alone like that . . . anything could have happened. What were you? You know . . . Kind of asking for it? Curious?"

"Not *that* curious," I said. "Two guys from school were assigned to follow us at a distance—see that we were okay. But you're right, that could have been dangerous."

"So . . . ," he said, and now I realized that his leg was pressing against my leg. I moved it. "Those other two guys . . . the ones assigned to protect you . . . your boyfriends?"

"No," I said, laughing a little too self-consciously. "Just friends. Part of the newspaper staff." I looked out the window again.

"You've got a boyfriend, though," he said, and his voice was softer. "Pretty girl like you has got to have a boyfriend." The leg was back.

This time I moved mine deliberately. "Yes," I said, in as businesslike a tone as I could. "I have a boyfriend at the University of Chicago, and I'm going to meet him after the wedding."

"Aha!" Doug said triumphantly. Then, more softly, "That's the real reason for the trip, right?" He was trying to get me to laugh, and he got a smile. "What's his name?"

"Never mind. You don't need to know that," I said, trying to humor him and turn him off at the same time, struggling to stay polite.

"Okay. How long have you known Mr. No-Name?"

"Forever," I said. "Since sixth grade."

"Sixth grade! Wow! Must be pretty hot stuff." He glanced around at the Asian man on the other side of him, checking, I suppose, to see if he was still sleeping. He was. Then he leaned over so far that his face was half a foot from mine. "So . . . what are you and Mr. No-Name going to do while you're in Chicago? Want some good places to go, I could name a few." He idly placed one hand on my knee.

I reacted immediately, picked up his hand and put it back on his own leg. He laughed.

"No, thanks," I said coldly.

He must have thought I was playing with him. He glanced again at the sleeping man beside him, and this time, when the hand came back, he squeezed my knee. "You know what I think?" he said. "I think there isn't any Mr. No-Name. And I'll bet I could show you a *really* good time in Chicago if you'd let me."

"MR. CARPENTER, WOULD YOU PLEASE TAKE YOUR HAND OFF MY KNEE?" I said, in as loud a voice as I could muster.

The Asian man opened his eyes. People across the aisle

leaned forward and looked over. A man in front of us turned around and looked over the back of his seat.

Doug immediately removed his hand and his face flushed. The flight attendant came quickly down the aisle. Doug picked up his book and his briefcase and stood up.

"Excuse me," he said, and climbed over the man in the aisle seat.

"Is everything all right here?" the attendant asked me.

"It is now," I said.

Douglas Carpenter never came back.

Uncle Milt met me at O'Hare. Flying to Chicago by myself was nothing compared to finding my way through the maze of endless corridors, overhead signs, entrances, exits, and escalators in the terminal. Miraculously, I finally found baggage pickup and, even more miraculously, saw my uncle in a bright yellow polo shirt, looking around him, head turning like a periscope.

He saw me before I could reach him, and a huge grin spread across his broad, craggy face. He held out his arms and gave me a bear hug.

"My favorite niece," he said.

"Your *only* niece," I reminded him. "Thanks for picking me up."

"How was the flight, honey?"

I wasn't about to tell him about Douglas Carpenter because he'd tell Aunt Sally, and she'd put me under protective custody for the duration. "Fine," I said.

"You never saw such commotion back at the house," said

Milt as we edged our way over to the conveyor belt where other passengers were waiting. "Carol's staying with us this week, so all the bridal stuff—bridesmaids' dresses, the favors, the bows, the ribbons—is everywhere. We tried to keep things out of the room where your folks will be sleeping, but it's a lost cause."

There was a bump and thud as the flaps at one end of the conveyor belt flew open and two suitcases toppled through, one falling over on the other. Passengers inched closer as more bags came through, and every now and then a hand reached out and caught one.

"What color is your suitcase? You see it?" Uncle Milt asked.

"Navy blue with a red stripe along the top and sides," I said. "I don't see it yet."

I studied my uncle as he leaned forward, watching for my bag. His face was a little thinner, and the skin under his chin was loose and flabby. His hair was thinner too, but he still had the same old sparkle in his eyes. He reached out once for a blue suitcase but pulled back when he saw a big green ribbon tied to the handle. I realized with a pang that every time I saw my aunt and uncle, they'd look a little older. The same must be true when they saw my dad. Changes I didn't notice from one day to the next would be far more noticeable to them.

The crowd began to thin out as people found their bags and left. The few remaining suitcases were going around a third and a fourth time, but my bag wasn't among them.

"What's happened to it?" I asked.

"I don't know," said Uncle Milt. "You had your name on it, right? Luggage tag and all?"

"Yes. And they ticketed it again when I checked it in."

"Got the stub?"

I gave him my carry-on bag to hold and searched my purse. The stub was in the pocket that held my cell phone, and I handed it to him.

"Let's see what I can do," he said, and went over to an employee standing by the conveyor belt. "Got any more bags back there?" he asked. "Still one missing."

"What color?" the man asked, and we told him. He went in a side door, and when he came back, he was empty-handed.

"Nope," he said. "No more bags back there."

6
THE LIST

My throat tightened, my temples throbbed. My shoes! My strapless bra! My cutoffs, sneakers, and . . . the lacy black pants and the condoms.

"I had our gift for Carol and Larry in it!" I cried. "And everything I need for the wedding."

"Was probably put on another plane," the employee said as my face registered panic. "Lots of planes leaving for Chicago. Go to the claim office and fill out a form. They'll put a tracer on it."

"The wedding's in three days!" I said, choking out the words.

"Oh, most bags don't stay lost that long," the man said, and directed us to the claim office.

We had to stand in line again, with other passengers look-ing as upset as I was. Uncle Milt had my carry-on bag over his shoulder, and I wished I'd put my "necessaries" in there. It did have my makeup, my curling iron, and hair dryer, but I could have used anyone's hair dryer. Could have bought makeup at any drugstore. Why hadn't I packed more carefully?

"May I help you?" a clerk said at last as we finally reached her desk.

"This young lady's bag is missing," Milt said, showing the luggage claim ticket.

"It's for a wedding in three days!" I said. "I've got to have it!"

The brown-haired clerk in the tortoiseshell glasses said, "You're not the bride, I hope."

"No, but I'm a bridesmaid."

"We usually locate a bag in a day or two," the woman said. "Briefly, can you describe the contents?"

"A wedding present, a pair of sneakers, shorts, a pair of beige sandals, some underwear—"

"Okay, that's enough. Any jewelry or valuables? We do have a limit on liability."

"No," I said miserably. We filled out the form and left.

"When we locate the bag, we'll deliver it to your Chicago address," the clerk said. And then, looking over my shoulder, "Next."

I rode back to Aunt Sally's in shock. I imagined the tag com-ing off my suitcase. Imagined airline employees going through my stuff, looking for an address. I imagined somebody calling Aunt Sally and telling her about the condoms. I even wondered if Doug Carpenter stole my bag just for embarrassing him on the plane.

Aunt Sally almost smothered me in her arms when we got to their place. "Oh, Alice, you look more like Marie every day," she said. "You've got her chin and cheekbones exactly!"

She was upset about my missing suitcase, but Carol simply shrugged it off. "If it doesn't come by tomorrow, Alice, my maid of honor will take you shopping and we'll get whatever you need. Don't worry about it. That's what maids of honor are for."

Carol looked fantastic. She always did have a nice figure, but she looked even better now. Tall, hair the same color as mine, though I think she'd added highlights. Right now it was tied in a ponytail, and Carol was wearing shorts and a tee.

"Let's go up and try on your dress to see if it needs alterations," she said. "We've got a seamstress standing by. Then we'll think about my bachelorette party. You'd look fine in what you've got on."

There was bridal stuff everywhere—a mountain of gifts in one corner of the dining room, boxes of bridal favors, baskets of bows. . . .

But the bridesmaid's dress wasn't at all what I expected. It was short. It was peach-colored. It was clingy, with little gathers where a wide band of peach Lycra circled the waist. There were narrow straps over the shoulders, with a bit of a ruffle along the edge, and the round neckline dipped so low, I'll bet you'd be able to see my nipples if you tried. It was more like a wisp of a sundress made for someone who wore a 36D bra.

"Wow!" was all I could say. Then, "Wow!" again.

Carol laughed at my astonishment. "It takes a while," she said. "The other bridemaids' dresses are lilac, apple green, and turquoise. Dad says we'll look like a seaside orchard."

"They're certainly summery," I told her.

"All my bridesmaids like them," she said happily.

"But won't your friend—the one who's pregnant—want this dress? It was supposed to be hers in the first place."

"Well, we're going to alter it for you. That neckline needs to come up a bit, don't you think? No, Joan and her husband are so excited about the pregnancy, it's the only thing on her mind right now," Carol told me. "The dress is yours for coming to Chicago early and helping me out."

Aunt Sally came up with her sewing box and soon had the shoulder seams pinned, the front taken in a little. The rest of the dress was fine, and I looked rather stunning in it, actually. I'd look even better in heels.

"Now," said Carol, when we'd finished, "the girls are coming to pick us up at eight, and I've got to wash my hair. Do you need anything at all? Makeup?"

"No worries. I've got a few things in my carry-on bag that should see me through this evening," I told her.

"Good. Shower if you like, but this is just going to be fun and casual."

Aunt Sally studied us uncertainly. "Remember, Carol, she's

underage. I've heard about these bachelorette parties. We don't want to have to bail you girls out or anything."

Carol gave her mom an affectionate kiss on the cheek. "We'll return her as pure as the driven snow," she promised, and then, with a wink to me, "although snow in Chicago doesn't stay clean for very long."

There were three other bridesmaids: Anne, who was the maid of honor, Heather, and Becky. They arrived in an SUV, driven by Anne's neighbor, an ex-Marine who was getting paid to be our designated driver and bodyguard for the evening, Carol had told me.

Charlie was a large, good-natured guy who said that it was his job to see that we had a good time, but if any of us got into difficulty during the evening, all we had to do was signal. I wished he'd been sitting on the other side of Douglas Carpenter on the plane ride to Chicago.

In the backseat Carol had to give up the T-shirt she was wearing for a special white shirt with BRIDE in big blue letters and a short veil that fell halfway down her back, held on by a headband.

At a dance club called Polly's Place, Charlie gave our reservation number, and we were led to a special room with a sign over the door saying GIRLS' NIGHT OUT. Another bridal group was just leaving, laughing raucously, and I figured this club must see a lot of bachelorette parties.

The manager welcomed us and said that by tradition, all

bachelorette parties began their evening in this room playing Pin the Tail on the Donkey.

Huh? I thought. But then we saw a large picture on the wall of a handsome guy in his birthday suit, minus one important piece of equipment. And we howled when the manager handed each of us a paper copy of "the equipment" and a thumbtack to pin it where it belonged.

One by one we were blindfolded, turned around three times, and gently shoved in the direction of the picture, to pin our "tail" where we figured it should go.

We shrieked when Heather placed hers on the man's left nipple. I got mine a bit closer when I attached it to his navel. Anne went too low and pinned it on his knee, and Carol's attempt got the biggest laugh when she pinned the man's penis to his right hand so that he appeared to be holding it.

I had worried that I might feel as out of place here as I'd felt at the bridal shower for Crystal Harkins way back when. But Anne was funny, Heather was warm and friendly, and Becky was as spontaneous as a ten-year-old, so we got along fine.

"Hey!" Becky had exclaimed when she'd received a paper penis and discovered that one of the testicles had been torn off.

"Oh, Becky, you've got a one-nut man!" Heather sympathized.

"Manager! Manager!" Anne called. "We've got an undescended testicle here!" and we howled with laughter.

When we'd finished the game, we went back into the main room. It had a bar along one side, small tables at the back. A band was playing at the other end of the dance floor. Charlie went to the bar and brought back beers for Carol and her friends, a Sprite for me. The manager had insisted, he said. Finally, after we'd danced for a while, Charlie reached into his jacket pocket and, with a flourish, pulled out a paper. "And now . . . ," he said, "*the list!*"

"Oh, no!" Carol cried, but I think she'd been expecting it, whatever the list was.

We had to crowd closer to Charlie to hear, because it was so loud in the dance club. "Do you, Carol, solemnly swear that you will fulfill the Eight Obligations of a Bride-to-Be, as listed on this sheet of paper?" Charlie intoned.

"Do I have a choice?" Carol said, to laughter, knowing the three other girls had written the list themselves.

Charlie read number one: "Collect four business cards from four men."

While we followed gaily behind, Carol went from one small table to the next, looking for good candidates for businessmen, apologizing for the intrusion, and asking if anyone had a business card. All of the men were amused. Some of their dates looked annoyed at first, but when they noticed the veil and the gaggle of girls following along behind, they laughed too. It took seven tries to collect four cards, but Carol carried them triumphantly back to Charlie.

We were distracted momentarily by the sight of a half dozen men hastily pulling out dollar bills from their wallets and lining up in front of another bride-to-be, this one red-faced, who was wearing a T-shirt with Life Savers taped all over her chest. Printed on the T-shirt were the words suck for a buck, and each man paid to bite or lick off one of the candies.

"Not to worry," Anne said when she saw the surprise on my face. "We're a bit more refined than that."

"Task number two!" read Charlie. "Get a man to sign your T-shirt."

Carol looked relieved that it was no more raunchy than that. She took the Sharpie pen Charlie handed to her and walked over to a short, smiling man at the bar. Of course, he wanted to know if he could choose the spot where he would sign, but Carol laughingly offered her shoulder. He obliged, then gave her a pat on the fanny.

We danced some more, and the other bridesmaids sang along to ancient songs I didn't know—"Our Lips Are Sealed" and "Should I Stay or Should I Go?" After Carol completed the next three tasks on the list—*kiss a bald man on top of his head; ask a man to buy you a drink;* and *persuade a man to give you his right sock*—Charlie told us it was time to move on, and we went to another dance club called Gossip.

"The men sure were obliging," I said, still wondering about the guy who would be half sockless the rest of the evening.

"Ha! You should see what she has to do next!" said Heather, and Carol made a dramatic little whimper.

It must have been Girls' Night Out all over Chicago, because we saw three or four more bachelorette parties going on at Gossip. There was a line outside, but Charlie must have pulled some strings because he got us in right away and brought more beers and my third Sprite of the evening. I was getting a little tired of trips to the women's room and was about to go another time when Charlie read task number six: "Use the men's room and scold the guys for leaving the seat up." It was such a good one that we couldn't wait to see Carol do it.

With my cousin gamely in the lead, we followed her into the men's room, where the two men at the urinals quickly zipped up, staring at us in disbelief, then amusement. A man coming out of a stall took two steps forward and stopped, but the toilet seat behind him was already down, so Carol had to give a sort of general admonition, and when all three men backed out of the room as fast as they could reasonably go, I begged her to stand guard while I used the john, and then we went back out to dance.

Two more tasks to go. It was almost midnight when Charlie read number seven: "Sit on the lap of a man named Steve."

When Carol approached the men at this bar and explained that she had to find a man named Steve, every Tom, Dick, and Harry in the place seemed to be named Steve, and they were all laughing and offering themselves to the bride-to-be.

"Over here, darlin'," said an older man, waving his driver's license to prove he really was a Steve, and Carol sat on his lap for about ten seconds and gave him a hug.

The band at Gossip was really good, and we even had Charlie dancing with us. But finally it was time to wrap things up, so he gathered us one more time and read off task number eight: "Coax a man into giving you a condom."

"Omigod!" said Carol. "You *guys*! Have a heart!" I laughed along with the others, but no one would let her wriggle out of it.

"And we get to choose which guy," Anne insisted. As we followed along behind her, she chose a plump, straight-faced man sitting at the end of the bar talking politics to the man beside him. The object, I figured, was to make Carol have to ask as many guys as possible before she found one with a condom.

"I'm sorry to interrupt," Carol said, and somehow her headband had slipped to one side, giving her veil, and Carol herself, a slightly tipsy look, "but I'm sort of on a mission, and I've got to collect a condom. Could you possibly . . . ?" She winced to show her discomfort.

The sober-faced man stared at her for a moment, then at us, and slowly, beginning to grin, he reached in his back pocket, pulled out his wallet, and handed her a little foil packet with the word TROJAN.

We cheered, and Carol thanked him with a peck on the cheek. As we headed back to Uncle Milt's in the SUV, I was glad *I* didn't have to relate the evening to Aunt Sally.

7

MR. AND MRS. LAWRENCE SWENSON

My bag was there when we got back. It was in the hallway, the luggage tag in place—a new routing slip taped to the top.

My eye went immediately to the small zipped pocket on one side of the suitcase. It was closed. As I reached for the handle, I let my fingers slide over the pocket. I could feel the outline of the box of condoms, the soft thickness where my black pants would be. All was well.

If God or Fate or Destiny had intended for me not to have sex with Patrick, that would have been the perfect time to intervene and have that pocket robbed. If everything in my suitcase was in order except the underwear and the condoms, I could take it as a sign that this was a bad idea, but now that they were here . . .

It was pretty stupid reasoning, and I knew it even as I began to lug the suitcase up the first flight of stairs to the landing.

"Let me help," Carol said, coming up the stairs behind me. She lifted the other end and we took it to the spare bedroom. The full set of table linens we were giving Carol and Larry was what made it so heavy. "Mom's going to let you sleep in here till Ben and Sylvia come, and then you'll sleep in my room. I'll pull out the trundle bed for you. Les gets the basement."

I was a little disappointed that I wouldn't have three nights of girl talk with Carol before she married, but I should have been glad she was staying here at her parents' in the first place. After she pointed out my towel and drinking cup on the bed, she motioned toward her room. "Want to see my gown?"

"Of course!" I followed her down the hall, past Aunt Sally and Uncle Milt's bedroom, to the room at the end, still decorated with Carol's high school and college stuff. She switched on a lamp. Her closet door was open, and a great bulge of tulle and satin poked out.

She reached for the padded hanger and lifted the gown. It was more frilly than I'd expected of Carol, but absolutely gorgeous. The top was ivory-colored lace, and strapless. It had a long torso dipping to a point, both front and back, and the tulle seemed to spring up and out from the bodice like a filmy cloud covering the slim satin skirt, so that you'd be able to detect the outline of Carol's figure beneath.

"Wow!" I said. "It's beautiful!"

"I was going to go for a sleeker look, but . . . I don't know. I put this on at the store, and Mom almost cried, she loved it so much. I like it too. It's just fairy-tale enough to please Mom and fashionable enough to please me." Carol looked at it a bit wistfully. "Mom and Dad didn't get a chance to celebrate my first marriage with me, so this much is for Mom."

As she hung it back up, Carol said mischievously, "Of course, Mom wondered about the propriety of my wearing white, but I told her that ivory doesn't count, and she's happy." She yawned. "I've got to get to bed, Alice. I'm pooped. Got everything you need?"

I told her I did and said I'd see her at breakfast. Lunch, anyway. There was a lot we could have talked about, but I was sleepy too, and when I woke in the morning, I discovered I'd slipped into bed in my pants—hadn't even bothered to put on my pajamas.

We were so busy on Thursday, I felt as though I were back in that Hecht's department store where I'd worked last summer. People kept coming in and out; packages were arriving; phone calls being made and received. . . . Carol seemed to be on her cell much of the time. I decided that I could be most helpful by staying out of the way, yet on the edge of activity so that I could help when needed.

Carol went to Anne's Thursday evening, where their hairdresser was going to propose some styles for the wedding party.

I figured this was Carol's last chance for a night with her closest friends as a single woman, so I ate a semi-quiet supper with Uncle Milt and Aunt Sally, glad to keep them company. I told Carol they could fix my hair any way they liked.

"I've dreamed about this wedding for years and years," Aunt Sally told me. "I guess every mother dreams about her daughter's wedding, and maybe it's a good thing her first marriage didn't last, or this Saturday wouldn't be happening at all."

I'm not sure that Aunt Sally's reasoning was any better than my thinking about God and Fate and Destiny and sex. If Carol's first marriage had worked out and she was still happily married to that sailor, there could be little grandchildren eating dinner with Aunt Sally right now.

But I just said, "She told me last night that she wanted a wedding dress you'd love too, and that's how she chose the one she did."

Aunt Sally's eyes glistened. "Really? She told you that?"

I nodded. I knew that even if I didn't say another word the whole time I was in Chicago, that one little sentence was what Aunt Sally needed most to hear.

Dad and Sylvia arrived on Friday, and Les was to fly in a few hours before the rehearsal dinner. I had to go to the church with Carol and other members of the wedding party, and Dad said he'd pick up Les at the airport in the rental car. We all met at the restaurant where the dinner would be held. Any family member from out of town was invited also.

Carol had arranged it so that everyone under the age of thirty was seated with her at our two long tables, the older adults at the others. Larry was sitting on one side of her, Les on the other, and we were telling the guys about the bachelorette party, making up stuff and exaggerating, of course.

"Naturally, we can't tell you everything, Larry, because after we locked Carol in the coat check room with a salesman from Detroit, we have no *idea* what happened," Anne said.

"Whoa! Whoa!" Larry said, and laughed.

"And then, when we made her practice throwing her bouquet, she, of course, didn't have one, so she took off her bra . . . ," continued Heather, and everyone laughed some more.

It seemed to me that Larry Swenson was always smiling. I don't know that he ever played football, but he looked like a halfback—big and boxy—and his hair was the color of honey. Every time Carol introduced him to somebody else, he gave that person his full attention. No wonder he was doing so well in hotel management.

I turned *my* attention to Lester. "Were you ever at a dance club when a bachelorette party was going on?" I asked him.

"Not if I could help it," he said. "But I remember one time . . ."

"Yeah? Yeah?" we coaxed, urging him on, and Larry rested his arms on the table, eager to hear Lester's story.

"A gal came up to me and said she had to get the tag off a guy's underwear, could I possibly help?" Les began.

We were cheering already.

"What did you do?" I asked.

"What *could* I do? I turned to the guy beside me and asked if I could yank the tag off his Jockeys for this nice young lady. He said no." The waiter who was bringing our coffee stopped to listen when we hooted some more.

"And . . . ?" Carol said.

"Well, I didn't want to make her cry, so I stood up, lowered my jeans enough to pull up the top of my boxers in back, and told her to go for it. She tried, but she couldn't get the label off. So I told her to wait, went to the men's room, and took off my jeans. Took off my boxers. I couldn't get the damn thing off either, so I did the only thing left to do. Pulled on my jeans, went back out, and handed her my shorts, label intact."

The girls screamed and pounded the table.

"I just knew I'd like this guy!" Becky said, leaning over toward Lester and giving his arm a squeeze.

Carol's wedding day was cloudy and a bit cooler, but after Aunt Sally checked the forecast on The Weather Channel, she said that her second prayer had been answered. Not only was Carol marrying a nice young man, but there would be no rain on her wedding day. I imagined God sitting up there in the clouds, pondering whether he should pay attention to fighting in the Middle East or the weather in Chicago.

I wasn't as nervous a bridesmaid this time as I'd been at Crystal Harkins's wedding. Or even at Dad and Sylvia's. In a way, I suppose, because I was a bridesmaid by default, just taking the place of someone else, I wouldn't be expected to do as good a job as she might do, I reasoned. But then, it had been sort of by default that I'd stood up for Sylvia, too, because her sister was supposed to have been her maid of honor, but she'd fallen seriously ill. And though Crystal always liked me, I had the feeling she'd asked me to be a bridesmaid to rub it in Lester's face that she was marrying someone else, since Les hadn't asked her.

Oh well. There were probably 250 people at the church; Carol and Larry had lots of friends. Some were neighbors of Milt and Sally's, and not all were coming to the reception, but everyone wanted to see Sally's daughter "married at last."

I stood solemnly beside Becky, who stood next to Heather, who stood next to Anne, who took Carol's bouquet when it came time for the exchange of rings. I almost started giggling when I thought how these women who looked so serious now were the same women who had been holding paper penises in their hands a few nights before.

Carol, though, looked as lovely and thoughtful as I'd ever seen her. This was the same Carol who had sent me clothes she'd outgrown all these years and helped give me a sense of style. The same Carol who eloped with a sailor, her parents not finding out till they got a postcard from her on her honeymoon in Mexico. The same Carol who had patiently answered my questions about . . . well . . . just about everything.

The night before, when I slept on Carol's trundle bed after Sylvia and Dad took over the guest room, we'd talked a little before we fell asleep. But I didn't ask her opinion of whether or not I should sleep with Patrick. I didn't ask if she thought it was right. Carol was tired and needed to be fresh and rested for her wedding day, for one thing. But also, I knew it was my decision alone to make, and maybe I didn't want to analyze it too much. Maybe I wanted to keep it spontaneous. Maybe I felt that this was perhaps my only chance to be alone with Patrick for a whole night, far away from his parents and mine, and I didn't want anyone, including my conscience, saying no.

I blinked and brought my mind back to the wedding.

". . . Then by the authority vested in me," the minister was saying, "I now pronounce you husband and wife. Larry, you may kiss your bride."

If you could hear smiles, you would have heard a happy buzz filling the sanctuary as Larry and Carol turned toward each other. He seemed to pause a moment, just drinking in the sight of her, then drew her to him, wrapped her in his arms, and . . . Well, that was the longest kiss I'd witnessed at a wedding. I even heard Aunt Sally whisper, "Oh my!" It was probably no more than six or seven seconds, but if you took the time to count *one one thousand, two one thousand . . .* , you'd see how long a seven-second kiss seems in church.

At last they drew apart and the organ pealed out the familiar "you can go now" music for bride and groom, and everyone was smiling—wide, happy smiles. Anne handed Carol her bouquet, we paired up just as we'd rehearsed, and I put my hand on the arm of a stocky groomsman in a black tux. We all went back up the aisle, through the foyer, out the door of the church and around the side, away from the crowd. Then Larry and Carol kissed again, and we broke into happy, relaxed chatter, glad it was over and that no one had tripped or sneezed. When the guests had departed for the reception at a nearby hotel, we dutifully went back inside to pose for wedding pictures, and I felt very beautiful and feminine in my wispy dress, which was now my very own.

Aunt Sally is one of those people who should never drink. In public, I mean. At her only daughter's wedding, in particular. It's not that she drinks too much. It's that she drinks so little, so rarely, that when she *does* drink—even half a glass of wine— she's not quite as reserved as she should be.

Dad gave a wonderful toast, and Uncle Milt brought tears to the eyes of everyone as he talked about the mixture of sadness and admiration he felt for his daughter when he first took her to college and said good-bye. That there was some of that same feeling now, but she couldn't be marrying a finer man.

If Aunt Sally had just left it there. If she had just understood that a father's toast represents both parents. But Aunt Sally finished her glass of wine, then dinged her fork against her empty goblet, and as everyone turned to see who was speaking next, she got to her feet, bracing one hand on Uncle Milt's shoulder.

I saw him give her an anxious look. He covered her hand with his own, a way of cautioning her, perhaps. But Aunt Sally just smiled around the room and cleared her throat.

"Milt loves . . . our daughter . . . as much as I do," she began, "but I didn't just miss Carol the day she went to college. A mother starts missing her daughter as soon as she goes to kindergarten, so I've been all through the 'missing' part." She stopped and dabbed at her eyes with a corner of her napkin, then placed it back on the table. "I even missed Carol when she went on her first sleepover, and that was back when sleepovers were just with girls."

There was hesitant laughter around the room, and Carol looked quickly over at her mother, leaning forward as though trying to catch her eye. But her mom barreled on.

"Now, I'm no prude," Aunt Sally continued, and I saw Uncle Milt pat her hand, giving her the "sit down" signal, but Aunt Sally didn't stop. "I just want Carol to know that while I never approved . . ."

Oh no! I thought. *Please, Aunt Sally. Don't lecture her now about moving in with Larry last year.*

Lester saved the day. He interrupted, standing up at his own table and raising his glass: "Oh, I know that story, Sal, and I hope you'll let me finish it for you, because after all these years I've just got to set the record straight."

Aunt Sally looked flustered, but Milt was tugging at her arm, persuading her to sit down, and Lester's smile in her direction finally convinced her that things would be okay. She sat.

I stared at my brother.

"I think we all know what devoted parents Sally and Milt have been to Carol," Les continued, "and though times are changing, some things are just too hard to accept. The night I invited Carol for a sleepover, I'll admit, was over-the-top."

There were more giggles, and Aunt Sally looked at him in surprise.

"I was eight years old," Les said, and now the room rocked with laughter. When it quieted down, he continued: "Carol was twelve—Alice was only one, so she doesn't count. The truth is that I wanted to watch a movie a friend had loaned me, but I didn't want to watch it alone. I knew that if I told Mom or Dad what it was about, they wouldn't let me see it at all. So I persuaded both sets of parents that Carol and I were going to play Monopoly, and we did, till about midnight. We were cousins, after all. But now, Aunt Sally, you deserve to know the truth. After everyone else had gone to bed, Carol and I watched *Vampires of the Deep*, not once, but twice, and neither of us got a wink of sleep the rest of the night." More laughter. "To Sally and Milt and my parents, my apologies. To Carol and Larry, may you have more memorable nights than that by far!"

The room erupted in laughter and applause, and I heard Aunt Sally say, both pleased and puzzled at the toast, "Why, I don't remember that at all!"

Carol looked gratefully over at Les, who was taking his seat again, and Dad was grinning too, and he gave Les the thumbs-up sign.

Later, when the bride and groom were dancing again and people were moving about the room, talking with each other, I slipped over to Lester's table and sat down on the empty chair next to him.

"I never heard that story before, Les. Carol never mentioned it either."

Les glanced toward Aunt Sally, then back again. "That's because it never happened," he said, and grinned as he downed the last of his wine.

8

MAX AND THE MED

Mr. and Mrs. Lawrence Swenson were off to Greece for their honeymoon, Les had flown back to Maryland, Dad and Sylvia were relaxing with Uncle Milt and Aunt Sally, and at 11:47 a.m., I stepped off a bus on Michigan Avenue across from Water Tower Place.

The weather had grown sultry again, and I was wearing my cutoffs and a halter top, sunglasses and sneakers. I had my jeans and other essentials in the carry-on bag over my shoulder, and I hoped that Patrick would be on time and I wouldn't be stranded in downtown Chicago.

Just thinking about Patrick, though, made my throat feel

tight with excitement. And there he was, sitting on a bench, a baseball cap tipped low over his forehead. A redhead, he'd always had to be careful about the sun, and his freckles got a shade darker in summer.

When he saw me, he bounced up, smiling broadly.

"What a coincidence!" he said. "I was just hoping somebody I knew would come along." And he kissed me. Then he took my bag and slipped the strap over his own shoulder. "Man, it's good to see you," he said, smiling down at me and putting one arm around my waist. "Have any trouble getting down here?"

"No. Uncle Milt offered to drive me, but his instructions seemed simple enough," I said.

"So, what do you want to do first? See the sights? Want to eat? To walk? What?"

"I'm not especially hungry," I told him. "Why don't we just walk, and we can stop for something when you like. I've already seen downtown Chicago. Not everything, but a lot."

"Bet you haven't been to the beach."

"Beach?"

He turned me around and we started walking the other way. We must have been facing the lake, because there was more of a breeze now on our faces, and it felt good.

Patrick leaned down as we walked, kissed me again, and then we walked on, both of us smiling, Patrick squinting against the sun. I felt absolutely exhilarated as we strolled past the fancy stores on Michigan Avenue along the Magnificent Mile, as it's called. I probably couldn't even afford a pair of socks from any of those places.

"So how did the wedding go? Anything dramatic happen?" he asked.

I told him about the bachelorette party, the rehearsal dinner, the ceremony, and Lester's quick save at the reception.

Patrick laughed. "Leave it to Lester," he said.

"So how's summer school? How many courses are you taking?"

"Three, but they're consecutive and very intense. The university doesn't want you taking more than one at a time."

"What are they?"

"I just finished Ancient Egyptian Language, Culture, and History. The next is American Law and Litigation, and the third is Introduction to the Civilizations of East Asia. This one deals with Japan. Tons of reading in all three, but they count toward my core requirements."

I tried to imagine spending my summer studying all that. "I don't know how you do it, Patrick. I don't even know why, but I'm glad you're you," I told him.

"Me too," said Patrick. "I'd hate to be anyone else."

The early-afternoon sun was hot, despite the breeze. The sky was opening up the closer we got to the lake, and after the next couple of blocks we entered an underpass. As we came out the other side, there it was: sand, water, sky, and people sunbathing all over the place, right along Lake Shore Drive. People in suits and ties holding briefcases on one side of the street; people in bikinis sitting on towels on the other.

"Patrick, I *love* it!" I said.

He held on to my arm as he balanced on one foot, removing one sneaker, then the other, and I did the same with mine. Our feet sank into the sand as we walked down to the water.

"This is so wild!" I said, looking around. "Seagulls and sailboats in one direction, skyscrapers in another."

"Would you believe some people live in Chicago for years and never know the beach is here?" Patrick said.

The water seemed icy cold to me—my toes hurt after only a few minutes, and there weren't many swimmers. But we sloshed ankle-deep along the shore, enjoying the warmth of the sand when we detoured for a minute or two, then went back in again, lifting our faces and closing our eyes against the breeze.

I nuzzled Patrick's shoulder to let him know how happy I was, and he gave my waist a little tug, pulling me closer. Once, when he kissed me, we almost lost our balance and toppled into the water, but we laughed and righted ourselves in time.

We found a pretzel stand and bought a couple to eat on a bench in the shade. For a while we just cuddled and watched three little kids chasing a seagull across the sand, like they really had a chance. Then we went in search of a drinking fountain and took turns squirting the water high over the rim while the other used it to rinse the sand from between our toes. Only half succeeding, we put our shoes back on.

"What next?" I asked.

"We're going to take the six—the number six bus—back to

Hyde Park. We'll be within walking distance of Max P.," Patrick said.

"Who's Max?"

He laughed. "Max Palevsky Residential Commons, to be exact. It's where they house all summer school students. Like a dorm. We'll stow your bag and then go someplace for dinner."

Everything was an adventure with Patrick. The walk, the traffic, the lake, the gulls, the bus rolling block after block, mile after mile to Chicago's South Side. I wondered if the other passengers were looking at us and thinking, *A guy and his girlfriend* or just, *A guy and a friend*?

At some point Patrick rested his hand on my leg. "It's hot," he said. "No more sun for you until you lather up."

"The sun will be down in a few hours," I said.

"And that's when the neighborhood really comes alive," Patrick told me.

I hoped I'd have a chance to clean up a little before we went to dinner. My feet were still sandy inside my sneakers. I wanted in the worst way to ask Patrick where I'd be sleeping, but I didn't want to sound too eager.

Max P. was a modern-looking building, not at all like the ivy-covered stone buildings that formed most of the University of Chicago campus. I signed the visitors' list at the front desk, and as we went up the stairs to the second floor, I heard what sounded like a flute and violin practicing together from somewhere.

Patrick unlocked the third door on the left, and we went into a small living room, sort of—a couple of chairs, a couch, a lamp. . . .

There were three more doors in this room—one led to a bathroom and the others were for the bedrooms, with two narrow beds in each.

He opened the door to the room he shared. A large guy with dark hair and thick eyebrows lay sprawled on his back on one of the beds. A notebook lay open, facedown, on his chest, and a copy of the Sunday *Tribune* was scattered on the floor. Patrick's roommate barely opened his eyes when he saw us and closed them again, his lips half open as he slipped back into sleep.

"Sorry," Patrick told him, and then, to me, "This is my room and that's Abe." As we backed out, he whispered, "Migraines. He says he gets one after every exam, and it lasts for a day or two."

After he closed the door, I said, trying to sound casual, "Hey, Patrick, where am I staying tonight?"

"A friend's checking with some of the girls. She said she'd call."

"When will we know?" I asked.

"Soon. You won't have to sleep out on the steps, I promise."

That wasn't what I was thinking about, and I wondered if Patrick could read my mind. He just reached down and kissed me—really kissed me. This was the first time we were truly alone together, and then he kissed me again. When he let me go a second time, he said, "You can clean up if you want. Kevin and Spence aren't back yet."

While Patrick sat down with the *Sun-Times*, I went into the bathroom and locked the door. You could tell this was a guys' bathroom. There were hair shavings in the sink and on the bar of soap. Damp towels were clumped together on the towel rack. Not all that different from girls' bathrooms, I guess, except for the hair shavings.

I undressed quickly and got in the shower. I didn't know when the other two guys were coming back or when Abe might wake up. So I washed quickly, all but my hair, and just as I stepped out, I realized I didn't have a towel.

"Patrick?" I called. "Do you have a spare towel?"

There was no answer.

"Patrick?" I called again, putting my mouth to the door.

Nothing.

I unlocked the door and opened it a crack. "Patrick?"

The living room was empty. Great! I locked the door again and studied the wet towels. There were only three of them, and all were wet and rumpled. Moldy-smelling, actually. There was no bath mat, only a dirty piece of a shag rug that needed washing.

I stood on the rug and did a little drying dance, trying to shake off every drop of water that I could. I could tell I'd got a sunburn despite the sunscreen I'd put on before I'd left that morning. My arms and legs would soon be dry, but there were other parts of me that needed extra drying. I was tempted to wipe off with toilet paper, but there wasn't much left of the roll. Even if the guys didn't need it, I surely would.

I was doing my shake-off dance again when I heard a door open and close, then Patrick's voice outside the bathroom: "Hey, Alice? I brought you a clean towel. Stick out your hand."

Gratefully, I did, and I was finally dry enough to put on my bra and underwear, my good jeans, and a tank top. I luxuriated in the feel of clean toes without sand between them.

"You're looking great," Patrick said when I came out at last. I knew I'd taken longer than I should when Abe came charging out of Patrick's room and immediately took over the bathroom.

"Sorry," I said as he shut the door behind him. And to Patrick, "He looked angry."

"It's the migraine," Patrick said. "Now . . . you hungry?"

"Yeah, I am."

"What do you crave?"

"What I'd really like, Patrick, is to just be you for a day. Go where you'd go to eat on a Sunday night, do whatever you do."

He grinned. "Hey, you're a cheap date. Okay, let's go to the Med."

"What? Sounds like a clinic," I said as he held the door open for me.

"The Medici," Patrick said. "My favorite hangout. A popular place back in the sixties, they say."

It was a beautiful night on campus. We walked with our arms around each other, hands in the other's hip pocket. Every so often Patrick gave me an affectionate little hug, pulling me closer, and we'd kiss as we walked. And yet, we were anonymous too. There were so many people out enjoying the evening that no one paid any attention to us.

Every time we made a turn, it seemed, there was a poster or a bulletin board promoting an organization or a lecture, a concert, a play. Being Sunday, there were notices about religious services and discussions, and I stopped to marvel at the diversity: Sacred Sites Field Trip to Hindu Temple of Greater Chicago; QueeReligions: Gay *and* Religious Identity Are Not Inherently Conflicted; Christian-Based Agriculture at Lamb of God Farm; Dogs, Zoomorphism, and the Sacred in Ancient India. . . .

"Look at all these amazing things you can go to, Patrick," I said. "How do students attend all this stuff and still find time to study?"

"They don't," said Patrick. "I guess one of the first things you're supposed to learn at college is to make choices."

The Medici was crowded and noisy, and the walls, the tables, the chairs were completely covered with graffiti.

"Wow!" I said. "They don't mind?"

"Not really. Not unless you carve through the tables. And, of course, they never have to paint the place."

"Hey, Pat!" a girl called, and we looked to see three people waving to us from a corner table. *Pat? Patrick is Pat here at the university?*

"Hey!" Patrick said. "How's it going?"

"Great. Sit down," one of the guys said, and the other pulled out a chair for me. Patrick got a chair from a nearby table, and everyone squeezed over to make room.

"We were all in soc together," Patrick explained to me. "The Egyptian class. Alice, this is Fran, Adam, and John."

"Hi," I said, and smiled around the table.

"You a student here?" Adam asked.

"No. I'm visiting from Maryland," I answered.

"Long way from home, aren't you?" said Fran, and I could see her blue eyes analyzing the relationship. She wore no makeup and might have been more attractive if she had, but she dressed simply, her hair pulled up off the nape of her neck and held in place with a clip.

"She wanted to get a taste of campus life, so I brought her here," said Patrick. "What's good tonight? We're hungry."

"I'd try the grilled tuna steak or the Moroccan ragout," said John.

"But you've gotta get the raspberry lemonade," said Fran, pointing to the word *Himbeersaft* on the menu.

"Or the Mexicana hot chocolate," said Adam.

I told Patrick to order for me—I wanted to try whatever he liked best—and John motioned the waitress over. After she left, Adam turned to me. "Where do you go to school? University of Maryland?"

I was flattered but had to say, "I'm a senior in high school."

"Oh," said Fran. "This your first visit to Chicago?"

"No, I have relatives here. In fact, my cousin got married yesterday, and my family's here for that. So I came over to see

Patrick. We've known each other for a long time." I wanted to get that said in case Fran had intentions regarding Patrick.

Adam knew someone who went to Frostburg, John said he had a brother in Baltimore, and then the conversation turned to private schools versus state universities, the quality of professors for first-year students versus fourth-year, and the food at Bartlett Hall, the student cafeteria.

"Well, the food here is fabulous," I told Patrick as we sipped our drinks and shared a platter of onion rings. Fran and Adam, it turned out, were freshman students like Patrick, while John would be a second-year student come fall.

The others finished their dessert and coffee, then excused themselves to go see a movie at Doc Films—one of John's friends was running the projector. They invited us to come along, but Patrick said he wanted to show me the campus, so we said good night.

"I'm glad to see that University of Chicago people take time out to have fun," I told him.

"Of course. What did you think?"

"But you still seem to be studying twenty-four/seven. . . ."

"Well, but when my third course is over in August, I'm going to spend some time in Wisconsin with my parents. Dad's brother has a house on a lake, and Mom's beginning to realize I'll be away at school for most of the time from now on."

"I've been realizing that for a long time," I said softly.

"Yeah?"

"Yes. Ever since you said you were coming here to school.

That's especially why I wanted to see you this weekend."

"Want to commemorate it, then?" he asked.

I guess I looked surprised. Did he mean . . . ? I smiled uncertainly. "How?"

He pointed to the tabletop, which was etched all over with names and dates. I'm not sure if I was relieved or disappointed, but some of them were really funny: *Nietzsche was here* and *Leave your appendix at Student Care*. One of them read, *I sold my car for Scav.*

"What's Scav?" I asked.

"It's a joke. The big campus-wide scavenger hunt each May. Here. Use this steak knife."

I couldn't think of anything original at all, especially not with Patrick watching. Not when other people sat over coffee discussing the Socratic method. But why should I try to be someone I wasn't? I took the steak knife and looked for an empty space. Then I dug deeply into the soft, once-polished wood of the table: *Alice and Patrick*, followed by the date.

Patrick looked at it, then at me. He got up and came around to my side of the table, and I scooted over to make room. Grinning, he firmly, though a bit raggedly, cut a heart around our names and added a piercing arrow.

9
THE NIGHT IN MAX P.

We walked all over campus afterward. The bookstore was still bustling—students sitting in the café section reading foreign newspapers over coffee, browsers in the book section in shorts and flip-flops.

"Want me to buy you a present?" Patrick asked.

"Why?"

"A keepsake! A memento!"

"Sure. What are you going to buy? A bookmark?" I teased.

Patrick picked up a heavy maroon coffee mug with UNIVERSITY OF CHICAGO etched in white Gothic letters.

"Too heavy," I said. "I've got to carry my bag back to Aunt Sally's tomorrow."

"Sweatshirt?"

"Same."

So he bought me a pair of earrings that looked like the Earth as a small blue marble. I took off the ones I was wearing and liked the feel of the new lightweight pair dangling from my earlobes.

After the bookstore we went to the Reynolds Club, which is sort of the university's student union, I guess. Of course I walked right across the university seal in the main lobby, but Patrick walked around it.

"*What?* Is it holy or something?" I asked, noticing that other students didn't step on it either.

"Superstition," said Patrick. "If you step on the seal, you won't graduate in four years."

"Go ahead and step on it, Patrick!" I said. "You're going to graduate in three anyway!"

Like most of the architecture on campus, the Reynolds Club was an old stone Gothic building half covered in ivy, with enormous high-ceilinged rooms. In Hutchinson Commons, the dining hall, portraits of past presidents—a long line of them on both sides—looked solemnly down on the rows and rows of long tables where students sat eating, studying, arguing, joking, just hanging out.

In another huge room, with a large fireplace, the students were more quiet. Some studied at the thick, polished wood tables or lounged on upholstered chairs. Not air-conditioned, the room's windows were open to the night, and some students stood looking out, trying to catch a breeze. One guy stretched out on a leather couch, dozing. As we walked by the row of computer kiosks, Patrick stopped and fed his address and password into a computer to check his e-mail, then took me to see the fountain, which had just been turned on for the summer, and to the C-Shop for ice cream. We strolled past Cobb Hall, where artsy-looking students were hanging out, smoking, and finally stopped to sit on a secluded bench near Botany Pond.

Patrick said that the pond was stocked with goldfish and that a family of ducks made a home in the reeds, but we didn't see any.

"What's it like, Patrick, living away from home?" I asked him.

"You should know that. You were a junior counselor once at camp, right?"

"But that was just for part of a summer. This is going to be your home for the next three or four years, practically." I snuggled against him, and we looked out across the darkened water of the pond.

"I guess it hasn't really sunk in yet," Patrick said. "Or maybe, because Dad was away a lot when I was growing up, it seems like the natural thing to do."

"Because of his work?"

"Yeah. Diplomatic Corps. Whatever the family routine, it feels natural if that's all you know. And we got to live in a lot of neat places."

We were quiet a minute or two. Patrick's fingers idly stroked the side of my face.

"I wonder how it will be for Dad when I'm at college," I said. "Maybe he'll be *glad* I'm gone. He and Sylvia can have the house to themselves."

"It's not like you're deported or anything. You can always go back for holidays, for the summer. They'll probably be glad to see you come and glad to see you go. It's what animals do, you know. Leave the nest."

"Maybe I've been too sheltered all my life. We haven't traveled around the world like you and your family. It's always been Dad and Les and me. And Mom, when she was alive. And suddenly it will just be me alone."

"And a roommate," said Patrick.

"How's that working out?"

"Weird. It's always weird, actually living with someone you hardly know. You just get used to weirdness, that's all. And after a while even that gets routine—guys laughing and talking in the next room half the night, using the wrong toothbrush, not washing their socks. Then you go home to neatness and order and stuff, and *that's* the weirdness."

"Would you ever want a life like your dad's, do you think— traveling and being away so much? My dad was always there for me."

"I don't know. Depends what I had to come back to, I guess. I don't think I want to live my life alone. I'm sure of that. Not many people do."

"Me either," I said.

* * *

Now, in the late-night stillness, sometime after eleven, I sat side-ways, my feet up on the bench, nestled in Patrick's arms. He caressed my arm, my neck, my breasts.

I loved that he was touching me. Loved that we were here on a bench in the darkness, away from everyone else. That I was experiencing part of his life at the university, that I was seventeen . . . I tipped my head back until my face was directly under his. He leaned down and kissed me, a long, sideways kiss, so that our noses could breathe and the kiss could go on and on.

His fingers moved gently, slowly, back and forth on the bare skin above my waistband, and I sat up for a moment and leaned forward so that he could unhook my bra. When we resumed the kiss, his hand moved up under the bra, over my bare breasts, and I could feel my nipples stiffen under his caresses.

A flood of warmth spread along my inner thighs. Patrick was breathing harder too.

I turned around and put my hand on the fly of his jeans. Surprised, Patrick withdrew his arm and unzipped them. Slowly I put my hand under his boxers and gently stroked him, the first time I had ever touched a boy like this. And suddenly his lips parted, his head jerked back once, twice, then again, and I felt warm wetness as he ejaculated in my hand. He leaned against me, murmuring my name.

I could feel my own wetness and wanted his hand on me.

"I need you," I whispered, and lay back in his arms again, my legs stretched out on the bench, and worked at unzipping my jeans. Patrick helped me tug them down a little, then gently slid his hand into my underwear and touched me. My throat seemed to be swelling in my excitement. I guided his fingers just where I wanted them, showing him how hard to press and how fast to do it, and a few minutes later, in the dark of Botany Pond, I came. When it was over, I curled up in Patrick's arms, and all I could say to him was, "Patrick."

I'm not sure how long we stayed there. I was surprised and not surprised by what had happened. Occasionally we heard distant voices, a footstep as someone came out of Regenstein Library, but no one walked in our direction.

"What are you thinking?" Patrick whispered at last, nuzzling my ear.

"How wonderful this was. How glad I am to be here. What were *you* thinking?"

"That I always wondered if we'd ever be like this. *Hoped* we would."

"So did I."

I cuddled even closer to him and kissed his neck. Is this what it would be like if Patrick and I were students at the same college? Would we spend weekends in secluded places in summer or search out an empty dorm room in winter? Or was this a special moment because Patrick was willing to take the time? Because I was a visitor and we hadn't seen each other for a month? Because . . . because . . . ?

He nuzzled my ear again. "Alice, it's after midnight. Almost one. We'd better get you to bed."

I disentangled myself from his arms. "Patrick, where am I going to sleep tonight? My bag's back in your room."

He stood up. "Let's go see if anyone left a message at the desk. One of the girls said she'd ask around and see if there was an empty bed."

I stared at his face in the darkness. "You don't really have a place for me, do you?"

"Well, maybe. She said she thought a girl was going to drop out before the second course. If she did, then her room—her bed, anyway . . ."

I didn't know whether to laugh or faint. "Patrick!"

"It's no biggie. We've got that couch in our suite. I could sleep out there and—"

"You want me to sleep in the room with your roommate?"

"It's a bed. He's not in it."

"Patrick!"

"He's okay. Abe's a nice guy. He'll be on one side of the room and you'll be on the other. I'll be right outside the door."

I almost laughed. How could a guy be so sophisticated and smart and sexy and still be so clueless?

"I don't *want* to, Patrick! I don't want to be in a bedroom with a guy I don't even know and listen to him breathe! Why didn't you tell me there wouldn't be a place for me to sleep?"

"Because there is! There's a bed! There's a couch!" Patrick put his arms around me and turned me toward him. "Because I was afraid you wouldn't come. I thought something would turn up, and if it didn't, I'd take the couch. I suppose I could always ask Abe if he'd sleep on the couch."

"He's having a migraine, Patrick."

"Yeah, I know. And it's sort of bad manners to ask your roommate to leave. 'Sexile,' they call it."

I thought of the black lacy pants and the condoms in my bag. I thought how impossible that idea had been all along. What had I been thinking?

Patrick looked crestfallen as he backed away from me, holding on to my arms. "There's something else I haven't told you," he said.

I think I stopped breathing. Not a girlfriend here at the university! Not the Fran we had met at the Med.

"What?" I asked shakily.

"I've got a class tomorrow at nine."

"Oh . . ."

"Alice, I really, really wanted you to come. I wanted to show you around and do everything we did today." He squeezed my arms. "*Everything.* I figured that one half of one day was better than no day at all. You told me you can stay till one tomorrow. I'm going to come back here over my lunch break and see that you get a cab to Water Tower Place. I'd go with you, but it's the first day of my second course, and I can't afford to miss it. I'm really, really sorry."

"I . . . I know," I said. "Is the rest of your summer schedule just as tight?"

"'Fraid so. These condensed classes are held every day."

I didn't want to hear about it, not really, but this was part of Patrick too—the focus, the intensity, the intellect, the drive. . . .

I reached out and stroked his face. "I know," I said again. "I'm glad I came too, even if it was only for half a day. And an evening. Don't forget the evening."

"How *could* I forget?" said Patrick. He pulled me to him again. And we kissed.

When we got back to Max P., there was no one now at the desk. A note with Patrick's name on it was under a stapler. He picked it up and we read it together:

> *Patrick, if your friend had come on Friday or Saturday night,*
> *I could have found a bed for her because some of the girls went*
> *home over the weekend. But everyone's back now, and the girl*
> *I thought might drop out didn't, so we're full up. Sorry.*

We walked up to Patrick's suite and opened the door to the living area. One of the guys was sitting on the couch eating a bag of corn chips. He quickly swallowed and wiped one hand across his mouth.

"Alice, this is Spence. He rooms with Kevin," Patrick said.

"Hi," said Spence. "You're the one from Maryland, right?"

"Yeah," I said, and smiled, glad to know Patrick had mentioned me.

"She's going back tomorrow," said Patrick, and glanced round. "Kevin still out?"

"No. He turned in early." Spence scooted over. "Want to sit down?" he asked me.

"Actually, I think we're going to need that couch," Patrick told him. "Alice needs a place to crash."

"Sure!" Spence picked up the chips and the book he was reading. "I'll go down to the lounge. See you later."

"Sorry about this," Patrick told him. "I thought we'd find a place in one of the girls' suites, but they're full."

"No problem. Nice to meet you," Spence said, and went out into the hall.

Patrick looked at me uncertainly. "Sure this is going to be okay?"

"Of course," I said, though I wanted him all over again. "Go to bed, Patrick. I'll see you in the morning."

He lingered. I lingered. We kissed again. He pressed against me, then pulled away. "Better not start something we can't finish," he said reluctantly.

"Okay," I told him.

I took my bag into the bathroom, washed my face, and brushed my teeth. As I pulled out my pajamas, my lacy black underpants came with them. I looked at them wistfully for a moment, then shoved them to the bottom of the bag.

When I came back out in my pajamas, there were two sheets, a pillow, and a light blanket on the couch. Patrick had made an effort to tuck one end of the sheets under a cushion. He stepped out of his bedroom, bare-chested.

"I'll leave my door open a little if you want. Scream if one of the guys tries to crawl in with you," he joked, and went on into the bathroom.

I got between the sheets and tried to settle down. This wasn't exactly what I'd had in mind when I'd suggested this visit. *Well, Dad*, I thought. *At least you'll be pleased at the way things turned out, I'll bet.*

I tried to be mature about it, because I'd invited myself, after all. It's not the weekend Patrick would have picked, with a new course starting the next day. It's not the night he would have chosen—Friday or Saturday would have been so much better. He could have told me, *It's the worst possible time, Alice. . . .* But he'd really wanted to see me, my family was here in town, so he made the best of it, and I should too.

I was lying so still when Patrick came out of the bathroom that he must have thought I was asleep already. I'd been sure he would come over and give me a final kiss, but he moved noiselessly into the room where Abe was snoring. I heard him stumble a little over his shoes, and then all but Abe was quiet.

Disappointed, I turned over on my side, my nose against the pillow. There was Patrick's scent, clear as anything. It was obviously Patrick's pillow. He'd given me his pillow! He'd probably given me his sheets! His blanket! I felt like creeping in there in the dark and covering him with the blanket, but the air-conditioning had been set on high, and I knew I'd need the blanket myself before the night was over. Maybe I should just crawl in bed with him, taking the pillow and blanket with me. But Patrick hadn't suggested that. He had a class. It was late. . . .

There was a clock with luminous hands on an otherwise bare shelf of a bookcase. One fifty-three. A door closed somewhere down the hallway. Laughter. A boisterous good night. Quiet again.

I sighed and nuzzled the pillow once more, drinking in Patrick's scent. I guess I'd never thought of him as having a "scent," but I could recognize it now. I sniffed the sheets. Perhaps it was there too.

A key turned in the lock, and someone came in the suite and turned on the light.

"Oops! Sorry!" Spence said, and turned the light off again. "I forgot." He bumped into the end table as he groped his way to the bathroom. At least he hadn't come in and sat down on me.

The sound of his urinating was remarkably loud, and I felt embarrassed that I was so close and couldn't avoid hearing. Then the sound of water running in the sink. The clunk of a plastic glass. The bathroom door opened more quietly, and Spence went into the bedroom he shared with Kevin.

He didn't flush, I thought. *Eeeuuu.*

I turned over again, but this time my knees bumped the back of the couch. I turned still again, straightened my legs, pulled the blanket up under my chin, and stared at the dark ceiling.

Patrick was already fitting into university life. He talked of "the Reg" and "the Quads," "Ida" and "Hutch," as though they'd been part of his vocabulary forever. New friends called to him to join their table. His dorm room looked like any guy's bedroom—like he was perfectly at home.

Patrick could fit in anywhere, it seemed, and I wondered if I would ever feel so comfortable living away from Dad and Lester. If I could find my way around a big city, go to movies with titles I couldn't even pronounce, pass a course on Egyptian hieroglyphics, and get from one side of campus to the other in time for class.

The next time I looked at the clock, it was after three. I wondered if Patrick was awake in the other room. If I didn't get to sleep, I was going to feel awful. I was going to *look* awful when Patrick kissed me good morning. Maybe he was planning to take me to breakfast.

I wondered if I should get up before the guys and get my shower first. Or save all the hot water for them. *Sleep!* I told myself. *Pretend you're at home and go to sleep.*

But I wasn't at home. I was lying on a couch surrounded by four guys, one of them snoring first softly, then loudly in sudden snorts. I really was tired. All that excitement. All that walking. . . .

I went over the day again in my mind. The way Patrick had smiled at me as I got off the bus. The way he had tugged at my waist as we walked along Michigan Avenue. The way our feet kept touching in the lake water, the sand squishing between our toes. . . .

I remembered his fingers touching me and felt myself growing wet just thinking about it. Then, miraculously, I fell asleep.

When I woke, the blanket was up around my ears, and there were voices and noises out in the hall. I tried to remember where I was, what room I was in, what bed. . . . I opened my eyes and peeped out. The bathroom door was wide open, but the room was empty. Both bedroom doors were open, but there were no sounds from either one. Sunlight poured through one window.

I sat up and ran one hand through my tangled hair. Listened some more.

"Patrick?" I called softly.

No response.

I threw off the sheet and got up.

"Patrick?" I called again, louder. No answer.

I peeked in Kevin and Spence's room. No one was there. I looked in Abe and Patrick's room. Everyone was gone. There were no sheets or blankets on Patrick's bed. Just a bare mattress, a couple of jackets he must have used as cover, and a rolled-up sweatshirt for his head.

What was I supposed to do now?

I had to go to the bathroom and found my towel on the floor. Someone had used it for a bath mat.

"Argggghhh!" I wailed, and plunked myself down on the toilet.

It was when I padded back to the living area that I noticed an envelope propped up on a chair. It read:

Alice,

Couldn't bring myself to wake you. Figured you must have had a pretty restless night. Either that or a fight with your blanket. All of us have nine o'clock classes, so we had to leave. Tried to do it quietly. I'll be back a little after twelve to see you off and

*have ordered a cab to take you back to Water Tower Place. I've
drawn a map to Bartlett, where you'll get a great breakfast.
Enjoy your morning. Wish I were with you.*

P.

I collapsed again on the couch and tried to think, my arms
dangling between my knees. The clock read 10:13, and I was
sitting here in a deserted male dorm, my towel on the bathroom
floor and a map to a place I had never been.

There was a mini fridge at one end of the couch, and I realized that the weird noise I'd heard in the night was the fridge
shutting on and off. I leaned over and opened the door. A half
can of Coke, a couple containers of vanilla pudding, one piece
of moldy cheese, and a ham and cheese sandwich still in its deli
wrapper, with a scribbled initial on top.

I studied the initial. It could have been an *S*, could have
been an *A*, could even have been a *K*. It certainly wasn't a *P*. I
knew that one of those three other guys had used my towel as a
bath mat. It would not have been Patrick. I figured that whoever
used my towel deserved whatever happened to this sandwich,
so I ate it, and topped it off with a vanilla pudding. That was
breakfast.

10
BOOTS AND BUTTS

I took a shower, washed my hair, and could single out Patrick's towel by the scent. I used that. Any moment I expected one of the roommates to come back and rattle the doorknob, but Max P. was quiet. Everyone, it seemed, had gone to class.

When I'd fixed my hair, I wiped up the stray strands I'd left in the sink and spread Patrick's towel over the shower rod to dry. Then I took the sheets and pillow and blanket from off the couch, went in Patrick's room, and made his bed up neatly. For a brief moment I thought of leaving the black lace pants I'd bought beneath his pillow, but then I checked myself. What we'd shared on the bench by Botany Pond was so personal, so intense, that it couldn't be summed up in a pair of pants. *"Alice,"* he had murmured. And, *"Patrick,"* I'd replied.

By 11:10 my stuff was packed and I had close to an hour before Patrick was due back to see me off. I walked around campus, memorizing each street name, every turn, so that I could find my way back to Max P.

It was obviously going to be another hot July day in Chicago, but I was enjoying the breeze on the Quads. Eventually I came to a huge stone cathedral, so I followed the curving driveway and found myself at the entrance to Rockefeller Chapel. One of the doors was propped open, and I breathed in the dark coolness that enveloped me when I stepped inside.

There must have been a wedding the night before, as there were still white satin bows at the ends of the pews near the front. A custodian was loading two large potted palms onto a cart for delivery somewhere else, I imagined.

I stood in a back pew looking up at the high arched ceiling, at the light filtering through the stained-glass windows, and wondered whether Patrick and I would ever be here together. Standing at the altar, perhaps? I guess it was just a weekend for wedding thoughts, with Carol's still fresh in my mind.

By the time I got back to Max P., Patrick was standing there on the steps, looking all around, my bag at his feet. There was a cab waiting at the curb. I was about four minutes late.

He looked relieved when he saw me. His shirt was damp, and I guessed he'd run all the way from his class.

"I'm sorry," I told him. "I just wanted to walk a little. I saw Rockefeller Chapel, and it's beautiful."

"That was on my list to show you," he said. "Glad you saw it. Things go okay this morning?"

"Yes, I'm all set. Will you have time for lunch?" I was worried it might have been Patrick's sandwich I ate after all.

"Class starts again at one. I'll get a burger on the way back," he said, and bent down to kiss me. I reached up and touched his cheek as our lips met. Lingered.

"Thanks so much, Patrick," I said. "It was a lot of fun. I'm glad it worked out."

He squeezed my arms as he held them firmly in his grip. "So am I," he told me, and it was like we were having a conversation with our eyes. And then, "I've already taken care of the cab . . . you don't need to tip."

He walked me over to the curb and opened the door for me. After I slid in, he leaned down again and kissed my cheek. "Bye," he said. "It was great having you here. I'll remember it all summer."

I smiled back at him. "Even longer," I said.

Patrick closed the door, and the cab moved away—past the Gothic buildings with the gargoyles that silently howled at the sky; past the ivy-covered arches and the students lounging on benches, sipping their coffee. We seemed to be heading toward the lake, because I could see only sky up ahead, and then, there I was, riding in the backseat of a taxi along Lake Shore Drive. Past the Museum of Science and Industry, past the rocky boulders along this stretch of Lake Michigan, past the parks and fountains, the uptown skyline looming ahead.

I leaned back and closed my eyes for a minute, wanting to make an indelible image of it all in my mind. *Alice . . . Patrick . . .*

Uncle Milt picked me up at Water Tower Place, and Aunt Sally had a lunch prepared for Dad and Sylvia and me before we left for the airport.

"Well, how was your trip to the university?" she asked as soon as I sat down and picked up my BLT. "Did you meet some nice girls? I remember when Carol went off to visit colleges in her senior year."

"It's a great university, but I doubt I'll apply here," I told her. "I just wanted to visit a friend and meet the people he hangs out with." *Ooops.*

Aunt Sally stopped chewing. "You were visiting a boy?"

I nodded, and Dad quickly interceded for me. "I've heard that the university's had some new buildings going up, Al. What are the dorms like?"

"Really nice," I said. "The one for summer school students, anyway. The dorm rooms are in clusters of three each—two bedrooms, a bath, and a living area. Two students per bedroom."

"Were there *girls* in the bedrooms?" asked Aunt Sally.

"Only in the girls' suites."

"And you slept with the girls?" Aunt Sally's not shy about asking questions, but I knew that Dad and Sylvia were waiting for my answer too.

"No, actually. I slept in Patrick's suite," I said, and before she could choke, I added, "On the couch." And then I added, holding back a smile, "Alone."

But that didn't satisfy Aunt Sally. "You mean you slept on a couch in the middle of four boys who could have walked in on you during the night?"

"Nobody stepped on me that I remember," I said.

Aunt Sally shook her head. "In *my* day, boys didn't visit girls in their dormitory rooms, and girls certainly didn't go to theirs. If a boy had to come upstairs for some reason, a girl would call out, 'Man on second!'"

"Sounds more like a baseball game," said Uncle Milt, and we laughed.

"Well, that gave us a chance to duck into our rooms and close the doors," Aunt Sally explained.

Dad couldn't help himself. "If a girl had come to my dorm and a boy yelled, 'Woman on second!' every guy in the place would have come running."

We laughed some more, and Aunt Sally looked about the table in exasperation. But this time Sylvia came to the rescue: "Isn't it great, Sally, how people are more relaxed with each other now? I'd never have let a guy see me in curlers or an old bathrobe. Now guys and girls hang out together in old baggy sweats, step right out of the shower with stringy hair, and don't think a thing about it."

"But . . . with a towel, I hope?" Aunt Sally said, knowing she was outnumbered.

"Most definitely a towel," I said. *But not necessarily her own.*

* * *

Back in Maryland we got in Dad's car at the airport, and I'd not been home for thirty seconds—hadn't even gone up the front steps yet—when Liz called to me from her driveway.

"Alice! You've got to come with me! Dad's letting me have the car. You've got to see something!"

"We just got in!" I called. "It can't wait?"

"No! Really!" She was obviously excited about something.

I looked at Dad and Sylvia.

"Go ahead," he said. "I'll get your bag." He waved to Liz, and he and Sylvia went on inside.

I walked across the street. Whatever it was, Liz was in a hurry. She hadn't even asked me about Chicago or Patrick or Carol's wedding.

"This better be good!" I said, getting in the passenger side. "They didn't give us so much as peanuts on the plane, and I'm starved. What's going on?"

"I won't tell you. You've got to see for yourself, but it was on the six o'clock news." She giggled, a silly kind of giggle.

I looked over. "You okay?"

"Yes! Of course! How was Chicago? The wedding? How's Patrick?"

"Great, great, and great, but watch out for that Jeep," I said. "We'll talk after we get wherever we're going. This is rush hour, you know."

It was five of seven when we got to the Metro parking lot, but as lots of cars were leaving, we found a space right away.

"Hurry up!" she said, getting out of the car.

"I don't have any money with me!" I said. "I left my bags with Dad."

"You don't need any," she called over her shoulder.

I followed her through the crowd toward the entrance to the Metro. I couldn't imagine!

As we got closer, I heard music. It sounded like "Country Roads," and when we rounded the corner, there they were near the bottom of the escalator: Keeno and Mark, wearing nothing but Jockey shorts, painters' caps, and work boots. Painted on the seat of their tightie-whities were the words NAKED CARPENTERS.

"What?" I gasped, and my mouth dropped open. *"WHAT?"*

A boom box provided the piano accompaniment, Mark played the harmonica, and Keeno stood with a long saw between his knees, and was playing it with a bow.

I could only stare.

With the handle of the saw gripped firmly between his legs, Keeno grasped the tip end of the blade between his thumb and forefinger, bending the blade almost ninety degrees, moving it slightly up and down, and with the other hand, he stroked across the straight edge of the saw with a bow as though he were playing a violin.

"When did . . . where did . . . why the . . . ?" I cried, looking incredulously at Liz.

But she had converted to a giggly eight-year-old, and our laughter was joined by the shrieks of young women coming down the escalator from the train platform, who had just caught sight of the two guys making music in their skivvies, a scattering of dollar bills in the open saw case at their feet.

"How did they think this up? Why the underwear? Why the *saw*?" I asked Liz.

She couldn't take her eyes off the guys, and I'll admit they were well endowed. "Didn't you ever hear about the guy in Times Square, the Naked Cowboy, who plays a guitar in his underwear? Well, Keeno figured if it worked for the Naked Cowboy in New York, then maybe it would work for him and Mark," Liz said. "That's the way Keeno explained it to me. They're trying to earn money to buy a car. Isn't this *wild*?" And then she told me how Keeno's great-uncle had taught him to play the musical saw, so he figured maybe he could cash in on that—he and Mark together.

I guess you could call it "wild," but it was also sort of weird. The way she described it, the Naked Cowboy in New York strutted about as he played, wearing cowboy boots and a Stetson and playing frat rock; but Keeno had to stand perfectly still to keep the saw in place. And the kind of music he played on the saw was nice, but it wasn't exactly hip or cool—"Moon River," "Summertime," and "Are You Lonesome Tonight?"

"Why are they playing this stuff?" I asked Liz.

"Keeno says you can't play anything fast on a musical saw or it loses its vibrato or something. At least these numbers are better than 'Ave Maria' or 'Silent Night,'" she answered.

Whatever, they drew a crowd—or their underwear did. Mark jazzed up each piece with his harmonica as best he could, and you couldn't help admiring their muscular backs and hot butts. Also, Keeno had been letting his hair grow, and by now it just touched his shoulders. So they made it a sort of comedy routine, smiling flirtatiously at the girls who laughingly dropped a dollar or two in the saw case and nodding and smiling at the men who cautiously stepped closer to study the saw as Keeno played.

When they took a short break, Liz and I moved in closer.

"You guys are hilarious!" I said. "Keeno, I never knew you could do this."

"Neither did I—not in front of anyone but family. But, hey! If the Naked Cowboy can do it . . . !"

"Mom and Dad were here about an hour ago and thought it was funny, though they didn't care much for the underwear," Mark said, and we laughed.

"I wouldn't try it in January," I told them. "Wow. I come back from Chicago and find out you guys are celebrities! You made the evening news!"

"Yeah, maybe we'll skip college and retire early," Mark joked, checking the money in the case. And then, as we heard another train come in overhead, they took their places and began another song.

Liz and I stayed forty minutes or so. Then I said, "Listen, I'm starved. I haven't had any dinner. I need to get back, but let's watch to see if they put the guys on the ten o'clock news."

"Huh? Oh . . . well, I suppose it's time I went home too," Liz said. "I think they're going to do the Glenmont station tomorrow night. See how it goes."

She still didn't move, and I realized she wanted Keeno's attention one last time. Keeno was playing "Love Me Tender," and when he looked over at her, they exchanged a lingering smile.

As we walked back to the car, Liz was still humming the song. I stole sideways glances at her, and she had a peculiar smile on her face.

"Liz?" I said. "Is it the underwear?"

She startled and flushed a little. "What?"

"The attraction."

"Don't be ridiculous."

I grinned. "The muscles? The boots? The saw? The butt? *What?*"

She grinned too. "All of the above," she said.

11
PEOPLE CARE

Liz told me that another local station included a shot of Keeno and Mark on the early news after they started showing up at Metro stops in the District and Virginia. A week later a brief story about them came out in the *Gazette*. If people weren't inspired by the music, they were at least amused, it seemed, and enough dollars accumulated in the saw case to persuade the guys to keep at it.

We were busy at the Melody Inn as fall orders began to come in from schools for choir music, band music, and rental instruments for orchestra. Dad was also looking for someone to hire to replace David, who'd be leaving around the middle of August. He'd be going back to college full-time and entering a seminary after he graduated to study for the priesthood.

"I've been wondering why you'd choose Georgetown over Catholic U?" I asked him.

"Georgetown's a little more open to controversy. Faith that's not challenged can grow dull, you know," he said.

"If you say so," I told him.

The first week back home for me went by in a blur of activity. A lot of paperwork had piled up the few days we were in Chicago, and I was tired in the evenings from just running around the store, glad to eat my dinner on the back porch, e-mail Patrick, or read the last of the assignments on my summer reading list, *Crime and Punishment*. Liz went to Metro stops with Keeno and Mark sometimes to help carry stuff, and Pamela was visiting her cousin in New Jersey.

My e-mails to Patrick were brief and to the point. I've known him long enough to understand that he doesn't much like small talk. He doesn't e-mail just to be doing something. He hates texting unless it's something important. Ditto for phone calls. I can see Patrick as CEO of some major corporation someday. But when I'd told him that on our walk along Lake Michigan, he'd looked surprised.

"That's about the last thing I'd ever want to do with my life," he'd said.

"Some get paid millions," I'd said.

"My point exactly," he'd answered. "Who needs millions?"

Miss u a lot, I e-mailed once. *Loved your scent on the pillow.*

I could smell your shampoo on my towel, he e-mailed back.

Gwen called that Saturday.

"You still on for next Monday? For the week?" she asked.

My mind spun like a pinball in a machine, and I finally remembered agreeing to work evenings in a Montgomery County soup kitchen.

"I'm still up for it," I said. "Pamela's coming back tomorrow. Have you reached Liz?"

"Yeah. I thought she might have run off by now with one of the Naked Carpenters, but I finally got her."

I laughed. "You've noticed too? Her thing for Keeno?"

"She's sure having fun, I'll say that," said Gwen.

"You know what? Since Brian quit coming around so much, Keeno's been hanging out with Mark, and Mark's a different guy. Have you noticed? I mean, who knew he could play the harmonica? Who knew he'd get up the nerve to play in his underwear?"

"What was he like before?" Gwen asked. She hadn't really been part of our group until high school.

"Sort of like . . . well, background music. A lot like his folks. Lived in Brian's shadow. I hope he and Keeno make some big bucks with their carpenter gig. Listen, we need to get together and catch up. Why don't you come by tomorrow afternoon—I'll get Pam and Liz if I can—and we'll just hang out on the porch."

"About three, maybe?" said Gwen.

"Perfect. See you then."

Pamela was slightly tanned and, we noticed, letting her blond hair grow longer. She was stretched out on our chaise lounge, where Gwen, in a wicker chair, was also resting her feet. Pam's pink toes against Gwen's brown ones looked like little edibles on a dessert tray.

"What year was it, Pam?" I asked lazily. "The year of the gum?"

"What?" asked Pamela.

"Your hair. You're letting it grow. I'm trying to figure out how many years it took you to get over Brian putting gum in it—how long since you cut it off."

"Seventh grade," put in Liz. "How could you forget?"

"More than four years!" I said. "That's a long time to hold a grudge."

"She should have cut off *Brian's* hair instead," said Gwen, giving Pamela's toes a nudge.

"I figured I'd start letting it grow this summer and see if I couldn't get it shoulder length by the time I go to college. Speaking of which . . ." Pamela turned to me and set her glass down on the bamboo table. "How did your visit go with Patrick? How did the wedding go? *Everything?*"

"Terrific!" I said. "And you wouldn't *believe* the bachelorette party."

"Oh yeah?" said Pamela. "I've heard about those parties. You went to a bar, right? And Carol had to unzip a guy's fly?"

I spit my ice cube back into my glass and coughed. "*No!* Nothing like that. But we played Pin the Penis on the Guy."

"*What?*" said Liz.

I laughed. "It was a takeoff on Pin the Tail on the Donkey. No guys involved. But she had to ask a man for a condom."

Liz was still looking wary. "She didn't have to put it *on* him, did she?"

"No. But she had to go in the men's room and lecture the guys about leaving the toilet seat up."

"Tame!" Pamela insisted. "I've heard of brides-to-be having to straddle a customer and give him a lap dance."

Liz sank back in her chair. "If I ever get engaged, guys, just forget it, okay?"

"Yeah? So what's with you and Keeno?" Pamela asked. "I go away for one week and come back to hear about you and a Naked Carpenter and a musical saw!"

"It's a lot of fun!" said Liz, and explained about the Naked Cowboy in Times Square and Keeno and Mark wondering if they could pull off something like that here. "I don't think they're going to do it much longer, though," she added. "Keeno says tips are falling off. Once people have seen them play in their underwear, they just smile and walk on by."

Gwen studied her. "But you like him."

"Keeno? Yeah, I like him, naked or not. We'll see where it leads." Liz was grinning.

"Speaking of which . . . ," Pamela said again, and turned

once more to me. "What did you and Patrick do? Where all did you go?"

"None of the touristy places," I said. "We walked to the beach at the east end of Michigan Avenue—it's almost like being at the ocean—sand and everything. Then we took a bus to the South Side and I saw his room. I took a shower and we did the campus. Met his friends at their favorite restaurant. Checked out the bookstore, the Reynolds Club, the library . . ."

"Where did you sleep?" asked Liz.

I told them about the three other roommates, the layout of Max P., and how I slept on the couch in their living area.

Pamela, Gwen, and Elizabeth all groaned in disappointment.

"And you two didn't get together during the night?" asked Liz.

"He had to get up early for class, and it was almost two when I got to bed," I said.

"Yeah, but . . . your one night at the university . . . ," said Pamela.

"The couch was pretty narrow," I told them.

Gwen was still mulling it over. "A girl . . . a guy . . . what's one night without sleep?" She studied me intently.

"Gwen, any one of those guys could have walked in on us," I said, but my face gave me away.

Gwen started to smile. "Then I'm going to suggest that possibly something went on between you and Patrick *before* you went to bed alone on the couch?"

I could feel the heat rising in my neck, my cheeks, and knew they'd seen it.

"Aha!" Pamela cried. "Look at her cheeks! Alice, if you ever tried to take a lie detector test, your face would give you away. What happened?"

I could have told them everything. I could have told them about the midnight walk around campus, about Botany Pond and the secluded bench that knew our secret. But this was something that belonged to Patrick and me, not to be divided up and parceled out for inspection among friends, however close we were.

I just smiled and leaned back in my chair. "Let's just say it was a beautiful night in the neighborhood, and I spent some of it in Patrick's arms."

"But . . . did you . . . ?" Liz asked, because we'd had this promise to tell each other when "it" happened.

"No," I said, and smiled again. "Subject closed." Then, for something we *could* talk about, I told them about Doug Carpenter putting his hand on my knee on the plane.

"Good for you, Alice!" Gwen said, when I told them how I'd embarrassed him. "Where did he go after he left your row?"

"Who cares?" I said. "Maybe the only seat left was the john, and the attendant made him sit there the rest of the way to Chicago."

On Monday at four in the afternoon, Dad let me off work early, and Gwen picked up Pamela first, then Liz and me, and drove us to People Care in downtown Silver Spring.

There was certainly nothing attractive about the building—the ground floor of a warehouse or something—but the volunteers who ran the soup kitchen had made it as welcoming as possible. There were blue-checkered curtains at the windows, which were barred from the outside, and a bouquet of artificial pansies on each long table. A big man—perhaps three hundred pounds—was setting up folding chairs, adding them to the assortment of wood chairs that already completed some of the tables.

"This is William," said the woman in charge—Mrs. Gladys, everyone called her. "He's our right-hand man. He's been helping out here for thirteen years, haven't you, William?"

The big man beamed. "You helped me, I help you. Simple as that," he said, and continued whacking the legs of each chair and standing them up with military precision.

There were nine volunteers to start—Mark and Keeno had said they'd come by later and help with cleanup. Mrs. Gladys assigned seven of us to help prepare the food; two others to set the tables and arrange the little trays of condiments needed for each table.

Gwen and Liz and I helped out in the kitchen, along with a guy named Austin—horn-rimmed glasses and dreadlocks; a smaller guy, Danny; and two girls. Shelley, the redhead, smiled continually; and Mavis, the tall, lean one, had a "let's get going" attitude. As soon as Mrs. Gladys explained the menu and what needed to be done, Mavis was chopping up chunks of celery and dropping them in the food processor.

Shelley and I set to work peeling the hard-boiled eggs for the tuna salad, and the others added veggies and pasta to the soup.

There was always soup, Mrs. Gladys explained. Even on the

hottest days, many of the homeless wanted soup. She guessed it was because it helped fill them up, and if People Care ran out of the entrée, a double portion of soup might satisfy.

"We appreciate you young people helping out," she told us, stopping a moment to wipe the perspiration off her forehead, where her hairnet had released one gray curl. She had a round face, wide as a dinner plate, and violet eyes that seemed to belong to a younger person. "Last summer was the first year we put out a call for young folks to relieve our volunteers for a week, and we were so pleased with the result."

"It's nice to be needed," I said cheerfully. "Gwen here is the one who rounded us up, made us sign on the dotted line. Two more guys will be coming by later this evening, I hope, to help with cleanup."

"We'll take whatever we can get," Mrs. Gladys said.

When Shelley and I finished peeling the eggs, I joined Gwen in layering the large rectangular pans for the bread pudding, the soup kitchen's signature dish. A mixture of white bread, raisins, milk, vanilla, and eggs, it was baked in the oven and served warm. Once its vanilla scent filled the kitchen, it undoubtedly drifted out into the street from the air vents.

The kitchen was hot, and the air-conditioning wasn't the best. I made a mental note to come in a skirt and tank top the following night, not the jeans and polo shirt I'd put on this time. Mrs. Gladys explained that she tried to direct the airflow to the dining room itself after people arrived, as this was perhaps the only place some of them could get cool during a heat wave. As it was, she said many came with everything they owned on their backs, summer and winter, afraid to take it off for fear it would be stolen. No matter what the state of their clothing or their hygiene, only those high on drugs or alcohol were turned away, and William, at the door, saw to that.

As it grew closer to opening time, we heard William say, "Y'all just wait now—just form me a nice straight line, and soon as Mrs. Gladys says she's ready, I'll let you in."

The men and women out on the sidewalk seemed to know the drill, and we heard only occasional murmurings, no protests, despite the heat. At last William moved his large body to let them pass. As I watched from the kitchen doorway, it seemed to me that many went directly to chairs they daily claimed as their own.

As some of the others served the soup, Shelley and Mavis and I arranged the egg slices on the platters of tuna salad, then dotted them with ripe olives someone had donated that afternoon.

"How did you hear about People Care?" Shelley asked me as we worked at the kitchen counter.

"Gwen, my friend over there by the window, told us about it. Her church had asked for volunteers," I explained.

"I heard about it at our church too," said Shelley. "I volunteer for lots of things." She turned to Mavis. "Are you from Gwen's church?"

"No, I don't go to church," Mavis replied. "I read about it on a bulletin board at the library."

"Oh." Shelley's hands paused over the tuna salad, then continued dropping the olives in place. "Well, you'd be welcome anytime if you ever wanted to come to mine," she said.

"Not likely, but thanks," Mavis told her. "I decided that a loooong time ago."

Mrs. Gladys took the platters we'd prepared and handed them to Austin and Danny to take to the dining room, gave us more to garnish, then went back to the stove to add peas to the soup.

Shelley glanced sideways at Mavis. "I'm just curious . . . I hope you don't mind my asking . . . but . . . what made you decide that? Not to go to church?"

"I just have a lot of questions, I guess, that the church can't answer. 'Because the Bible says so' was never enough for me."

"My church could answer them, I'll bet," said Shelley.

Mavis smiled a little. "Well, I'm not a betting person but—" Just then she got a whiff of the pepper I had sprinkled on top of the tuna salad and sneezed.

"God bless you," said Shelley.

"No, thanks," said Mavis.

Shelley looked uncertainly at the rest of us, but the kitchen was hot enough without getting into *that* at the moment.

12
SHELLEY'S SERMON

One of our jobs at People Care was to smile a lot and make everyone feel welcome. Shelley was especially good at smiling, and because her red hair was on the wild side, she got lots of smiles in return.

We watched from the kitchen doorway as Mrs. Gladys pointed out some of the "regulars": Miss Ruth, who wore gloves when she ate to protect herself from germs; Gordon, who was recovering from a leg amputation and used a crutch; Wallace, who lived under a viaduct; Mrs. Strickler, who had been claiming for the past three years that her son would be visiting soon.

Some of our diners were drug users; some were alcoholics;

some had been conned out of their savings, crippled by illness, fired from their jobs, forsaken by family, or had such a run of bad luck that they were simply out of hope.

As I passed from table to table pouring coffee for those who wanted it, more than a few of them thanked me politely.

"Much appreciated. I'll take me a second cup."

Some gave orders: "Fill it to the top," a scowling man told me. "You never fill it to the top!"

Some explained: "I have to have three sugars and one sugar substitute for my diabetes," one woman told me, confused.

And to each, Mrs. Gladys had instructed, we were to be polite and as accommodating and patient as possible, realizing that for some, a full cup of coffee was the only request they could expect to be granted, the wait staff the only people they could count on to be kind.

Most nights, Mrs. Gladys told us, clients lined up to be handed a plate from the serving table. But on nights when there was an abundance of volunteers, she liked her men and women to be able to sit at a table and be served restaurant-style. Tonight was such a night, and we carried platters of tuna salad around, serving to the left of each plate, ladling soup out to those who asked for it, and distributing rolls from a basket.

When all the seats had been taken, we heard William say at the door, "I'm sorry, now, but we don't have any more room in there. Just wait a bit, and we'll take you in; long as the food holds out."

And when one man's voice rose in argument, William said,

"Y'all just have to get here a little sooner, that's what. Door opens at five o'clock, you know that, Dennis. Gotta get the legs movin'—git yourself over here."

We didn't try to hurry anyone, but we did tell those who had obviously finished eating that others were waiting for a chair, and slowly the room began to empty. The oilcloth-covered tables were wiped clean, and more diners were led in.

When all those in the second seating had been served, Mrs. Gladys said that half the volunteers could go out back for a break—the others would get a rest after everyone had gone, before cleanup began.

There was an old loading dock behind the soup kitchen and low concrete walls on either side. The tall buildings along the alley channeled the air down our way, and I sat on one of the walls, leaning my head back to offer my face and throat to the breeze. I thought of Patrick and our walk along Lake Michigan.

We talked a little about what else we'd done over the summer, and Mavis mentioned that in June she had gone to Ohio to help out a town that had been virtually flattened by a late spring tornado.

"I *saw* that on TV!" Shelley said. "Like the plagues in the Old Testament. Those people were poor already, and then there was a drought, then a fire in a warehouse, and then . . . the tornado. It's hard to understand God's plan sometimes, but there's always a reason."

"What?" said Mavis. "God's plan was to burn eleven men to death in that fire and kill two babies in the tornado?"

Shelley was resolute. "God has the whole world in his hands, Mavis."

"Then he's criminally insane," Mavis said. "Personally, I don't believe in God."

Shelley looked startled, and even Liz turned her head.

"You can't mean that," said Shelley.

"No offense, but I do."

"But you went to Ohio to help the tornado victims, you're here volunteering at a soup kitchen . . . Why would you do these things if you don't believe in God?"

Mavis shrugged and smiled a little. "Because they need to be done. Because I want to help. Is that so strange?" She looked around at Liz and me.

"I don't think it's strange," I said.

"But you could be at the beach or spending all day at the mall," Shelley said.

Mavis laughed this time. "I do those things, too, but *this* week I want to be here."

"You're serving God, then, whether you know it or not," Shelley told her.

"If that makes you happy, then believe what you want, but I'm an atheist," Mavis said.

I'm not sure I'd ever met an atheist before—not a bona fide atheist who admitted it, I mean. Like Shelley, I guess I'd have to say that the last place I'd expect to find one was a soup kitchen serving the homeless, but then, why not?

"I just don't see how—," Shelley began.

"There's lots of things I don't understand, but that's not one of them," said Mavis.

Mrs. Gladys stuck her head out the kitchen doorway. "Ready for cleanup," she called. "Let's give the other volunteers a break."

We moved slowly back inside as Gwen and Pamela came out, fanning themselves, glad to exchange places with us on the wall. Austin and Danny followed with bags for the Dumpster. They had already cleaned the tables and scraped the plates. It was our job to wipe off the chairs and fold them up so that William could mop the floor.

Shelley and Mavis went out to the kitchen with Mrs. Gladys to help with dishes, and Liz and I did the chairs.

"Do you think she means it? About being an atheist?" asked Liz. "I'd be afraid to even *say* it."

"But if that's what she really believes . . ."

We were both quiet then as we each folded the chair we'd been wiping off and started on another.

Mark and Keeno didn't come by at all. Mark called me later after I'd gotten home and said they weren't getting much action at the Farragut North Metro station, so they'd gone all the way out to Shady Grove, but by then most of the commuters had come through. They figured it was too late to stop by the soup kitchen. Maybe they'd make it the next night.

But they didn't make it on Tuesday either, and maybe it was a good thing, because Shelley came armed for argument this time. There was a different mix at first break. Gwen and Austin and Danny came out to the back wall with Liz, Shelley, Mavis, and me. Pamela stayed inside with a couple of new kids who didn't know the ropes.

As soon as we'd sat down on the low walls, some of the guys straddling them, Shelley said, "I just want you to know, Mavis, that I'm praying for you. Really."

"What's this?" asked Danny.

"Shelley's trying to save my soul," Mavis said. And then, more seriously to Shelley, "I don't know why it bothers you so much what I believe or don't believe."

"Because I'm a Christian, and I *have* to be concerned," Shelley replied. "I'd feel terrible if . . . well . . . if I got to heaven and you weren't there, Mavis. If I could have done something about it and didn't."

It seemed sort of presumptuous that Shelley would just assume that *she* would be in heaven, but I wasn't sure I was invited into the conversation. It was certainly a conversation I'd never hear at school, I felt sure.

"Whoa!" said Gwen. "When did all *this* start?"

"We're just continuing a discussion that began yesterday," Shelley told her. "Mavis says she's an atheist, and I'm trying to understand, that's all."

"So what exactly do *you* believe, Shelley?" I asked.

"Basically, that the only way you can be saved is to be born again in Jesus Christ. That's what I believe."

"Isn't that sort of condescending to other religions? To me, for example? I'm Jewish," said Danny.

Shelley shrugged helplessly. "If we're right, we're right."

"And if Jews or Muslims believe *they're* right?"

"Then there will be conflict until the Second Coming, that's all."

"What about all the people who lived *before* Christ?" asked Gwen.

"I'm sure that God has made some provision for them," Shelley said. "But in our church practically everyone who was born again can tell you the day and the hour we gave ourselves to Christ."

"I went through First Communion," Liz said.

Shelley smiled uncomfortably. "I'm sorry, Elizabeth, but . . . it doesn't really count. I mean, it's important and all if you're Catholic, but when I was ten years old, I made a definite commitment. I just got down on my knees and turned my life over to God. Now, whenever I have to make a decision, I ask myself, 'What would Jesus do?' Life is so simple and beautiful this way." She focused on me. "What do *you* believe, Alice?"

"I guess I've always assumed there was a God, but I don't understand him. For starters, I don't understand why we need to pray for someone who's sick, like we have to beg and plead with God to help him. Doesn't he already know?"

"You pray to remind yourself he's Lord and Master, and he decides where you'll spend eternity," said Shelley.

"So you really believe in heaven and hell?" Danny asked her.

"Yes, I really believe."

Pamela and the other kids drifted out of the kitchen then,

eating slices of the cooled bread pudding. "What's the debate?" Pamela asked.

"Religion," said Mavis. "Or lack thereof."

"I've got a bus to catch," said one of the guys.

"See ya tomorrow."

"To be continued," said Shelley cheerfully.

I'd driven the girls down in Sylvia's car this time, so I was the one driving home. We were still discussing the debate.

"Shelley's so sincere," Liz said thoughtfully. "What if she *is* right?"

"Then what? Catholics are wrong?" I asked.

"I don't know. Maybe you really do have to have a special moment when you're 'born again,' as she says. We use a Catholic Bible. I was never really confused before."

I smiled at her in the rearview mirror, but of course she couldn't see. "I know a time when you were a little confused. Don't you remember when you wanted to have Pamela's breast blessed by a priest?"

"*What?*" cried Gwen, and Pamela whooped.

"That guy on the train!"

"Right," I said, and explained it to Gwen. "The three of us were on Amtrak going to Chicago. Big trip. Dad even got us rooms in the sleeper. Some man was flirting with Pam."

"You mean Pam was flirting with *him*!" said Liz. "He thought she was in college and invited her to have dinner with him. We had to sit across from them in the dining car and listen to all that bull!"

I continued: "Later, he edged his way into her sleeping compartment, kissed her, and evidently touched one of her breasts before she got away."

Pamela got in the act then: "And when Liz found out, she wanted me to go to a priest and have it blessed—'made whole again' is the way she put it."

"And Pam kept saying, 'It *is* whole! He didn't take a bite out of it or anything!'" I added, and we shrieked.

Liz was laughing too. "Come on, you guys. I was a naive twelve-year-old."

"And two years later at camp, she lets Ross feel her boobs," said Gwen. "Hey, girl, you grew up fast!"

"It still doesn't solve the question of who's right about God," said Liz.

"Who *ever* knows for sure?" said Gwen.

Keeno and Mark came by on Wednesday about an hour before we closed up the soup kitchen. The guys were fully dressed, of course, and said they'd spent the evening busking at Gallery Place.

"How did it go?" I asked.

"About the same," said Keeno, but Mark made the thumbs-down sign.

We introduced them to the other volunteers, and Mrs. Gladys said, "We're happy to have you guys, whenever you can come. We need those two large garbage cans emptied in the Dumpster near the alley. And then, William's hurt his back, so if you could mop the floor for him after the chairs are wiped down, I think he'd appreciate it. And if some of you want to wash those front windows, it would be helpful."

Mavis was studying Keeno. "Hey, aren't you the guys who were on TV last week—one of the local channels?"

Gwen and Liz and Pamela and I started grinning.

"You *are*!" Mavis said, and Keeno tipped his cap.

"The Naked Carpenters!" another girl gasped.

"What's this?" said Mrs. Gladys.

"The guys who play the musical saw and harmonica in Metro stations in their skivvies," said Mavis. "A couple of TV stations had them on the early news."

William came over, one hand on his back. He was smiling too. "You the one who plays 'Amazing Grace' on the saw?"

"He's the man," said Mark.

"Well, for goodness' sake," said Mrs. Gladys. "Why don't you play some songs tomorrow night for the dinner folk? I'll bet they'd love to hear it. We don't have performers coming by here very often."

"Ain't *never* nobody come and perform for us," said William.

Liz looked at Keeno. "Do it," she said.

Keeno looked at Mark.

"Why not?" said Mark. "Sure. We'd be glad to."

13

A HEATED DISCUSSION

The weather turned a little cooler on Thursday, and the men and women waiting in a long line to get inside People Care weren't as irritable as they'd been the day before.

Two of the volunteers who had started out the week failed to show, but we were surprised when Justin Collier walked in.

"Justin!" I said, looking past him to see if Jill was trailing behind, because they're usually joined at the hip. He was alone.

"I've had to work the last three nights, but I've got the rest of the week free," he said. "What can I do?"

"You chose the right day to come," Mrs. Gladys said. "I've got some coolers on the floor of the kitchen that need lifting up to the counter. And then, if you could help William with the chairs . . ."

For a guy who lives in a big house in Kensington, whose family has made millions in real estate, Justin comes off as a regular Joe. A regular *handsome* Joe. Both Mavis and Shelley looked for ways to work on whatever job he was doing.

"Jill coming?" Liz ventured.

"I don't think so. I told her this would be my substitute for working out at the gym." He grinned.

Mark and Keeno—dressed, of course—arrived just after the first group had started to eat. There was no saw case on the floor this time, open for tips. Some of the diners watched disinterestedly as Mark connected the boom box to an amplifier and put in the CD of piano music, and Keeno got out his saw and bow. Others hunched over their soup, eyes on the bread and crackers, and didn't watch the activity at all. But a few put down their spoons and stared.

One man, with stubby, gnarled fingers, came over to Keeno and examined the saw. "Whatcha going to do with *that* thing?" he asked. "That ain't no regular saw. Too long and the teeth are too straight. Supposed to be one pointing thisaway, the next pointing thataway."

Keeno just winked at him. "It's *not* a regular saw. You'll see."

Mrs. Gladys came over too. "How would you like me to introduce you?" she asked.

"No introduction," Keeno said. "We'll just play."

This time Keeno sat on a folding chair to perform. When Mark started the recorded piano music to "Ramblin' Man" and joined in on the harmonica, William, who was keeping order at the door, called out, "You go, boy! Hit it!"

The people at the tables looked on in surprise at the sight of a violin bow sliding skillfully over the straight edge of the saw, tilting this way and that. Smiles spread across some of the faces, puzzlement over others. One man tapped his foot loudly on the floor.

When the first song was over, William and the volunteers clapped loudly, and so did some of the diners. Mrs. Gladys stepped out of the kitchen.

"Friends, we have a special treat for you this evening. These young men came by to play some music for you. You know the harmonica, of course, but I wonder if any of you have seen a musical saw. . . ."

"My grandfather played the saw," one man called out.

And another said, "Used to myself, till my fingers stiffed up."

"Well, I hope all of you enjoy the music," Mrs. Gladys said.

Keeno, it turned out, had quite a repertoire, mostly old songs I'd never heard. But when he played "My Bonnie Lies over the Ocean," a *really* old number, several people joined in the chorus:

Bring back, bring back,
Oh, bring back my Bonnie to me, to me. . . .

The problem was that what began as an orderly line along the sidewalk outside became a crowd at the door, all trying to see over each other's heads, waiting to come in.

"They're just dawdling with their food now," Mrs. Gladys observed, watching from the kitchen doorway. "No one wants to leave. I've got to make an announcement."

And after a quick consultation with Keeno and Mark, she said, "We have another crowd to serve, ladies and gentlemen, so I hope that you will finish your meal and let us clean the tables after this next number, 'Amazing Grace.'"

This time we had at least a third of the room singing along. It was a terrific evening, especially when the second group came in and turned expectantly in their chairs, not toward the servers, but toward Mark and Keeno.

Afterward, when the pots and pans were washed and put away, the kitchen scrubbed, the folding chairs wiped down, and the kitchen closed down for the night, we volunteers took our paper cups of coffee and slices of cold bread pudding out back where we could cool off.

"Did you notice the man in the green flannel shirt?" I asked the others.

"Far table? Second seating?" asked Gwen.

"Yes. When Keeno began to play and everyone turned to watch, this man started taking rolls off the other plates as fast as he could go. I had to stop him."

Everyone laughed.

"The guy in the bright orange shirt? I don't think he stopped tapping his foot once," said Mark.

"We'll only be here for three more nights. It'd be nice if you guys could play for all three," I said. "You'd wow 'em."

"You know what?" Shelley said to Keeno. "Looking at the faces in there and the way you lifted their spirits, I couldn't help but think that this was meant to be."

"Aw, shucks!" said Keeno, a sappy look on his face, and we laughed.

Shelley smiled too. "I mean it! You guys could have been off playing golf this week. We all could have been at the beach. Instead, each of us was drawn to this soup kitchen, and *somebody* was pulling the strings so that Keeno and Mark showed up here."

"It's called 'tanking,' Shelley," Keeno told her. "We tanked at the Metro stops and had nowhere else to go."

Shelley shook her head. "And you don't see God's hand in this? If you 'tanked,' maybe you tanked for a reason."

"Just like God's hand was behind that hurricane in New Orleans and the tsunami in Indonesia?" said Mavis, and her eyes looked angry.

"What?" said Pamela. "What does that have to do with anything?"

"Shelley believes that God is behind everything that happens, good or bad," Mavis explained. "I decided years ago that if I've got a mind, I'm going to use it, and the only sane conclusion I can come to is that we are on this Earth by chance, and if this is the only chance we've got, we'd better make it count."

"But why do you choose to do good?" Shelley argued. "Why not choose to be the most powerful, like animals do? Survival of the fittest?"

"Not everyone *does* choose to do good," said Mavis. "I figure my choices come from family and environment. But you can't go attributing everything that happens—good or bad—to God. That's a cop-out."

"God doesn't *make* bad things happen, he *lets* them happen because a lot of them are our own fault," Shelley said hastily.

"Tornadoes and hurricanes are our own fault?" I asked, astonished. I began to wish I were taking notes. If the subject ignited so much feeling here, maybe it was a topic we could explore in *The Edge*.

"Some things He causes and some things He just lets happen?" asked Mark, studying Shelley, his legs dangling off the wall. "He just sits up there and *lets* that mother drown her four daughters, one by one? Lets that man kill his wife?"

Justin was looking from one of us to the other.

"Here's the way our minister explained it," said Shelley. "He brought a tapestry once to church—something his wife was working on. On one side of the cloth was a lighthouse against a rocky shore. It was all so clean and neat, you could see the whitecaps on the waves. But when he turned it over and showed us the other side, all you could make out were knots and loose threads that seemed to go nowhere. Nothing made sense. You had no idea that there was a lighthouse on the other side. And that's the way life is. From where we sit, all we can see are the knots and tangles and threads that seem to go nowhere. But from where God sits, everything is where it should be according to His plan."

We sat for a few moments thinking that over. It was a good analogy, I'll give her that.

"Look, Shelley, you can prove almost anything by saying we can't understand it now, but it's God's plan," said Austin. "If something good happens, it's God. If something bad happens, well, it's part of His mysterious plan. Crap! You win no matter what. I could claim there's a great horned toad controlling the universe, and no one can disprove it."

"You're a nonbeliever too, then?" Shelley asked in a small voice.

"Maybe I believe in a God who created a world and then washed His hands of it," said Austin. "But whatever, I'm the one who decides what religion is right for me."

"You can't just pick and choose a religion like you're buying a pair of shoes! Scholars have been studying biblical history for centuries!" said Shelley.

"And they've been studying the teachings of Buddha even longer," said Danny. "What makes you think Christianity is the one true way to go?"

"Because I *know*!" Shelley said. "I *feel* it! I live it! It's my faith, my life!"

"And if someone else feels the same way about *his* religion?" Danny asked. "A Jew? A Muslim? A Hindu?"

Shelley shook her head.

There was a commotion somewhere down the alley, and we could hear two men shouting at each other. Three, maybe.

"You braggin', thievin' son of a bitch!"

"You're full of it, brother."

"Uh-oh," said Liz. "Maybe this isn't a great place to be after dark."

The yelling continued. "You took my damn tarp!"

A third man's voice: "Just take it back, Eddie, and let's go."

"Like he was takin' rolls there at the table. You seen that, didn't you? Wasn't the first time he done that."

"Someone from here?" I asked the others.

A yell. "Get your hands off me!"

"C'mon, Eddie . . ."

A cry of pain. A scream.

Austin and Keeno were on their feet.

"Don't go down there!" Pamela said as Mark jumped up too. "They could have knives!"

But Justin followed and so did Danny. All five guys ran out into the alley and disappeared around a building.

"Hey!" we heard Austin shout.

"Get out your cell phones," Gwen told the rest of us. "We may need to call 911." We held our breath, listening for shots, wondering whether to wait.

Another yell. A string of expletives. Indistinct voices. More swearing. More conversation. Gradually the loud voices grew softer, Austin's and Keeno's voices a little louder. Three minutes went by. Five. We heard one of the men mention "Red Sails in the Sunset."

"M'God, they're talking music!" Pamela said. "Did you hear that?"

"One of Keeno's songs!" said Liz.

"Music soothes the savage beast," said Mavis wryly. We waited for Shelley to say something about God, but she didn't.

When the guys came back about ten minutes later, they were smiling. "The case of the missing tarp," said Keeno.

"Had one buried at the bottom of his cart, didn't see it—or want to see it. But everybody's happy now," said Austin, sitting down again and reaching for his coffee cup, draining the last of it.

Someone started talking about a fight he'd seen once at a Nationals game, but Shelley sat transfixed on the wall.

"You can't tell me that God didn't have a hand in what just happened in the alley," she said.

"Oh, Shel, knock it off," said Austin.

Pamela was getting impatient. "You can't prove scientifically that there's a God, Shelley. All you keep saying is you know He's there. Enough already!"

Shelley only smiled. "You can't prove scientifically that you love someone, either. You can't measure it. But you know it's there."

"Then why can't you just let people find their own way, their own religion, Shel?" asked Gwen. "Why can't Buddhists be Buddhists and atheists be atheists and Catholics be Catholics without you trying to put your own particular stamp on how they're supposed to worship?"

"Because it wouldn't *save* you!" Shelley said earnestly.

I just had to do a feature story for our school paper in the fall, I decided. Maybe a series of questionnaires called "Sound Off" or something. If University of Chicago students could talk about Christian-based agriculture at a Lamb of God farm, why couldn't I write a feature on what *our* students believe about heaven and hell, for example? Stem cell research? The death penalty?

Keeno finally got into the conversation. "What you're saying, then, Shelley, is that it's not enough just to be a good person, you have to believe in God."

"Absolutely."

"And it's not enough to believe in God, you have to be a Christian."

"Right."

"And you can't just be a Catholic Christian, you have to be Protestant," said Mavis.

"Well . . . yes, I guess so."

"And not just a Protestant Christian, but a Protestant born-again Christian," said Gwen.

Shelley suddenly began to cry, and then I felt terrible. "That's the way I *believe*! Jesus told us to preach the gospel, and *you're* not being tolerant of *me*!"

"We're really not trying to change you," Gwen said. "But if you're going to argue religion, Shelley, then you have to be prepared to listen to what other people think."

"And now that we've discussed it, and we've more or less told you how we feel, can you let it rest?" asked Austin. "Hopefully?"

Shelley fished in her bag for a tissue and wiped her cheeks. "If you reject what I've told you, then I've done all I can. All I can say is that I'll pray for you."

"Don't feel bad, girl," Gwen said, and put one arm around her. "Tonight *I'm* going to pray for *you*."

"Whew!" Pamela said when we got in the car. She was staying with her mom for the week, and her mother had let her use the car. "Justin probably wonders what the heck he walked into."

"But this is how it all begins," I said. "Wars. Persecution. Burning people at the stake."

"Everyone wants you to believe that *his* religion has the answers," said Gwen. "The One True Church; Believers versus infidels; Christ and the Antichrist; God's Chosen People versus everyone else; The Righteous and the Left-Behinds . . . It goes on and on."

"So . . . what are you saying? That all religions are a bunch of nonsense?" Liz asked.

"Maybe they're all right in some things and wrong in others," I offered.

"You're a religious person, Gwen. Do you believe in God?" Liz persisted.

"Yes, because I want to believe there's justice somewhere in the universe. I want to believe I can make a difference. I don't believe in God because I'm afraid that if I don't, I'll go to hell."

"You're waaaaay beyond me," said Pamela, turning the car west toward Gwen's neighborhood. "To tell the truth, I don't worry too much about all this. If there's a God, I figure at some time in my life he'll give me a sign and I'll know for sure we've connected."

"A sign?" I asked.

"Yeah. A direct answer to prayer or something. A voice in the storm, a light in the sky, something supernatural."

"I don't know, Pamela. I think God's more subtle than that," said Liz.

"What about your miscarriage?" I asked Pamela.

"I didn't pray for a miscarriage. I prayed that I wouldn't be pregnant in the first place."

"Pamela, by then you already were!" Liz said.

"So? He could have zapped my uterus or something. How would I know what he could have done?"

"But . . . in the end . . . you didn't stay pregnant."

"Yeah, so I figure it's sort of fifty-fifty whether or not my prayer was answered. The one thing in my life I've really prayed hard for was that Mom would give up her lousy boyfriend and come back to the family. Well, she gave up her boyfriend, but Dad wouldn't take her back, and now he's engaged to Meredith. Was that an answer to my prayers or not? I don't think it was part of God's plan for Mom to run off with her boyfriend in the first place, or God's got a weird sense of humor."

"Sometimes I think the whole idea of God is weird," I said.

Liz looked at me worriedly. "You're beginning to sound like Mavis."

"Really?" I shook my head. "Mavis seems so sure of being atheist. I'm not sure about anything, except that I wish I were."

We drove with the windows down now that the evening had cooled off. The scent of freshly mowed grass reached our nostrils, the scent of mulch. Pamela had one of her favorite CDs in the player—a song about love and taking chances.

"How's your mom doing, Pam?" I asked. "Still working at Nordstrom?"

"Yeah. She seems to like it. Likes dressing up, anyway. Says she likes to go to work 'looking like somebody.'"

"Is she going out with anyone?" asked Liz.

"I think she's been out to dinner a couple of times with some manager from another store. I don't know the details. I don't ask. But at least she has friends."

"And . . . what about her daughter?" Gwen asked slyly.

"Me?"

"Who else?"

"I'm taking a break from guys this summer, not that anyone's been calling. I've got to start thinking about what I'm going to do after graduation. College? Some kind of theater arts school? Costume design? Questions, questions . . ."

"Well, tonight was a nice change of pace for the soup kitchen," Gwen said as we approached her driveway. "And I think Mark and Keeno really enjoyed playing for those people."

"Ha. Keeno wasn't playing for the soup kitchen, he was playing for Liz," said Pamela. "His eyes follow her around the room. I could tell that from the get-go."

"All the more incentive for him to come back again, then," said Gwen. "G'night, guys."

When I got home later, I went slowly up the steps to our front porch and sat on the glider awhile before making my way inside.

Dad was still up reading.

"Getting home sort of late, aren't you?" he said, looking up. "You've had a pretty long day."

"The usual," I said. "Discussing God and the universe. That took some time."

14
MARKING TIME

Keeno and Mark came back the last three nights of our volunteer work at the soup kitchen and played for the diners. But on Sunday we said our good-byes to Mrs. Gladys, who asked us to remember her and People Care anytime we wanted to help out.

Now I didn't feel at all energetic. I just wanted to glide through the last week of July with my brain set on "pause." When Sylvia asked me to help her make peach preserves one evening, it was all I could do to say yes.

"I picked up this wonderful little basket of ripe peaches at a roadside stand, and we can't possibly eat them all before they spoil," she said. "There's not much work making freezer jam, especially if there are two of us working."

"You freeze it instead of cook it?" I asked.

"You cook the syrup that goes over the peaches, and then you freeze it. The preserves have that fresh-off-the-tree taste that I love," she explained.

We sat across from each other at the kitchen table, peeling the peaches, the sweet juice running down our fingers and into a bowl. Every so often we couldn't resist cutting off a slice and popping it into our mouths. Sylvia, her hair in a short ponytail, already had peach stains on her old striped shirt.

"If these were the olden days," she said, "we'd be standing in a steaming kitchen with a pressure cooker bubbling on the stove. We'd have to sterilize the jars, melt the paraffin, pour it over the jam once the jars were filled, put them in the pressure cooker. . . . What an ordeal!"

"Why did you have to do it?" I asked.

"Actually, I didn't. Mostly I just watched my grandmother do it. She said that her preserves were better than any you'd find at the store, and she was right. But she didn't have the delight of tasting frozen peach preserves. She never had that big a freezer. She prided herself on the long rows of canned fruits and vege-tables in her cellar. Shelf after shelf, and she arranged them all by color. Reds here, greens there . . . Yellows had a special place, and of course purple plums were right there on top, all of them waiting for winter and the hypothetical blizzard that was sup-posed to trap us inside for two weeks."

"Did your mom make stuff like that?" I asked, picking up the next peach in the basket.

"No, she didn't much care for kitchen work. Believe it or not, my mother prided herself on her laundry."

"Laundry?"

Sylvia nodded and paused to eat another slice. "She'd set an entire day aside just to iron. My sister and I would come home from school to find a rack of Dad's shirts, all starched and pressed; our own shirts and blouses hooked over door handles, waiting for us to take them upstairs. Ours was a freshly pressed house, let me tell you—tablecloths, even sheets. I guess I take pride in my knitting. I like to open my sweater drawer and check out all those I made myself. Strange, isn't it, how much satisfaction we get out of making something with our own hands?"

I tried to think what I made with *my* own hands. Not much, unless I considered the articles I wrote for *The Edge* at school. And, yes, I did take pride—leafing through my album, page after page encased in plastic protectors—proud of all those bylines: *By Alice McKinley, Staff Writer*. And this coming year all my bylines would read: *By Alice McKinley, Features Editor*.

"I wish I could remember more things about my mother," I told Sylvia. "Mostly it's what other people tell me about her. That she was tall, which I'm not. That she liked to sing, which I can't. I love to make pineapple upside-down cake, like she did, and I have her hair color. But my memories of her get all mixed up with Aunt Sally, since she took care of Les and me for a while after Mom died."

"I wish I could help," Sylvia said. "But I know that Ben loved her very much. Once in a while he even calls me 'Marie' by mistake."

I glanced up at her. "Don't you ever get jealous?"

"Of Marie? Actually, I take it as a compliment—that he must be feeling especially close to me, just as he did with her."

The peaches were all peeled now, so we began chopping them up into tiny pieces. I asked my next question without looking at her: "Do you ever feel jealous of anyone else?"

"Other women?"

"Yeah."

"Not really. I know that women seem to like your dad, and I understand that, because I like him too! He treats them warmly, courteously, and he treats me the same way. But once in a great while I'm a little jealous of you."

I actually dropped the paring knife and it clattered to the table. *"Me?"*

"Yep. I see him trying so hard to understand you sometimes, to figure out what's bothering you if you seem sad or distant. He wonders if he said or did the right thing, whether he should have done something else. And I have to remind him that you have two parents now, and I can carry some of the load. But he still feels that he's the one responsible for how you turn out."

"Wow! I . . . had no idea I was such a big deal!" I gasped.

"You're a daughter, his *only* daughter—so it's natural, completely natural. But you asked if I was ever jealous, so I had to admit that sometimes, yes." She made a funny face at me. "Never think of *me* as a rival?"

I smiled a little. "I suppose maybe I was jealous a little right after you moved in with us. Dad wanted you to love the place— the house—Les and me. It was always 'Sylvia this and Sylvia that' with him. As if your opinion was all that mattered." I couldn't believe that Sylvia and I were actually having this conversation. "So there!" I said, and made a funny face back.

"You know, biological mothers and daughters get jealous of each other sometimes too," Sylvia said. "Mom admitted that to me after I was grown. She said that much as a mother may love her daughter, she's a little envious when her own body starts to wrinkle and sag a bit while her daughter is looking young and beautiful. She *wants* her to be young and pretty, of course, but she also wants to stay the same way herself. These relationships can get very complicated."

"I guess so," I said. "If I ever get married and have children, though, will you hate me because that makes you a grandmother?"

She laughed and I did too.

"How could I ever hate the girl who introduced me to my husband? I'll never, ever forget the night you and Ben came to pick me up for the Messiah Sing-Along, and your dad thought he was just picking up a friend of yours."

We were actually talking about it! All this time, Sylvia and I had sort of gone on pretending that she hadn't known how hard I'd tried to set her up with my dad.

"So . . . ," she said. "Are you sorry?"

I grinned at her across the table. "I'd do it again in a heartbeat. Only I'd be a little more subtle."

* * *

Wednesday evening, just as we were starting dinner, the phone rang.

"I'll get it," I said, only because Dad and Sylvia had already sat down at the table. I went into the hall and picked it up.

"Al!" came Lester's voice. "How you doing?" And then, before I could answer, he said, "Look. I've got to ask a big, big favor. This is huge."

"Your car broke down on the Beltway and you want—"

"No. Listen. Paul and George and I are taking this trip to Utah, remember?"

"Yes . . ."

"We're leaving Friday, and we'll be gone ten days, and we had this friend who was going to stay here—keep an eye on the place in case Mr. Watts needed anything."

"Yeah . . . ?"

"He can't do it. His dad's sick and he's flying to Florida. We can't go on this trip unless we have someone here at night—that was our rental agreement. Could you and Gwen possibly stay here? I'd feel better if there were two of you, and Gwen's the most levelheaded one of your friends."

I tried to take it all in. "Gwen and I both work!" I said.

"I know. Daytime's no problem. Mr. Watts has an aide from eight until six. But someone has to be here after six."

My mind was jumping all over the place. Ten days in a bachelor apartment? Ten days on our own, away from parents? Was this a trick question?

I tried to control myself. "Yeah, but I think there should be three girls, Les. I can't guarantee that one of us wouldn't have to go out for something, and if Mr. Watts fell, it would take two girls to pick him up."

"Okay, then, but make it Liz."

"All right, Lester, but if Gwen and Liz and I stay there for ten days and exclude Pamela . . ."

"I don't trust Pamela in the apartment, Al. You know she'd be in every drawer, every closet."

"She wouldn't! She's grown up a lot. We'll even make her sign an agreement!"

"Al . . ."

"Four girls or we won't come."

"There are only three beds."

"Three *double* beds, Les. Pamela can sleep with one of us."

Les gave a long sigh. "All right, providing she sleeps with you. I want you to keep your eye on her while she's there, Al. No booze, no boys, no smoking for any of you. Okay? Absolute promise?"

"Promise."

"I'll run it by the Watts family, but I think they'll say it's okay. You're all going to be seniors this year. Tell me I can trust you."

"Are we getting paid?"

"You're getting the use of our apartment, whatever food's in the fridge, the phone, the water, the lights. But first you've got to find out for me if Gwen's available. I want to know that she's on board."

"I appreciate your confidence in me."

"Please, Al?"

"I'll call you back."

I was grinning when I put down the phone and thrust one fist in the air. "*Yes!*" I whispered, not wanting Dad and Sylvia to get wind of it yet. I called Gwen's number. She talked it over with her dad and said yes. I called Liz. She talked it over with her mom and said yes. I called Pamela. She said yes without talking it over with anyone. I decided to tell Les we'd do it before I brought it up with Dad so it could be a done deal.

Then I phoned Lester. "We're on," I told him.

"Good," said Les. "I've already run it by Dad and Sylvia."

15
SETTLING IN

When we unlocked the door to Lester's apartment and went inside, we walked right into a cardboard sign dangling from the hall light fixture. We dropped our bags on the floor and looked around.

There were signs everywhere:

SMOKE ALARM GOES OFF FOR BURNT TOAST.

IF MR. WATTS WANTS YOU TO BUY DOUGHNUTS, DON'T.

USE YOUR CELL PHONES. IF WE CAN'T REACH YOU ON THE APARTMENT PHONE, YOU'RE DEAD.

PLEASE USE UP ALL THE BROCCOLI.

"Well, here we are!" I said. "We haven't been here since . . ."

"Valentine's Day," said Gwen. "When we came over to decorate Lester's car."

"And almost got ourselves arrested," Liz remembered.

"I get dibs on Lester's room!" said Pamela, heading straight for it. She knew which one it was, because we had helped him unpack when he first moved in.

"We're sharing the bed, then," I told her. "And you signed an agreement that you wouldn't go through his stuff."

"I won't touch a thing that's not mine, but it's not a federal offense if I open a drawer by mistake, is it?" said Pamela.

"For you, yes," I said.

"I'll take this room," said Liz, poking her head in George's bedroom. "He's the one getting married in September, isn't he?"

"Yeah. The last big bachelor trip."

"Then I'll take Paul's room," said Gwen.

While the others dropped their stuff in the bedrooms, I checked the fridge to see what the guys had left us. Not much, but it was a good start—a package of four small steaks and a few containers from Boston Market.

"Can you believe this?" I said, beaming. "We've got a furnished apartment for ten days, absolutely free. This is definitely the way a summer should go!"

"Except that we can't party," said Pamela.

"Not with guys," I said.

"What exactly are we supposed to do about Mr. Watts?" asked Liz. "Does he need to be bathed or what?"

"No. He has an aide all day. She helps him shower and dress in the morning, gives him his medicine during the day, goes for walks with him in the afternoons, then cooks a little dinner for him before she leaves at six. Les says that all we have to do is go down about nine o'clock, see that he takes his medicine and gets safely in bed. If he needs us during the night, he'll ring a cowbell. Les says we'll hear it, not to worry."

"I think we should all go down with you tonight and say hello so he'll know who's here," said Gwen.

"Good idea," I said.

It was incredibly exciting having an apartment all to ourselves. It was like we were career women, renting our own place, cooking our own dinner, except then we'd probably have wine with the meal. We found the cupboard where the guys stashed their stuff, but we'd promised no booze and we'd stick to it.

Pamela set the table, Liz tossed the salad, I opened a container of roasted potatoes and another of scalloped apples, and Gwen broiled the steaks.

"Delicious!" I declared as we each raised a glass of sparkling cider, which Liz had thought to bring along.

"To our first apartment or our first real jobs, whichever comes first," said Pamela. "You know, if we were just starting out, we probably wouldn't be having steak, especially if we lived in New York," said Pamela.

"If we lived in New York, we wouldn't even be able to afford an apartment," said Gwen.

"Yeah, just look how old Les and his roommates are," I said. "George is the only one out of school, and they're not even paying rent yet." I sighed. "It'll be forever before we're completely on our own."

"Paul's the one who fascinates me," said Gwen. "You can learn a lot about a man just by the books he reads. I checked out his bookcase, and he's got books on geology and physics. He's got Veblen's *Theory of the Leisure Class* and Huxley's *Brave New World*. I mean, that guy is all over the map."

"Well, I'm glad I'm not marrying George, then, because most of his books are about finance," said Liz. "Stocks, bonds, investment strategies . . . Bor-ing!"

"Yeah, but he'll be the one who gets rich," said Pamela. "As for Lester, he's got a whole shelf of comic books, along with *The Sane Society* and *War and Peace*. And . . ." She got up from the table and went into our bedroom—Lester's room—and came out a minute later with a mischievous smile on her face. ". . . *this*!" She held up a book titled, *The Erotic Drawings of Mihaly Zichy*. "*Now* let's see you try to describe Lester!" We laughed.

"He told me you'd snoop," I scolded her.

"Yeah? What else did he say about me?"

"She's had a crush on Les ever since your family moved in," said Liz.

"If he told you I'd snoop, he must have been thinking about me," Pamela said.

"Girl, sit down and finish your steak," Gwen said. "We're going to tie you up if you don't behave yourself."

But now that Pamela had brought the book out, of course we all had to look at the pictures before we put it back.

We went downstairs so I could reintroduce the girls to Otto Watts. I didn't know if he'd remember Liz and Pamela from the time we'd brought a surprise supper to Les. That was the night we'd discovered Les was having a party, so we gave the food to Mr. Watts instead.

"Well," he said now after we rang the bell. "What'd you bring me this time?"

"An invitation for dinner tomorrow night," I told him. "How about if we make the dinner and bring it down? We'll eat here and do the dishes afterward."

"Can't argue with that! Come on in," he said.

"This is Gwen Wheeler," I told him. "The only one of us you haven't met."

Lester had already told Mr. Watts we'd be here, of course.

"Glad to have you," the old man said, waving us toward the chairs in his high-ceilinged Victorian living room. "You know the rules, right?"

"No boys, no booze, no smoking," said Pamela.

Mr. Watts looked surprised. "He didn't tell you the rest?"

"There are more?" I asked.

"Of *course* there are more. This is my house, isn't it? No card playing, no TV, and lights-out after ten o'clock."

"What?" we exclaimed.

Then he began to laugh, and as we finally relaxed, he said, "Gotcha, didn't I?"

"Be serious now," I told him. "Do you need anything before we go back upstairs? Have you taken your medicine?"

"Got my medicine. Even got my jammies on," he said, pointing beneath his robe. "If you want, you could bring me a glass of milk and a doughnut."

"'Fraid not," I said. "Lester says no doughnuts."

"And Lester's full of baloney," Mr. Watts declared. "He keeps talking like that, I'll have to kick him out of that apartment." He glanced at the clock. "Don't want to rush you girls now, but I've got to watch *CSI*. You can stay if you want, but you can only talk during the commercials."

We laughed.

"We're going," said Gwen. "Windows all closed?"

"Everything's shipshape," the old man said. "If you get too noisy up there, I'll just take out my hearing aid."

With a new CD playing in the background, we sat around Lester's living room talking about our summer—the good, the bad, the boring—and Pamela suggested that we make a prediction where we'd all be when we were twenty-five.

Jill and Justin? Married. Penny? Engaged, probably, to a golf-playing businessman. Karen? Real estate. Yolanda? Single. Hairstylist. Brian? Working for some Wall Street broker his dad knows—divorced and paying child support. Patrick? Teaching political science at Ohio State.

"We ought to be writing all this down to keep so we can open the envelope when we're twenty-five," said Liz, and got her pen from her bag.

"Remember the time capsule our class buried back in seventh grade?" I reminded her. "We're all supposed to come back when we're sixty and open it up. Read those letters we wrote to our sixty-year-old selves."

"I don't even remember mine," said Pamela. "Okay, who's next? Mark? What do we say for Mark?"

"He and Keeno will own a car dealership," I guessed.

"When they're only twenty-five?" asked Gwen.

"Okay, they'll be operating a car repair shop, saving up to buy a dealership."

"Married?" asked Pamela.

"Definitely married," said Liz. "Well, Keeno, anyway."

"What about you?" asked Gwen. "Teacher, I'm guessing. Married. Child on the way."

Liz giggled. "And you'll still be in medical school. Alice will be a reporter for the *Washington Post*. . . . And Pamela?"

"Massage therapist," Pam joked. "Men only."

"I wish we could stay here in Silver Spring and keep our gang together," Liz said wistfully. "Go to each other's weddings and raise our kids together. Teach them to swim at the Stedmeisters' pool. Drive to the Mall on the Fourth of July. I hate to think of everyone scattering to the winds. . . ."

"I get sad if I think we *won't*," said Pamela. "I'd like to come back for reunions and stuff, but, hey, sister! I want to live in

New York! I want to see Paris! I want to be pinched by a guy in Rome and kissed by a bullfighter in Barcelona! Come *on*!"

I figured that my chance of being kissed by a bullfighter was about one in a billion even if I spent the rest of my life in Spain, but it would be nice to see the world as long as I could keep in touch with everybody.

The apartment phone rang, and I reached over to the magazine table and picked it up. Les had told me that although he and George and Paul all had cell phones, they'd kept the apartment's landline and listed number for business calls.

"Hello?" I said, answering in as businesslike a voice as possible.

There was no response, but I could tell someone was on the line. Possibly Mr. Watts. "Hello?" I said again, a little louder.

"Uh . . . Could I speak with Lester?" came a woman's voice.

"I'm sorry, but he's not here. May I take a message?" I replied.

Another pause. Then, "Do you know when he'll be back?"

"Not for ten days. He's in Utah."

"*Utah?*" The voice sounded incredulous. It was a young woman's voice. "May I ask who you are?"

"I'm Alice, his sister."

"Yeah, right," said the voice.

My eyes widened in surprise. "Who are *you*?" Gwen, Liz, and Pamela turned toward me, listening.

"I'm a friend, I *think*," the woman said. "Listen, are you his girlfriend? Because if you are, I need to know."

"His girlfriend? I told you, I'm his sister."

Liz had one hand over her mouth. Gwen was smiling, and Pamela was laughing silently.

"Yeah, and I'm a duchess," the woman said. "You're his wife, aren't you?"

"No! What's this all about, anyway?"

"Well, I can't believe he said I could call him, and then I get you," she said.

"When did he tell you that? Where did you meet him?"

"A couple of nights ago in a bar. He was really nice. . . ." She paused. "I'm getting him in trouble, aren't I? What's he doing, playing around?"

"Look, whoever you are, I—"

The woman hung up, and I put down the phone.

"Who was *that*?" the others wanted to know.

"Some woman who met Les in a bar, and she thinks I'm his wife."

"His *wife*?" Pamela screamed with laughter.

"Girlfriend, anyway. She says Les told her to call."

Pamela playfully shook her head. "A heartbreaker, I knew it. That's Les—love 'em and leave 'em."

"That doesn't sound like Lester," I said.

"Do you have his cell phone number? You could give her that if she calls again," Gwen suggested.

"Are you nuts? And ruin his vacation?"

"Well, ask him about it anyway."

"I will," I said.

* * *

Gwen and Liz went grocery shopping on Saturday, and we made lasagna that evening for dinner. I put together a pineapple upside-down cake, the only cake I can make without a recipe. I cut five slices from the pan and put them on a plate to take downstairs. We also brought a salad and a long loaf of garlic bread. Mr. Watts ate like a bear.

"How do you stay so healthy?" asked Gwen.

"I don't," he replied. "Why do you suppose they give me a nurse's aide?"

"Well, you certainly have a good appetite," Gwen told him. "At ninety-two, you must be doing something right."

"Here's the secret," he said, lowering his voice to a whisper, as though no one else could hear. "I do everything they tell me not to do."

We laughed.

"Sugar? I love it. Red meat? Bring it on. I gave up gin and cigars a long time ago, but I watch any show on TV that'll raise my pulse, and I skip any program with 'nature' in the title. Puts me to sleep."

We cleaned up the kitchen after dinner, then played poker with Mr. Watts till Liz said she was sleepy.

"Bunch of deadbeats," Mr. Watts said, but I noticed him yawning too. "Go on up, then," he said. "I'll turn on my TV, but there's nothing good on Saturday nights. Might have to watch a nature program yet."

We waited till he'd put on his pajamas and was out of the bathroom. Then we followed him into the bedroom and made sure he took his nightly medicine.

"He's a riot," Liz said on our way up the side steps. "Did he ever marry?"

"His wife died a long time ago. Has the one son in Atlanta and some sisters somewhere. That's his family," I told her.

We all had calls to make when we got upstairs. I had a message from Patrick on my cell. Gwen called her grandmother to say her nightly good night. Liz called Keeno, and Pamela called home.

"Patrick missing you?" Liz asked after I came back out of the bedroom.

"I hope so," I said. "But even if he were back here now, we couldn't have guys over, so I'd really be bummed."

"How's he doing in his summer courses?" asked Gwen.

"Acing them, of course. I don't even ask. With Patrick, it's all or nothing," I said. "Everything gets his best shot."

"Well, when he ever decides to really go for you, girl, watch out," said Gwen.

We played cards and talked about having a backyard party on Sunday afternoon or evening. Shortly after midnight Liz went to bed, and the rest of us followed.

I don't know what time it was, but I was awakened by Pamela, shaking my arm.

"Alice!" she whispered.

I could hardly get my lips to move. "Huh?"

"Listen!"

My mind kept retreating back into sleep, and I had to work to focus on Pamela. *Footsteps.*

My heart jumped. I opened my eyes and stared up into the darkness.

All was quiet. Then a couple more footsteps—the soft, stealthy kind, not the quiet of bare feet padding into the bathroom. These were accompanied by creaking floorboards, with pauses in between.

I bolted upright and swung my legs over my side of the bed. Groping my way around it, I followed Pamela and we crept out into the hallway, where we bumped into Liz, feeling her way along.

"S-someone's in the apartment!" she whispered, then hissed, "Gwen!" at the doorway to Gwen's room.

Gwen must have heard it too, because she was already sitting up. We could see her silhouette against the window. She got up and silently came out into the hall.

"Someone's in here!" Liz repeated. My heart was beating so fast, it hurt. Hadn't we locked the door? I was sure that we had. A window? Here on the second floor?

Another couple of footsteps. There's nothing more sinister than the footsteps of someone you don't know in the middle of the night.

Pamela was pushing me into the bathroom, the only room in the apartment with a lock. Gwen and Liz pressed in after us. We closed the door as quietly as we could and locked it. I felt sure I could hear their hearts beating along with mine.

"Did you hear anyone come in?" I whispered to the others.

"I thought maybe I heard the front door close, I'm not sure," said Liz. "I think that's what woke me. Then I saw the beam of a flashlight going on and off and heard the footsteps."

"Call 911," I said shakily.

"Who's got a phone?" asked Gwen.

"We don't have a phone?" gasped Pamela. "We're locked in a bathroom on the second floor and don't have a cell phone?"

"Someone's out there!" I squeaked in panic as the footsteps came closer, then receded, then came closer again. Pamela clamped one hand over my mouth until we heard a floorboard squeak farther down the hall, but maybe that meant there were two of them!

"Let's all scream," Liz suggested. "Let's open the window above the tub and all scream together."

"And bang on the pipes!" Pamela whispered. "If we bang hard enough, maybe it will wake Mr. Watts. Do we have anything metal?"

I felt along the top of the sink and found a plastic deodorant container and my can of mousse.

"Two of us can bang on the pipes and the other two scream out the window," Gwen instructed.

Gwen and Liz stepped into the tub and tried to raise the window, but it was stuck.

Someone rattled the doorknob to the bathroom, and that's when we panicked. All four of us screamed for Mr. Watts, and I banged as hard as I could on the pipe under the sink with the spray can.

And then, above the noise, we heard someone yell, "Will you stop that infernal racket?"

We stopped, looking around us, and the voice outside the door said, "What did you do? Lock yourselves in?"

"Mr. Watts!" I gasped.

Gwen turned on the light and opened the door.

He was standing there in his robe, holding the pan of pineapple upside-down cake in one hand, a flashlight in the other.

"What are you *doing* up here?" I said, as though it weren't perfectly obvious.

He looked sheepishly down at the pan. "Got a little hungry, I guess."

"You climbed up all those steps?" said Liz.

"How did you get in?" asked Pamela.

"I *do* own the place, you know," Mr. Watts said, and jingled the key looped over one finger.

"But why didn't you just call us and ask for some more cake?" Gwen wanted to know.

"If you wouldn't bring me a doughnut, you wouldn't give me more cake, so I decided to help myself." He squinted as he stared at us. "What were you yelling about, and how come you're all in here?"

I took the pan out of his hands. "It's a long story, and it's two in the morning. Sit down at the table and we'll cut you a piece," I told him.

16

A WOMAN CALLER

We all slept in on Sunday. We'd each made our own car arrangements for next week, but for this weekend, we were using my dad's car. I'd told Liz she could have it to go to Mass, or Gwen could drive it to church, but I think we were all too exhausted from our middle-of-the-night visitor for anything.

Gwen got up around noon and made omelets for the rest of us. One at a time we roused ourselves and sauntered into the kitchen.

"If we're going to have a party, we'd better get with it," Gwen said. "How about inviting Molly over too? I haven't talked with her for a couple of weeks."

"Sold!" I said. "Let's order pizza and invite anyone who's

around. I see a volleyball net there in the backyard. No one said we couldn't have guys over if they stayed outside."

As it turned out, almost everyone was available except Brian. We called, but no one was home. Keeno thought he and his parents had flown to Vegas for a week.

Molly drove over in her mom's car, and she looked great. We all told her so.

"I feel pretty good too," she said. The chemo was over, and her hair was beginning to grow back in. She looked like a blue-eyed Peter Pan, and we almost hugged the breath out of her. "I'll know for sure how I'm doing when I see the doctor in two weeks and take a blood test. I've been accepted at the University of Maryland, so . . . fingers crossed!" She held out both hands, and we all did the same.

Keeno picked up the drinks for us—Cokes and near beer, as the guys call the nonalcoholic kind. I'd made that clear. Mr. Watts let us have all the ice in his freezer.

Justin came with Jill, Karen came with Penny, and Gwen invited Yolanda, her friend from church, as well as Austin from the soup kitchen.

"How did you get his number?" I asked, surprised.

"He gave it to me," Gwen said nonchalantly. "Can't a girl have friends?"

We were all glad to see him. He was a big guy—muscular big—and with his dreads and his horned-rimmed glasses, he made quite a first impression.

"This is where you live, huh?" Austin said as he came around to the back of Mr. Watts's large house with the wraparound porch.

"No, it's where my brother lives, in the upstairs apartment with two roommates," I said. "Mr. Watts, the owner, lives downstairs. We're apartment-sitting for the week."

"Cool," said Austin, and went over to join the volleyball game.

We'd brought down three folding chairs from Lester's apartment, and Mr. Watts loaned us his lawn chairs. He sat on the screened porch in back, watching our game, cheering when we got a good volley going. He also agreed to let the guys use his bathroom when needed.

When the pizza was delivered, we sat wherever we could find shade, stealing over to another group occasionally to see if they had any sausage pizza left or trading a green pepper and anchovies for a mushroom.

I was sitting with some of the girls, and I'll admit I got satisfaction out of Penny's expression when Liz announced, purposely, I'm sure, that I'd been to Chicago to visit Patrick at the university. Do you ever get over the jealousy of someone who stole your boyfriend for a while? When you're not even sure if she initiated it or he did? But I saw her eyes studying me, and I liked that I was "the girlfriend" again.

"Really?" said Jill. "How's he doing?" And without waiting for an answer, "Where'd you stay?"

"In his dorm. The guys have a suite. Pretty common there."

"Hey!" said Jill, and smiled knowingly.

I smiled too. "It's a fabulous university, and Patrick fits in well. Three summer courses, one after another. You know Patrick. We had a great time."

"I can imagine," said Karen.

"What have you been up to lately?" Pam asked Penny.

"Not much of anything," Penny said. "I had surgery for an ingrown toenail, but I expect it'll be healed by the time school starts."

I noticed the bandage around one toe. Could I ever be that honest? I wondered. Could I sit there like Penny listening to a girl talk about being close to a guy I once liked and then admit that I'd just had surgery for an unglamorous ingrown toenail?

"You won't believe what the Colliers have done to try to break up Justin and me," Jill told us bitterly, not waiting for us to ask about her. "The more they try, the more determined we are that they'll never get their way. You heard about them whisking Justin off to the Bahamas over spring break—they made it sound like a spur-of-the-moment thing, celebrate his grandmother's ninetieth birthday, no advance warning, bags all packed. Well, we fooled them! When Justin found out what they'd done, he got a ticket for me the very next day, and you should have seen their faces when I showed up in the hotel next door. His mom absolutely detests me, the old witch, and the feeling's mutual."

"But you and Justin have been a couple practically forever," said Pamela. We didn't mention that he used to like Liz.

"Why does she hate you so much?" I asked. Jill has never been a favorite person of mine, but I don't hate her.

"I think she wants him to marry some high-society girl from a prominent family. She tells Justin I'm just attracted to him for their money, and when she's *really* feeling mean, she refers to me as 'GDJ,' he says—Gold Digger Jill. 'Going out with GDJ again?' she'll ask him, so it sounds as though that's my name, Geedee Jay."

"Nice of him to tell you all that," said Gwen. "Sort of fans the flames, doesn't it?"

"Well, I asked him to tell me. I want to know everything the bitch says about me. She could have played the queen in *Snow White*."

"And . . . you're Snow White?" I asked, against my better judgment.

Jill ignored it. "Well, it's not going to work, because Justin and I have a plan."

"What?" asked Liz.

Jill only smiled. "You'll know it when it happens."

"You're going to elope when you're eighteen, I'll bet," Pamela guessed.

Jill continued smiling. "My lips are sealed."

Was it remotely possible they'd do something as stupid as a suicide pact, to keep them "together for eternity" or some other dumb thing? I wondered. Fill a car with carbon monoxide and die in each other's arms? Jill seemed too self-absorbed for that, and Justin, I hoped, too intelligent. But you never know.

* * *

As dusk set in, we wanted to play one more volleyball game while we could still see the ball. Molly especially wanted a turn.

"I'm feeling great these days," she said to Gwen and Liz and me. "I'm this close"—she held up her thumb and forefinger—"to a remission."

"Go, Molly!" Gwen said, and we cheered.

It was about eight forty-five when we heard some car doors slam and voices coming around the side of the house. Four guys showed up, three of them with beers in their hands. It was obvious these weren't their first beers of the evening.

"Heeeeey!" one of them called. "Keeno, buddy!"

One of the guys was wearing a St. John's T-shirt, Keeno's school.

Keeno stared at them a moment or two. "How ya doin', Jake," he said, surprised. "What's up?"

"Saw your car out front, man! Sounds like a party! 'That's Keeno's Buick,' Bill says. 'We gotta check this out.'" He looked around. "Nice place."

Keeno nodded toward me. "Friend of mine," he said. He didn't invite them to stay, but they were obviously people he knew from school.

"It's . . . sort of a private party," I put in, wondering if that was rude. "For . . . uh . . . Molly." I had to make up something.

"Well, hey! Which one's Molly?" said one of the four, his eyes coming to rest on Jill, who happened to be sitting on a lawn chair with Penny and Karen on the grass beside her. Justin ambled over and put one hand on Jill's shoulder, staring unsmiling at the intruders.

The guy laughed and glanced away, then suddenly reached out and knocked the volleyball from Mark's hands and tossed it to one of his buddies.

"We'll play you!" he said over his shoulder to Mark. "Come on, Keeno. Let's have some fun."

"Uh . . . dude, this isn't my party," Keeno said. "We're sort of wrapping things up."

"Bill! Catch!" the second guy said, and the four boys propelled the ball rapidly back and forth among them, one of them playing single-handed, still holding his beer can.

I resented having our party end this way. The ball flew out-of-bounds and hit Penny on the side of the head. The larger of the guys retrieved it. "Sorry, babe," he said. "Wanna get in the game?"

"Yeah, bring your head over here, I'll rub it for you," the larger guy said as Penny ran one hand over her cheek. Her drink had spilled onto her shorts.

"You can give *us* head whenever you want," said another guy, and they laughed.

"Jake, come on," Keeno said. "Knock it off."

The newcomers only laughed and hit the ball even harder.

Austin and Mark went over to the volleyball net and started taking it down while Keeno began folding up the chairs.

"Game's over," Mark said.

"Whassa matter?" said Jake. "Hey, get a look at Mr. Party

Pooper here! His pants are full of it." Then, "Hot potato!" and he forcefully threw the ball to Bill, who immediately tossed it back. They threw faster and faster, their yells louder, more raucous.

"Jake, it's time for you guys to go," Keeno pleaded. "Come on. Clear out."

Suddenly Mark moved in and intercepted the ball, tucking it under his arm. "I said, party's over," he told them.

"Just go!" I said.

"Aren't you going to offer us a little refreshment first?" one of the guys asked, picking up his beer can and draining the last of it.

The fourth boy was opening the lids of the five pizza boxes there on the folding table. He lifted out a large slice of mushroom. "Food!" he called to the others. And to me, "You got any more inside?" He moved toward the back steps.

"Don't go in there," said Austin.

"Yeah? You the caretaker?" the boy responded. I saw Austin's jaw clench.

"This is a private house and this is a private party. Just keep out," Austin repeated.

"Hey, what's with you guys? What are you so upset about?" Jake asked, turning to me.

"Here!" shouted the fourth guy. "There's more in this box." He threw a large slice of pizza to Jake. It landed on the ground.

I heard a car door slam, then a second, and my heart pounded, my hands felt cold. I knew how quickly a crowd could grow. But moments later, two police officers came around the side of the house, and I was never so glad to see the police in my life. For a moment I was afraid they might be the same ones who had caught us in the cemetery, but they weren't. Suddenly all the raucous laughter stopped.

"Shit," I heard one of the new guys mutter.

"Got a complaint from a neighbor about noise back here," one of the officers said, and I closed my eyes. All I could think of was what Les would say. A party, boys, booze, neighbors' complaints, and the police showing up. All in Mr. Watts's backyard. I opened my eyes again when the policeman asked, "Anyone want to tell me what's going on?"

It was Mark who volunteered.

"Yeah, our friend Alice is giving a party, and we have four uninvited guests who won't leave," he said, nodding toward the four who were standing between the pizza boxes and the back steps.

The second officer was walking around, checking us out, looking for booze. One of the guys had his hand behind his back, trying to set his beer can on the table behind him, but he missed.

"Who brought the beer?" the officer asked.

"The guys who crashed our party," I told him.

The officer turned to Jake and his buddies. "IDs, please."

In slow motion, disgust on their faces, the four pulled out their wallets.

"Hey, man, we're not hurting anybody. We go to St. John's with Keeno over there. Just wanted to stop by, see what's happening, that's all," Bill said.

The officer didn't answer, just checked his license. "Which one of you is driving?" he asked.

"I am," another guy answered.

"Come out front? Take a Breathalyzer test?" the officer said, an order more than a question.

The guy looked at his friends and finally agreed.

"Where'd you get the beer?" the first officer questioned.

"From home," said Jake.

"All four of you, around in front," the officer said. And then, to the rest of us, "Sorry for the interruption. Enjoy your party," and he escorted the intruders back around the side of the house.

We stared at each other in amazement.

I was hyperventilating. "Omigod, if Les finds out . . ." I sat down on the steps. "If they'd gone inside and trashed the place . . . or hurt Mr. Watts . . . Who do you suppose called the police?"

The screen door opened behind me, and Mr. Watts looked us over.

"I'm so sorry," I told him.

"Those were guys I know at school," said Keeno, "but I sure didn't invite them."

"They just started taking over," said Liz.

"That's when I called the police," said Mr. Watts.

We all stared at him.

"The police said that a neighbor—," I began.

"*I'm* a neighbor! I'm *your* neighbor, aren't I?" the old man said. "I didn't give the police my name—just said some ruffians had invaded a party next door and someone was about to get hurt. I gave them the address and hung up."

"Mr. Watts, you're a wonder!" said Gwen.

"And I need some doughnuts to calm me down!" he said.

Keeno volunteered to go get some, and I didn't stop him.

"It's on us, Mr. Watts," Keeno said. "What kind do you want?"

"Bring back a dozen," Mr. Watts told him. "You know the kind with raspberry centers? Get two of those. The glazed chocolate? Make it three. Couple cream-filled, a jelly center . . ."

Justin, who had trailed behind the officers, came back to report that the guy who'd been driving had evidently passed the Breathalyzer test, because the police let him drive his car and the others had got in with him.

"You don't think they'll be back again, do you? Vandalize the house?" Liz asked.

Keeno shook his head. "No, they're jerks, but they're not that bad."

We stayed in the yard until the mosquitoes became impossible, going over what had happened that evening, thinking of all the what-ifs, marveling at Mr. Watts and his call to 911.

I had my eye on him and the doughnuts, however. He had a chocolate-coated doughnut in one hand and a raspberry-filled in the other, but he deserved them.

Molly left before the others, giving us each an exuberant hug. The guys set up the volleyball net again for future games, took the chairs inside, and we cleaned up all the trash. Soon the yard showed no trace of a party.

Gwen walked with Austin out to his car, and Liz lingered awhile with Keeno. I went inside with Mr. Watts, saw that he took his medicine, and helped him find his pajamas.

"You all set?" I asked before I turned out the light.

He just lay there grinning. "More excitement these last two nights than I've had in ten years," he said. "What's on for tomorrow?"

"Don't count on anything," I told him. "We're going to have a quiet week."

I think my heart rate was almost back to normal as I went up the side steps to the apartment. Liz, Gwen, and Pamela were inside now, feet on the coffee table, checking out late-night movies on TV. The apartment phone rang, and Pamela answered.

"Hello?" she said. There was a pause in which she turned to me and rolled her eyes, pointing to the phone. "No, I'm not Lester's sister. I'm Pamela . . . I'm just staying here for a while." Her voice suddenly became irritable. "Who is this?" she demanded. Then she slowly put the phone down. "She hung up," she told us.

"I'll bet it's the same woman who met Les in the bar," I said. "Did she sound young? Could you tell?"

"I think so," said Pamela. "First she asks for Lester. Then she wants to know if I'm his sister. When I said my name was Pamela, she just said, 'What the hell . . . ?' and hung up."

"Seems like Les has a lot of explaining to do," said Liz.

"As for you, girl," said Gwen with a smile, "I saw you and

Keeno getting pretty chummy. Sitting there in his lap. Feeding each other pizza."

"Omigod, don't tell me they're at the feeding stage now," said Pamela, rolling her eyes.

"We were eating two different kinds of pizza, that's all," Liz said. "We just traded bites."

"Next thing you know, he'll be rubbing her back," said Gwen.

"Carrying her lip gloss for her in his pocket," said Pamela.

"Hugging her when she forgets her jacket," said Gwen.

"Lucky Liz," I said wistfully.

Gwen looked over. "Patrick's not coming back before the fall semester starts?"

"I don't think so. He's going to Wisconsin with his parents over his break, but I miss him."

Lester called that evening to see how things were going. Did he have mental telepathy? I wondered.

"How's the bike trip?" I asked cheerily.

"Fantastic! My legs are already sore, but we took a sweat bath last night and that helped."

"A sweat bath?"

"Like a sauna. Made a fire, heated up some rocks really well, then put a tent around it and we all sat around these hot rocks. Dirt and sweat just rolled off."

"Lester, that's about the grossest thing I ever heard. When guys get together, they do the most disgusting things."

"Eleven guys and three girls. The girls enjoyed it too."

I couldn't imagine any girl I knew enjoying a sweat bath, but then, I don't know all girls.

"Scenery's gorgeous, weather's great, food is good—we've got a chef traveling with us. Can't complain. How's it going there?"

I told him about Mr. Watts coming in our apartment in the middle of the night, looking for pineapple upside-down cake, and he laughed.

"You dangle something sweet in front of that guy, he'll do most anything. Just keep him away from doughnuts. He's addicted to doughnuts."

"Uh . . . too late," I said, and realized I can't keep anything from Les. Before I knew it, I'd told him about the party, just so he wouldn't hear it from anyone else.

I heard him sigh. "Al, tell me this: Do you think I can go the rest of the bike trip without worrying about what's happening there?"

"Absolutely," I said. "If we have any more trouble, I'll call Dad." And then, to change the subject, I said, "By the way, a woman's called here twice."

"About a job?"

"Uh . . . no."

"Who was it? She say what she wanted?"

"She wouldn't give her name. She just wanted to talk to you. I told her you were in Utah for ten days, but I don't think she believed I was your sister."

"And she didn't say anything else?"

"She said she met you in a bar a couple of nights ago—that you were really nice to her and told her she could call you."

"*What* bar? What *night*? I haven't been in a bar for a month! I've been working on my thesis and getting ready for this trip."

I was relieved to hear it, but puzzled. "If she calls again, should I try to get her name and phone number, say you'll call her?"

Lester seemed to be thinking it over. "Get her name and phone number, but don't promise anything."

He talked a little more about the bike trip—how George had fallen off his bike and might have a bump on his head at his wedding. Finally he signed off, and I clicked END on my cell phone.

"Les says he has no idea who the woman is who's calling," I told the others.

"Anyone who believes *that* will buy the Brooklyn Bridge," said Pamela.

"*I* believe him," said Liz.

"Then how did she get his name? How'd she get his number? Hey, a guy has to defend himself," said Pam. "This is Lester's life, and we're not supposed to pry, right? What else *could* he tell us?"

When I went to the Melody Inn on Monday, Dad said he was closing up for two hours at noon so we could have a farewell party for David, even though he'd be working two more weeks while Marilyn took a vacation. We were sort of celebrating something else, too: Marilyn was pregnant! She was so happy about it, she seemed to be giving off sparks.

"Are you going to be a full-time mom after the baby comes?" I asked her.

"I'm hoping to keep my job, if Ben will have me," Marilyn said, looking across the table at Dad. "He's giving me three months of maternity leave, and after that, my mom's going to take care of the baby during the day. Jack will take over a lot of the time, because most of his gigs are in the evening. We'll just have to play it by ear and see what works."

Dad's going-away gift to David was a book of sacred solos for the baritone voice. I could tell that David was pleased. He thumbed through it, exclaiming over a few of the titles, humming some of the others. "I'll be joining the choir at Georgetown," he said. "That's something I really look forward to doing."

I looked from him to Marilyn. "You two are going off in such different directions. Momhood and priesthood."

"There wouldn't be any priests if there weren't any mothers," said David, taking a big bite of custard pie.

"You're going to miss me, David," I said. "Who else will keep poking her nose into your business?"

"Oh, you'll find someone else to torment," he joked. "But where will I ever find another person who asks whether a girl slept in my tent on a camping trip?" We laughed.

"Well, now that you're giving up girlfriends, I guess nobody would even think to ask," I said.

* * *

I dropped Dad off at home after we'd closed up shop that day, and when I got to Lester's apartment, I picked up the mail and brought it upstairs. A note from Gwen said that she was stopping at the store and would be back by seven, that Liz had called and would be eating with her family, back by eight. Pamela was in the shower.

I could hear Mr. Watts's aide bidding him good night out on the back porch, and I sat at the kitchen table sorting the mail between Les and Paul and George—bills, advertisements, sports magazines.

A blue envelope slipped out of a circular when I picked it up. It was addressed to *Mr. Lester McKinley*, and down in the left-hand corner, underlined, was the word _Personal_. I looked up in the top corner to see who it was from: *Crystal Carey*, it read.

That was her married name. It used to be Harkins. And she used to be Lester's girlfriend.

17
THE UNTHINKABLE

A woman who'd said she'd met Les in a bar had called twice, and Les's old girlfriend—a *serious* girlfriend who had wanted to marry him, a *married* girlfriend—was writing him letters and marking them <u>Personal</u>.

Maybe I didn't know my brother as well as I'd thought. Maybe Pamela was right when she said he was the sort who would "love 'em and leave 'em." I wouldn't open the letter, of course, but if Les called again, I was going to ask him about it. I didn't care if it *did* ruin his vacation.

I put Paul's mail on the desk in his bedroom. Same with George's. I put all Lester's mail on his desk, but tucked the blue envelope beneath a gray sweater in the bottom drawer of his dresser so Pam wouldn't see it.

In fact, the only problem we had with Pamela now was that she ate her lunch and snacks in the living room and left her dishes where they were.

"Pamela, is this your cereal bowl?" Gwen would call. "It's got crud ossifying on it."

"Just fill it with water," Pamela would call, her feet on the coffee table, remote control in hand.

"Why don't you do it yourself? C'mon, girl, you've got three days' worth of dishes all around the place," Gwen would say.

Gwen, on the other hand, irritated us by leaving her shoes where she kicked them off, and if we went from one room to another in the dark, we'd stumble over them.

My worst fault, according to the others, was taking too long in the bathroom.

"Alice, could you possibly dry your hair in the bedroom?" Liz would call.

And Liz, in turn, was scolded for taking a fresh glass each time she wanted a drink, so that she could use four or five different glasses in the course of a day and the cupboard would soon be empty. Ten days at Lester's apartment was a preview, I guess, of what we could expect when we had apartments and roommates of our own someday.

I was still wondering about Lester as I set the table that evening. Did I really expect him to tell me what was going on between him and Crystal? And what about that woman who'd called?

"Something wrong?" Gwen asked me at dinner. Pamela had brought home some Chinese cashew chicken, and we were dutifully eating the broccoli in the fridge.

"Just . . . life," I said. "Half the time I don't even know what's going on and the other half I don't understand."

"Well, *I* had a good day," Gwen said. "Guess who showed up and took me to lunch?"

"Would his name start with an 'A'?" asked Pamela.

Gwen smiled. "Yeah. He's just a thoroughly nice guy, you know? Just a guy friend. Just buddies. I like that."

And Pamela, for once, didn't argue.

Liz came in a little before eight with a dessert her mom had made for us. We were still sitting at the table an hour later, talking, watching the clock to make sure we checked in on Mr. Watts, when there was a knock at the apartment door.

"If it's Mr. Watts wanting doughnuts, the answer's no," I said as Liz got up. "Tell him they're gone. He shouldn't be climbing those stairs anyway."

We couldn't see the door from where we were sitting, but we heard Liz say, "Hello?"

A woman's voice asked, "Who are you? Alice or Pamela?"

"I'm Elizabeth," said Liz.

"What *is* this?" the woman said. "Lester have a harem or something? The man downstairs said this is Lester's apartment."

"Omigod!" I said to Gwen and Pamela. "It's *her*!" I scrambled from my chair and called, "I'll handle it, Liz." I padded barefoot to the door.

A woman of about twenty-five or so—maybe older—with dyed hair and too much makeup stood there on the outside stairway staring first at Liz, then at me.

"I'm Alice, Lester's sister," I said, and felt a little sorry for her, she looked so confused. "Would you like to come in?"

"I'd like to talk with Lester, if possible," she said.

"He's in Utah," I said, "but please come in. My friends and I are house-sitting for Les and his roommates."

"Are his roommates female too?" she asked, looking around uncertainly as she stepped inside.

"No. Two guys." I led her to the living room and took some magazines off the couch so she could sit down. Liz went back to the kitchen.

"I can't figure out if this is a joke or what," the woman said.

"I'd sort of like to know that myself," I told her. "When did you meet Lester?"

"Last week." She sat a little too stiffly, hands on her bag. The cherry red polish on her fingernails was chipped. She was wearing sandals, jeans, and a jersey top. "Tuesday, I think it was. Les was there with a couple other guys."

Paul and George? I wondered. Had he lied to me?

"They invited me to their table, and we really hit it off. All three of them, actually—the short one and the tall one too—but I liked Lester the most. And he was flirting back. As they were leaving, I asked him if he was planning to come back to Henry's. Y'know, maybe we could have a drink or something. He said sure, that I could call him anytime. But he didn't give me his phone number. All I knew was that he lived in Takoma Park, and I found his name in the phone book."

It had to be Les.

"Where is Henry's?" I asked.

"Fourteenth and K, somewhere around there." She glanced at the bookcases along one wall. "This where they live, huh?"

"Yeah. For a couple of years now. He's a graduate student at the University of Maryland."

"Yeah, that's what one of the guys said. That he went to the U. I just had one year of college, but I went to secretarial school. I work at Verizon."

She was looking over at a photo of Les and Paul and George on one of their ski trips. "Is that Lester?" she asked, and fished in her bag for a pair of glasses.

"Yes." I went over to the bookshelf and brought the photo back. She held it in both hands.

"Well, I don't see him," she said.

I looked at her, then at the photo, and pointed him out. "That's Lester," I said. "That one's George and there's Paul."

She stared some more and shook her head. "This isn't any of them. None of these guys is Lester." And suddenly she teared up. "It was all a big joke, wasn't it? I *wondered* why Lester didn't give me his number. Just a bunch of shitheads goofing off."

That was it exactly, and I felt so bad for her. "I'm really sorry," I said. "When Les called home the other night, I told him about your call, and he said he hadn't been in a bar for at least a month, certainly not in the last week."

"Well, I was stupid to fall for it. To have called in the first place, and now I was a fool for coming out here. He seemed so sincere, and it was all a big act."

"Don't feel too bad," I said. "You ought to hear what happened to us the other night." And I told her about how we heard footsteps and locked ourselves in the bathroom without a cell phone. She didn't laugh, but at least she smiled at me before she left. And she never did give me her name.

After the door closed, I went out to the kitchen and sat with the others. I knew they'd heard everything we'd said.

"I hope I'm never that gullible," said Liz.

"I hope I'm never that stupid," said Pam.

"I hope I'm never that desperate," said Gwen.

"I hope I never meet up with the guys who played that trick on her," I told them. "But Les will be glad to know he's off the hook."

He called again that night to say that for the next few days they'd be in a no-service area, so this was his final check for a while. Had I managed to get through the day without the police coming by? Yes, I said, but then I told him about the woman who came over, and he was as angry at the guys who did it as he was sorry for her, whoever she was.

"Any idea who would do that, Les?" I asked.

"There are a couple of slimeballs who might pull something like that, but I wouldn't call them friends," he said.

For a minute I thought I wouldn't have a chance to tell him

about Crystal's letter because Liz was in the room with me, but then she went out to the kitchen to help Gwen look for microwave popcorn.

"Les, I was sorting through the mail today and you got a letter from Crystal. Crystal Carey," I added, just to emphasize the fact that she was married. "It was marked 'Personal' on the front. I put it in the bottom drawer of your dresser. I wanted you to know where it was."

There was complete silence from the other end of the line.

"Did she . . . did you open it?" he asked.

"Of course not. But I couldn't help wondering why . . . Well, she's married now—"

"Yes, I know. Look, Al. I want you to take a pen and, in bold letters, write 'Return to Sender' on the front."

"What?"

"'Return to Sender' over my address. Then mail it."

"You're not even going to read it?"

"No. I read the last one and wished I hadn't."

"Then it's . . . not the first one she's sent."

"No, the second, and I should have sent the first one back too. I'm not going into details, but Crystal's a woman who always wants what she can't have. And whatever problems she's having—with her marriage or with herself—she should be talking them over with Peter, not with me."

"'Return to Sender.' Got it. And, Les," I told him, "we're having a fabulous time."

* * *

The rest of the week was uneventful, as I'd predicted. Austin called Gwen once or twice, and Keeno came over a few nights to see Liz. Each time she went out and sat with him in his car.

We cleaned the apartment on Saturday for Lester's return the next day. Liz made a batch of brownies for the guys to find when they came home. We'd scrubbed the bathroom and kitchen and were waiting for the floors to dry. Gwen and Pam and Liz had taken their iced tea out on the side steps overlooking the street, and I was about to follow when the apartment phone rang.

I answered. "Hello?"

A pause. *Not again!* I thought.

"Hello? Is someone there?" I said.

Another pause. Finally a woman's voice said, "*Alice?* Is this Alice? This is Crystal."

Omigod!

"Crystal!" I said. "How *are* you?"

"I'm okay," she answered, but she sounded distant. "What are you doing at Lester's?"

I knew right away that when I told her we were staying here for the week, she'd know it was me who returned her letter. "Lester's in Utah on a bike trip, and I'm here apartment-sitting with some friends," I said.

"Oh! Well, I don't know if that explains things or not," she said.

"Explain?" But I knew *exactly* what she meant.

"The letter, Alice. Did you return my letter?"

"I was following Lester's instructions, Crystal. When he

called home, I told him what mail had come, and he asked me to return your letter."

"He . . . didn't even want to read it first?" she asked.

I shook my head, then realized I had to respond. "No. I asked the same question, but he said he should have returned the first one too." *Oops.*

There was a pause, so long I thought maybe she'd quietly put down the phone, but then she asked "Did *you* read it?"

"Of course not!"

She sighed. "Well, I never thought he'd just send it back. I don't have anyone else to talk to."

I knew I shouldn't get involved, but I took a chance. "You have Peter."

"Is that what Les said?"

"Actually, yes."

"What else did he say?"

I could feel my pulse throbbing in my temples. Did I dare? This was so *not* my business, but I wanted to help Lester out.

"He said . . . whatever problems you're having . . . with your marriage or with yourself . . . you should be talking them over with Peter, not with him."

"Look, can I ask you something? Does Les have a girlfriend? Is this why he won't talk to me? I could always talk more easily with Les than anyone else."

"I don't know, Crystal. He doesn't tell me the details of his private life. But I think I know him well enough that if he sends your letters back, he means it."

"What did he mean by . . . problems with myself?"

"You'd know that better than anyone, I guess."

"I can guess what he thinks. He told me once that I always want what I can't have. And if I *do* manage to get it, he said, I want something else."

I shrugged, then remembered again that she couldn't see me. I wasn't sure how to respond. "Is that true?" I finally asked.

"If he'd married me, I don't think it would be true."

I didn't answer, and because I didn't, she said, "Thanks, Alice, for being honest with me. How are *you*, incidentally?"

"I'm doing fine, Crystal. This will be my senior year, and I'm features editor for the school paper. I'm excited about that."

"Wow! I should think so!" she said.

"How is your little boy?"

There was a pause, and then she laughed. "He's great, Alice. But you know, now I want a little girl, so . . . well, maybe Les has a point. Anyway, tell him hello from me. Tell him there won't be any more letters. Tell him if he wants to get in touch, he knows where to call. No, don't say that. Just tell him that Crystal said . . . good-bye. Tell him that, will you?"

"Sure."

I think that Mr. Watts hated to see us go. He said we were more fun than a barrel of monkeys—insane monkeys, but fun anyway.

Les called from the apartment to tell me they were back, that the place looked great, thanks for the brownies, and that he looked forward to sleeping in his own bed. He'd tell me all about the trip later. When I mentioned that David Reilly wouldn't be there for the big Labor Day sale at the Melody Inn, Les said he'd plan to come in that day and help out.

We were approaching the middle of August, and I was eager for school to begin. It would start later this year, not until after Labor Day, but I wanted to be busy again. I wanted to work on my ideas for *The Edge* and take my mind off Patrick and whether or not he'd make it home before Thanksgiving.

Gwen and I were the only ones working in the same places we had the summer before—I at the Melody Inn, Gwen continuing a high school internship at the National Institutes of Health. She must have impressed them, because this was her third stint there, and she had definitely decided to go for a medical degree once she got out of college.

Pamela was clerking in a fabric store; Liz was working mornings in a day-care center at her church; Keeno worked for his dad in a hardware store; and Mark pumped gas at a service station. I wasn't sure what the others were doing. It was as though all of us inhabited separate worlds during the day that had nothing to do with any other part of our lives, and we didn't come back to our own bodies until we got together in the evenings— at the movies, the mall, bowling, or the Stedmeisters' pool.

We didn't talk about what we did during the day. Pamela never said, *Do you want to know about my afternoon at G Street Fabrics?* and Mark never said, *I must have pumped three hundred gallons today.* Work just was. Play just was. We just were—

enjoying the second week of August, knowing all too well how intense things would get in our senior year.

"It's fun seeing Elizabeth laugh," I said to Sylvia the following Sunday after I'd watched Liz and Keeno horsing around together on her porch. "She laughs a lot more around Keeno. And he seems a little more serious. Like they sort of meet on middle ground."

Sylvia had finished the peach preserves and was starting to make grape jelly; Les and Paul were thinking about a new roommate after George left to get married; Carol sent a thank-you note for our wedding gift. . . .

And then . . .

Tuesday evening, August 18:

6:00 p.m.: Dad and I closed up the store and drove home.

6:30 p.m.: Sylvia made grilled pecan chicken, and Dad and I made the salad.

7:00 p.m.: We ate our dinner out back on the screened porch, and Dad dished up the ice cream. It was a gorgeous night and all the windows in the house were open.

8:00 p.m.: Patrick called and we talked on my cell phone for twenty minutes. I figured he was lonely.

8:22 p.m.: I had ended my call with Patrick and had started downstairs when the house phone rang. I didn't bother answering because I thought Sylvia was still in the kitchen and would pick it up. But the phone kept ringing, and I heard Dad yell, "Al, would you grab that, please?" I realized they were outside inspecting the shrubbery.

"Got it!" I yelled back, clattering on down and grabbing the hall phone. "Hello?"

There were great gasping sobs from the other end. "Hello?" I said anxiously. "Who is this?"

"A-Alice!" came Elizabeth's voice. "Oh, A-Alice! I've been trying to call you!"

"I was on my cell with Patrick," I told her. "Liz, what's wrong?"

"Alice . . . ," she said again, and her wail was so awful, so full of grief, I couldn't stand it.

"What?"

"Mark's dead!"

I screamed. "Liz! No! Oh, God, no!"

"K-Keeno called me. He t-tried to call Mark." She was crying so hard now that I mistook my own tears for hers, wetting my hands. "It . . . happened around six thirty . . . somewhere near . . . Randolph Road."

"Oh, Liz! Oh, Liz!" I sank to the floor, leaning over on one side, bracing myself with one elbow.

"He was just *sitting* there, Alice, waiting to make a left t-turn! He wasn't doing *anything*!" We sobbed together, and I felt I couldn't listen to the rest, but I had to. "He was sitting at the light behind an SUV, and a truck came up from behind and d-d-didn't stop. . . ."

I could only cry.

"A neighbor's there at the Stedmeisters' taking calls. He told Keeno that Mark didn't have a ch-chance. He was trapped! He wasn't d-doing *anything*!"

Dad and Sylvia came through the front door just then, talking about turning on the sprinkler, and Dad saw me there on the floor.

"Alice!" he yelled.

"D-Dad!" I cried. "Oh, Daddy! Mark's dead."

18

BELIEVING. OR NOT.

We sat on the long couch in Elizabeth's living room—Liz and Gwen and Pamela and I. It might have been nine or ten or even eleven o'clock, I don't know. Keeno sat bent over in the chair next to us, head in his hands. Dad and Sylvia and Mr. and Mrs. Price were grouped around the dining room table. Little Nate was asleep upstairs.

Dad had called the Stedmeisters and talked briefly with Mark's dad. The minister was there at the house, Dad was told, and Mrs. Stedmeister was on sedation.

Everything seemed surreal. I had been in Elizabeth's living room hundreds—perhaps thousands—of times since we'd moved here, but now the colors didn't look the same. I stared at details I'd never noticed before: a frayed corner of the carpet; two bookends shaped like halves of a globe; a spot on an armchair; a grandparent's picture.

The tissue in my hand was so wet, it was useless, and I reached for the box on the coffee table. When any of us spoke, our noses sounded clogged. My eyes traveled from one friend to the next, and I wondered if tomorrow someone else would be missing. I'd called Patrick as soon as I'd been sure I could speak, and I knew without asking that he was crying. He wanted to know when the funeral would be, and I promised to find out.

I had just seen Mark the day before! I was thinking. We'd all gone to Gepetto's for dinner that evening. Mark had been laughing. He'd been alive. He'd been wearing a white shirt with broad black stripes on it and a large seven-digit inmate's number on the back, which had made us laugh. Keeno had told us that if he and Mark could earn half the money toward that old car they wanted to buy, his dad would donate the rest. Then Keeno had dramatically pulled off his baseball cap and passed it around the table.

It was as though, if I closed my eyes, I could step back a day in time and make things turn out differently—get Mark to go another route, get the light to change, get the truck to stop. . . .

"If ever there was an example of just being in the wrong place at the wrong time . . . ," Mr. Price mused from the dining room.

"But if his blinker was on, as the police said it was, how

could the truck driver not have noticed?" Sylvia said. "Was the man on drugs, I wonder?"

Did it make any difference? I thought. *Mark is dead.*

"Traffic is awful around Randolph Road and Macon during rush hour," Dad said.

"As usual, though, the truck driver survived. It's always that way, it seems—always the other person who's killed," said Elizabeth's mom.

And Mark is dead, I repeated to myself.

Pamela was sobbing softly, and Liz began to cry again. Keeno got up and sat down on the arm of the couch, putting one arm around Liz. She buried her face against him.

I found I could cry without making a sound. Without even knowing it. I could feel tears on my arms, my hands, and I looked down to see spots on my shirt.

"I've talked to one of their neighbors, and they're starting a list for dinner deliveries to the Stedmeisters," said Sylvia. "I signed up for next week."

"I'll call tomorrow and put our name on the list," Mrs. Price said.

I didn't want to think of food. Didn't think I could swallow. Elizabeth's mom had made coffee and put out a plate of cookies, but no one touched a thing. Food couldn't help, I thought. *Mark is dead.*

Mark wouldn't be buying a car and fixing it up. He wouldn't be going back to school. He wouldn't attend homecoming or football games or band concerts or the prom. He wouldn't be going to Clemson. He would never marry, and there wouldn't be any grandchildren to keep the Stedmeisters company.

Mark is dead, and he's not coming back.

Wednesday evening:

It was dark about nine. Liz came over to ride with me. We picked up Pamela, then drove to Gwen's to get her and Yolanda.

When we got to the Stedmeisters', there were already cars stretching along the curb down the block, friends leaning against their cars, talking in soft voices. Liz walked along the row, distributing the tiny battery-operated candles she'd borrowed from her church, which they use sometimes on Christmas Eve.

The upstairs of the Stedmeister house was dark, but there was a light in the living room and another on near the back.

Every person we could think of who had ever swum in Mark's pool had been asked to come by on this evening. There were the five of us girls; there were Keeno and Brian. Jill and Justin. Karen and Penny. The only person missing from our group was Patrick, but some other kids from school, all of whom had been at the Stedmeisters' to swim at least once, gathered there with us in front of the house, eighteen in all.

We made no sound. Didn't speak. Didn't sing. We spread ourselves out about four feet apart from each other and formed a semicircle around the house, facing the front, holding our lighted candles. Just stood—a silent tribute from the old gang, gathering there one last time.

A tribute to all the years Mrs. Stedmeister had given us food, served us drinks, cleaned up after our messes on their patio, mopped up their bathroom after we'd changed out of our wet suits.

For all the times Mr. Stedmeister had vacuumed the pool for us, tested the water, scrubbed the coping, put on the cover. For every year, every summer, this house and patio and pool and yard had been our gathering place, our home.

For all the things they would miss now that Mark was gone. For all the things we would enjoy that he would never know.

I'm not sure how long we stood there. Forty minutes, perhaps. Maybe an hour. Cars drove slowly by in a silent parade. Neighbors stood quietly on their porches, possibly expecting us to do something. But there was nothing we could do except *be* there, offering a sad thank-you to the friends these two parents had been.

The door opened. We did not expect it, but we welcomed it. Mr. and Mrs. Stedmeister came hesitantly out on the front porch. Mark's dad looked gray and older than he'd ever looked, but he had one arm around his wife's shoulder.

She came to the edge of the porch and looked around at all eighteen grieving friends. Then, in a trembling voice we had to strain to hear, she said, "It was so nice of you to come. I wonder if you would all walk around to the pool and just sit there for a while. I would so love to see that. And please . . . may I give you some lemonade?"

For me, the next few days went by in slow motion. It took forever to get out of bed. Once in the bathroom, I'd stand under the shower till the water turned cold; eat half a slice of toast, then quit. At work I moved on automatic. I answered the phone and found the sheet music or guitar strings that a customer wanted, but I felt exhausted, frayed.

It wasn't just that we had lost a longtime member of our crew or a place to hang out. It was also that the risk factor for staying alive had altered. We always knew that if we drove too fast and went off the road, we could die; that something could go wrong inside our own bodies that could kill us; that if we went to dangerous places, we might get caught in a cross fire. But none of us had seriously considered that we could be minding our own business, sitting perfectly still, in fact, and end up dead. If Mark had been in the "wrong" place at the "wrong" time, couldn't every place we had thought of as okay turn out wrong?

Gwen drove us by the spot where Mark had died. Each day the little memorial at the side of the road grew larger: flowers, teddy bears, wreaths, and even toy cars—for the car Mark and Keeno had wanted to buy. Someone added a car's headlight; then someone contributed a hubcap. MARK, WE WILL NEVER FORGET YOU, read a hand-lettered sign, streaked a bit by rain.

But we knew Mark. People who didn't would glance over at the sad little collection and think, *Another drunken teenager. Another kid driving too fast.*

"I miss him, but I can't really think what I miss most," Liz said.

"His smile?" I suggested. "Mark had a great smile."

"He was always up for anything," said Pamela.

"Whatever you wanted to do, Mark was ready. That's what I liked about him."

Liz said it best: "He was just an average guy—wasn't a jock or star student or anything—but somehow, if Mark was missing, we knew it. We just needed him there."

"Did you see what he did at the party—just moved in on those guys and took the ball?" Gwen asked.

I let out my breath. "After bringing Keeno around, Brian's virtually left the gang, Keeno's stayed, and Mark . . . he seemed to be changing, more sure of himself. . . ."

"And then things changed forever," said Pamela.

There was a brief story about the accident in the Metro section of the *Post*:

SILVER SPRING YOUTH KILLED IN ACCIDENT

A sixteen-year-old boy was killed Tuesday when his car was struck from behind by a delivery truck. Mark B. Stedmeister was pronounced dead at the scene of the accident, which happened around 6:30 p.m. when his vehicle, waiting to make a left turn onto Randolph Road at Macon Drive, was propelled into the rear of an SUV. The truck's driver, Rodney Johnson, was taken to Holy Cross Hospital with non-life-threatening injuries. The results of drug and alcohol tests are pending. The driver of the SUV was unhurt.

Sixteen-year-old just didn't say it. It didn't say sixteen years of the Stedmeisters looking after their only son—welcoming his friends, worrying about some of them, watching him slip, watching him thrive, and then, suddenly, losing him. Things can be dismissed so easily with words. Words can be so full or so empty.

We called or texted each other every day—five or six times. Sometimes all we said was, "You okay?"

"How are you doing?" I asked Pamela when I called her on Saturday. I was paying special attention to Pamela because she and Mark used to go out together.

"All cried out," said Pamela. "I just feel flat. A sort of nothingness. Like the whole thing was beyond anyone's control, so what's the use?"

"The use of . . . ?"

"Of anything! If you can't plan for anything—you can plan but you can't guarantee—why bother?"

"No one can guarantee anything, Pamela—not ever. But you still have to plan for a life or you won't have any at all."

"Yes, you will. I could just sit around forever. Eat, sleep, pee, and I'd exist. But what's the point?"

"To see how long you can live before something zaps you, if nothing else."

"Mark was just starting to get his act together," Pamela said. "He and Keeno had become a team. That crazy Naked Carpenters thing. They were good at fixing up old cars. Mark could have started his own business, I'll bet. And then some bastard of a truck driver plows into him. . . ."

"I know." We were both quiet for a moment. "Dad said that the driver's blood tests turned out negative. He's a sixty-seven-year-old man, and they think he may have fallen asleep or had a ministroke or something." We'd even been robbed of a reason to hate the driver.

"Oh, God . . . I just can't figure it out," said Pamela. "All *I* seem to want to do is sleep."

"Me too. Do you want us to drive you to the church tomorrow?"

"Dad's driving. He said he'd go with me."

"We'll see you there, then."

Patrick was there. He had flown in Sunday morning, and a neighbor was taking him back to the airport right after the service because there was a birthday celebration for Patrick's father that evening. We hugged each other in the church foyer.

I hate funerals. When my grandfather died, it was so sad. I hate the long faces, the dark suits, the funeral men who speak in soft voices and direct traffic. I hated having to look at all the scrapbooks and photos of Mark on display to show people all we'd miss now that he was gone. I just didn't want to do this. Didn't want to be there, didn't want it to have happened. But it did and I was and I would and I did.

Patrick and I sat together holding hands. Dad and Sylvia and Les, looking sad and tired, sat on the other side of me. A lot of friends from school were there—those who weren't on vacation, anyway.

Most of us had brought a single flower and had placed it on the casket. I tried to steer my mind away from what was inside. Tried not to think of Mark's body smashed between the back of an SUV and the front of a truck. Tried not to wonder what Mark had been thinking about as he waited for the light to change. If he had looked in his rearview mirror and seen the truck coming. If he'd realized he was trapped. I hoped he'd had the radio on full blast and hadn't seen the truck coming up behind him; hadn't heard it and had felt nothing because the impact was so swift and sudden. Hoped he had felt no panic, no fear, no pain—one moment music, the next moment nothing. It was over for Mark, yet all of us there at the service were going through the horror of it again and again.

The minister did his best and said all the right things, but it wasn't enough. Nothing would ever be enough. But when he asked if anyone would like to share a memory of Mark, I knew it wouldn't be me. I couldn't trust myself to speak at all.

An uncle of Mark's went to the microphone and spoke for the family. Told how Mark had always liked mechanical things. How he'd once taken a clock apart, then couldn't get it back together the right way, and it was a day before the family realized that the clock wasn't working.

Low chuckles traveled around the room, people glad to have been afforded an emotion they could deal with. The Stedmeisters themselves didn't speak, and I knew they couldn't. Mrs. Stedmeister wept continuously into a handkerchief she held to her nose. Mr. Stedmeister had one arm around her and kept patting her shoulder. But his face looked old and lined, his head too heavy to hold up. A neighbor shared a few memories and told how Mark used to climb the fence to get to her apple tree and once asked her, as a small boy, why she didn't grow apples without worms in them. More appreciative laughter.

"Is there anyone else who would like to speak before we conclude the service?" the minister asked.

I felt Patrick's fingers disengage from mine. He got up and walked to the front of the church.

When Patrick turned to face the audience, he looked taller than I remembered him just a month before—his shoulders more broad, perhaps because of his suit jacket. His red hair had become more brown, and his face, despite the freckles, looked more mature.

"My name is Patrick Long, and I've been a friend of Mark's since the fourth grade," he said. "I hope I can speak for many of his friends when I say that Mark's death has changed our lives in ways we didn't expect. It has made us appreciate the life that we have, however short or long it may be; the friendships we've made; the loyalty of friends like Mark; and the generosity of his parents.

"Mark was nothing if not loyal; if ever a friend was steady, a 'there for you' kind of friend, it was Mark. He wasn't showy, wasn't loud, but he was there. You could count on him completely."

And then, when Patrick ended his eulogy, I cried. We all cried. "Wish you were here, buddy. We'll miss you."

Patrick's voice trembled on those words, and I saw him blink as he came back to our row. I think every girl there reached for a tissue. I saw Keeno press two fingers into the corners of his eyes to hold back tears. From somewhere a few rows forward came a deep, choking sob, as though someone were holding back as long as possible before another sob could escape. I was surprised to see that it was Brian Brewster, his head in his hands.

Patrick sat back down, and we leaned against each other. I squeezed his hand. His fingers squeezed back. I was glad he was here. Grateful he had come. Sad that he had to fly back to Wisconsin that same afternoon. But most of all I was angry at God. If I hadn't had a personal relationship with him before, I did now. I was furious.

Patrick had to go back to the airport, but I went to the cemetery with the others. Each of us tossed a handful of dirt on Mark's coffin. Slowly, almost without sound, the coffin was lowered into the ground, the bands that held it slipped away. Mrs. Stedmeister couldn't look. She and Mark's dad sat on folding chairs at graveside, and she buried her head in his shoulder until the casket was out of sight. I hugged them both before we left and could feel her tears against my cheek.

As I walked back to the car with my friends, Keeno with his arm around Liz, I said, "I think we should all take turns stopping by the Stedmeisters' each week just to talk with them, see how they're doing."

"We should," agreed Gwen. "Just talk about every good or funny thing about him we can remember."

"Mrs. Stedmeister told me she wants to give away some of his things to his friends," said Keeno. "I'm afraid she'll be sorry later. I didn't know what to say."

"Let's do whatever makes her feel better," I said. "And if she gives something away and then wants it back, she can have it."

Neighbors were preparing food at a community center for anyone who wanted to drop in, but most of us were wiped. I just wanted to go home and sleep. We were exhausted from the week and had already had our time alone with Mark's parents the night we gathered around their house and pool. This was a chance for the adults to talk.

I lay down on my bed and fell asleep. When I woke, I felt really good and rested for a minute or two until I remembered, and then I just wanted to stand at the window and scream at the sky.

"I don't believe in God anymore," I said to David Reilly at work the next morning—a great thing to tell a would-be priest when he just stops by the Melody Inn to pick up his last paycheck. Dad had an eye appointment and wouldn't be in until noon, and Sylvia was at school; teachers had to be in their classrooms getting ready for the fall semester. So I'd taken the bus in, and Marilyn and I alone were holding down the fort.

"Because your friend died?" David asked me.

"Because if God could have saved him, he didn't, and he should have," I said. "Because of all the horrible things that happen to innocent people."

"It's okay to be angry," David said.

"I didn't say I was just angry, I said I didn't believe."

David only nodded that he understood, but he didn't say anything. He started helping me pack up an order for a school.

"How do *you* explain it?" I challenged him.

"I don't," said David.

"Well, it doesn't make any sense to believe there's a God watching over us when he lets something like this happen," I said.

"It does if your faith is stronger than your doubt," David said. "And I want to believe in God, so I do."

"How can you talk yourself into that?" I demanded. "I would love to believe in a God that will watch over me, but I can't. There's too much evidence to the contrary."

"It may seem that way to you, but I see evidence of God in everyday beauty and kindness. I can't imagine a world without God, so I'm going to live as though there is one," said David.

"Well, I can't believe in something just because I *want* to, David."

"I understand that too," said David.

"Good, because I don't understand anything at all."

19
GOOD-BYES AND BEGINNINGS

No one talked about getting together the coming weekend, the last weekend of August. No one suggested a movie, a restaurant, a card game, bowling. It was as though we couldn't find comfort in each other, as we had at first. We were drained. No matter what a person said, it didn't work. Didn't help.

I was upset that neither Liz nor Pamela nor Gwen offered to have a sleepover where we could at least be together and *talk* about not talking. Why was it always me, it seemed, who invited them here? I used the computer at work to check my e-mail, but there wasn't a message from any of them. No text messages on my cell.

When Liz did finally call on Friday, it was to ask if I had seen the article about teenage accidents in the *Gazette*.

"No," I said crisply. "I have not."

"What's wrong?" she asked.

"What's *wrong*? You've forgotten already?"

"About Mark? Of *course* not!" she said. And then she just hung up.

I didn't care. Why would I want to read an article about teenage accidents? Why on *Earth* would I want to read that *now*?

I called Pamela to complain about Elizabeth, and her dad said she'd gone to the mall. I couldn't believe it. The *mall*? As in *shopping*?

I decided not to call Gwen. Let her call me.

We had takeout for dinner and it wasn't very good. Sylvia had used a coupon for a new Thai restaurant, and I left half the food on my plate.

Dad looked over. "You planning anything for tonight, Al?"

"No, and neither is anyone else, evidently," I said sullenly.

"Want to play Scrabble with Ben and me? Play cards? Rent a movie?" Sylvia asked.

"Not particularly, but thanks," I told her.

Then Dad said, "Les is coming to the store tomorrow to help out, since David's gone and Marilyn has a doctor's appointment. Things will probably stay slow until the holiday sale next weekend, though, so if you'd rather stay home tomorrow—take a day off—you can."

"Yeah. I think I'll do that," I said.

I sat in front of the TV that night flipping channels, not able to focus long on anything. I'd thought that Gwen and Pamela and Liz and I were so close. I'd always considered them my best friends. What was happening to us?

It rained that night. After weeks of dry weather, it poured off and on, and I slept fitfully, waking several times to listen to the rain, then drifting off again. It was only in the morning that I slept deeply, and I woke to find that Dad had already left for work. A note from Sylvia said that she was putting in a few hours in her classroom.

I went out on the back porch in my pajamas. There was a touch of green to grass that had been a dull yellow-brown. Flowers had opened their petals. I felt a little better, but still, the knowledge that I was still here and the world would go on was tempered by the fact that a longtime friend was gone. That rain would still rain and snow would still fall, but Mark wouldn't hear or see it. And that I could stand this only because I had to.

I had lunch in place of breakfast, and halfway through the afternoon I texted Liz and Pamela and Gwen: *It's cooler out. Does anyone feel like a walk this evening? To anywhere?*

Pamela answered: *I'm up for it.*

Gwen texted: *What time?*

Liz answered: *Yes.*

Gwen drove over, and we stood awkwardly in front of my house, discussing where we should go. No one suggested a park because those are too crowded on summer weekends. When

Pamela said, "The playground?" we headed over to the old brick building where Liz and Pam and I had gone to grade school. There was nothing picturesque about it, nothing special except the memories, but Gwen gamely walked the perimeter with us, just as we used to do with Mark and Patrick and Brian. Finally we walked across to the playground equipment and sat down.

"It's hard," I said at last, forcing the words from my lips.

"I know," said Liz.

"Even talking about it."

"I don't *want* anyone asking how I feel because the answer is . . . numb," said Pamela. She was perched on the low end of the teeter-totter facing downhill, feet resting on the hand bar. "Yesterday I went to the mall and just walked. I think I went down every hallway, looked in every shop, but I didn't go inside any of them. I just wanted to be distracted—window after window—shoes, toys, lawn mowers, greeting cards . . . it didn't matter."

"Did it help?" asked Gwen.

"Not much."

I was strangely quiet. Gwen and I were sitting on the swings. She sat with her legs stretched out in front of her, but I was turning slowly around and around, the chains above me twisting until they wouldn't turn any farther. But I didn't uncoil as I used to do back in sixth grade, letting myself whirl around, then back again. I uncoiled myself slowly, letting my feet make a circle in the dirt.

"I just . . . I keep going to Google, looking for stuff about road accidents," said Liz, from a bench at one side. "First I think

I'm looking for statistics to tell me Mark's accident was one in a million, a freak sort of thing, and it's highly unlikely it would ever happen again to anyone I know. And then I think I'm reading to reassure myself that Mark wasn't alone—that this happens more often than we think. I just keep looking and looking and reading and reading and never find anything that makes me feel more accepting of it."

The flatness I'd been feeling was giving way to surprise. But when Gwen didn't say anything, I asked, "What about you?"

She sighed and let her shoulders drop. "I feel like I'm not feeling enough. All of you knew Mark longer than I did. I just feel sort of left out—all the memories you have that I don't."

Just the word *memories* made me tear up. My mouth turned down at the corners. "I'm just so . . . incredibly . . . sad . . . for the Stedmeisters," I said, and began to cry.

Pamela got off the teeter-totter and came over and hugged me.

"So how have you been dealing with the sadness, Alice?" Gwen asked. "Until yesterday I hadn't heard from you all week."

I wiped my eyes. "Well, I didn't see any e-mails from you. Any of you. Nobody called. I've been miserable, if you want the truth. Just flat. Hollow. I thought that at least *one* of you would know how I felt."

"Alice, is it that hard to ask for help?" asked Gwen.

"Yeah, why didn't *you* call *us*?" said Liz.

"You were there for me when I got pregnant," said Pamela. "You were there for me when Mom left and I had fights with my dad."

"Yeah, Alice. You stayed at the hospital with me when Mom

was having Nathan," said Liz. "You didn't freak out when I told you I'd been molested. Why can't you call us when *you're* down?"

I didn't know why. Why it seemed easier somehow to give comfort than to ask for it.

"I guess . . . I didn't think any of you felt the same way I did. I mean, when I called your house, Pam, your dad said you were at the mall, and shopping was the last thing I wanted to do."

"But I wasn't—"

"I know."

"Even if she *was* shopping, Alice, we grieve in different ways," said Gwen. "Is that so hard to accept?"

"We go to different churches," said Liz.

"We don't wear our hair exactly the same way or look good in exactly the same clothes," added Pamela. "We even have different bad habits. Once you're in the bathroom, for example, you set up housekeeping and stay in there forever."

That made us smile.

"Well, I've really been needing you guys," I told them. "I've just felt I was down in a hole and couldn't climb out. That it was up to you to figure out what to do about it."

"One thing we *can* do is visit the Stedmeisters," said Gwen. "What about tomorrow?"

That seemed so right. Doing anything constructive seemed right.

"I'll bake something for them," said Liz.

"I could take them some of Sylvia's flowers," I said.

"Then I'll drive," said Pamela. "Pick you up about three, Gwen?"

Amazing how one idea led to another. As we walked back toward my place, I knew what I was going to write for the first issue of the school paper. A feature article, "Memories of Mark."

As we turned at the corner, Liz said, "Keeno was supposed to come by last night, but he didn't."

Uh-oh, I thought.

"You know where he was?" she continued. "He went to the soup kitchen at closing time and gave William a lesson on the musical saw."

I just turned toward her and grinned.

"William was so psyched. Keeno says he's a natural, and he's going to stop by again sometime and let him play some more."

"I think I like Keeno," I told her.

"I know I do," she said.

At the Stedmeisters' on Sunday afternoon, Gwen gave Mark's parents a photo someone had taken of the night we'd all stood around their home—the candles little pinpricks of light in the darkness.

Mrs. Stedmeister closed her eyes for a moment and held it close to her chest. "Thank you so much," she said. "Thank you."

Later, Mark's dad took us out in their backyard and showed us a tree he had just planted in Mark's memory. It was a maple sapling, and it stood right at the back of the driveway, where Mark used to tinker with old cars. The leaves would turn orange-red in October, Mr. Stedmeister said, and a tag on one of the branches read, OCTOBER SUNSET.

"It's going to be a beautiful tree," I told him. "We'd like to come back when the leaves turn and see it."

I felt like a tree myself, newly planted, changing color. Like I had survived the summer heat and was dressing up for fall. Even after the girls left, the feeling stayed with me.

I'd received an e-mail from David, saying he was visiting his folks in New Hampshire and already had seen a few trees start to turn—that nothing was as glorious as New England in the fall. Then he added: *I miss you and the Melody Inn already—all our good discussions. You've been through a tough time lately, but I'm trusting that as the weeks go on, you'll feel better. Astonishing things can happen to people who hope.*

I noticed he didn't say *believe*, he said *hope*. I wondered if they were the same. If they *could* be the same. Since no one really knows what or who God is, or whether God is at all, why can't God be hope? I couldn't understand that, either, but I liked that David wrote to me.

There was an e-mail from Patrick, too—Patrick, who hates to e-mail. He wondered if I had been wearing the blue earrings he'd bought for me in Chicago—the ones shaped like little globes. Could someone take a picture of me wearing them, he wondered, and send it on to him?

I was feeling really good. Sylvia was making spareribs for dinner, and the aroma drifted through the house. I was rearranging my dresser drawers and desk after having hung a framed photo of the candlelight vigil at the Stedmeisters' on the wall—glad that I had gone to visit them before school began.

And *then*—as though the day couldn't get any better—Molly called and said she was sorry she hadn't called me on Friday, but she'd seen the doctor and her blood work was great; she could start the fall semester at the U.

"Hey, Molly!" I cried. "That's the best—the very best—news of all!"

"I'm in remission, no guarantees. But I'm going to give it all I've got," said Molly.

"Your best has always been better than anyone else's," I told her. "I can't wait to tell the others. No, I'm going to let you do that yourself. It's too exciting."

When I put down the phone, I went out on the back porch, where Dad was working the *New York Times* crossword puzzle.

"Dad, about religion . . . ," I said.

He was mouthing the letters as he filled in the little squares on the paper. "Yes?" he said at last, looking up.

"I don't know if I'm a Christian or not. I don't even know if I believe there's a God. If somebody asked me what religion I was, I'd probably say I'm still finding out. All I know is I want to be part of everything that's good and true and real. That's sort of what's happening with me, just in case you're interested."

Dad patted the cushion beside him. "That's a terrific place to begin," he said, smiling. "Help me finish up this puzzle and we can talk about it some more."

So we sat there rocking on the glider, smelling the spareribs, and figuring out forty-eight down and fifty across.

Already looking forward to Alice's senior year?

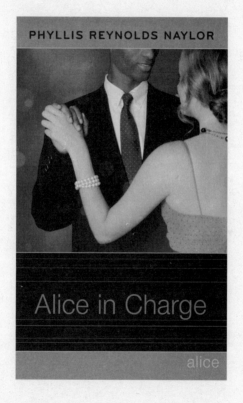

PHYLLIS REYNOLDS NAYLOR

Alice in Charge

alice

Here's a sneak peek!

STARTING OVER

It was impossible to start school without remembering him.

Some kids, of course, had been on vacation when it happened and hadn't seen the news in the paper. Some hadn't even known Mark Stedmeister.

But we'd known him. We'd laughed with him, danced with him, argued with him, swum with him, and then . . . said our good-byes to him when he was buried.

There was the usual safety assembly the first day of school. But the principal opened it with announcements of the two deaths over the summer: a girl who drowned at a family picnic, and Mark, killed in a traffic accident. Mr. Beck asked for two minutes of silence to remember them, and then a guy from band played "Amazing Grace" on the trumpet.

Gwen and Pam and Liz and I held hands during the playing, marveling that we had any tears left after the last awful weeks and the day Liz had phoned me, crying, "He was just sitting there, Alice! He wasn't doing *anything*! And a truck ran into him from behind."

It helps to have friends. When you can spread the sadness around, there's a little less, somehow, for each person to bear. As we left the auditorium later, teachers handed out plastic bracelets we could wear for the day—blue for Mark, yellow for the freshman who had drowned—and as we went from class to class, we'd look for the blue bracelets and lock eyes for a moment.

"So how did it go today?" Sylvia asked when she got home that afternoon. And without waiting for an answer, she gave me a long hug.

"Different," I said, when we disentangled. "It will always seem different without Mark around."

"I know," she said. "But life does have a way of filling that empty space, whether you want it to or not."

She was right about that. Lester's twenty-fifth birthday, for one. I'd bought him a tie from the Melody Inn. The pattern was little brown figures against a bright yellow background, and if you studied them closely, you saw they were tiny eighth notes forming a grid. I could tell by Lester's expression that he liked it.

"Good choice, Al!" he said, obviously surprised at my excellent taste. "So how's it going? First day of your last year of high school, huh?"

"No, Les, you're supposed to say, 'This is the first day of the rest of your life,'" I told him.

"Oh. Well then, this is the first minute of the first hour of the first day of the rest of your life. Even more exciting."

We did the usual birthday thing: Lester's favorite meal—steak and potatoes—the cake, the candles, the ice cream. After Dad asked him how his master's thesis was coming and they had a long discussion, Les asked if I had any ideas for feature articles I'd be doing for *The Edge*.

"Maybe 'The Secret Lives of Brothers'?" I suggested.

"Boring. Eat, sleep, study. Definitely boring," he said.

From her end of the table, Sylvia paused a moment as she gathered up the dessert plates. "Weren't you working on a special tribute to Mark?" she asked. Now that I was features editor of our school paper, everyone had suggestions.

"I am, but it just hasn't jelled yet," I said. "I want it to be special. Right now I've got other stuff to do, and I haven't even started my college applications."

"First priority," Dad said.

"Yeah, right," I told him. "Do you realize that every teacher seems to think *his* subject comes first? It's the truth! 'Could anything be more important than learning to express yourselves?' our English teacher says. 'Hold in those stomach muscles, girls,' says the gym teacher. 'If you take only one thing with you when you leave high school, it's the importance of posture.' And Miss Ames says she doesn't care what else is on our plate, the articles for *The Edge* positively have to be in on time. Yada yada yada."

"Wait till college, kiddo. Wait till grad school," said Lester.

"I don't want to hear it!" I wailed. "Each day I think, 'If I can just make it through this one . . .' Whoever said you could slide through your senior year was insane."

Lester looked at Sylvia. "Aren't you glad you're not teaching high school?" he asked. "All this moaning and groaning?"

Sylvia laughed. "Give the girl a break, Les. Feature articles are the most interesting part of a newspaper. She's got a big job this year."

"Hmmm," said Lester. "Maybe she *should* do an article on brothers. 'My Bro, the Stud.' 'Life with a Philosophy Major: The Secret Genius of Les McKinley.'"

"You wish," I said.

In addition to thinking about articles for *The Edge* and all my other assignments, I was thinking about Patrick. About the phone conversation we'd had the night before. Patrick's at the University of Chicago now, and with both of us still raw after Mark's funeral, we've been checking in with each other more often. He wants to know how I'm doing, how our friends are handling things, and I ask how he's coping, away from everyone back home.

"Mostly by keeping busy," Patrick had said. "And thinking about you."

"I miss you, Patrick," I'd told him.

"I miss *you*. Lots," he'd answered. "But remember, this is your senior year. Don't give up anything just because I'm not there."

"What does that mean?" I'd asked.

I'd known what he was saying, though. We'd had that conversation before. Going out with other people, he meant, and I knew he was right—Patrick is so reasonable, so practical, so . . . *Patrick*. I didn't want *him* to be lonely either. But I didn't feel very reasonable inside, and it was hard imagining Patrick with someone else.

"We both know how we feel about each other," he'd said.

Did we? I don't think either of us had said the words *I love you*. We'd never said we were dating exclusively. With nearly seven hundred miles between us now, some choices, we knew, had already been made. What we did know was that we were special to each other.

I thought of my visit to his campus over the summer. I thought of the bench by Botany Pond. Patrick's kisses, his arms, his hands. . . . It was hard imagining myself with someone else too, but—as he'd said—it was my senior year.

"I know," I'd told him, and we'd said our long good nights.

In my group of best girlfriends—Pamela, Liz, and Gwen—I was the closest to having a steady boyfriend. Dark-haired Liz had been going out with Keeno a lot, but nothing definite. Gwen was seeing a guy we'd met over the summer when we'd volunteered for a week at a soup kitchen, and Pamela wasn't going out with anyone at present. "Breathing fresh air" was the way she put it.

There was a lot to think about. With our parents worrying over banks and mortgages and retirement funds, college seemed like a bigger hurdle than it had before. And some colleges were more concerned with grades than with SAT scores, so seniors couldn't just slide through their last year, especially the first semester.

"Where are you going to apply?" I asked Liz. "Gwen's already made up her mind. She's going to sail right through the University of Maryland and enter their medical school. I think it's some sort of scholarship worked out with the National Institutes of Health."

"She *should* get a scholarship—all these summers she's been interning at the NIH," said Liz. "I don't know—I think I want a really small liberal arts college, like Bennington up in Vermont."

We were sitting around Elizabeth's porch watching her little brother blow soap bubbles at us. Nathan was perched on the railing, giggling each time we reached out to grab one.

"Sure you want a small college?" asked Pamela, absently examining her toes, feet propped on the wicker coffee table. Her nails were perfectly trimmed, polished in shell white. "It *sounds* nice and cozy, but everyone knows your business, and you've got all these little cliques to deal with."

"Where are you going to apply?" Liz asked her.

"It's gotta be New York, that much I know. One of their theater arts schools, maybe. Somebody told me about City College, and someone else recommended the American Academy of Dramatic Arts. I doubt I could get into Cornell, but they've got a good drama department. Where are you going to apply, Alice?"

I shrugged. "Mrs. Bailey recommends Maryland because they've got a good graduate program in counseling, and that's where she got her degree. But a couple of guys from church really like the University of North Carolina at Chapel Hill. . . ."

"That's a good school," said Liz.

". . . And I've heard good things about William and Mary."

"Virginia?" asked Liz.

"Yes. Williamsburg. I was thinking I could visit both on the same trip."

"You could always go to Bennington with me," said Liz.

"Clear up in Vermont? Where it *really* snows?"

"It's not Colorado."

Just then a soap bubble came drifting past my face, and I snapped at it like a dog. Nathan screeched with laughter.

What I didn't tell my friends was that lately I'd been getting a sort of panicky, homesick, lonely feeling whenever I thought about leaving for college—coming "home" at night to a dorm room. To a roommate I may not even like. A roommate the complete opposite of me, perhaps. I don't know when I first started feeling this way—Mark's funeral? Dad's worries about investments and the store? But at college there would be no stepmom to talk with across the table, no Dad to give me a bear hug, no brother to stop by with an account of his latest adventure.

It was crazy! Hadn't I always looked forward to being on my own? Didn't I want that no-curfew life? I'd been away before—the school trip to New York, for example. I'd been a counselor at summer camp. And yet . . . All my friends had been there, and my friends were like family. At college I'd be with strangers. I'd be a stranger to them. And no matter how I tried to reason myself out of it, the homesickness was there in my chest, and it thumped painfully whenever college came to mind, which was often. I didn't want to chicken out and choose Bennington just to be with Liz or Maryland just to room with Gwen. Still . . .

Nathan tumbled off the railing at that point and skinned his knee. The soap solution spilled all over the porch, he was howling, and we got up to help. That put an end to the conversation for the time being, and time was what I needed to work things through.

The school newspaper, though, kept me busy. Our staff had to stay on top of everything. We were the first to know how we'd be celebrating Spirit Week, because we had to publish it. We had to know when dances would be held, when games were scheduled, which faculty member had retired and which teachers were new. We were supposed to announce new clubs, student trips, projects, protests. . . . We were the school's barometer, and in our staff meetings we tried to get a sense of things before they happened.

We were also trying something different this semester. Because of our newspaper's growing reputation and the number of students who'd signed up to work on *The Edge*, we'd been given a larger room on the main floor, instead of the small one we'd been using for years. Here we had two long tables for layout instead of one. Four computers instead of two. And on the suggestion of Phil Adler—our news editor/editor in chief—we were going to try publishing an eight-page newspaper every week instead of a sixteen-page biweekly edition.

We wanted to be even more timely. And because the printer's schedule sometimes held up our paper for a day, we were going to aim for Thursday publication. Then, if there was a snafu, students would still get their copies by Friday and know what was going on over the weekend.

"I've got reservations about this, but it's worth a try," Miss Ames, our faculty sponsor, told us. "I know you've doubled your number of reporters, and you've got an A team and a B team so that not everyone works on each issue. But you four editors are going to have to work *every* week. That means most Mondays, Tuesdays, and Wednesdays after school. Can you can swing it?"

We said we could. Phil and I and Tim Moss, the new sports editor (and Pamela's old boyfriend), and Sam Mayer, the photography editor (and one of my old boyfriends), all wagged our woolly heads and said, yes, of course, no problem, we're on it. All completely insane, of course.

It will keep me from thinking so much about missing Patrick, I thought. But each day that passed brought me that much closer to D-day—decision time—and what I was going to do about college.

* * *

It was through *The Edge* that I found out about Student Jury. Modeled after some counties where student juries meet in city hall, ours would be a lot simpler, according to Mr. Beck. He decided that if more decisions and penalties were handed down by students themselves—overseen, of course, by a faculty member—maybe Mr. Gephardt, our vice principal, could have more time for his other responsibilities, and maybe the offenders would feel that the penalties were more fair. Students guilty of some minor infraction would be referred to the jury and would be sentenced by their peers.

The Edge agreed to run a front-page story on it, and I found out that I'd been recommended by the faculty to serve on the jury.

"No way!" I told Gwen. I had assignments to do. Articles to write. If anyone should serve on it, she should.

"So what have you got so far on your résumé?" was her answer.

"For what? College?"

"Well, not the Marines!" We were undressing for gym, and she pulled a pair of wrinkled gym shorts over her cotton underwear. "Extracurricular stuff, school activities, community service. You've got features editor of the paper, Drama Club, the Gay/Straight Alliance, some volunteer hours, camp counselor . . . What else?"

"I need more?"

"It can't hurt. You've got heavy competition." Gwen slid a gray

T-shirt down over her brown arms and dropped her shoes in the locker. "Student Jury—dealing with kids with problems—might look pretty impressive, especially if you're going into counseling."

I gave a small whimper. "I told you the paper's coming out weekly, didn't I? I'm still working for Dad on Saturdays. I've got—"

"And William and Mary is going to care?"

Gwen's impossibly practical. "You and Patrick would make a good couple," I told her.

"Yeah, but I've got Austin," she said, and gave me a smug smile.

Later I whimpered some more to Liz and Pamela, but they were on Gwen's side.

"I've heard you need to put anything you can think of on your résumé," said Pamela. "I'm so glad you guys talked me into trying out for *Guys and Dolls* last spring. If I was sure I could get a part in the next production, I'd even jump the gun and include that."

They won. I told Mr. Gephardt I'd serve on Student Jury for at least one semester.

"Glad to have you on board," he said, as though we were sailing out to sea.

Maybe, like Patrick, I was trying to "stay busy" too. Maybe it made a good defense against going out with other guys. But I *did* keep busy, and whenever I felt my mind drifting to Mark, out of sadness, or to Patrick, out of longing, or to college, out of panic,

I wondered if I could somehow use my own musings as a springboard for a feature article: "When Life Dumps a Load," "Long Distance Dating: Does It Work?" "Facing College: The Panic and the Pleasure"—something like that.

Amy Sheldon had been transferred from special ed in our sophomore year and had struggled to go mainstream ever since. I'm not sure what grade she was in. I think she was repeating her junior year.

It's hard to describe Amy, because we've never quite decided what's different about her. She walks with a slight tilt forward and is undersized for her age. Her facial features are nonsymmetrical, but it's mostly her directness that stands out—a childlike stare when she talks with you about the first thing on her mind . . . and the way she speaks in non sequiturs, as though she's never really a part of the conversation, and I suppose in some ways she never is. Somehow she has always managed to attach herself to me, and there have been times when I felt as though I had a puppy following along at my heels.

The same day I said yes to Student Jury, Amy caught up with me after school. I had taken a couple of things from my locker, ready to go to the newsroom, when Amy appeared at my elbow.

"I've got to wait till Mom comes for me at four because she had a dentist appointment and then I'm getting a new bra," she said.

"Hey! Big time!" I said. "What color are you going to get?"

She smiled in anticipation. "I wanted red or black, but Mom said 'I don't think so.' She said I could have white or blue or pink."

"Well, those are pretty too," I told her. I realized I'd closed my locker without taking out my jacket and opened it again.

"I went from a thirty-two A to a thirty-two B, and a year ago I didn't wear any bra at all. I hate panty hose. Do you ever wear panty hose?"

"Not if I can help it," I said.

"I wouldn't want to wear a rubber bath mat around me," Amy said.

I blinked. *"What?"*

"Grandma Roth—she's my mother's mother—used to wear a Playtex girdle when she was my age. She said it was like wrapping a rubber bath mat around her. She even had to wear it when it was hot. I hate summer, do you? Am I asking too many questions?"

I tried to dismiss her comment with a quick smile but saw how eagerly she waited for an answer. "Well, sometimes you do ask a lot."

"My dad says if you don't ask questions, how do you learn anything? You know why I like to ask questions?"

"Um . . . why?" It seemed she was going to follow me all the way down the hall.

"Because people talk to me then. Most of the time, anyway. Most people don't come up to me and start a conversation, so I have to start one, and Dad says the best way to start a conversation is to ask a question. And you know what?"

If I felt lonely just thinking about college, I imagined how it must feel to be Amy, to be lonely most of the time. "What?" I asked, slowing a little to give her my full concentration.

"If somebody just answers and walks away, or doesn't answer at all, you know what I say? 'Have a nice day!'"

I could barely look at her. "That's the perfect response, Amy," I said. "You just keep asking all the questions you want."

I was deep in thought, my eyes on the window, as Phil went over our next issue. We could give free copies to all the stores surrounding the school, he said, just to be part of the community and maybe help persuade them to buy ads; the art department had suggested we use sketches occasionally, drawn by our art students, to illustrate some of our articles; and we still needed one more roving reporter in order to have an equal number for each class. A few reporters from last year had graduated, and some had dropped out for another activity.

I suddenly came to life. "I'd like to suggest Amy Sheldon," I said, and the sound of it surprised even me.

There was total silence, except for one girl's shocked *"Amy?"* Then, embarrassed, she said, "Are you sure she can handle it?"

"I don't know," I said honestly. "But I'd like to give her a try. She's good at asking questions."

There was a low murmur of laughter. "Boy, *is* she! Remember when she went around asking other girls if they'd started their periods?" someone said.

"Now, *there's* a good opener," said Tim. More laughter.

"Everybody likes to be asked questions about themselves, and if she bombs, we don't have to print it."

Silence. Then Phil said, "Can you offer her a temporary assignment—so she won't get her hopes up?"

"Sure, I could do that." I waited. The lack of enthusiasm was overwhelming.

I watched Phil. I'd met him last year when I joined the Gay/Straight Alliance in support of my friends Lori and Leslie. He'd been a tall, gangly roving reporter before, but now that we were seniors, he was head honcho and looked the part. It was weird, in a way, that all the people who had run the paper before us were in college, and now we were the ones making the decisions.

"Okay," Phil said at last. "We'll give it a try. But have a practice session with her first, huh?"

"Of course," I said, and realized I'd added still one more thing to my to-do list.

"In the same spirit," Miss Ames said, "I'd like to suggest an article now and then by Daniel Bul Dau." When a lot of us looked blank, she added, "He's here from Sudan—you may have seen him around school. He's eighteen, and his family is being sponsored by a local charity. I think he could write some short pieces—or longer ones, if he likes—on how he's adapting to American life, his take on American culture, what you have to overcome in being a refugee . . . whatever he wants to write about. He's quite fluent in English."

We were all okay with that. More than okay.

"Feature article, right?" Phil said, looking at me, meaning this was my contact to make.

"Give me his name and homeroom, and I'll take care of it," I offered, and wondered if there would be any time left in my schedule for sleep.

Daniel Bul Dau had skin as dark as a chestnut, wide-spaced eyes that were full of either wonder or amusement or both, and a tall, slim build with unusually long legs. On Tuesday he smiled all the while I was talking with him about the newspaper and the article we wanted him to write.

"What am I to say?" he asked.

"Anything you want. I think kids would be especially interested in what you like about the United States and what you don't. Your experiences, frustrations. Tell us about life in Sudan and what you miss. Whatever you'd like us to know. I'll give you my cell phone number if you have any questions."

"I will write it for you," he said, and his wide smile never changed.

Gwen and Pam and Liz and I were talking about teachers over lunch. Specifically male teachers. Who was hot, who was not, who was married, who was not. We were trying to figure out Dennis Granger, who was subbing for an English teacher on maternity leave.

"Married," Pamela guessed. "I wouldn't say he's hot, but he's sort of handsome."

"Not as good-looking as Stedman in physics," said Gwen.

"I caught him looking at my breasts last week," said Liz.

"Stedman?"

"No, Granger."

"Kincaid looks at butts," said Pamela.

"Kincaid? He's as nearsighted as a person can be!" I said.

"That's why he has to really study you from every angle," said Pamela just as Dennis Granger approached our table and looked at us quizzically as we tried to hide our smiles. I think he deduced we were talking about guys and jokingly ambled around our table as though trying to eavesdrop on the conversation. He leaned way over us, pretending to mooch a chip or a pickle from somebody's tray, his arm sliding across one of our shoulders. We broke into laughter the moment he was gone.

"The best teacher I ever had was Mr. Everett in eighth grade," Liz said when we recovered. "I wish there were more like him."

Pamela gave her a look. "Yeah, you were in love with him, remember?"

"Crushing, maybe," said Liz.

"One of the best teachers I ever had was Sylvia," I told them.

"And then your dad goes and marries her," said Liz.

"Well, she couldn't be my teacher forever. I liked Mr. Everett, too. But I totally loved Mrs. Plotkin. Remember sixth grade? I was so awful to her at first and did everything I could to be expelled from her class. She just really cared about her students."

"That's why I want to be a teacher," said Liz.

"You'll make a great one," I told her.

"And you'll make a great counselor," said Liz.

Pamela rolled her eyes. "While you two are saving the world, I'll be working for a top ad agency in New York, and you can come up on weekends."

"With or without boyfriends?" asked Liz.

"Depends on the boyfriends," said Pamela.

"I thought you were going to a theater arts school," said Gwen.

Pamela gave an anguished sigh. "I just don't know what to do. I used to think I'd like fashion designing, but I've pretty much given that up. So it's between theater and advertising. I'm thinking maybe I'll try a theater arts school for a year to see if they think I have talent. If I don't measure up, I'll leave and go for a business degree somewhere. Of course, then I'd be a year behind everyone else."

"Pamela, in college that doesn't matter," said Gwen. "Go for it."

Liz looked wistfully around the group. "You'll be off doing medical research, of course," she said to Gwen. "Remember how we used to think we'd all go to the same college, sleep in the same dorm, get married the same summer, maybe? Help raise each other's kids?"

"I'm not having kids," said Pamela.

Gwen chuckled. "Hold that thought," she said. "We'll check in with each other five years from now and see what's happening."

When you need a friend who *really* understands . . .

because

normal

is **WAY**

overrated

ten

miles

past

normal

frances o' roark dowell

EBOOK EDITION ALSO AVAILABLE

From Atheneum Books for Young Readers
TEEN.SimonandSchuster.com

Sydney has the choice . . . but can she make the decision?

every little thing in the world

nina de gramont

every little thing in the world

nina de gramont

POWERFUL

BOOKS ABOUT STRONG YOUNG WOMEN

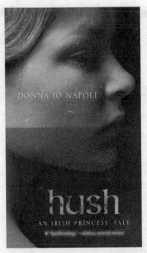

HUSH: AN IRISH PRINCESS' TALE
by Donna Jo Napoli

OUTSIDE BEAUTY
by Cynthia Kadohata

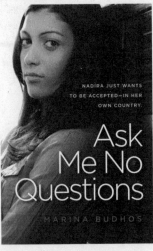

ASK ME NO QUESTIONS
by Marina Budhos

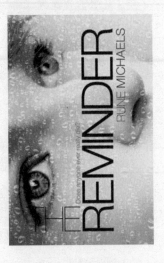

THE REMINDER
by Rune Michaels

From ATHENEUM BOOKS *for* YOUNG READERS
Published by SIMON & SCHUSTER